Ortiz Lane

BENJAMIN LEAVENS

To Mrs. Bailey, whose red ink cut deep in my adolescent heart...
Where would we be without our teachers?

CHRISTMAS 2015

Rain was finally coming to the Ozarks. In an unusual move, NOAA hydrologists predicted record flooding from a storm that would hit southwest Missouri on Christmas Eve and continue through the weekend. Emergency management teams in Newton County's Shoal Creek river basin could not ignore the dire prediction. It was going to be a dramatic end to a long dry spell.

Christmas or not, volunteer teams from the Redings Mill VFD still went door-to-door to warn residents in the floodplain to seek higher ground. At least the number of affected properties was relatively small, and the task was completed within nine hours. Then the VFD chief called the regional water rescue team.

Newton County Rescue and Recovery's (NCRR) chief reported they were ready and waiting except for Boat 42. NCRR was funded through private donations and limited county support, so there simply wasn't enough money to replace the motor. It was hard to get people to understand the need for a new outboard when the sun was shining and previous floods were distant memories, so Boat 42 would remain out of service.

Until the storm hit, there was little left to be done but continue to warn citizens through mass media, put out the usual reminders not to drive into floodwaters (even though someone always did), and go enjoy the holiday as much as possible.

Throughout Christmas Eve, the sky turned from clear and sunny to rolling clouds and gradually darkened until the first drops of rain began to stir up miniature clouds of dust on the Tipton Ford public river access at the end of Ortiz Lane. Bone dry, the gravel road and approach to Shoal Creek would take quite a bit of rain before the dust settled and turned to mud. Gray clouds covered the sunset and the western sky turned black as daylight faded.

Newton County Deputy Terry Pusser was headed home and had already radioed in to sign off when he heard a disturbance call for the Tipton Ford access. He lived nearby, and it was close enough to check it out before going home. Christmas sometimes brought domestic situations to a head, and Pusser didn't want a potential person in distress to have to wait for one of the two cars on patrol that night to get across the county.

"Newton 11 to Dispatch. Show me active and en route to Tipton Ford access."

"Dispatch to Newton 11, copy 16:40."

Pusser sped up a bit as he turned off Highway 71 and headed down Scenic Drive toward the access. Scenic Drive was the remnant of Old Highway 71 and had been the main highway from the '20s through the late '40s. He followed the road over an ancient bridge that would soon be underwater if weather predictions were right, and flicked on the wipers which only smeared the dusty windshield of his old Crown Vic. He was in line to get a roomier Tahoe soon, but not in time for Christmas. Nice to know there were better days ahead, though. It was only a few short years ago that deputies in Newton County had to supply their own cars and equipment.

Five minutes later, Pusser's headlights flicked on automatically when he pulled into the empty Tipton access parking area and dust surrounded his cruiser for a moment. Squinting through the smeary windshield, he could see a little bit of dark, oily material glistening on the gravel near the boat ramp. Whatever the dark stuff was, it wasn't shiny from the spattering rain. Probably oil, but he would still check it out. He keyed the mike on his shoulder.

"Newton 11 to Dispatch. Show me out of the car at Tipton Access, no other vehicles present."

"Dispatch to Newton 11, copy 16:48."

Rain pinged loudly on the car roof as the sky finally opened. Instead of putting on his Smokey Bear hat, which the rain would ruin, Pusser slipped on an NCSO ball cap and slid his service Maglite out of its holder as he stepped from the car.

He cringed as the cold water ran down his neck and hunched forward to keep the rain off his face and chest as he trotted over to the liquid on the ground. Usually, he would put on a nitrile glove before touching something unknown, but the rain pounded harder, making him careless. He touched the liquid with his index and middle finger as he shone the bright LED beam on it, and darned if it didn't look like blood!

"Well, shit!" It might really be a crime scene, and the evidence was washing away before his eyes. He removed his hat and laid it over the blood, flinching as water ran down his neck.

Back at the car he popped the trunk, opened a big Tupperware container holding his evidence kit and grabbed a piece of plastic to cover the blood better. Rolling his eyes, he wiped his hands with a wet wipe and slipped on a pair of nitrile gloves. *Last time I forget that!*

He trotted back to get his hat and covered the blood with the plastic. A gust of wind shifted his hat, and as he reached to grab it, the plastic peeled off and sailed away, tumbled down the boat ramp, and flattened in the river.

"Crap!" Rain mired the blood into grey silty chert rock slush and the wind blew harder. He snatched a handful of gravel, trying to protect it in his fist. His cap slipped again, and the Maglite banged against his skull as he reached to stabilize it with his other hand.

"Dispatch to Newton 11. 10-18." They were checking to see if he was okay.

Sighing in exasperation, he ran back to the trunk and held it up against the wind with his head as he pulled his glove off inside out, but there was little left to trap inside. The whole thing was becoming a waste of time.

"Newton 11. 10-19. Dispatch, I need a case number."

"Dispatch to Newton 11, case number 15-1669."

"Newton 11, copy." He did have a good memory for numbers and such, so he didn't feel the need to write the case number down right away.

"Dispatch to Newton 11. 16:55." He shoved the glove into a baggie and dropped it in the trunk, put on his service poncho, and shut the trunk lid.

With the poncho keeping him mostly dry now and his hands free, he scanned the area more carefully. Water smoothed the gravel, and the boat ramp was clean and shiny-wet. A quick search of the surroundings showed nothing out of the ordinary. While most of the river was pretty shallow, there was a deep, normally still area ten yards downstream now dimpled with rain, but he could see no disturbances on the grass or in the mud near the bank. There was nothing to indicate a struggle—no shell casings or other signs of trouble.

With nothing to photograph or collect, he returned to the cruiser to write a brief report into his notebook as the rain continued its cacophony on the roof. He called his sergeant to make sure there were no related calls in the county that might shed light on the source of the blood, but nothing turned up. They decided just to make a report and toss the baggie and glove.

The matter was properly filed and dropped as the rain fell down and the rivers came up.

The resulting flood set new records in the Shoal Creek basin, inundating the control room at the gas pipeline pumping station on Old 71 Highway and several nice homes along the river's edge. Ten feet of rushing water covered the Tipton Ford access, cutting deep grooves in the gravel, tearing down signs, and taking out many large oak and sycamore trees along the bank.

Newton County Rescue and Recovery was fully activated and performed eighty-four water rescues in a thirty-six-hour period. While transporting a gentleman who had just been rescued with his dog, the motor on Boat 41 also burned out in the middle of a half-mile-wide area of the flood-swollen river. Replacing motors suddenly became a top priority, and a county commissioner put the replacement on her personal credit card.

Rescues included a train crew who were stranded when the tracks washed out, twenty-seven high-dollar show horses in a low-lying barn, and hundreds of people trapped by the floodwaters. The damage was widespread, but no one in Newton County was reported missing, and, thankfully, no lives were lost.

CHAPTER ONE
A LONG TIME AGO IN MISSOURI

Poonboy brought bad news to their house at 9:00 p.m. Drawn by his urgent knocks on the door of their housing authority apartment, Sharon and Rose watched from the hallway as he finally let himself in. Light from the foyer briefly supplemented the muted television's flicker. Dazed from lying on the couch all afternoon, their mom Lisa roused herself to a slouch at Poonboy's shaking. His burning ammonia smell made their noses wrinkle as they watched, listening closely for any mention of food.

"Lisa, wake up!"

"Wha-" Lisa's voice was blurry.

"They got Lenny again."

Her voice sharpened, "What the fuck?"

"The shake-n-bake exploded, and the car burned up. I ran, but fuckin' Lenny tried to put it out, and the laws got him."

"Why? It wasn't even our car!" Lisa wiped the sleep out of her eyes.

"Fuck if I know. I think he was trying to save the stash, but now they'll get him on the car, too." Poonboy shook his head.

Sharon and Rose heard a grating moan from their mom, contrived of late to express the worsening back and hip pain from the life growing in her belly. The girls vaguely understood that Lenny, their dad, cooked his "product" and traded some for "oxys" to help mama's pain. Without the oxys, they knew the irritating moans were gonna get longer and louder. They winced as she whined, "What the fuck're we gonna dooooooo?"

Lisa's whine faded to another moan. She hunched forward on the worn ocher-yellow cushions, her legs spread, and lightly beat her huge belly with her wrists, her fists clenched in pain. Squeaky old springs punctuated her movement as she whined, "I need my oxys!"

"I dunno. We'll figure something, but I gotta go take a shower." Poonboy's tone was just as whiney as hers as he sought to quickly placate her, but his annoyance still came through. He lived at his sister's on the second floor, which was against the rules, and turned to leave.

"I just wanna cut 'em out. It hurts so bad, all the time!" The girls knew she was talking about the babies in her belly. She called them twins, triplets, or quintuplets depending on how much pain she had, and lately, she was threatening to *cut 'em out*.

He spun back to face her, eyes wide with shock. "You can't cut em out!"

"Jeeze, Poonboy!" Lisa sighed loudly. "I'll be fucking fine."

The girls' eyes met as Poonboy made his exit. It wasn't looking good for supper.

Lisa got up and made her way down the hall to the bathroom, kicking toys and clothes out of the way, and the girls retreated to their room and listened as she peed. They shadowed her back to the kitchen, ever hopeful, but their faces dropped as she popped two more oxys with a swig of booze and laid back down on the couch. The television's flickering was joined by the reality show's dramatic narrative as Lisa laid on the remote, but she didn't notice. She moaned gently now, forgetting she might have an audience.

It wasn't much of an audience, either. The girls were still in their nightgowns, faces unwashed, teeth unbrushed, and hair tangled and stringy. Lisa had forgotten morning chores and breakfast, and though they'd eaten the last of the soggy Cheerios and split a cheese sandwich on stale, crispy-edged bread for breakfast, they were now starving.

When drunk and stoned out, Lisa might lock them in their bedroom or worse if they roused her, but hunger drove them silently into the kitchen. Rose carefully scraped a chair across the floor as Sharon, peeking around the room divider, watched their mom. She bumped the chair against the fridge and crawled up to open the freezer door and remove the Hungry Man fried chicken TV dinner they'd scoped out. It was that last of the food.

She handed it down to Sharon, who could read. "Six to eight minutes," she whispered.

Rose crawled down and slid the chair loudly down the short counter to the microwave while Sharon shushed her as she watched their mom from the edge of the living room. Rose put the dinner into the microwave and shut the door as quietly as possible, but the keypad made terribly loud beeps. Lisa stirred, and Sharon urgently shushed Rose again, who entered eighty minutes instead of eight. She crawled down and went to take a look with Sharon.

"I'm telling you she moved!" Sharon whispered into Rose's ear. Lisa's eyes were half-open, but she wasn't seeing anything. She gave a long, low moan and shifted on the couch. Her shirt slid up to expose her fish-white belly with its dark veins.

"I still got to start it," Rose whispered back. "Even if she wakes up, she'll just go back to sleep. When I hit start, we'll run to our room."

"Okay then," Sharon, alert for danger, kept her eyes glued on her mother.

Rose climbed back up and pushed the start button. Sharon watched as her sister scrambled off the chair and back across the kitchen. Rose took her hand, and they ran to the bedroom, bouncing up and down like little fawns as they navigated the debris in the hallway.

"Little fuckers!" slurred Lisa.

The girls cowered behind their rickety bunk beds in the corner of the room, hoping she wouldn't rouse enough to investigate. They also knew she might take their food. Her voice came up the hall.

"I'm gonna beat your asses if you don't let me sleep!"

The girls waited, but couldn't hear any movement, only the faint hum of the microwave. Rose, always braver, got up to turn out the bedroom light and gave a little scream when she came face to face with Lisa. The door slammed behind her as she scampered back to Sharon, and they heard the outside lock click into place as Lisa muttered, "*Fuckers.*"

There wouldn't be supper now, and Sharon had to pee.

*

Lisa's coughing fit roused her enough to realize the shriek of the smoke alarm wasn't a fucking dream. And it wasn't the June heat she felt as adrenaline overcame her narc-induced stupor—her apartment was on fire! She flopped off the couch, and the cushions followed her, tangling with her limbs. Pushing them clumsily aside, she rose to her knees, belly pendulous as she crawled to look down the hallway, blocked by dark smoke boiling from the kitchen. The narcotic haze made it hard to focus, but this was bad! Fuck, fuck, fuck!

Flames from the microwave and its cabinet shimmered through the smoke, and she screamed down the hallway, "Girls, GET OUT!!!" Coughing interrupted her effort, and the shrieking smoke alarm kept her from hearing any reply, so she crawled towards the front door, coughing, head spinning, and strength fading. She knew she had to get to the door, and it wasn't much further . . .

*

Poonboy and his sister Angel lived one floor up and across the central stairway of the six-plex. He'd just dozed off under a sheet on his sister's fake leather couch when the common smoke detectors went off. Despite earlier beers and blunt, he quickly hopped off the couch and hurried to the door. Smoke filled the hall and stairwell with a plasticky burnt smell. *More fuckin' fire! Twice in one night?!?*

He yelled at Angel to get out while he went to check on Lisa and the girls. Scantily clad residents had started to fill the hallway amid shouts of "Fire!" and "Get Out!" Shrieking smoke alarms made everyone yell louder.

Poonboy fought through the fleeing tenants and jumped down the steps to Lenny and Lisa's on the ground floor. Smoke was seeping around the door, but the handle wasn't hot, and the door wasn't latched as he shouldered the door inward. Acrid smoke flowed out as the door hit something soft and heavy. Momentarily confused, Poonboy spotted the fingertips pinched under the door and cringed.

The fingers jerked away as he pulled the door back. He heard cursing over the alarms—which meant Lisa was alive. "Get out!" Poonboy yelled again as Angel came up behind him. He pushed the door back in more gently.

Lisa's scraped hand grabbed the edge of the door as she rolled herself out of the way. Smoke billowed as the door swung open. It stung his eyes and burned his nose and throat, forcing an involuntary cough. Poonboy instinctively dropped to his knees as Lisa cried out, "My girls, my girls, my girls—" before coughing interrupted her plea.

Fire flared in the kitchen as oxygen rushed in from the door, and Poonboy didn't have any maternal instincts to overcome his fear of fire. He loved the girls, especially Rose, but not enough for him to try to be a hero. Lisa was struggling to breathe, so he began to awkwardly drag her out, glad her apartment was on the ground floor by the exit.

Another resident stopped to help, and they slid, then half-carried her to the sidewalk out front. She was sobbing between coughing fits, and other residents circled her, spouting little bits of medical knowledge. Poonboy stooped, and Angel cradled her head.

"She needs oxygen," insisted a large older woman. "She can have mine."

Soon the prongs of a nasal cannula were in Lisa's nose, and the woman turned her oxygen concentrator as high as it would go. Lisa was coughing less but sobbing more as she began to catch her breath, "My girls, my girls!"

"Did you see them?" Poonboy asked.

"Noo-oooo!"

Poonboy looked towards the smoke billowing from Lisa's living room window. He saw that the girls' open bedroom window was not billowing smoke and the window screen was lying crooked on the meager hedge below the window.

"They might be okay! Angel, you stay here with Lisa, I'm gonna look for 'em. They might'a got out!"

He ran to the bedroom window. Faint smoke drifted out, and he leaned his head inside the dark room. "Rose! Sharon!" he called. He leaned further in and called again. Nothing. He climbed over the ledge and quickly checked the closet and under the bed with his hands, calling their names loudly. He knew better than to open the bedroom door.

"Poonboy!"

He started, relief instantly flooding his heart as his throat tightened. He closed his eyes in a quick, silent prayer of thanks. Never had Sharon's little voice sounded so precious. Her little head was silhouetted in the streetlights behind her as she looked into the room from outside. "Oh, thank God! Your mama's going crazy!"

He practically fell out of the window and picked her up in a bear hug. Her stringy, tangled hair felt so sweet against his face. "You're my special girl! Where the fuck were you?"

"We snuck out the window to pee. Mama locked the door again. We thought we were in trouble when we saw the smoke…"

"God, no! I'm just glad you're alive!" He kissed her on top of her head, something he had never done in public. Rose came in for a hug, too, and he picked them both up, one in each arm, the adrenaline rush giving him strength. He carried them back over to Lisa.

"Get outta my way! I found the girls!"

Lisa rolled to her side and leaned up on an elbow. The girls hopped down, and she hugged them as close as she could. "Thank God, thank God, thank God." She broke into coughing and laid back on the sidewalk, Angel doing her best to cradle Lisa's head. Rose slipped her hand into Sharon's as they seemingly escaped any punishment. Joplin Fire arrived, along with police and ambulances, further protecting them from any wrath.

With her big belly and fluid on the sidewalk now indicating broken water, paramedics seemed surprised that Lisa couldn't name an OB doctor. They quickly got her on a gurney and started rolling. Sharon and Rose stayed close to Angel while Poonboy, a known dealer, quietly faded into the background as the police arrived. If the firefighters found his stash, he could end up in the pokey with Lenny.

Angel wasn't about to be stuck with children, and the girls knew they were going into foster care again when they heard her telling the policeman about Lenny going to jail and Lisa in labor. They just hoped whoever they ended up with had food!

*

As the adrenaline wore off, Lisa became aware of her pain again, especially as contractions began. By the time they reached the hospital, her moans were long, loud, and twice as irritating. A rapid ultrasound in the emergency department revealed triplets, and an OB was snagged.

"I need something for the fuckin' paaaiiiin," she pined, then coughed several times, pulling off her oxygen mask. "It's a ten!"

"Okay, look, we are going to be giving you a spinal pretty quick, which will help with the pain. You gotta keep the mask on, though. You're having a miscarriage. It looks like your babies are about twenty-six weeks, but they might make it. We're gonna try." The doctor's voice was clipped. Rating pain was a common ploy of addicts, and Lisa had been faintly repeating *ten*. "We're going to take you for a C-section, ma'am."

"Save my babies! Please save my babies!" Lisa focused on the babies for a moment, then her eyes rolled back in a narcotic lull before the next contraction roused her to resume the moan. "Ten... ten... ten."

*

The NICU team did their best, but the third baby out of Lisa's womb was the only survivor. Once the first two girls were declared dead, all efforts focused on number three, and she was immediately taken to the NICU on life support.

Social services named the child Jane Doe when she became a ward of the state, and as the four illicit substances began to clear her system, Baby Jane thrived under the NICU's shepherding. Lisa, recovering from the C-section, was wheeled by the unit each day to look at Baby Jane through the incubator's plastic and post to Facebook. When it became clear the baby wouldn't be coming home with her, she lost interest. On day three, after the nurses made her walk to the NICU, she quit coming at all.

She was overheard talking with Poonboy on her phone, begging for a fix, on the day before her discharge. Seeming distracted, she forgot to walk down to see the baby that day. She calmed some after he visited that night, and before discharge the next morning during a social worker visit, she crudely exerted her motherhood by insisting her name be spelled Jain, not Jane, and the last name be Smith, not Doe.

It had been less than a week, and Lisa's apartment was being repaired, so she moved in with Angel, taking an air mattress on the living room floor while Poonboy continued to sleep on the couch. His meth kept her mostly on schedule for her visits with Sharon and Rose, who remained in foster care, but she was intimidated by the NICU, and after a few calls to check on Jain, she made no further efforts to see her.

Despite no home, no income, a history of drug use while pregnant, and pending charges for child endangerment, reunification with Lisa was the official goal for all three girls. Her meth-fueled visits with Sharon and Rose every week continued through the winter, always with promises to get them home soon. Clear signs of meth use went undetected, and it began to look like they might come home after Lisa got back into her own apartment. The girls were happier in foster care and were certainly better fed, but they were too young to have a say in the matter.

While she continued to ask about Jain, the threat of prosecution for child endangerment and more stringent requirements for reunification—including random drug tests and strict housing requirements—scared Lisa off, and it seemed clear there would be no further action against her if the baby stayed in state custody. She insisted she wanted Baby Jain to come home, but eventually quit asking.

With Lenny in prison, Lisa moved near Springfield, Missouri, to live with her mother, and Sharon and Rose were transferred to a foster home there while reunification efforts for them continued. Thriving Baby Jain was placed directly into an adoptive foster home south of Joplin in October after twelve and a half weeks in the NICU. Sharon and Rose, their lives directed by a court system focused on "reunification," went home to Lisa just in time for Christmas.

CHAPTER TWO

CATNISS DIES

IT WAS No Hump Wednesday at Joplin Pet Care, and the morning crew of three veterinarians, three veterinary nurses, and seven support staff members had just knocked out forty desexing surgeries, mostly on dogs. Pete Kramer, lead veterinarian and clinic owner, started Low-Cost Spay/Neuter Days years ago after having to euthanize hundreds of unwanted pets when the carbon monoxide chamber quit working at the local humane society. Low-Cost Spay/Neuter Days evolved into a community tradition that was hard work and a money-loser, but it generated passion in the staff and community goodwill as local euthanasia numbers declined.

"Well, we really knocked that out!" Pete exclaimed as the last patient of the morning was gently carried off to recovery. He pulled his zebra-striped surgery cap off and ran his hands through his sandy blonde hair as he glanced at the clock then headed out of the surgery suite. He had a big, open face and large gentle eyes that were poor at hiding emotion and quick to express kindness. His skin was smooth and only lightly tanned in these waning days of winter, with freckles over his nose and arms. He was trim and lithe, despite his large frame, from years of daily swimming.

"Fuckin' A!" Mikki grinned. She was a born-again RVT who lived for veterinary medicine, and surgery in particular. Even though she had dark skin, dark hair, and full lips and eyes that appeared slightly Hispanic, she was a German-American girl. She was the driving force behind the Spay/Neuter (S/N) operation, and she had everything from presurgical to anesthesia induction and recovery to clean up running like clockwork that morning. "Hell, we might even get to eat lunch today!"

"Great, you just cursed us!" Pete knocked on his head like it was wood. Joplin Pet Care was an extremely busy veterinary hospital that had grown tremendously from when it started out with a doctor, a receptionist, and an assistant twenty years before. It was rare to make it through lunch without interruption by an emergency or urgent care case. Still, hope sprang eternal.

"I'm buying today, Monterrey Mexican's on me!" A little cheer went up with Pete's sudden declaration. Casey, another assistant, began to take orders from everyone. By the time callbacks to patient's owners were finished, and the two-table surgery room and treatment/prep areas were cleaned up, several sacks of piping hot Mexican food were being laid out on the treatment room tables.

"You should enjoy this." Pete's eyes were twinkling as he teased Mikki about her Hispanic appearance.

Mikki flipped him off casually as she lifted a taco to her mouth. Kelli, one of the receptionists, came into the treatment room as Pete returned the gesture. He was embarrassed to be caught... Kelli was quiet and didn't generally join in their crudities.

"Someone just called in a dog emergency. I think they're almost here."

"What is it?" asked Pete, the concern in his voice instantly alerting everyone.

Kelli shrugged, "Don't know, they hung up."

Tension rose in the treatment room, as it always did when an unknown emergency was coming to the clinic. Food remained, but lunch was over, and equipment and supplies for the incoming patient quickly replaced salsa, chips, and tacos.

Many of the people working at JPC thrived on emergency medicine, like Mikki, who had previously worked in a metropolitan veterinary emergency facility for many years. As a fellow emergency junkie, Pete had worked as a critical care Respiratory Therapist in a human Level One trauma center throughout and before veterinary school. Together, they were equipped to handle almost anything.

Pete and his wife, Prissy, had built JPC into several historic old downtown brick buildings in south Joplin and had included a large enclosed parking garage in a connected warehouse. At 12:26 p.m., Kelli watched an old white Ford F-150 pickup bounce into the parking garage and come to a halt by the entrance door to the clinic. Sitting in the bed of the truck were a disheveled red-headed woman and a teenage boy, who cradled a large yellow Lab wrapped in a blanket.

"They're here!" Kelli shouted from the front desk.

Casey and Mikki immediately headed to the waiting truck, followed by Pete. A man in worn jeans and an older khaki work shirt slid from behind the wheel as they approached.

"We don't know what happened," he said. "We got up this morning, did our chores, ran into town, and when we got home, she was collapsed on the garage floor."

He spoke quickly, and his voice trembled, "We can't stand to see her sufferin'. She looks real bad!"

"Let's see what's going on," Mikki said. The man opened the tailgate of the truck, and Mikki climbed into the bed. "And who is this?" she asked the young man holding the limp dog.

"Catniss," he replied, shakily patting Catniss' head. Brown diarrhea stained the blanket she was wrapped in, and the dog made no response except to blink as Mikki ran her hands over the cold body under the blanket.

"And you just found her this way this morning? She was normal before that?"

"Yeah. She came home last night, ate some, then barfed a bit later. We found puke by the garage door," the woman replied. She glanced at her husband, then said, "But she felt okay, just a little slow, so we didn't do nothin'. I should've brought her then!"

"No, it's not your fault. Were there any other symptoms?"

"No, she seemed fine except just not very playful. I should've known! She never throws up!"

"If there were no other signs, we just would've told you to wait and see before bringing her in," interjected Pete. He was worried Mikki might inadvertently say something judgmental.

Mikki said, "Let's get her into the treatment room." Pete ignored her quick stank eye for interrupting. They all got down out of the truck and slid Catniss, who was on a large piece of cardboard, to the edge of the tailgate. The boy and his mother stepped back, and as the boy awkwardly put his arm around her shoulder, she began to tear up. Pete and Mikki scooped the yellow Lab up carefully, straining as they took on her weight.

Kelli held the door as the man watched, and they shuffled through the entrance door and started past the counter, the mother and boy in tow. The man was slow to follow, so Kelli went in, leaving him to find his way.

"We're going to take her back to the treatment room and get started on her. If you guys would stay here and give Kelli some information, we'll talk once we get her more stable." Pete used his firm doctor voice.

"Sure." The man replied as he came in. Kelli led them to a private exam room for the paperwork. Pete and Mikki continued to shuffle towards the swinging door that separated the reception area in the front from the treatment room in the back.

As they hefted Catniss up onto the grate of the closest "wet table" that doubled as an exam table, she let loose with some more diarrhea, and foul-smelling brown liquid flowed into the crook of Mikki's arm.

"As usual," Mikki said sarcastically, rolling her eyes. She was a magnet for gross excretions, and everyone knew it.

"Hey! You should'a asked for the front end!" Pete smiled.

"And if I had, she would've puked instead." Mikki immediately started hosing off her arm and lathering it with scrub soap, a small sneer of disgust crunching her nose and upper lip.

They got the blanket out from around Catniss, and Mikki began washing diarrhea from the golden hair of her rump. Pete started reassuring the dog as he carefully examined her. His hands ran down the head and neck, checking for enlarged lymph nodes, lumps or bumps, sore spots from trauma, abdominal tenderness, free movement of limbs, and any external parasites. There was some mild tenderness in the abdomen, generalized weakness—she couldn't, or wouldn't, stand—and fleas and lots of embedded ticks, not uncommon for Ozark country dogs.

Mikki slid in a thermometer when she finished cleaning up Catniss's rear end, and Casey clipped the hair on her left front leg to start an IV.

"Pulse 180; respiratory rate is about 35-40," Casey reported.

"Temperature's 99.5," said Mikki.

"Poor old girl," Pete soothed as he finished his exam, he cupped her chin in one palm and patted her head with the other. Dogs should be at least 101. Catniss gave a tiny wag of her tail. "How are you doing, darling?"

Pete stepped to one side while Mikki automatically stepped to the other to help hold the dog in position for an IV. "You're a good dog," he said, then raised her lip to reveal white gums.

"Gums're pale and jaundiced... and dry." Catniss burped, and he turned his face away. "And horrid breath that smells like rotten meat!"

He pulled out his stethoscope and listened to her chest with a frown. "She does have a grade one systolic heart murmur. More of a flow murmur... Lungs are clear."

As he quit listening, they let Catniss slump back down after sliding a heating pad under her.

"Okay, girl, now the fun part," Mikki said to Catniss as Pete slipped on a glove. The rectal exam just revealed more brown diarrhea, and Pete smeared a slide for microscopic examination. Pete nodded as Casey questioningly held up a bag of LRS, and she started the IV fluids.

"Get some O2 going at ten and start a STAT screen when you're done drawing blood. Verify with a PCV and TPP." These were all blood tests that would quickly provide more info. "And bump her with a touch of hydromorph for the pain. I'm gonna chart quick." He handed the fecal smear to an assistant who was already at the microscope.

Kelli was coming from the exam room with a clipboard. "How old is she?" he called out as he entered vitals in the computerized chart.

"Two years," Kelli answered. "Intact female. The Roys are signed in and ready to be talked to about Catniss. I put them in room two."

"Roys? Okay, I'll be right in to talk with them," Pete replied as he finished charting. Kelli kept walking towards him until she could lower her voice.

"No money. At all." She looked concerned since dealing with money issues often fell to her.

Pete nodded. He saw Catniss was in the clinic system while charting, but she had not been seen since she was a puppy. Usually, that indicated money problems rather than ignorant neglect. Apparently, Kelli's interview had verified that.

Mikki spoke across the treatment room, relaying results from the blood work. "Her PCV's eight, and the serum's dark yellow. STAT screen's almost done. Urine's red and clean except for some increased casts and USG is 1.015." Pete smiled to himself. He'd forgotten the urine, but Casey and Mikki had collected it without comment and ran it automatically. Urine was supposed to be yellow, and the low USG, which measures urine concentration, along with the "casts," meant Catniss had active kidney damage occurring as well.

"Uffda. Well, I'd better talk to them now and see what they want to do. Thanks!" Pete headed for exam room two.

The woman and her son were sitting on the bench in exam two, and the man was standing in the corner. They appeared relieved to see Pete. "We're so thankful you were here!" the woman said, looking at him intently.

"Well, Catniss is looking a tiny bit better for the moment. We've started fluids and a warming pad, and something for pain. She's responding some to the treatment." As he spoke, he realized she was Lexi; they often passed her place as they floated down the river on kayaks or canoes. He paused, unable to recollect the other names.

"My name is Dr. Kramer, Pete Kramer." He put his hand out to the man.

"I'm George, and this is our son, Joseph." They shook hands briefly. "We're neighbors, right? Ya'll live in the ol' Swanson place on Shoal Creek?"

"Yes… I recognized Lexi. I should since my daughter used to stay with you during the day sometimes! Just couldn't remember your name. Ya'll just live upstream from us on the other side of the river, about a river mile, right?"

"We're the first place east of you, yep."

"Then I recognize Miss Catniss! She comes and swims alongside our kayaks sometimes. Usually a dog or two with her, right?" The Roy place was a bit worn, and the dogs were typical country dogs, running free around the property and minimally cared for at best. Pete had never been inside their house, though his wife Prissy must have since their daughter, before they lost her, had spent the night there a few times.

"Yup."

"Sorry we have to meet like this."

"What's goin' on with Catniss?" asked Lexi. Anxiety made her voice tense, and her face was closed, guarded, eyes intent on Pete.

"Right now, she's a pretty sick dog. What we know is that she's dehydrated and quite low on blood. She's destroying her blood cells, which makes her turn yellow. Her kidneys are damaged by this process as well, so she's in kidney failure, too. We can't tell what's causing this, but the most common things around here are tick diseases. And she's struggling to breathe."

"We know she's got a few ticks, but we treat her with that stuff we got at Wal-Mart. The ticks'er really bad this year!" George said.

"Yes, but nothing is 100%, and she does have ticks attached to her, so we can't rule out tick disease at this point. It would be the best thing for her to have because we can treat that. But it could also be other things, like bad infection, auto-immune disease, or cancer."

Pete let the implication that it might not be treatable sink in for a moment. With money being tight and the man not very emotionally invested in Catniss, unless he was reading him wrong, he wanted to prepare them for the worst.

"I have to ask you a few questions now, just to be sure about some things. Is that okay?"

"Yes, that's fine," replied George, and Lexi licked her lips and nodded once in earnest.

"Okay, so Catniss was normal until last night?"

"Yes," Lexi said.

"And she just ate a little last night before she threw up?"

"Yes."

"And you live in the country... Have you seen Catniss or the other dogs drag anything home to eat in the last week, or have they been in the trash pile at all?"

"No, not that we know of, but she could certainly find dead animals in the river or in the bottoms. And there's always the neighbor's trash pile, but she don't roam much."

"Other dogs okay?" Pete was trying to figure out what the heck was wrong with Catniss, looking for any clue.

Lexi tensed as the new concern emerged. Her eyes narrowed, trying to see the answer inside him. "Yes, are they gonna get sick?"

"Let's figure out what's wrong with Catniss first, and you may not have to worry. Right now, she's really short on blood. She's gonna need a transfusion, x-rays, IV's, and a lot of inpatient hospital care. She's in tough shape, but we can sure give it our best shot."

George and Lexi looked long at each other, and Pete knew what was coming. He'd listed expensive-sounding things to test the waters.

"What're her chances, Doc?" George asked. "We know she's pretty sick, but we ain't rich.

"Her prognosis isn't great based on how she's looking right now. It's not entirely hopeless, but if we're going to try to save her, we need to get that transfusion going, and it's going to cost a fair bit. We'll get you an estimate while I recheck her, and we'll get some x-rays, okay?" It would cost more to save her than they could afford, even with a neighborly discount, but they had to digest that a bit.

"Yes, okay," Lexi said before George could object.

"I'll do my best."

"Thank you!"

Pete left the room just as Mikki started to open the door from her side.

"She's looking worse," she whispered.

Pete approached, and Catniss was in dire straits, gasping for breath. No dog could keep that up, and Casey had cranked the oxygen wide open and was trying to keep the mask over Catniss's nose and mouth as she struggled. Another assistant help keep her in position on the table. Not needed at the moment, Mikki had sent the other staff about their business to prepare for the afternoon appointments that would begin to show up soon.

"Hey, girl. Hang in there." The dog didn't, couldn't, respond. A moment later, she burped, and something foul escaped around the oxygen mask, so rank that Pete didn't want to breathe himself. Between the odor and the extreme distress, he knew she was already dead.

"Get 10cc of Sleepaway ready, please," he sighed deeply. "And bring the owners back here." He didn't look up, momentarily swimming in defeat and dreading the emotions that would follow as they helped the owners through the process. Mikki moved silently to comply, equally discouraged.

Pete was waiting, stroking Catniss's head as she lay on her side when Casey and Kelli brought the Roys into the treatment room. Instinct told them it was bad. George slowed down, but Lexi broke into tears as she and Joseph rushed to hug their friend. Joseph buried his face on her side as Lexi put her face to Catniss's, only to draw back at the odor coming around the mask. "She's taken a turn for the worse, so I had them get you right away. She's lost too much blood and is dying right now. It's too late even for a transfusion. I'm so sorry."

Joseph's face was still buried in the soft fur of her flank as he shook in grief. Lexi slipped her arm around him and leaned to kiss him on the exposed cheek. "What should we do?"

She looked at Pete. Pete stepped back as George approached the other side of the narrow table and reached to comfort both Lexi and Joseph. "We need to let her go, so she'll stop suffering. If there were any chance of pulling through, we'd intervene more, but she's not gonna make it," he paused. "I'd like to give her some medicine that's basically an overdose of anesthesia to put her to sleep so she'll quit suffering if that's okay," Pete explained. "She's really struggling."

Catniss, in full shock now and barely conscious, was without the strength to respond to them. Her tail was limp on the table. Pete offered a box of tissues, and Lexi gathered herself, wiping her nose and eyes. "Yes, that's the best thing. There's nothin' you can do, right?" she asked, her eyes searching his again.

"It's just a dog," George said, quiet but tense. "We can't afford heroics."

"There are things we could do," replied Pete, ignoring George's insensitivity. "Nothing that would help, though."

"If you agree," Pete continued after a moment, "there's this permission form to sign, but I can sign it for you. I just want you to know about it."

"No, it's fine. I can sign it," Lexi stated firmly through her tears. Blocking George, she took the clipboard and bravely scribbled her signature at the bottom of the page.

Mikki handed Pete the syringe with the pink euthanasia solution.

"She already has an IV in place, so I'll just give the medication through the IV. Y'all don't have to move; you can just comfort her as she passes." He paused to give them a moment. "I'll go ahead and give her the medicine if that's okay."

He wasn't trying to rush them; he just didn't want Catniss to suffer any longer. Lexi and George looked at each other and then Joseph.

George closed his eyes and nodded. "Okay," Pete explained, "I am going to give the medicine, pentobarbital, directly into her IV, and she'll immediately relax. It should be very peaceful."

The Roys nodded their heads.

"I'm going to push the medicine now." He inserted the needle into the injection port on the IV line and pushed the Sleepaway in. Catniss immediately relaxed and quit breathing. Despite the quiet sobs of the Roys and the tears in everyone's eyes, the tension flowed out of the room.

The hiss of the oxygen stopped as Casey quietly turned it off and slipped the mask from Catniss's face. The room filled with a foul odor again as the gas from Catniss's stomach escaped through her mouth.

Once a few moments passed, and the Roys collected themselves, Pete asked them if they wanted scripture read. They did, and Mikki, who had retrieved the Bible from the chapel, handed it to Pete. He read aloud his favorite Psalm for animals, 36:6:

Your unfailing love, Oh Lord, is as vast as the heavens;

Your faithfulness reaches beyond the clouds.

Your righteousness is like the mighty mountains;

Your justice like the ocean depths.

You care for people and animals alike O'LORD,

How Precious is your unfailing love, O'God!

"Because he cares for them, and all creation, I believe all animals do indeed go to heaven at the restoration of all things. I think you will see Catniss again, except restored and not suffering," Pete said.

Everyone hugged, and Pete said a short prayer for the Roys and Catniss, then walked the Roys out to the pickup in the parking garage. As Lexi and Joe got into the truck on the passenger side, Pete quietly asked George if it would be alright to do an autopsy.

"It'd be good to know what was causing that smell since you have three other dogs. It may be something she was exposed to on your land or roaming nearby. I'd be willing to do it for free… I have dogs, too."

"Just don't say nuthin' to Lexi. Might get upset. She don't have good sense about pets. Loves them too much… wastes too much money on 'em, too." George said it like Pete was his confidant.

"Okay, thank you. I'll let you know if we find anything significant." Pete went back into the clinic to the treatment room, where Catniss was already being transferred into a body bag.

"Hey, we're going to do a necropsy as soon as we can, but we have to get through the appointments first," Pete said to Mikki and Casey as they bagged her up.

Mikki shifted her eyes in a way that indicated there was something she wanted to say but was nervous about it.

"What?" Pete grinned.

"You took so long in the room earlier; we were able to get x-rays while you were talking…" Mikki and Casey looked a little sheepish.

Pete rolled his eyes, "I wasn't in the room *that* long…"

"You *might* want to take a look at them when you get a chance." Mikki and Casey lifted the wrapped body to carry it out to the cooler while Pete went to the radiology room. Around them, the clinic was rapidly picking up the pace. It would be a busy afternoon, and Pete's first appointment was in fifteen minutes.

He clicked on the computer mouse to bring up the most recent digital radiographs, and an antemortem x-ray image of Catniss's abdomen popped up on the screen. Pete studied the image, his arms crossed and his chin in one hand, eyes narrowed and focused. It was interesting because there were metallic foreign bodies in the stomach, as well as some bony-looking junk. Extra gas, whose miasma still contaminated the air, was present as well.

"What do you want us to do with the rest of the blood? You still want the CBC and chemistry profile?"

"Yes, please." He was curious and, even though he would need to pay for it himself, it might be a good learning experience.

"Okie dokie," said Mikki.

Case after case left everyone exhausted at the end of the day. JPC was opened from 7:00 a.m. to 7:00 p.m., and 7:00 p.m. rolled around very quickly that evening. By 8:00 p.m., everything was caught up. Pete had the body brought back inside, now stiff and cool from the freezer. Mikki and Casey helped slide it off the cart, out of the bag, and onto the wet table's grate. Everyone cringed, mentally, if not visibly, as the odor returned.

"So, what do you think is going on with the anemia?" Mikki asked as she walked by, crunching up her nose.

"It's a mystery, but it might be related to what's in her stomach, so we gotta check."

"Well, get this done, cuz she stiiii-inks!" He rolled his eyes. Like he couldn't smell Catniss himself. It *was* going to stink up the whole clinic if he didn't work fast, so he laid Catniss on her back, exposing her stomach for the procedure.

He slid the towel and the empty body bag over onto the cart and immediately grabbed the electric clipper and buzzed Catniss's belly, removing the hair from her chin clear down to her inguinal region, so it wouldn't stick to the guts when they were removed.

Once he was done, hair was everywhere, and her belly was smooth and bare. Her skin was already beginning to discolor where the oozing intestines and organs were beginning to stain the inner body wall. He vacuumed the hair up carefully and used the sprayer to rinse her skin and clean her mouth out, then dried her with the towel that had been over her. Pushing and tying her stiff legs outward to the cleats on the table's sides, she was quickly positioned for exploration.

Pete put on nitrile gloves and made a broad, fast scalpel cut, starting at her pubic bone, at the very hind part of her abdomen, and extended the incision on the midline all the way to her mid-sternum. The linea, a tough white band of connective tissue holding the two halves of the abdomen together, was completely exposed in one long incision. A quick stab penetrated the linea, and Pete quickly opened the abdomen from the sternum to the pubis.

In deep-chested dogs, like the large yellow Lab that Catniss was, the stomach resides high up under the rib cage. Pete went ahead and carefully extended the incision towards her head to better expose the stomach. This meant cutting through the xiphoid and up through the cartilage that joins the ribs to the sternum with a heavy scissor, allowing the chest to be spread open a bit to better expose the stomach.

He then inserted his hands and pulled the chest apart with force. Cold, gristly tissue finally ripped as the sharp edges of the ribs tried to cut through his gloves. Mottled and purple, the stomach and the overlying liver were revealed beneath the opening he had created. Gas made the stomach appear smooth and rounded, but Pete could feel chunky, grindy stuff inside.

Careful inspection of the rest of the guts in the abdomen and found nothing else irregular except for severe inflammation in the pancreas. Little vesicles of life in her uterus would have been puppies in another seven weeks or so, which gave him a flash of despair. Not wanting the loss to distract him or cause him to reveal his grief, he gently pushed the uterus back.

It was time to check the stomach contents, and Pete slipped his damaged gloves off and tossed them in the trash. After donning a surgical mask for odor protection, he pulled on double gloves. Mikki and Casey came near, eager to see what was inside.

"Get ready for a stink, I think!" Pete scooped up the stomach in one hand and held the scalpel ready in the other. He stabbed. First, a tiny hiss, then a putrid brown/black ooze as he extended the incision with a scissor. A dreadful rotten meat odor invaded the room.

"Ewwww!" Casey and Mikki echoed on cue. "That's horrible!" They were drawn closer, but Pete sensed most of the remaining staff rapidly thinning out and heading home, their curiosity overwhelmed by the odor of rotten death.

"Smells like possum roadkill shit stew left out in the sun ten days!" he gagged.

As Pete directed the warm, soupy fluid into the wet table, sinewy white bone and some black metal objects surfaced, and he reached in to extract whatever was there. He pulled out a bracelet of what appeared to be coins. Tangled in the loop were some bones: a partial wrist and some finger bones.

"Is that what I think it is?" Mikki said, eyes wide and leaning in despite the stench.

"Looks like it."

Mikki held out a towel for Pete as he lifted the material aside. He gently separated the bracelet with two corroded coins from the bones and meat, making two small piles. He reached back into the stomach and pulled out a few more bones and one loose penny—Abe's head was visible on the black corroded surface.

"This is either from a washed-up grave, or she came across a body in the woods. Maybe from the river since they live on Shoal Creek… Take my cellphone for a camera and get the investigations box from the surgery room."

Mikki brought the box, used for when they were called to assist with abuse investigations, and they rinsed and photographed carefully before placing the bracelet and the bones into two separate big baggies. All three coins were pennies. Catniss had left her mark: The clamp that had held the loose penny was chewed and bent, and several bones showed crushing. What was either the main carpal bone or the end of the radius appeared to be shattered on the free edge.

Pete decided not to explore the chest further and quickly sewed up the stomach and then the linea and skin as Mikki washed the odious soup down the drain. Casey and Mikki worked the body and gross towel back into the body bag, and this time tied it tight and attached both an identification tag and a hold tag so it wouldn't be cremated.

"So, what do you think is going on?" Casey rolled a cart close so they could take the body back to the freezer.

"Well, they're body parts from someone. Who knows?" They slid the bag back onto the cart. "Her anemia was probably from the zinc in the pennies," Pete continued, his deep distraction by the body parts causing a neutral tone as he gave the automatic reply. "I knew zinc was bad, but I thought it would just kill little things, like cats," Mikki replied. Pete was already intensely focused on implications raised by the wrist bones. He shook off his distraction, and his eyes cleared as he tried to focus. Pete appreciated Mikki's tenacity with the medical aspects of the case and her constant desire to learn, but he was surprised she wasn't obsessing about the bones as well.

"Well, that's normally true, but the bracelet was tangled with the hand parts, and those were too big to immediately pass out of the stomach. When zinc's in stomach acid, it's quickly dissolved, absorbed, and poof—hemolytic anemia out the butt," Pete explained.

"So, if it had gotten into the intestines, then it wouldn't have been so bad?"

"Right, they would have passed through. Still may have gotten pancreatitis from the rotten stuff, though." Pete considered for a moment, then looked at her a little incredulously and said, "Don't you even care about whose wrist that might be?"

"Well, duh, but that isn't really what killed Catniss, is it?" She seemed to not appreciate his tone, adding, "Isn't that a police thing, not a medical thing?"

He rolled his eyes, but not so she could see. He had to admire her focus, though, and tried not to sound sarcastic. "I'll go call the police and let them know then. Probably oughta tell the Roys, too."

He washed up his hands and tempered his excitement about the find by stopping at his computer to chart. Once the x-rays and the photographs were transferred to Catniss's patient file, he typed in complete notes and entered the tentative diagnoses as heavy metal poisoning and pancreatitis. It was almost 9:00 p.m. when he placed the baggies into a brown paper sack and sealed it with a sticky label with Catniss's information.

Mikki and Casey, the last two standing, headed out the door as his phone vibrated with a text from Prissy.

Where are you?

He felt a flash of irritation he knew to be inappropriate. It *was* getting late, after all.

Interesting case, almost done. TTYL.

"Interesting" was their private code word for difficult situations.

Despite the clinic's location in the City of Joplin in Jasper County, Pete knew the case would fall to Newton County authorities where Catniss lived and would have encountered the body, or body parts. He picked up the phone and called his brother from another father, who ran tracking hounds and was also a deputy at the Newton County Sheriff's Office. Allen Miller was from his mother's first marriage, born fifteen years and three marriages before Pete took his first breath.

"Bro?" Allen never wasted words.

"Hey, bro." Pete cut to the chase, "Look, I have something to for you."

"Oh?"

"Yeah, this is kind of weird-sounding…" Pete began as he flicked his index finger against the brown evidence bag he'd carried back to his desk.

"Well, that's okay, considering the source."

Allen was soon headed over to pick up the "evidence." While he was waiting, Pete printed up the chart as well, then sat back and threw his feet on his desk, staring out the window as he considered the day's events.

CHAPTER THREE
FORGIVEN

PETE'S CELL PHONE alarm woke him quietly at 4:30 a.m. Thursday. He placed a kiss on Prissy's brow and stroked her dark hair before carefully sliding out from under her velvety olive-skinned thigh. She gently stirred, graceful even in slumber. A naturally beautiful body remained, but he was glad her eyes, long hardened from hurt, stayed closed. It was painful to see the dull coldness that had replaced their once lively radiance. Also, Prissy would need her sleep; settling a new foster child required lots of extra energy.

Last night around 11:00 p.m., he had just finished relating the details of the Catniss death and postmortem when a caseworker called with a placement. Prissy reluctantly said yes, a word not often on her lips or in her heart, to the placement request. His heart leapt—it had been years! Almost twenty years since they'd lost Jain. Since then, *Prissy's* enthusiasm for fostering, and even life, had been diminished, not his. Then her eyes had met Pete's, and he knew she was seeking derision that only existed in her heart for the foolishness of exposing them to another potential loss.

She found no scorn or rejection in his kind gaze. He was hoping only enthusiasm shone out. It seemed like a new day might be dawning. Every foster was a potential loss, but it was how you handled that loss that really mattered. Until Jain, his faith had always carried them both, and it still carried him past the parting that came with almost every child they took in. After Jain, something broke in Prissy, something he couldn't fix. There was no explanation for the call last night unless Prissy had run into a social worker somewhere and not mentioned it to him. There were rare calls for placements, and they had become even rarer as the years went by, but meeting an old worker might spark something. Foster homes were scarce, and workers were often desperate.

After his morning bathroom chores, he tip-toed out of the master suite and down the river house hall past two empty bedrooms, his heart buoyed by the prospect of the old Prissy rising again. After hosting forty foster kids over the years, the other bedrooms had laid empty since seven-year-old Jain, whom they raised almost from birth, had been removed from their home unexpectedly several years prior. In a ruthless application of family reunification policies, a judge in another county decided to ignore the recommendations of everyone involved and sent Jain back to her biological mother at the TPR hearing.

Termination of Parental Rights, the last step before Jain's adoption into their family, was to have been finalized that day. But the judge was inebriated and had family ties to the biological mother, Lisa Hartley. He decided to give her another chance at motherhood with a daughter she'd only visited twice in seven years, leaving everyone stunned. That was the soul injury from which Prissy had never recovered. Neither did the judge, whose drinking led to a fiery encounter with a bridge abutment out on the interstate a few years later that put him, or what was left of him, in the grave. But his demise brought no joy for Prissy; her "yes" the night before had been the first flicker of light he'd seen since then.

Pete's six-day-a-week work and emergencies only on Sundays had saved him, more or less, but Prissy had retreated into a post-traumatic shell no one could penetrate as she did her best to prepare her daughter in the two weeks the court allowed. Since then, Pete was left without a spiritual partner, much less a sensual one.

On the way to the front door, he saw he was losing the thermostat war and smiled to himself. He left it at seventy, where Prissy must have set it in the night. He preferred sixty-six, or even sixty-four. Their two Golden Retrievers and a cross-bred Collie greeted him quietly as he headed out the front door then around the side of the house towards the picnic table on the lawn overlooking the river. Their feet and bellies were wet, and he gently corrected Peeta, the bigger Golden, when he tried to put his soppy paws on Pete's leg. Once they all got some petting, they happily glomped off to explore the morning.

With the clinic open from seven to seven, early morning was about the only time he could get alone. It had rained in the night, but if there had been thunder, he'd slept through it. A cacophony of frogs and toads filled the river bottoms each night, but the spring morning now cooled their song to a gentle, random croak. Swollen buds on trees and plants gave a faint green cast to the otherwise brown and gray river flora this time of year, and dawn tickled the eastern sky. Pete sat on the damp bench of the picnic table to reflect. His habit was to meditate on the most important things first and work to the least important ones last; his God, his life, and the day to come, in that order. It helped remind him of priorities, even if he often failed to live his life according to them.

Coming to an enlightened knowledge of Jesus was the most important day in his life. Though it seemed like a lifetime, it had only been fifteen years… that day had changed everything. Pete slowly shook his head, and a smile played on his lips as he recalled times prior to that day: his former self.

Back then, his most moving personal spiritual experiences were all related to sex. His world had shifted when the pulsing pleasures of his first orgasm flowed through his body and soul, bringing the promise and fear of being able to make a new life. Later, when he and his first girlfriend's sweaty-slick bodies melded in a deep ecstasy that seemed to last forever, his world shifted again as he understood the fires of passion from which that new life arose.

Indeed, a child did come from that first union, and his mother, so active in foster care and adoptions but warring with God, was, ironically, who finally convinced her teenage son and his girlfriend to abort. Early term fetuses were not babies, she assured them. Destruction of the child so passionately forged was like a spiritual divorce for the young couple, and they fell apart soon after. Their deep spiritual scars were never acknowledged, and hence never addressed or resolved.

Prissy was his gift from God. While Pete's mom had been an avid foster parent, even taking in kids off the street from Houston's Fourth Ward where Pete grew up, Prissy's parents had been alcoholics. Sexual abuse by older siblings resulting from the neglectful parenting, combined with intermittent physical and regular verbal abuse in her chaotic childhood, led her to depression as a young adult. After years of struggle, she longed to go and be with Jesus but awoke in the ICU after her first and only suicide attempt. Apparently, Jesus wanted her to be with Pete, and the months of inpatient therapy she'd chosen made that possible when they met while he was in veterinary medical school.

Even before they were officially married, they were trying hard to get pregnant. Prissy was able to mostly surrender herself to Pete's loving arms, even more so after they tied the knot, but severe endometriosis lurked around her womb. While the resultant hysterectomy interrupted their reproductive plans and sex life, it pushed them more towards the foster parenting Pete had experienced throughout his childhood.

As a believer, Prissy prayed for Pete and even led him to church. It wasn't until after the hysterectomy that he had a vision. He had been praying to a God unknown for comfort for his Prissy, a way to fill their need and desire for children, and for guidance on where their lives were to go from here. When a shining angel came to him and told him they would have a vet clinic in a month and then a large family to boot, he knew the vision was true even if he couldn't conceive how the promise would be fulfilled.

To his surprise, Prissy believed his vision and seemed more at peace. He didn't understand why she, or anyone, would allow that a person could have a real vision, much less accept it as truth, unless they had experienced it as well. The vision made him consider that God might be real, and the Jesus stuff might not be crap, but still, he wasn't sure.

Until enlightenment came to him one Sunday, Pete had not much considered the loss of his first child, and certainly, it had nothing to do with why he came to church with Prissy. But that morning, during the singing, he looked up at a metal support beam in the high vaulted ceiling of the sanctuary. Suddenly, he couldn't sing. Deep remorse overwhelmed him as he recalled the murder of his baby years ago. A black desire to die, to end it there, was all-encompassing. *Jesus, fucking save me, what have I done!?!*

And then a brilliant light pierced the beam, and a path opened directly into what could only be heaven itself. Looking down was his daughter, whole and beautiful, smiling gently upon him, and he knew he was forgiven. Jesus flooded his heart, soul, and mind with the Holy Spirit, and he was released from his crime, indeed all his crimes, and knew the ecstasy of redemption and the source of all truth for the first time in his life. *It wasn't crap!*

He laughed out loud that he had once considered his sexual experiences to be the most important spiritual things in his life—they were only weak reflections of knowing and being fully known by this living God. Prissy glanced at him, saw his emotion, and squeezed his hand with a smile as she continued singing. Pete realized that no one else had seen the light and wondered why God held him so dear. It dawned on him that it wasn't just him, and that's why people still faithfully gathered in churches throughout the world. His heart laughed again, and he rejoined the song as the last verse wound down.

Sitting there on the bench, all these things passed through his mind while the river quietly flowed by towards the ocean as it had for thousands of years. Re-establishing these foundational things in early morning stolen time invariably filled him with gratitude. When the river of life became a flood of good or bad, that gratitude and the resulting peace served as a spiritual bedrock, anchoring his soul in what mattered. One new foster kid wasn't a flood, but it was a good time to take stock of where he was, where Prissy was, and where they were going. The years since Jain had been like a spiritual winter in their relationship and life together, a hiatus, hopefully of healing. Maybe that would prove out in the days to follow.

He put his face in his hands as he asked God for help not just with Prissy someday moving past the loss of Jain so long ago, but also for her as she managed the new child. He prayed for himself as he faced another day without warmth from Prissy, his wife and guide to his salvation. Mother to their many children. Supposedly she was his companion for life, yet he had never been so lonely. Then, he focused on his deep gratitude for all the good wrought from all the bad, which seemed to bring God close, then asked again for help for today and all it would hold. He took in one last breath of the wet, life-filled river scent and opened his eyes as a cardinal flew past, and the moment of closeness with the creator of creation was over.

The high cirrus clouds were livened with peach flame in the morning sky, and a fresh breeze was coming out of the southwest as he drove up the river road to his morning swim before work. Thursdays after No Humps were crazy with catch-up at the clinic, and the seemingly incessant demands of veterinary medicine would dominate his thoughts and actions for most of the day.

CHAPTER FOUR
FINAL RESTING PLACE

WHERE IT RAN south of Joplin, Shoal Creek cut a meandering path through the land to create the entire Shoal Creek Valley, a space with open bottomlands and mixed hardwood forests along the river's course. Thurman Branch, named after a preacher who once baptized there, joined with Shoal Creek just past the Roy place. Another small creek, Beef Branch, joined shortly after that, along with numerous springs and seeps.

Further down the valley, where it narrowed somewhat, Shoal Creek had a defined course. But that meandering confluence of tributaries in the widest part of the valley was unknown to most people. Forest surrounded the area of tributaries, keeping them hidden. The combination of trees and tributaries created humps, dips, and small oxbows throughout this two square mile area called "the bottoms."

From the roads that run through the valley, or from the small cliffs and hills along either side, there is a deceptive appearance of open farmland interspersed with woods. Sometimes the river is visible through the trees, but none of the tributaries are. Those who braved the river on kayaks or canoes discovered a beautiful Ozark stream with a gravel bottom interspersed with some deep, slow-flowing wide spots.

Numerous fallen trees and gravel bars gave the river its name and complicated passage, and portaging around the blockages was not uncommon.

If you got in trouble and hiked out from the river to the nearest road, the distance was never more than a mile, but in the bottom areas that were surrounded by forest, you might have struggled through up to a half-mile of briars, brambles, fallen trees, and stagnant water to get to clear land.

In other places, farm fields came right up to the creek's edge, and walking out was easy. Near the Roys' place was where the bottoms began and ran for about two river miles downstream. This narrow band of difficult land was a dog's paradise, with unlimited things to discover and explore in the tangled habitats. Those bottoms, and the nice flat open farm and ranch fields interspersed with them, had become a search grid laid out by the sheriff's department to make sure every square yard of the area was covered as they looked for the source of the body parts from Catniss's belly.

In Newton County, Deputy Allen Miller had been running cadaver and tracking dogs for decades and was the first person who came to mind when grids needed to be searched. Allen was tall and thin with leathery skin like golden sable. He always wore a straw cowboy hat, blue jeans, and a pearl-buttoned cowboy shirt. And like most persons in the search and rescue (SAR) community, and dog handlers in particular, Allen was eccentric.

Eccentricity was a plus—normal people do not spend large portions of their lives training dogs for a highly specialized task, maintain that training on a regular basis, subject their lives to disruption at a moment's notice day or night, and do it all for no pay or reimbursement of any kind. They may have traveled a few miles, as was the case with the trip to the Roys' place, or a few thousand miles in the case of a major event, like 9-11 or an earthquake in Asia.

Unless he was dying, Allen would show up when called almost anywhere in the world. With a cowboy's sense of humor and love of a good prank, he could be a lot of fun. He liked Irish whiskey when he wasn't working, but when he was on track, he was focused and serious. Because he was a dog handler, he also had a strong sense of perspective on life.

Allen found living children and adults, and sometimes a critical piece of evidence in a criminal case, but for the most part, dead people and children were what he searched for: cadavers. He only endured this by keeping the bigger picture in mind. Finding a lost loved one, even if they have died, brought closure for their family and those left behind; closure that was much harder to find without having their remains. His work and life were a labor of loving devotion to help people in their time of loss, built on the premise he had read in a detective novel: everyone counts, or no one counts.

Allen prepared for this task with relentless training. It took years to develop a good tracking and cadaver dog. Many things were required to achieve the goal. First, he must pick a young dog with a disposition for tracking work and a love of learning. Then the dog's long-term health potential was evaluated by Pete. If health issues showed up that would shorten the dog's useful life, he had to reconsider training the dog even if he had already become fond of it.

Developing a close working relationship with the dog was critical over the next two to three years of training and conditioning and went something like this:

"Hide" the little baggie of cadaver scent (often a paper towel with some dried and rotted blood drawn from his own arm) in plain sight, give intermittent rewards, verbal praise, or a tiny treat for the "finds," then repeat. Intermittent, or Pavlovian, rewards are used because they are much more effective than constant rewards when training animals.

Weeks, sometimes months of easy, plain sight finds were mixed with substrate acclimation that advanced over several months and years, like learning to climb through debris and over trash and rocks. Different lead and harnesses would be used, and there might even be trips on police or medical helicopters and small airplanes.

Then the cadaver scent gradually became more hidden. Over time, it was placed under rocks and vehicles, in the soil, up high in a tree, or down low in a crevice. Maybe Allen would place a bag deep in one of the many caves found in the Ozarks, or down an old mine shaft. All the while, new experiences are added. Like with the mailman, search calls come in the early morning, late evening, or nighttime, and during rain, sleet, snow, and hail. Both dog and handler must be prepared.

Later, climbing and rappelling must be included in the dog's repertoire, along with boating, flying in an airliner, and being around any environment that might accompany a disaster: sirens, shooting, yelling, fire smells, and chemical smells. The dog had to become comfortable with veterinary exams and decontamination from chemical exposures (usually with a fire hose and lots of soap).

Years went by, and during the process, many dogs learned to detect other things that were considered a whole different ball game. Some dogs could track a scent, detect drugs or other substances, find electronic storage devices containing illicit documents, photos, or videos, or perhaps find explosives at an airport. Sometimes, a dog learned personal protection for its handler. No matter what, you teach, reward, then reinforce often.

Allen usually trained and developed his dogs as trackers and Human Remains Detector (HRD) dogs over those first three years. After that, if they didn't flunk out for one of many reasons, he could work the dog for six to seven years on average, or less for larger dogs whose bodies wore out faster. With all his dogs over the years, he maintained a lifelong daily relationship of training and reinforcement of work habits, with more intense practice exercises of some type on at least a weekly basis.

Allen lost his wife to cancer many years ago and lived with usually just one primary dog and one dog in training. His house was on forty acres spotted with random piles of debris like what he would encounter on a search, and he almost always kept human tissue on hand to use for training reinforcement. His relationship with his dogs got instinctive over time, each knowing what the other would do in almost any situation or work environment. Their closeness became almost that of a married couple—a married couple living in poverty due to the shared passion that made them work for free, but a married couple nevertheless.

And then, the relationship ended quickly. As each dog neared the end of their useful life, about five or six years into a full working capacity, the next puppy must be found, and training started anew. His older dog wore out relatively fast and soon enters retirement. Arthritis, heart disease, and cancer all took their toll, and the dog either passed or was put to sleep to end its suffering.

Because of the underlying financial issues (eccentric people who devote hours to training SAR dogs are often not the greatest wage-earners), many dogs that enter service are not properly evaluated from a medical standpoint.

In the past, Allen sometimes had to retire young dogs due to serious, undetected medical problems, losing years of invested love and training. Once his brother, Pete, became a vet, almost all his veterinary care became free, not just for Allen and his dogs, but any serious working dog trainers—an unexpected bonus.

So, Allen's eccentricity was accompanied by a deep sense of perspective. He knew that the time he had to help people with a good dog was very limited, and he knew the fragility of life and how quickly it could be lost. While he got satisfaction from finding the object of a search and the appreciation of the people on the day of the discovery/recovery, there was rarely any public thanks for what he did, nor did he expect any. His relationship with the dog and the closure that goes with a job well done was enough.

Allen's current relationship with Dutch was about as good as it gets. Dutch, a Redbone Coonhound, was cliché in appearance and personality. His big, floppy coonhound ears and his long bony body were covered with soft red hair. He was a friendly dog when not working, with huge brown eyes, a big head dominated by his snout, and long bony legs. He was a certified Human Remains Detection (HRD) dog, and was also one of the best trackers in the region.

Although he often appeared sluggish and uncoordinated, Dutch could sail through the air and move very quickly through almost any type of terrain. Injuries were completely ignored when he was on scent, and water was no obstacle. Nor were briars, brambles, blackberry bushes, or the huge tangles of debris often found along the Shoal Creek bottoms. Getting cut was a real threat from all the sharp things that were found in these tangles, but it was rare for that to happen. Like magic, he usually came through the worst tangles unscathed.

Allen knew that when seeking a body or other evidence, the search began at the last known place of contact. In this case, that was the Roy farm. From there, the easiest way to find the body belonging to the hand was for Dutch to track Catniss's scent, hopefully straight to the original source. Dutch's nose was home to millions of nerve endings that could detect microscopic items.

To help people understand what Dutch "sees" with his nose, Allen would have them imagine looking at the trail of a person with muddy feet on a clean white floor in a shopping mall. The trail was very visible at first, and extremely easy to follow. But over the course of time, other people walking over the muddy tracks, air currents, carts, and mall cops on their Segways would dilute down the trail by gradually spreading out the bits of mud until they became mixed with all the other soiling on the floor.

For Dutch on a scent trail, Allen would tell them to just imagine that muddy trail of footprints in fine detail with each particle, even the ones too small to see, having its own scent. Dutch's nose told him where there were more scent particles and where they started to fade. The particles were as clear to his nose as the muddy footprints were to the eyes. Over time, the trail got fainter and fainter, but it could last for days, depending on the weather.

When a dog like Catniss lived on a farm in the country, she created a myriad of scent trails everywhere she went. However, a tracking dog could tell which trails were fresh and which were stale. It was not a difficult task for Dutch. Training Dutch to communicate what his nose was "seeing" to Allen was the hard part. The difference between a decent tracking dog and a great tracking dog was the relationship between the handler and the dog, as well as the experience level of each one.

Dutch's HRD skills came into play when they looked for cadavers. Instead of tracking a ground trail, Dutch followed the direction of the strongest air scent of the cadaver. Cadaver dogs attempted to lead you to the source of the corpse. In this case, he might've been able to detect the trail of cadaver scent that was probably on the outside of Catniss, even if the corpse was far away, so both his skills, tracking and cadaver detection, would be useful. Actually, conditions had been good to preserve a ground scent. Either way, scenting cadaver in the air or on a trail along the ground, Dutch and his nose would hopefully lead them to a larger smell coming from the body itself.

*

It was late, but a mysterious death case couldn't wait. Allen stopped by Sheriff Burgen's house after meeting with Pete the night before to brief him on the findings and the location of the Roy place. He left the evidence bag in the sheriff's care so the sheriff could give it to the detectives who would then take it to the crime lab first thing in the morning as they began to work the case.

When the midafternoon call came for Allen Miller and his dog the next day, he was ready. He had been with the sheriff's office for decades, as had the sheriff, and had seen just about everything imaginable. While finding human body parts in the countryside was not unheard of, it was very uncommon. Pet owners would often call the sheriff's office with a concern, but generally, the parts dogs brought home ended up being from a deer or some other wild animal. And human remains had never been found *inside* a dog before.

From their experience living in the country, they both knew it was not unusual for scavengers like marauding dogs, coyotes, skunks, possums, or vultures to spread body parts from dead animals over a large area. Parts could be carried a hundred yards or further away from the carcass to a place where the scavenger could stop in relative safety from the other predators or scavengers to gnaw away at the part they'd obtained. To complicate it further, a dog like Catniss could have roamed several miles, so the main body might be nowhere near the Roy residence.

It was a thirty-five-minute drive from Allen's home to the Roy place. Allen made it in twenty-three, one of the perks of being in law enforcement. Gateway Drive, also known as Old Highway 71, was a long downhill run going south from Joplin that eventually flattened out into the river valley. It had been repaved and designated a business route for the new I-49 highway a few years back, but after the road flattened out into the valley, it crossed two bumpy old bridges that remained from the original highway.

The bridges were narrow and aging, with large concrete guard rails close against the pavement, leaving room for only two narrow lanes and no sidewalks. The first bridge crossed Thurman Branch, and the second crossed Shoal Creek. The two waters flowed together about a half-mile downstream to the west, where their confluence led to the meandering web of channels and islands throughout the wooded river bottoms.

Barbed wire fencing ran along the highway, but it was clearly not in good shape. The poles were bent over from the flood last Christmas, and debris gathered along the strands of barbed wire, which had been pulled into fields several yards in some places. Part of the fence had been cleaned up and restrung, but most was still down.

Just after the bridges, the Roys' driveway was marked with a battered mailbox on a leaning pole. There were no numbers on the mailbox, but a weathered VFD marker on the pole matched the Roys' place, so Allen turned down the rutted gravel driveway.

Only one small patch of arable land appeared to be in fescue, but certainly not enough to make any money. It had clearly not even been cut last year; it was still dry and brown. He followed the driveway about a quarter mile around and through a small grove of mixed river bottom trees of sycamore, ash, and elder. The trees were tinting green with buds, and forsythia blossoms were blazing a brilliant yellow. Eventually, the driveway curved back into a clearing that led up to a higher area where the house was situated.

Allen had noticed debris stuck in some of the tree branches about eight feet off the ground coming up the driveway. As he drove up to the house, he estimated that the ground rose another three or four feet and had probably just cleared the big flood last Christmas. In the back seat, Dutch alerted to some dogs half-heartedly barking inside an aging pole building and poked his head out the open window. Allen was enjoying the first warm day of spring after a long brown winter. It felt good to his old bones.

He parked his old F150 crew cab in the shade for Dutch's sake, who was now sprawled across the back seat. Several Crown Vics from the sheriff's department and two Tahoes from the state police were parked nearby. Allen got out, lit a Camel, and walked to the sheriff's unmarked car.

"Howdy partner," he said, blowing a lungful of smoke off to the side as Burgen got out.

"Hello, dog man," Burgen replied. "Glad you could make it!"

"Glad to be here. What's the plan?"

"Let's get with the others, so I don't have to repeat myself. There's new information from the crime lab."

They walked toward a patrol car that was parked under a small ornamental pear tree just entering its spring blossom. It was running with the A/C on, and two patrol deputies got out. Allen, thankful he didn't wear a vest, nodded to his old friend Deputy Terry Pusser.

A tall folding table had been set up near the open trunk of the patrol car, and two state troopers walked over. Greetings and some banter were exchanged as the Newton County detective on the case came over and set a laptop on the table and pulled up a Google map on the screen. Allen stepped back to listen as the sheriff nodded at the detective to start.

"This is not for public release. Preliminary crime lab inspection shows the damage to the tissue from the dog, as expected. But it looks like turtles and fish may have chewed on the tissue that was left, and they saw little shells and algae under the microscope that are consistent with the sample having been in the water at some point.

"The most interesting thing is the shattered end of the arm bone, which was still attached to the wrist bone. They found fragments indicating a high-speed impact, and there was a lead trail on the x-rays. In other words, the arm, most likely from a woman, was damaged by a gunshot wound."

"Didn't expect a bullet," said Allen, letting smoke out as he talked.

"That's what I know so far," the detective answered. "We were going to search in the house and barn here, but that's probably not necessary since our victim is most likely on or near the river." That explained the presence of state patrol, which was responsible for investigating water deaths.

He then zoomed in on the Roys' farm.

The land included forest and some open pasture, and both sides of the river for a distance. Most of the river was in the bottoms, where access was difficult. But in the early spring, leaves were sparse, and except for the tangles and rafts of river debris, much of the low land had been flushed relatively clean from the recent flood.

Tangles could sometimes cover several acres and be well over six feet deep. In some places, tangles were like a thick raft or mat of very small twigs and sticks, soft and mulch-like. In other places, there could be deep piles of larger branches and even tree trunks interspersed with cast-offs and float-aways from human activity. Televisions, chairs, tables, pallets, railroad ties, and even a large security safe had been found in the tangles on Shoal Creek.

Sometimes a dead animal would be in the debris somewhere, usually wildlife or a big bird, and the reek of death nearby in the summertime could be almost disorienting. It was not unheard of for an old vehicle to mysteriously appear after a flood and then disappear in the next flood, never to be seen again. Unless there was a report or the vehicle was in sight of a road, such findings were rarely investigated.

If nothing was found on the Roys' land, then there were two other farms where they would have to get permission to search next. They decided that Allen would begin the preliminary sweep with an outside search in the house and garage buildings to rule out a cadaver scent in those areas. He was to be accompanied by a backup officer in case there were any unexpected confrontations and to provide ready communications. Once the buildings were cleared, Dutch would begin to sweep the yard and surrounding areas.

After that, they would begin a slow, methodical grid search of the farm, which could take several hours, even days. Grid searches produced results but could be extremely tedious. Either way, Allen was in it until it was finished. He'd either find it or clear the entire farm, or even the valley if he had to. He twisted the rest of the Camel under his boot and went to his truck and let Dutch out, who relieved himself on Burgen's tire. Allen grinned.

He hitched a leather lead to the collar and walked Dutch, now alert and focused in his excited, playful way when searching, as he lunged against the lead. Allen picked up his pace, and Pusser trotted along behind him. Dutch barked and was making multiple hits around the attached garage on the house and in the driveway, then all around the pole building. He was excited and eager to keep looking, but Allen quickly realized he would have to sweep off lead. There were too many hits around the buildings, and Dutch could best sort it out on his own.

Taking hold of his collar, he unclipped the lead and released him, saying, "Dutch, find it!"

Dutch took off in a sweeping pattern back and forth through the farmyard. At the edge of the yard, towards an adjacent open area by the fescue field, he circled a spot and let out a deep-throated bark and sat. Allen walked quickly to him and found a loosely formed pile of dog poop, or maybe puke.

Pusser followed him and stuck a small marker flag next to the dog pile, and Allen led Dutch back to the middle of the yard near Burgen.

"Pretty good shit detector."

"Yeah. If he could just help me get *my* shit together . . ." Allen returned Burgen's banter as he redirected Dutch towards the opposite side of the yard, repeating the find command. Dutch wagged his big tail and bounded back to his sweeps. If the off-lead sweeps didn't provide direction, the next step would be to begin the dreaded grid search.

CHAPTER FIVE
DUTCH'S PERSPECTIVE

SPRINGTIME WARMTH RAISED a vast array of earthly scents. Dutch ran eagerly back and forth, sorting the added dimension revealed by his nose, looking for the scent Allen had let him sniff and, bam, there it was again—a faint trail leading off through the woods. He could smell both the dead thing Allen wanted and the Catniss odor against the backdrop of the other dogs' scents. "Seeing" the scent trail clear as day, he erupted with his classic hound dog bay, a beautiful sound that vibrated his chest and echoed out across the Shoal Creek valley as he chased the scent.

He could hear Allen and the other men following him, but he was much faster and eager on the scent, which led along a game trail towards the river. The game added a scent dimension Dutch knew to ignore. Excitement drove him through the lowland copse, occasionally stopping to circle when the dog scent would split off from the dead scent Allen had given him, then erupting with another resonant bay when he found the track again.

He punched right through a briar patch, escaping injury as he followed the deadness along the game path's low tunnel. When he erupted out the other side, he heard Allen and the men looking for a way around. He called to them again in his deep baying voice, "This way! This way!"

On the other side of the briar patch, the way opened out into thinner woods along the river, and Dutch continued to follow the scent. He was excited and periodically let out quick, deep barks to let Allen know where he was. He went about two thousand yards west along the river, keeping the river on his right and open pasture on his left. The ground became a gravel riverbank, and the trail was not as clear, but he stuck to it, following until the river turned sharply south in front of him.

The river was fairly placid just before the turn, but where the scent had led, the river was flowing fast as it narrowed down. Bottomland on the opposite bank had been cut deeply by the river's action, and the turn had collected a tangle of trees and debris about eight feet tall. Dutch trotted out into the water, which was only a few inches deep at first, and then decided to cross the water and look for the scent on the other side.

He plunged into the deeper icy water that was flowing fast towards the tangle against the steep opposite bank; its iciness unnoticed in his eagerness. Soon it was over his head, and he started swimming for the other bank as the current carried him quickly towards the tangle. He crashed into a big log that was jammed across the current and was quickly carried underneath it.

Dutch was a powerful dog and loved to swim, but colliding with branches and debris while submerged was not fun. His big red head finally popped up in the middle of the tangle on the other side of the log. He kept paddling and eventually found a way through, clambering up onto the far bank. He paused, something he rarely did while on scent, and showered his surroundings with water as he shook and collected himself. He then silently began sweeping back and forth again, searching for the scent.

Dutch heard Allen's encouraging cry, faint across the rushing water, "Go, boy!"

He gave a tiny nod, flicking his eyes and face towards Allen (an acknowledgment only Allen would perceive), then beckoned forward with a jerk of his head back to work as he instinctively moved upstream in big half circles. And there it was! Dutch hit the scent and let out an excited bay, "It's here!" as he ran off through the woods to the west. The trail became stronger as Dutch followed it through the thin bottomland woods.

It was still death smell mixed with Catniss and the other dogs, but now the dead thing smell was stronger and seemed to be all around him in the afternoon air. He paused and circled back once with his nose high, then cut back and forth across the scent trail he had been following. He ran through the woods with his head higher now, baying several times in excitement.

Dutch covered about three hundred yards through the woods when he came to one of the huge debris rafts, or mats, that were hidden in various spots in the uneven topography of the river bottoms. The layers of collected material made a huge carpet of twigs and debris that was soft and spongy to walk on. It was quiet and almost like a sanctuary in the woods where these mats occurred. Dutch became instinctively calm as he walked out on the edge of the mat and paused as he took in the scent environment.

The dead thing was everywhere, overwhelming. Dutch circled around, trying to get a bearing on the source. Sometimes his foot would slip in up to his trunk, and he would quickly pull out with his other legs. He circled around again, and the scent grew weaker, so he stumbled out into a larger circling.

Suddenly, there it was. A disturbed area of mat about a foot across. Dutch stuck his snout into the hole and could taste the dead thing he was supposed to find. Damn the silent sanctuary! He raised his head and let out a quick, excited bay, and then a long series of bark alerts that shattered the peace. He walked back and forth and continued to bark, then sat looking at the hole, barking excitedly, thinking only of Allen's praise and the tasty treat it might bring. He wasn't even tired.

CHAPTER SIX

CHASING DUTCH

ALLEN WAS THE first to catch up close enough to see him. Despite the Camels, he was in good shape, and he was only mildly winded as he trotted along, his boots making little squishy sounds. He'd seen Dutch go underwater at the big log, and his heart was still pounding from the thought of losing the big red dog, even though he'd seen him come up on the other side. Dutch got louder and louder as Allen approached, and about a hundred yards away, Allen began to smell the death himself.

As he approached the debris raft, the smell was strong and almost overpowering. If he hadn't known they were after a human body, he would assume it was a cow that had died and been deposited here. Dutch was about ten feet onto the raft, barking down at a small disturbance in an area where the mat was well-formed and smooth. "Hey, Dutch! Good boy." He tossed him a treat.

"Leave it!" he commanded. Dutch immediately shut up, stood, and walked over to Allen, swallowing the treat as he came. Allen gave him another for leaving it so quickly.

Allen knew the area was a crime scene, but he needed to verify the find, so he walked across to the disturbed spot. Dogs or wildlife had been digging into the mat, and a long bone was exposed. There was some tattered cloth deeper in around the bone, some tissue, and edges of leathery, curled skin. He couldn't dislodge a piece of sheet metal material across the bone; it blocked everything other than what he was seeing, but not the odor.

Allen never showed a response to finds, always trying to keep a poker face, but his nose wrinkled and mouth pinched shut tightly to clamp out the stench as he stepped back and then walked off the mat, moving several feet away to a wide patch of early grass. He tipped back his hat, then lit up a Camel. Dutch came over and sat at his side, panting mildly. Allen took a big drag, then a smaller one, and dug in his jacket pocket for his cell phone. He knew the others would not be far behind but may not have crossed the river yet. He called Burgen and waited while the phone made a connection. Service was weak in the valley.

"Dutch found the body."

"That was quick! Where are you?" Burgen panted. He was still on the far bank of the river.

"About three hundred yards west through the woods. It'll be a fun recovery; it's deep in a debris raft." Allen took another drag, collected now.

"Okay, we're headed your way." Allen disconnected and slipped the phone back into his jacket pocket as he kneeled, putting the Camel back in his mouth. He cradled Dutch's big head in his hands, then stroked his head and ears. He began a brief scan, checking over Dutch's body when he noticed fresh blood in the grass.

He instinctively checked himself with a glance, but quickly found a large cut across the underside of Dutch's right wrist. The accessory pad was hanging by a thread, and blood was running freely down his foot. Allen didn't know how he missed it before, but the excitement of finding the body must have distracted him. He quickly clamped off the bleeding with his bare hand over the wound, and Dutch pulled back a little in response.

"Easy boy." Allen thought hard as he kneeled there. He didn't have his search pack because Dutch found a trail faster than expected and had taken off, but he was wearing a T-shirt and belt. He quickly took them off, getting blood on his outer khaki shirt, and pulled out his side knife and started cutting strips from the sweat-dampened cotton shirt.

The wound was bleeding heavily, and now Allen could see a blood trail leading back to the mat. Dutch must have cut his wrist on the sheet metal over part of the body because he didn't see a blood trail leading from the river. He wrapped the wound firmly but gently.

After he flicked the cigarette from his mouth to the ground and pressed it out with his wet, oozing boot, he wrapped a few more layers and called it good. Allen hooked up the leather leash so Dutch wouldn't go running off and patted him on the head again. "Good boy, Dutch." He put his shirt back on.

It took Burgen and Deputy Pusser about five minutes to wade across the river and through the woods to the edge of the debris mat. Pusser's ballistic vest made him hot, and they were both breathing heavily as they approached Allen and Dutch. They saw the blood on Allen's shirt and hands, then noticed the bandage on Dutch's foot. "What happened?" Burgen asked.

"He cut his wrist pretty good, I think on some appliance metal against the body. I've got the bleeding controlled, but I need to take him to Doc to get sewn up."

Allen gestured towards the mat with his eyebrows, and they needed no more direction as the stench led them the rest of the way. Burgen took a long gander, then his face scrunched up, and he returned to Allen.

"Thanks for your help! That might've taken days without you and Dutch. Let's get him back; I'll help you."

"Naw, I can carry him across, and if I cross upstream a little, it should be pretty easy."

But Burgen, even though he wasn't a water rescue man, knew enough to know that water crossings should be attended if at all possible, in case something went wrong. "It's no problem. Pusser'll stay here and tape the site, and I'll bring the patrol and coroner back."

Allen conceded. "All right, then."

They paused on the riverbank, and the stench lingered though they'd left the body behind.

"I'll take a cigarette."

"Thought you stopped?" Allen paused and shook out two, lit his, then handed Burgen the lighter. He kneeled to check the bandages.

"Yeah, but that shit stunk."

Allen chuckled, despite his concern for Dutch. "Pussy."

Allen scooped up Dutch in his arms. Dutch had trained to be carried and/or harnessed in a variety of ways, and he accepted Allen's comforting words with a small whine as they waded into the water and made their way across.

He set Dutch down and walked back towards the farmhouse with Dutch on the short lead. He was still limping a little, but as they walked briskly along, the foot seemed to work better as the makeshift bandage adjusted, and the limp became almost unnoticeable. They spoke little as they walked back, each considering their next moves. Back at the yard, Burgen veered off to the command center while Allen went to his truck.

Allen put Dutch in the back seat and pulled out his phone to call the clinic. Shaking his head, he hit "dial" as he drove from the yard, glancing at Dutch through the rearview mirror as the phone rang.

Pete's clinic answered quickly, and Allen recognized Mikki's voice., "Hey Mikki, it's Allen Mitchell," he said.

"Oh hi, Allen! How's Dutch doing?" He loved how she always remembered to ask after Dutch right away.

Allen explained about the cut and told Mikki he was on his way in to get it taken care of.

"Okay, we'll be expecting you." Even though it was getting later in the day and afternoon rush was in full swing, Pete would surely clean up and suture the wound tonight. They would just have to fit it in, even if it meant staying late.

CHAPTER SEVEN

RECOVERY

It was a long, cold night on the creek for Pusser, who burrowed in his sleeping bag on the grassy knoll close enough to guard the crime scene, yet far enough to escape the worst of the odor. Frosty air and the smoke smell from his small fire helped keep the odor down, too. There were plenty of owl hoots and screeches and rustling of tampering animals to keep him up much of the night. Right when he would doze off, another sound would rouse him. He managed to sleep some between false dawn and 6:00 a.m., but then birds began chirping. Lighter skies revealed mist drifting through the bottoms, thick here, thin there. A rooster crowed over the faint sound of the river as he started rolling up his sleeping bag.

A few hundred yards away as the crow flies, Burgen and Allen soon arrived in the Roys' yard, which would become a staging area. "How's old Dutch this morning?"

"Doing good." Allen smiled in thanks for Burgen's concern. "He had surgery last night, and Pete called early to let me know he was doin' fine."

Burgen nodded, and they both became distracted as an ambulance pulled up into the Roys' yard. They had come for rehab, which meant support for the personnel that would soon be showing up to assist with recovery of the body.

"Thanks for coming," Burgen said, always polite. He and Allen both took a cup of coffee from the steaming containers the paramedics set out. Going back to Burgen's Tahoe, they sat inside and talked about the case and the possible identity of the body. There wasn't much to discuss at this point, so they soon switched to the subject of the upcoming election and who might run against the sheriff.

Around 9:00 a.m., they got out of the Tahoe as teams from Newton County Rescue and Recovery and Redings Mill VFD arrived and began preparing for the recovery. State Police had returned along with the coroner to take charge of the body once it was recovered. Soon, everyone had joined Pusser on the little bluff near the body, having carried equipment and supplies across the cold river in stages.

Allen, Burgen, and the VFD chief mostly just watched as the team dug and sifted through covering debris. Pusser stood with them, free to go but reluctant to leave before the body was uncovered. They were soon discussing how the body ended up there.

Although a body swept by the river was usually found within a few dozen yards of its entry point, Allen favored the distance theory in this case. During a large flood with high volumes of water, it was certainly possible that a body could be carried a long way, even miles, from its entry point. This person had clearly been in the water for some time, probably long enough for it to be from the time of the Christmas flood.

"In fact, there's no doubt about it," Allen said, "because that flood was the last time water was high enough put the body into debris this high, and the flood before that was almost a year ago. He shook his head and said, "There's no way it's from before last summer. Has to be from the Christmas flood."

"Which means that the body could have come from Gateway drive, or it could have come from Neosho," the fire chief added, nodding in agreement. Neosho was about ten miles away.

"And there are dozens of access points between Ritchie and here," Burgen agreed. It was going to be like finding a needle in a haystack to locate where she went in the water. Pusser stood rubbing his chin and finally spoke.

"I remember a call down to Tipton access on Christmas Eve," he said slowly. "Some disturbance. When I got there, it was raining hard, but I remember finding something like blood on the ground." They all were looking at him, and he shrugged. "It got washed away, though. Never amounted to anything, but it may have been related."

Meanwhile, the sheet metal was revealed to be an old storage cabinet lying across the body. With no doors, it was quickly removed, exposing almost all the body, which was in fairly good shape. The group was somber as a petite woman was fully revealed, still crowding in a bit despite the smell.

There were still blue jeans around her hips and legs, with only minor tears. Tatters of a shirt were still covering her torso, and a bra was visible under the shirt, but it was torn and not properly positioned. Her hair was mostly gone, and her facial features were lost along with the skin of her head, but the woman's teeth were clearly visible. Some were missing, and decay was visible on the ones that remained.

The shattered left radius was plain to see, and there was a large tear in her shirt over where her left breast had been. A small jagged hole was in the exposed rib cage where it joined the sternum. No identifying features or obvious artifacts were immediately detected. Allen could see there would be no usable fingerprints, most likely leaving only DNA and teeth as possible identifiers. With no local hits on missing persons in the past year, identification would be tedious if her DNA and teeth were not already on file somewhere.

Her body was carefully folded into a body bag and carried back to a funeral home van that would transport it to forensics.

It was just before 11:30 a.m. when Burgen and Allen gathered everyone near the fire truck so the sheriff and coroner could express gratitude and dismiss the volunteers. "We'll holler if we need anything else. Thanks again," Burgen said.

While the various teams and personnel stowed equipment and gear, their faces were closed, and their eyes were down as considerations of mortality damped the simple pleasure of a job well done. Cleaning and checking the gear would happen at the various stations later in the day. Decompressing their feelings often came later as they cleaned, but today, the Newton County Rescue and Recovery chief, Grady, invited his team to lunch at the Undercliff, a small grill a few miles away on the banks of the river. The men and women who'd done most of the digging and moving of the body stepped lighter as they moved to their vehicles and started to depart.

Burgen stopped to talk with reporters, who were waiting in the Roy's yard. He kept it simple for the news media, advising them that a female body had been recovered by a local search team in debris probably from the Christmas flood.

More information would be released once the body was identified, and her next of kin notified. He asked that anyone with any knowledge of the woman please contact the sheriff's department. Because they could recall no one missing recently, and their own research yielded nothing, the few reporters seemed to assume the body was probably drug-related, so there wasn't much excitement.

"Do you know how old she was?" A lone reporter made an effort, maybe sensing a need to make the body count somehow.

"I think she was an adult. The corner should have a better idea after the autopsy." The sheriff nodded his thanks for the question.

"Do you recall any missing persons who might match her?" Her tone indicated she was either losing interest or nervous about pressing. The other reporters were already fading away. Drug bodies were fairly common in these situations, and not very newsworthy.

But Burgen gazed at her with his full attention, giving her question respect. It never hurt to build relationships with the press, and no matter who the body had belonged to, it mattered to him that the unknown subject found closure. He answered, "I don't, but if we find out, I'll let you know."

She nodded thanks and turned to dismiss her cameraman. Burgen approached her and said, "If you have a card, I'll be sure and let you know if I find anything out." He looked down at the card she produced. "Thanks for the questions, Candee Thomas." His eyebrow raised involuntarily at her name.

She nodded as she shook his hand, grinning slightly as she said, "Thank you, sheriff."

He stepped away towards his Tahoe and saw Allen driving off with a wave as he left to pick up Dutch.

CHAPTER EIGHT
ANOTHER JANE DOE

ON FRIDAY AFTERNOON, Pete was home for lunch, sitting at the long counter along the kitchen island, chewing a sandwich between words as he filled Prissy in. It was his first chance to sit and talk with Prissy since she'd said yes to the caseworker. The three-year-old boy had come yesterday morning and had left by three.

A kinship placement had been found, and that had been that.

"It was kind of a relief," reflected Prissy. "I wanted to try again, and then I didn't, so it was like dipping your toe in and pulling it out when the water's too cold. But the water wasn't cold, really."

"Scary?" asked Pete as his gentle eyes met hers. "Class V white water?"

She smiled and looked down as she replied, "Maybe Class II." Reticent was her way, and Pete didn't push much. He still felt guilty for the enthusiasm he'd shown for foster and adoptive care, the results of which had left her so wounded, even though she'd once shared his enthusiasm.

"I'm a qualified rescue swimmer." His reply was brief but brought a tiny eye roll and another genuine smile. He longed for more of that.

The conversation turned to the body recovery as Prissy asked about the bracelet that had been in Catniss's stomach, and their momentary closeness seemed to fade.

"No telling what the three pennies meant." With the sandwich now gone, he wiped his lips and rested his chin in his hand as he watched her take his paper plate and give the counter a wipe.

She didn't glance up as she put away the sandwich makings. "What about identifying the body?"

"DNA's the only real hope. And for it to work, it has to match someone in the system. Same with dental records." He raised his head slightly off his hand as he spoke so his chin could move.

"So, we may never know who she was?" She finally looked up at him.

"Correct. Just another Jane Doe." Prissy flinched as he realized what he had just said. Jain, the daughter they'd lost to a callus judge's decision so long ago, had been a Jane Doe at first. Her poly-addicted mother, Lisa, had changed the spelling to Jain and the last name to Smith when she exercised her only remaining power after losing her at birth. It would have been changed again, to a love name, if the Kramers had been able to adopt her. "I'm sorry, Priss. I didn't mean it that way."

While he had strongly advocated for their becoming foster parents years before, the truth was she was much more emotionally invested than he was, and part of what she was going through was really his "fault." Her eyes met his, and he felt a stirring of compassion for her that his resentment had blocked for a long time.

"Really." He had walked around the counter and now put a hand on her shoulder as tears filled her eyes. She stood there with him and leaned into an embrace. As she gave a dry sob, he realized she hadn't cried in years. He held her, but nothing else came. "You wanna lie down for a while?"

She nodded against his chest, and he smelled her clean sweat as he buried a kiss on her neck.

Pete cradled Prissy in his arm as they walked to the bedroom, and she clicked on the overhead fan, which he knew she hated. "Thanks for the fan."

"I can always add a blanket."

They spooned on the bedspread, getting comfortable, and the closeness and her smell brought desire that he dared express only by gently caressing her hair and shoulder as they drifted off to sleep. She was still a beautiful woman, but her troubled spirit that had driven him away so long wasn't going away on its own. Fucking Jain. Fucking kids in general!

Wakefulness came slowly an hour later. Prissy had pulled up a blanket from the foot of the bed and had it loosely draped over her. His breathing must have changed once awareness returned, and Prissy rolled to face him, adjusting her pillow. They laid face to face, far enough apart to look into each other's eyes as he slowly resumed stroking her hair across her forehead. She put her palm on his cheek and temple as they lay there, feeling the moment.

His eyes scrunched a little as the gesture made him smile, and a faint smile reflected back. She slowly leaned in to touch his lips with hers, gently tasting. When love was in her eyes, she was a flawless beauty. He moved his fingers ever so gently in her hair, barely touching her lip with his tongue. They held like that, and he waited, pushing no further without encouragement, which didn't come. It was like a flower that had opened for a moment, then gently closed, nectar withdrawn after a taste, and held within for a coming day. Somehow, he hoped there was a way opening that could save them. Here at home, he could take the time she needed until their bodies could become a healing thing, singing their song together.

She broke the kiss, shifting to get up and leaving him yearning. "I have to go pee." She rolled up and went to the bathroom.

Pete's passion faded to frustration, so he gave a mental eye roll and got out of bed.

Back in the kitchen, they got some water.

"Why'd you decide to take in another kid?"

"I don't know." She sipped the water. "I've been reading a guy named Kushner, a Rabbi, and he says that what people do matters. Either human actions are connected to what happens in the universe, or they are not. And if everything is connected to everything else, then sooner or later, everything matters... Maybe Jain mattered in some way bigger than us all. Maybe it was time. I don't know. It sure didn't last long."

Pete could see her eyes, having lost their earlier glimmer of love, were now almost dull. It was like her spirit had escaped a dungeon only to be drawn back in by the chains of remorse and regret that neither Pete nor Prissy could seem to break.

He drank down his water and rose to leave. "I don't know, either. But I know if people stopped mattering, it wouldn't be a good world. We matter. *You* matter, Priss, and what you had with Jain mattered. I'm sure it mattered to her, too. In her life, we were foundational, and you were most of that." He hugged her gently, but it was barely returned. Then he was gone, leaving her alone with her thoughts.

CHAPTER NINE
DREAMS OF CHILDHOOD

Cicadas chirred long and slow. She felt a pleasant urgency between her legs, spreading them slightly as her mind was roused to another gentle caress on the outer folds of that mysterious place. Whiskers scratched her cheek as roughened lips gently touched hers, and a hot tongue slid between her lips. Her back arched slightly as she opened her legs a little more, but whiskers... itchy?

She reflexively opened her eyes in the dim light from the hallway and saw Mr. Roger's face close to hers. His breath reeked of tobacco, unbrushed teeth, and beer. She scrunched her little face up and pushed him away, awake now, but everything dreamy still. He came closer again, whispering some platitude, but she couldn't focus. Seeming to pounce on her stupor this time, the touch between her legs was rough. His finger jammed into her, painful and dry, and she growled and pushed him away again.

His impatient huff was a hot stench, then he stood alongside her bed and began stroking himself. Fear paralyzed Jain as she realized she was naked, and her t-shirt was pushed up, exposing her. She tried to understand what she was seeing, knowing it was wrong and dangerous. His hips started thrusting back and forth over her, and she let out a gasp of fright as hot ejaculate spattered on her thigh, belly, and t-shirt. The smell was weird to her, and his words came through the sedated fog that still held her, "You're beautiful, baby. Beautiful." He caressed her face and flaxen hair gently as she lay frozen, afraid to breathe.

Then, she slapped the hand away with a louder growl and sat up abruptly, panting. Her brain spun, and the cicadas were loud as she grabbed her head, unintentionally pushing Eddie roughly aside. The tent shook as he leaned back with a snicker that sounded derisive to her.

"Shhhshhhshh! Easy girl, easy," he whispered as a whippoorwill called nearby. "Where were you?"

"It's not funny, dickhead." Jain had no reason to be harsh to Eddie, but Mr. Rogers, one of her biological mother's "boyfriends," was only now beginning to fade from her mind.

"Hey, it's me, Jainy. Keep it down." Eddie's gentle eyes tried to hold hers as she flashed him anger.

"What were you doing to me? Dick!" She wanted to push him away and run, but the tent's confinement restrained her, causing her to remember where they were. If she kept it up, she would wake everyone in the camp. This was Eddie, her friend, confidant, and guiltily…her foster brother.

He whispered faintly in reply, "Nothing. We dozed off, and you were having a bad dream and woke me up. I was just petting your hair."

"Everything okay in there?" A male counselor's light lit the inside of the tent, and Jain could see Eddie's wide eyes.

"Yeah, just a bad dream." Her eyes met Eddie's, and she saw laughter bubbling up. She grabbed his head, covering his mouth to stifle the laugh, and shoved it down low to hide his silhouette. His carefree manner was a delight, but she feared discovery.

"You need to talk? I can get one of the women to come by." Even if Eddie weren't here, Jain didn't think anyone would understand what drove her nightmares, which had become worse since she had drawn closer to her new foster brother with these sexual explorations.

"No, I'm okay. Thanks."

The light moved away. When they heard the counselor's tent flap zip closed, they relaxed as they lay face to face, sharing her pillow. He reached up to stroke her face and hair, but she closed her eyes and moved her head away, still unwilling; the badness of the dream conflicted with the pleasant urgency of her estrogen-driven passion.

"What's going on in your head?" In the dimness, his eyes felt intent, probing, despite the gentle whisper. She wondered the same thing and only had some of the answer. Try as she might, much of her past was blurry, and the dream was swirling as the sweat dried on her forehead.

"I... I don't know; it was just a dream. Don't worry about it." She didn't quite know how to talk about it. He watched her face and didn't reply. Their stolen tryst had been headed somewhere, but the moment was now lost, and he seemed to sense that. He silently got to his knees and prepared to leave.

He leaned in to squeeze her shoulder, but she pulled away as faint anxiety remained from her nightmare. "It's okay, *sis*." She had been placed in his foster home only a short time ago. There had been an instant mutual attraction, intensified by social isolation at their schools, and stolen intimacies at Kayak Camp now drew them closer.

He reached up to quietly unzip the tent flap and quickly snuck back to the senior high side, which was just across the camp road. He was fifteen and nervous with the older kids, and she was thirteen going on twenty, ill at ease with the younger children she matched only biologically. Most of the kids at camp shared tents, but both were loners in the small tents their fosters had provided. Morning devotions came after an almost sleepless night, and birds called in the trees, celebrating a new day.

A cloudless bronze sky reflected the heat of the summer sun by the time they set out on the river. Juniors left about fifteen minutes before seniors, but long days on the river allowed a loose mixing of the two groups. Eddie was much braver than Jain when they stopped for lunch at a nice jumping rock. She jumped feet first with the other kids while he managed a triple flip on his second try before they sat on the hot river gravel to eat icy fresh-sliced pineapple and peanut butter sandwiches. Afterwards, Jain drifted back in the pack of kayaks and was soon alongside Eddie.

They were laid back, feet resting on the bows, and had rolled towels fashioned into pillows. Counselors were almost always in sight, though distance allowed them to hold hands in the water between the boats. The beating sun reminded her of childhood days with the veterinary family—her first foster family, who had been avid kayakers.

But fond memories of growing up in their river house conflicted with her loss. They forced her to leave their home when she was almost seven, telling her it was for the best. A strange woman took her away in a car to go live in near Springfield with her "belly" mother, a woman called Lisa she had never known. Her life had been hell since then, even though recent placement with Eddie and his family had brought relief.

"Are you still mad they made you come to camp?" she teased, remembering their stolen kisses and petting before her nightmare.

He sighed, but his gentle hand squeeze said otherwise. "Yeah."

His hand was giving her a thrill, not to mention the intimacy they shared. She kept her voice casual, "I'm not."

The kayaks twisted slowly in the quiet water, sometimes cooling in the welcome shadows of overhanging trees. They had to stay between the lead and tail counselor kayaks, but there were 70 campers and ten counselors now stretched along a mile of river. With a hundred yards or more between them and anyone else, the distant shouts of other kids playing around the next corner and the quiet lapping of water around them gave them a privacy of sorts. His head fell sideways, and he looked at her, all serious now. "What were you dreaming about?"

Dreaming? Lots of history *always* lingered dream-like on the edges of her mind…

By the time her period started at ten years old, she'd been repeatedly exposed to sexual activity during multiple attempts at reunification with Lisa that were ordered by judges. Lisa and her boyfriends—intoxicated, inebriated, or both—would have sex on an old stained mattress on the floor while Jain either laid on the couch or listened from her bedroom. The johns, or clients, would sometimes come to Jain's bed. What they were allowed to do depended on what they would pay, but Jain didn't fully comprehend the negotiations she witnessed that could involve currency, drugs, or both. Sometimes they paid nothing if Lisa was passed out on the mattress. Jain now felt guilty over the occasional erotic warmth she'd experienced while she was either watching or being used by others.

Benzos, slipped to her so she would sleep while Lisa turned tricks, left a surreal aftertaste and confused impression of what sexuality truly meant. When she was in foster care, her passion was her own, private and sensual.

When she was with her "mother" Lisa during the "reunifications," it was a foggy experience imposed by adults, callous and empty.

Dreamy talk of finding a "forever" home was the official line she heard from caseworkers over the last few years, but reality brought transience as she bounced through homes that denied any meaningful family relationships. With no healthy touchpoints, she withdrew, and an outward appearance of sullen adolescence made her unattractive to adoptive families.

Despite her high intelligence, there was no hard shell of teen sarcasm to crack, yet they failed to appreciate her lack of active hostility. Sullen wasn't hostile; sullen was just having no reference point of normalcy to create a need for discussion of her abnormal emotional circumstances. She was isolated by her shell of loneliness and yearning, and skeptical of any feelings that might stir a desire to build trusting relationships with parental figures.

Morning camp devotions had been about Jesus telling Satan to "get behind him." The counselor leading the discussion encouraged them to put Satan behind them and enjoy the camp by living in the moment. Now she was alive with feelings for this boy/man floating alongside her. She felt the beginnings of a fearless intimacy she'd not known since being betrayed by the veterinarian family in the river house so long ago.

More like a nightmare! What she did know was that she was thrilled to be holding his hand. Here. Now. The sweet sensation pulled her back to the precious present.

"Nothing," she lilted playfully, testing him.

"You were busting a sweat over nightmares about nothing?" He gently caressed the inside of her thumb with his, his eyes intent under furrowed eyebrows, belying the grin curling a corner of his mouth.

"I don't know. It was hot. Maybe." She smiled a mystery at him, then deflected the intimacy. "What do you dream about?"

"You." He smiled back desire, his eyes revealing his interests.

She let that lay there awhile in the lazy afternoon air.

Playful shouts roused them as the current picked up, and they approached a rapid that had overturned several kayaks in a jumble.

For the rest of the afternoon, the river brought mild water challenges as it picked up its pace, and she had no further opportunity to "purple," as the counselors called it when boys (blue) and girls (pink) mixed. At the river take-out point, separate buses picked up junior and senior high for the ride back to camp.

In both camps, there were devotions each morning and vespers each evening. Each night, their whispering was a love song, seeming to fulfill emotions awakened by the evening meditations, and their explorations brought electric pleasure to her budding physique.

Passions raised by their brushing thighs in the dark during the final night's bonfire service culminated in her tent as she received gentle, ultimately pleasurable penetration, not forced upon her, but freely chosen for the first time. Peace held her like a blanket, and their breathing slowed together as he lay half on top of her afterwards, cradled in her arm as she softly stroked his dark hair.

Her quiet moans and his echoes drew a counselor. She heard the approach and slid out from under Eddie, wrapping her blanket around her as he clumsily pulled on his shorts. He hadn't zipped the flap all the way, and his face glared white when the flashlight clicked on.

"Are you okay in there?" The counselor's voice was quiet, concerned.

"Of course, we were just talking," she said quietly. But as the counselor pulled the flap back, Jain's flushed face revealed her lie.

"I thought he was your brother..." His eyes widened as the counselor realized what he had interrupted. "You'd better get back to your tent."

Her green eyes met Eddie's with regret and shame at being caught. "Sorry." She whispered and gave his arm a squeeze.

"Me, too." He caressed her shoulder then scuttled out.

Anxiety replaced the sweet peace she'd so briefly found and worsened in the days that followed as her placement was disrupted once again. Love's double-edged sword pleasured her body but pained her heart. Love was a two-faced bitch; she smiled pleasure on your body, only to leave you bleak and alone as her grimace ravaged your heart. Intimacy through sex led to separation and loss, a lesson she would not soon forget. Jain realized she had to learn to ride the pleasure and dodge the pain.

CHAPTER TEN

ANOTHER MOVE

Tied as usual in a thick plastic trash bag, she slung her clothes and meager possessions over one shoulder and carried her Box to the front porch of the DFS office to wait for her ride. The Box, a bland-appearing plastic file box with a carry handle in the lid, was a treasured part of her identity prepared by Prissy in the river house and was never violated by foster parents, nor by Lisa. It contained all the important documents of her life.

From it, she knew she'd been born a triplet, but her sisters hadn't survived. She'd named them Eliza and Hannah back when she was still in the river house. She knew she had an IQ of one hundred forty, and she knew that despite her feelings of abandonment and lingering resentment towards the Kramers, they tried to adopt her throughout the time she lived with them. She knew they were Christians and churchgoers. Bible verses she had written down as a child reminded her of Sunday school and children's church. A reading award from kindergarten came because Pete read to all the kids each night on their big couch and discussed the stories with them like they were adults.

When she was ten, she started a log that she kept in a file in the Box, recording each family she could recall and a thing or two about them as she moved through life in the system. Names weren't recorded, except for the Kramers, because she couldn't remember them when she started the list from memory. She was now leaving her eleventh placement, so in her log, the next entry would be: Twelve. Grade Nine Fosters. A few facts about them would follow in her neat, tiny handwriting. She always hoped it would be the last family on the list, but dreams of a "Forever Family" faded with each move.

When Grade Nine Foster mom picked her up, Jain tossed her trash bag into the back but set the Box carefully on the floor beside her in the mildly cluttered but clean minivan. Clean was usually a good thing, but mildly cluttered meant cleanliness wasn't overboard. "I'm Marsha," Grade Nine mom said with a firm but friendly authority as they drove away. They spoke little until they arrived at the house, and Jain appreciated the space. Lots of fosters felt the need to ask a lot of questions or make conversation.

Grade Nine mom led her inside. "We have two other children right now, twin girls, and you'll meet them later. In the meantime, I'll show you your room."

It was an entirely normal-appearing bedroom with a nice bed and a headboard and chest of drawers. "This is *mine*?"

"Yep. The whole thing. You have your own closet and share a bathroom with the girls."

"How old're they?"

"Eleven. We adopted them when they were five, but it almost didn't happen."

"I wish someone would have adopted me. They've been moving me since I was seven."

"Oh, Jain, I'm so sorry. The system isn't nice to kids or parents sometimes."

Jain snorted. "More like all the time."

"Look, honey, we don't have a lot of rules, but you'll learn them if we have to apply them," said Marsha, facing Jain with a now serious expression. Her brown hair fell slightly forward as she continued. "If you behave responsibly, we shouldn't need to apply them much. We have some fun, but we're not a real exciting family. You might say we're boring."

Marsha used both her hands to brush her hair behind her ears. "Bedtime is by nine during the week, sometimes later on weekends. Let me know if there's anything you need. We'll trust you until you give us a reason not to." She waited and watched until Jain gave a small nod of acknowledgment.

"You can set up your room how you like but ask for help if you want to hang things on the wall. Bathroom is across the hall." She pointed and then left her there, gently closing the door behind her.

Jain set down her trash bag and explored. There were hangers in the closet, on a rod at her level, and the floor was clean and empty. She'd never had a closet to herself before, and rarely a room, but this was number twelve—she knew better than to get her hopes too high. She went ahead and hung her few shirts, put the rest of her clothes in the dresser, and then carefully put the Box in the corner of the closet.

Boring wasn't as bad as it sounded, and after a check-up at the family doctor, routine except for STD testing, she fell into the home's summer routine. Grade Nine Foster dad, Jim, worked each day. Marsha ran a home business during the week and provided activities for all three girls. Weekends were for family, rarely for church, and never for work.

Though younger, the twins, Sharon and Bella, reminded her of the triplet sisters she never knew, but she didn't share their moderate Fetal Alcohol Syndrome characteristics. Lisa had been in prison in her early pregnancy and used other drugs, but not much alcohol when she got out. She knew from the Box that she should have died along with her sisters and only a miracle, she imagined, had kept her alive despite the four substances found in her system and being ten weeks early. But still, the twins' presence offered her some comfort as she imagined a life where her sisters had survived.

Fourth of July came and went before she realized she had missed her period.

"Are you okay?" Marsha asked one morning after breakfast. Jain had eaten well but was quiet and reflective as she helped clear the table and load the dishwasher. Fantasies of triplets somehow redeeming her preoccupied her more each day. She imagined Eddie and her raising them in a home like Marsha's. Strangely, she found herself unconcerned about the responsibilities of raising a family. In her fantasy, that would just happen effortlessly.

"Yeah," she said. "Just thinking about Eddie and camp and stuff."

"Stuff…" Marsha seemed thoughtful. "Speaking of stuff, shouldn't you have had your period by now?"

"I don't know." She felt her flush revealing the lie, "I guess." Fear began to rise, but Marsha's voice held calm assurance.

"You guess? Oh my." She felt Marsha's stare and looked up into compassionate eyes. "You're not guessing—you're pregnant, aren't you?"

Her heart leaped as Marsha spoke the p-word, "Yes… I think."

She liked saying yes, but reality suddenly set in, and fear rose higher as her thoughts raced. She'd need baby clothes, but had no money; a house of her own, but had no job; a car, but was too young to drive… Diapers, baby shampoo, a crib, groceries, formula, and *lots* of help. She'd need Eddie most of all, and Eddie was gone, threatened with jail if he ever saw her again. Hot tears spilled down her cheeks, and she looked down, suddenly numb and overwhelmed, unable to face Marsha's compassion and feared her judgment.

But relief flooded Jain when she simply felt a kind hug. Sobs wracked her as Marsha stroked her long flaxen hair and held her gently, their hips leaning against the counter together in the sunlit kitchen. As she calmed, she realized Marsha was calm as well, and she knew Marsha would help.

In the days that followed, she took two pregnancy tests, both confirming what she knew inside. Grade Nine dad took the twins to a Saturday morning daddy breakfast the following weekend to give Jain and Marsha time to talk.

They sat at the kitchen table with coffee and bagels as Marsha gently led their conversation in what at first seemed like a sales pitch for abortion.

"Your fears are real, Jain, and logical. You're thirteen, and you're smart enough to know you don't have the resources to raise a baby."

"But can't you help me?" She smiled, adding, "And it's bab-*ies*. Triplets, like me."

"You don't know that, and thinking like that only makes the decision harder," said Marsha. "We aren't going to raise any more babies, but more importantly, you've got a whole life ahead of you, and the brains to change the world." She had been leaning on her arms towards Jain across the table, her hair falling forward some. Now she leaned back and brushed her hair behind her ears, then shrugged, "You can choose freedom. Freedom to finish high school, go to college, find a good, boring husband, and raise kids in a stable household."

"But Eddie could be a good husband. Once I'm sixteen, we could get married." Jain thought of him often, clinging to his gentleness and the stolen sweetness they'd shared. "Don't his feelings matter?"

Marsha looked at her carefully and spoke softly this time, "They do, but Jain… Remember when we went to the fireworks?" Jain nodded reluctantly. "He was there. He saw us, and you, but he was with another girl. They went the other direction." She paused, and Jain waited, sensing what was coming. "Later, they were kissing by a car. Hot and heavy."

Jain felt tears running down her cheeks again as reality collided with her dreams.

Marsha held her hand. "He'd clearly moved on. I'm sorry."

Marsha's will prevailed as Jain realized it wasn't a cold sales pitch, but caring guidance from the heart. It hurt to hear and consider an abortion, let alone abortions if there were triplets. Still, it seemed the best path to follow and the only one to free her from the past. Even though the thrill and ecstasy that night in the tent sure didn't feel like sin, the shame it brought did, and abortion offered liberation from that as well.

Freedom, then, became her motivation that evening to submit to Marsha's advice. "Babies would be a lot, and especially tough to handle on my own." Jain looked up into Marsha's eyes, seeing only relief at her decision, not triumph as they sat side by side on the living room couch. It seemed Marsha's concern for her future was sincere, which helped further overcome her continued reluctance, and she said, "If you're willing to help me, I'm willing to do it."

Marsha slid closer, and Jain welcomed the embrace she found surrounding her. She buried her head on Marsha's bosom and felt the vibration of her words, "It, or they, really are just a fetus right now, Jain. It'll be like they were never there, and your life can go on. And so can mine," Marsha sat back to look into her eyes and continued, "but I'll be there to see you through this and after, as long as it takes."

No foster had ever made a long-term promise, and Jain felt more secure in her decision, taking ownership of it. She accepted Marsha's commitment, at least for now. There was no one else to get her through this thing.

When the pre-procedure ultrasound at the out-of-state clinic revealed just one fetus, instead of the triplets she'd willed, it seemed to confirm that her dreams of keeping the babies were unattainable fantasies. Unbidden and uncontrollable tears came as events seemed to unfold and carry her along.

She swallowed a sedative kindly given, and her feelings swirled. Neither refusing nor consenting as the baby was removed, she lay in a benzo-induced fog of passivity where hazy memories of Lisa's Mr. Rogers lived. Evil rose around her, but she felt powerless and overwhelmed.

Benzos didn't relieve her pain, just dulled her response, and wrenching agony in her uterus seemed like penance for surviving birth without her sisters. "Hannah," she moaned. "Eliza... so sorry..." Her heart was drowning in tears, but only one went down her cheek. After-bleeding soon came freely, like anguish seeping from her soul.

An extra-large sanitary pad and a blue absorbent underpad protected Marsha's car seat on the way home, and the bleeding subsided as they rode along. Marsha carefully helped her to her bed, and as she laid there, the afternoon sunlight was like the bright, hard truth forming inside her: Attempting intimacy through sex led to separation, pain, and loss, a lesson she would not soon forget. Rather than freedom, the abortion chained her to her past forever.

Staring dully at her Box of memories over in the closet, the reality of that decision that set in. As the evening wore on, the room slowly became red with the sunset. Foggy from the day, its events, and medications, fresh, silent tears ran across her face and into her pillow as she faded to sleep, her life forever changed.

CHAPTER ELEVEN

GRADUATION

By the time August came, and ninth grade loomed, her body felt normal, but her spirit was barren. Her baby had been ended, its importance marked by the emptiness it left behind; an emptiness that consumed the tears when they came unbidden those first weeks. It was like a void that sucked her in, a black hole of emotion that needed repair.

She had no desire to fill the hole with another baby and, instead, began to look to the Box. Her search for meaning seemed to lead there, where old attachments that influenced her spiritual identity were reinforced in her heart, becoming a healing balm of sorts.

Deep down, the Kramers were her original Forever Family, and the Box brought idealized memories that served to support the primal bonds formed in the river house. Sometimes she dreamed of finding them, but the abandonment she still felt brought a fear of rejection, and the dream turned gray.

Yet the deep Christian values the Kramers instilled remained, and when Marsha helped her get a contraceptive implant, it seemed like a failure to protect her innocence. This "freedom" opened a door for sexual experimentation without abortive consequences and felt like a violation of implied family trust.

"So…" Jain began when she hopped in the car after the procedure. Swelling and bruising from the implant brought minimal pain, especially compared to the abortion, and the anesthetic block they had injected allowed her to painlessly finger the thin tube beneath her skin. "Sex is okay?"

"Maybe not okay, but it's what kids are gonna do. The urge is incredibly strong."

"It's not a sin?"

"I don't really know about that, but I'm not sure it matters. Kids are gonna experiment, and parents can't stop them, obviously." She glanced at Jain as she steered the car. "Not even church camp could stop you, and we can't watch you 24/7."

"So, you just give up trying to stop me?" Almost unconsciously, Jane hoped not.

"How could we stop you? Birth control at least stops pregnancies, and we know you learn about safe sex in school. I'm not sure what else *we* can do."

"Tell me not to?" Her tone was a little biting. To Jain, no sex was safe sex. Someone was gonna get hurt either way, and Marsha was right about the urges. Still... *free love?*

"Okay, don't have sex, *Jain.*" Marsha's sarcasm bit back, and Jain shut up. The honeymoon was over.

Busy with the placement of a toddler in their fourth bedroom, Marsha and Jim backed away emotionally in response to Jain's passive resistance to deeper family interactions. She remained in her room, reading and compliant in her chores. She was dutiful in her interactions with the twins, but now more guarded against the now poignant memories they evoked of her long-lost sisters.

Her emotional distance grew in the months after the abortion/birth control events, but there was no significant outreach by the busy Grade Nine Fosters either, no full perception of the depth of her despair, and no direction towards counseling and the help it might have provided. Life went on relentlessly, as it does with children.

Being nominal Christians, the family rarely attended church. When they did, family follow-up was lacking. No Bible study on the couch, no discussion of the sermons, no prayer, and no daily living out the Christian life—things that were routine in her time at the Kramer's river house. So spiritually, Jain drifted as well, seeking no intimacy with God, and finding no encouragement in that direction. She lived in their house and was obedient in her interactions.

Despite the past rattling around in her spirit and knocking at her emotional doors, her brain allowed her to get excellent grades after she landed with the permissive Grade Nine Fosters. But brilliance had its downsides, and her success in school and intelligent insights revealed in term papers and teacher evaluations caused her depression and reclusiveness to go unnoticed. She was just interpreted as being a "quiet," personal girl.

What attachment Martha's previous kindnesses fostered resulted in only passive defiance towards them as she explored Goth, then drifted to the gentler fashion and raw emotional music explorations of the emo-kids movement. Earbuds grew in her ears, and she listened to the genre's heavy lyrics for long hours each day. Her good grades left them relatively unconcerned, and they were glad to see her passionate Pete Kramer-induced interest in pet overpopulation and contraceptive science lead to first-place science fair projects in the ninth and tenth grades.

Jain enjoyed the pleasures and thrill of rare, stolen sex and of being held for a bit, yet physical intimacy failed to penetrate the hard-learned emotional reserve that kept her isolated. She feared pregnancy and wanted birth control's freedom, but she didn't like the lump in her arm or the hormonal disruption it brought. But since an early sexual partner had ingrained that condoms were like wearing a raincoat in the shower, she grudgingly lived with the lump as she researched and explored birth control for those science fair projects.

When the implant wore out near the end of eleventh grade, her tenth-grade research led her to insist on an IUD instead of a new lump. Marsha was willing and even helped her arrange the change. Heavier periods with their natural mood swings followed, and she found them liberating and feminine, even though they were dulled by the medication in the IUD.

When her performance in school allowed her to skip some of her finals one day in May, Marsha prepared a quiet lunch for them, and they sat munching nachos and Marsha's wonderful chicken enchiladas. Uninterrupted time together was rare, and there was pleasant small talk until Jane brought up a concern that had been simmering inside her.

"Do you think three years of fake hormones and almost no cycling hurt me?" Her internet-fueled research had fostered cynicism towards the big industries that developed drugs. She saw how they focused on maximum profit with minimal hassle, promoting incomplete science. And people were like sheep, going where "science" and the companies shepherded them, unwilling to question the "experts."

"Hurt your body? Probably not. I would assume they wouldn't let kids use them if they were harmful." It was frustrating how Marsha just accepted the junk like everyone else.

"Who is "they"? I think a man must have invented that shit," declared Jain. "Having real periods makes me feel like a woman again." A nice forkful of enchilada emphasized her words. She savored its juiciness and the texture of the chicken inside.

"Language, Jain." Marsha's correction was automatic but showed that she still cared about Jain. "Some people think fewer periods are a good thing."

"But we're not made that way," she countered. "It's not right."

"And unwanted babies are?" Marsha flicked her bangs aside with a little jerk of her head. Her glance seemed triumphant to Jain, negating the loss she still struggled with.

"Who says they're unwanted?" Jain's flash of emotion surprised even her.

"So, you *want* babies every time you f—have sex?" Jain sensed venom, underlying anger, and... *jealousy?* Her eyes widened slightly with comprehension, then narrowed.

"You dislike my freedom?" Jain didn't usually pick fights, but deeply held resentments apparently festered, and hormones lowered her natural reticence. "Well, thanks, cuz you gave it to me."

"I gave you the freedom to make choices I've never had. You're welcome." Marsha's eyes were suddenly wet. It gave Jain pause, and she looked down at her plate, no longer seeing the food as she now perceived a scarlet thread pulling from Marsha's past.

"Well... thank you." Her modulated tone implied regret, and they hugged, tentative at first, then more tender. It had been awhile. No longer hungry, they cleared the dishes and cleaned the kitchen quietly together.

Her brief flare of hostility receded to her previous passivity as quickly as it rose. She returned to her outward quiet self-sufficiency, requiring little attention, and receiving that in return. The Grade Nine Fosters were busy with the twins and often took other placements to fill the home's fourth bedroom. And Grade Nine dad was careful to never be alone with her, making their bond shallow. It was more like living in a kindly boarding house for the pass-through fosters.

For Jain, it was not much more than that as her senior year passed. Her bond with Marsha, bittersweet because Marsha led her to loss but also freedom in a sense, had slightly improved after she had felt the thread pulling from Marsha's past, even though they'd never explored that together. She could at least sense the burden that drove Marsha's values and interactions with her, but the distractions of life in the home precluded any further bonding.

Her stolen moments increased as she followed the setting sun out her window some nights. They had no idea she even went to parties where emo music resonated in her heart, although they had noticed her clothes changing from black to include more earthly tones as the months passed. Never did they see her study or bring books home. When graduation from Ozark High School rolled around, they were surprised to learn she was at the top of her class, and her ACT score of thirty-five meant her options were wide open for university.

In their home, life had been like a wide, deep river as it slows to a lazy mirrored movement behind a dam. Here and there, a leaf drifts listlessly, a water boatman beetle might paddle past, and from time to time, raindrops might cause ripples that disappear as the water smooths back out to reflect brilliant summer sunlight again. And then there's broad movement beneath the surface as the water builds and swells, swifting towards the watershed.

On this river of life, there was no safety barrier, no little rope of floats, and no buoys to grab hold of. Her soul and spirit were being swept along by time and events, and the safe shores of state custody would no longer be hers, there in the whitewater of adulthood below the dam.

She was glad when the Grade Nine Fosters decided, two weeks before graduation, to have a little party to mark the event. Five years in one house was a record for her, but she had always regarded them as a service, paid by DFS. Now she allowed that the roof and sustenance provided over the years, and the attention now, might be seen as spiritual comfort.

"Have you decided on a plan for after graduation?" Marsha opened the line of inquiry as they sat around the kitchen table eating homemade graduation cake. Grade Nine dad was there as well, and the twins. Another two placements who Jain had mostly avoided, just as she had all their other placements over the years, were enjoying the cake and company as well.

"Well, kind of. I applied to the University of Florida last fall."

"Gainesville?"

"Yeah."

"And?" Marsha was focused, eyebrows raised and hands momentarily clasped in expectation.

"I got an acceptance letter and an honors scholarship. My counselor at school said it was a full-ride. Apparently, it's a little harder to get full-ride scholarships there for out-of-staters, but because I was a foster kid, I qualified."

"Sweet," exclaimed Marsha. She smiled broadly. "I'm so proud of you."

Grade Nine dad smiled too and said, "So, what're you gonna study?"

"Biology, for now. They're doing a lot of research in birth control, which you know I like," she grinned. "And they also have a big pet population control program at the veterinary school there."

"Are you going to go to vet school?" Marsha watched Jain's eyes.

It was a question that brought emotion, and Jain felt hot tears form as she choked up. *Marsha remembered her details!* Everyone stared at her, and she quickly regained her composure. She pushed her hair back over her ears. "No."

"Why not?" Grade Nine dad's voice was gentle.

"Cuz I could never kill puppies and kittens." She wiped her eyes with her napkin

Authority crept into his voice. "That's not the only thing vets do, Jain."

"Yeah, but I could *never* do that. Besides, even you know that I'm interested in birth control for people." Her reproachful glance included them all. "If I could do something to help stop unwanted babies, abortions, and help pets at the same time, that would be the best," she said firmly.

"What do you mean 'even *we* know?'" Marsha asked. Jain knew she was triggering Marsha with her little jabs but kept on.

"You haven't exactly shown an interest in my life until now when you find out I'm a brain." She couldn't seem to stop; it was like she was resisting the closeness of the celebratory moment. She blew her nose and dropped the napkin on the cake, leaving it half-eaten.

"We've always been here for you, Jain, you're the one who has kept the walls up, honey." Marsha's lips were pursed as she defended herself and her husband.

"And you never tried to knock 'em down, did you?" She didn't know where her anger was coming from. Maybe the images of puppy and kitten piles from the Kramers brought back the loss she still felt when her baby was torn away. She felt the hot tears welling up again and pushed her cake away. *Dammit!*

Marsha placed a hand on her shoulder, and she didn't resist, reaching for another napkin from the holder on the table instead. The other two fosters, years younger, were becoming restless, and Grade Nine dad instinctively led them away. "I know we've never been very close. We've always felt like you were just passing through, not wanting any closer connections." She leaned back, opening her hands and shrugging slightly. "Maybe we should have pushed harder, but it seemed you were pretty resistant."

"I'm sorry. I didn't mean to spoil the party. I was remembering things in my past, and I really didn't want to right now."

"Some time, some way, you're gonna have to."

"It's not like that. I just miss them."

"Who? Your parents?"

"No! God, I hate them! I don't even know them. I miss my *original* foster parents. At least the first ones I can remember." Even saying their name seemed too intimate to share.

"The veterinary family?"

"Yes." She was still surprised Marsha even remembered those details.

"Look, it's okay. I just got choked up. I'm really glad you made me a cake, and I'm really thankful you let me stay all these years. You gave me privacy, which is what *I* wanted."

"Maybe, but now I'm worried we gave you too much privacy. I hope you're emotionally ready." Her expression was open and concerned.

"I'll be fine, *mom*," she'd never used that word before, and spoke it with kindness, making Marsha blink. It didn't sound right or sit well, though. Despite the years, the Kramers were her foundational family and had shaped much of her identity, *not* the Grade Nines. She was determined to hold to that narrative.

In her heart of hearts, she longed to sit on the Kramer couch and snuggle while they read the Bible, Patricia Polacco books, and other stories to her; to lie on the grass in the yard while one of their big dogs licked her face in the late summer sun; to smell and taste Play Dough during craft projects on Sunday mornings at church. She held those distant memories close, but the intervening years now left her spiritually adrift without a name or family she could call her own.

Intellectually, her insight helped her understand the emotional pain that kept the Kramers from tracking her down and coming to her rescue. Legalities, institutional social service indifference, and distance were also barriers. Still, because of the unconditional love she had received, she felt betrayed when she never heard from them again. Loss and hurt left her distrustful of her Christian past also; in her eyes, God had let her down just like the Kramers. Flowing along her river of life, she yearned for a deep spiritual anchor as she faced the open sea.

"God…" she began that night, wrapped in a blanket in the dark of her room. She groaned, unable to articulate further. She needed a place to snuggle a dad who would never fade away but didn't know how to find one. She yearned for home but knew it not and feared she never would.

CHAPTER TWELVE
UNWORTHY

JAIN FOUND A room in an apartment building in Gainesville on a well-kept, tree-lined street close to the arts and sciences facilities. The building surrounded a small central courtyard where a huge oak tree grew, shading many of the apartments and bringing peace to the atmosphere. A thirty-hour Greyhound trip ended with a city bus connection that dropped her near her new home. All her possessions were in the duffle bag strapped to her shoulders, all her past in the Box she carried by her side.

She was pleased to find the red brick apartments tidy and well-maintained on the outside, and the neighborhood was very quiet in the early July morning. Humidity brought a glow to her face, and beads of sweat were on her upper lip by the time she reached the walkway outside the third-floor apartment door. Her hair was already limp, but the deep shade of the oak tree brought relief, and the dangles of Spanish moss enabled by those conditions were enchanting. She had never seen moss before.

She knocked timidly at the metal door to apartment 306, saw the peephole darken, and the door swung back to reveal a friendly face with wideset dark brown eyes. Cornrows set off her hair like a stylized helmet, and her smooth mahogany skin was made darker by her white cotton blouse. Her bare toes wiggled as she introduced herself with a smile, "I'm Camille. You must be Jain."

"I am. It's so nice of you to meet me. I hope I'm not making you late for work!"

"No, I don't have to be there until 8:00 this morning, so we're good for another fifteen minutes, which should be long enough."

Camille stepped aside as Jain entered. She led her across the open living/dining area to a bedroom door, one of three in the mostly furnished apartment designed for student living. Jain's room was a corner room, giving her two windows that looked off to the southwest towards the sprawling UF campus. The king-size bed looked huge but wasn't imposing and had a nightstand with a lamp on the side nearest the door. A small computer work desk was in the corner of the room, off the foot of the bed.

"You get the corner room," said Camille. "Neither one of us wanted to switch rooms when Georgia left, so you lucked out. There's even a small balcony."

"Sweet." Jain stepped into the room and plopped her duffle on the floor. "This is a lot bigger than I expected!"

"Yeah, these're some of the nicest apartments around, but the building's a little older, so people don't find it as attractive. I sure like it here. It's a really quiet place." Jain felt Camille's eyes checking her out.

"Perfect," Jain said, turning to face her.

"Make yourself at home. Each bedroom has its own key, but all the keys work on the front door. A closed door means privacy, but we ain't offended if you lock it. Bottom shelf in the fridge is yours, and we share the veggie drawers. An' your cupboard is marked with an 'A.'" Camille's eyes were friendly, her face open.

"Great. Thanks." Jain was immediately comfortable with her easy movements and speech.

"Okay, I gotta go, but I hope to get a chance to know you some later. This is a good neighborhood, but keep the front door locked just in case." Her eyes widened, and she said, "Cuz ya never know!"

Camille made her way out, and Jain was left alone with a faint smile. Her skin felt gritty from the long bus ride and sweaty humidity, something she'd never experienced in Missouri. She unpacked a few things and headed for the shower and then to bed, where someone had thoughtfully placed clean sheets. She fell into the flowing sheets and slept until mid-afternoon, linens crisp against her skin in the air-conditioned room.

She woke up later, momentarily confused at the quiet sounds of cooking outside her room. She oriented herself and dressed before entering the common area to find a deeply tanned blonde girl in her early twenties. Her blue eyes smiled a greeting as she put the lid back on a pot she was checking. "Hello there."

"Hi. I'm Jain, your new roommate, I assume."

"Yeah, and I'm Bobbie. I'm the one you talked to on the phone." Bobbie was wearing khaki shorts and a loose chambray sleeveless shirt buttoned nearly to the top. She had a heavier build than Jain or Camille, and her hair seemed too light to be natural. She wore makeup and turquoise jewelry at her throat and wrists.

"Nice to finally meet you. I seem to have slept the day away." Jain yawned and rubbed her eyes briefly.

Bobbie glanced at her. "Yeah, how long was the bus ride?"

"Thirty hours, and almost no sleep!"

"Uggh!" she said as she stirred the pot. "I'm making student supper, my spiced-up mac-n-cheese and tuna if you're hungry. There's plenty."

"Wow, thanks," said Jain as she looked first at Bobbie, then leaned to look at the mixture and sniff. It actually looked good, but Jain was a little anxious to learn about her surroundings and get a little space to adjust. "It looks and smells good, but I think I'll go out for a walk and get to know the area a little. Is it safe around here?"

"As safe as any university neighborhood. You're a beauty," Bobbie's tone was friendly, "but usually, no one will bother you too much."

Long legs, graceful form, and smooth flaxen hair set off a slightly freckled, naturally tanned face she knew was "pretty." But in the mirror, where she seldom dwelt, lonely green eyes looked on a girl of sorrow whom life had given only a stupid name from a mother who never was. She blinked away the compliment, which rang hollow and brought the threat of intimacy if accepted. "Sounds good. See you around then." She headed towards the door, hoping she didn't seem impolite.

"Okay. Bye, Jain." Jain slipped barefoot into her sandals and smiled back at Bobbie as she shut the door and set out.

Her walk confirmed, with relief, that she was only a few blocks from her work-study job in the biology department. Her scholarships more than covered her expenses, but it would be nice to have extra spending money. Work-study also gave her the opportunity to make closer connections to the faculty.

The old university neighborhoods, shaded with tall, gangly live oaks and towering pines, were amazing to her, especially the moss hanging every-where. Unlike the dry Ozarks back home, everything seemed moist and teeming with green. She made her way back to the apartment by a different route and found her roommates lying together on the couch watching a movie.

They seemed comfortable with each other, even in close proximity, and when she realized they usually shared the king-size bed in Camille's room and used Bobbie's room for a study area and closet, it soon became clear they were lovers. The only couples she had ever lived with had been straight foster parents, but the same-sex-ness of the couple gave her little pause. They lived and acted like most couples she had known over the years.

Jain lost contact with her Grade Nine Fosters, ignoring their weak out-reach seemed the most practical action as she began to establish herself in Gainesville. She continued to hold close the Box, its record of her life and few meager memories that had been started by the Kramers. In the days before classes started, with no friends or connection and lots of free time, she reviewed its contents and updated the log sheet she'd maintained in the placement file. After Grade Nine Fosters, she wrote "The End" in her neat block script.

She created a new manila file called "College," her latest placement, where she filed her acceptance letter and scholarship information. Hope-fully, this chapter would bring healing, a path away from the inner loneliness that had plagued her since the loss of Eddie to circumstance so long ago. Remembering him brought a lump to her throat and a pang to her heart.

As she looked at the Box, she realized there was no file of friendships. Cordial with her roommates, they were a friendly way to share expenses.

But no close bonds formed—they were into each other and their lives, and she didn't want to intrude. It was a loose trust of convenience, for the most part. Struggling with her identity and its broken connections, her Gothic clothing motifs returned.

Recreation of the dark barrier from her adolescence was a shield from further pain, but in college, Goth was rare, and she wasn't into the rest of the Goth scene. Earth tones gradually mixed with her loose-fitting Goth clothing again as she remained alone, outwardly brilliant, quiet, and self-sufficient, and inwardly searching for connection and meaning. She wanted to overcome her reticence, feeling awkward when she tried without success.

She even went to church a few times during her freshman year at Florida, but she imagined disapproval of her lifestyle and appearance at each one she found. While the people often seemed nice, she couldn't surmount her barriers. She often cried as her spirit moaned to God in the night, but in church surrounded by strangers, she couldn't open her heart. After a few random Sunday morning churches that fall, she tried Christmas Eve midnight mass with the Catholics.

St. Augustine Church was candlelit and majestic inside as families and groups of friends gathered. Apparently friendly, many quietly nodded in greeting to her, and when she sat towards the back of the crowded sanctuary, folks quickly moved to make room. But frequent kneeling, standing, and sitting were unfamiliar, interrupting her brief times of reflection. Then, she swallowed the wafer awkwardly as she recalled she wasn't supposed to take communion if she wasn't Catholic. Her violation of the rules wasn't intentional but made her feel even more unworthy.

God of rules, God of guilt, God of unattainable love... After that Christmas, she quit going to churches at all.

CHAPTER THIRTEEN

BLEAK REALITY

MEN WERE DRAWN by her head-turning beauty, even in her loose-fitting clothes, but many women seemed to somehow resent it. Aware of her visage, yet inwardly empty and self-loathing, mating attraction was the only reason she imagined any man would approach her. Free to respond but fearful of empty motivations, her looks became a barrier to attachment, and even the call of sensuality went unfulfilled.

She turned inward and backward to her past, cycling through items in the Box, and rediscovered a safe companionship living in her child-self's imagination. Even while still with the Kramers, she had fantasies of her two lost womb mates. Hannah and Eliza were present in her play, and a child's distant hand had drawn one of the few things in the Box that recorded her personal memories. "Hana," "Liza," and "Jain" in clumsy letters labeled the three stick figures, black on the white paper. They floated in a canoe at the river house.

In her childish play, she'd always favored Hannah, who was the brave sister, first to emerge from the womb. Now, Hannah became her friend and guide as she imagined life today with her in the lead, and Eliza was always close as well. They became inseparable yet separate and followed her everywhere. Often, she followed Hannah's imaginary lead as she navigated a course through university institutions in pursuit of higher learning.

Her current situation was rocky. Tossed by emotional waves all autumn as her past and present isolation consumed her, her fall semester grades were deeply average. Her inattention had produced predictable results and, summoned by email, she walked through the January sun to her advisor's office. Imagining Hannah alongside calmed her as she gave a tentative knock on the door jamb.

Dr. Skinner glanced up, then focused as she watched her beauty catch his eye. "Yes?"

"I'm Jain Smith." Her name had grown more distasteful over time and saying it bothered her now. Hannah sounded much better. "You emailed me." Dark blue eyes in a tanned, rugged face showed interest but not recognition. "You're my advisor. Biology 102?" She saw it click, and his eyes became kind as he connected the dots.

"Oh, yes!" He stood briefly and was a head taller than her as they shook hands. She felt a guilty thrill, fueled by loneliness, despite his ten year's seniority. "One of my full-ride scholars. Sorry, it took a second."

"No problem, Dr. Skinner." She followed his lead and sat at the only other chair.

He clicked on his keyboard, and she could see herself pop up on his screen. When they'd met last August, he'd taken her picture holding her hand-printed name on a sheet of paper. He'd said he took a mug shot to learn each student's face, and that was fine. But seeing 'Jain Smith' below her face grated, just as saying it had a moment ago. "So, Jain. I wanted to make sure you were doing okay. You have an almost perfect ACT score and were first out of four hundred in high school. Your Biology 101 grade was okay, but you didn't do so well in your other classes. What gives?" He leaned back from the screen and faced her directly.

Something hummed behind his eyes, an intensity that was alive and attractive. It seemed to suggest a purpose, from which this discussion distracted. Yet he gave her his full attention, which was a little unnerving. "I was having trouble, but things are getting better now. I think this semester will be better."

"What sort of trouble?" his tone was interested, not accusing. Focused now on her, his intensity made her want to respond.

"I'm… I was…having some trouble adjusting to being alone here. In Florida." She looked around the office.

"Where did you come from?"

"Missouri. Ozark, Missouri."

"And what brought you here?"

"Well, it's kind of a long story," she paused. "I have an interest in pet overpopulation and contraceptive science."

"I have time."

"What?" She felt her eyebrows rise, then scrunch together as she dipped her chin towards him. *Why do you care?*

"I have time. This is my advising hour, and you're the only one in line today." Stroking long fingers through his dark, unruly hair, he leaned back and put his hands behind his head. "Tell me a short version of your long story."

No one had ever wanted to hear her story, short *or* long version. Reluctant of how much to reveal, she tried to channel Hannah's confidence. It seemed clumsy, unsure to her, as she tried to lay out an abbreviated version that included the Kramers and the Grade Nine Fosters, but little in between. It was enough to explain her interest in pet overpopulation and birth control without risking too much.

"So, how many homes?" His intensity was still humming, undiluted by her story.

"What?"

"How many foster placements before you graduated?"

"An even dozen." She knew because she'd been dwelling in the Box.

"I had half that. An even half-dozen." His eyes caught hers as he faced her squarely, waiting.

"Oh." Her eyes widened and focused on his as perception dawned.

"I'm glad you survived the system. I know it wasn't easy."

It wasn't, and now her head was spinning at this unexpected duality: an urge to run contrasted against an almost erotic urge to draw closer. More than ever, she needed Hannah, who was hiding, leaving her exposed. She smiled a bit at her reliance on her imaginary sister.

"It wasn't so bad…" *It was hell, and still is!* She didn't know what else to say as she unconsciously leaned away from him and looked down.

"I'm sure it was hell." Like he'd read her thoughts! She looked back up. He changed the subject as if he sensed the fear rising in her. *Was it on her face?* He went on, "Yet here you are. Here *we* are. You seem to understand why your grades were marginal. Are you feeling better about the coming semester?"

She sat straighter but couldn't lean forward again. She had been feeling better before. "I-I think so."

"Okay." He sat straight again, addressing her squarely. She could suddenly smell a faint cologne. It was woodsy and very…male. "We have a lot in common, Ms. Jain Smith. I look forward, perhaps, to getting to know you better. For now, our hour is up. If you find yourself getting overwhelmed this semester, reach out. You're not alone."

They both rose.

Revelations of her past to an almost total stranger brought a disorienting rush, worsened by a visceral thrill when their hands touched. Certain he felt it, too, and she was relieved to see his wedding band. Then it was over, and she made her way out of the biology building.

Walking home, she was sure Hannah's stomach wouldn't have been churning at the memories of foggy, twisted sexuality brought on by the older man's masculinity. She ran across the street into McCarty Woods's green sanctuary just in time to empty her stomach behind a Chinquapin's wide trunk.

Pain sharpened her despair as she pressed her forehead into the bark. It was like the wall between her and the world, between her and God: hard, unyielding, and insurmountable. *Where* was Hannah? Where was Eliza? Why had she been left alone, a mistake wandering lost in this unforgiving world? She put her hands to her head and ran them through her hair as she stepped back in a melancholic fog. She wiped the wet from her face and lips on her sleeve and sat against a nearby maple as eternity demanded consideration. If it brought the childhood promise of joyful relief from this bleak world, maybe to die, for her, would be gain.

Her mind tossed and turned with her spirit. She envisioned a razor cutting her arms, warm blood draining the pain and assuaging the years of desolation and unrequited past that plagued her soul. Hannah and Eliza were free—she could join them. A warm bath in a clawfoot tub wouldn't be that bad. She could drift away, slip beneath the surface as her spirit eased into that same everlasting freedom in the presence of God, unattainable here.

Freedom's vision calmed her as she sat with her arms around her knees, staring down at the ground between her legs. Time returned when the bark grinding into her lower back became uncomfortable. An old pickup without a muffler roared past on Newell Drive. She'd felt Hannah and Eliza, but now they faded again, and the urge to join them receded. If she could just *be* Hannah, here and now, she might not feel so afraid and out of control. But Hannah was elusive as an awareness of bleak reality returned.

CHAPTER FOURTEEN
HANNAH ELIZA CRAMER

ADDING THIRTY HOURS of classes for the spring semester and volunteering at the nearby St. Francis Pet Care clinic for homeless people's pets brought verdant activity to ease that bleak reality. Considerations of suicide and realization of the power to choose that option somehow diminished the desire to join her sisters.

Hannah was the only name they knew her by at St. Francis, and she liked the sweetness of it spoken aloud. Compassion for the homeless, and the plight of their pets, broached her disinclination to touch the hearts of others, but her isolation was an abyss that drowned emotion, leaving only a dull inward yearning for connection.

Her grades returned to the monotonous A's of high school, raising no flags as she signed a full slate of classes in June, and the abbreviated summer class schedule left time to consider her situation. While the initial bump from hearing Hannah spoken at St. Francis diminished, its smoothness to her ear and meaning in her heart made the name 'Jain' spoken in her other life a grating racket, harder and harder to speak or write down. Her biological mother, Lisa, should have never been allowed to reproduce, much less name a child.

She reckoned it was time for her to begin to claim her identity and define herself by something that might help her fill the void that plagued her. Jane Doe, the name given to her in the hospital to protect her identity, was not a name of love but of DFS-imposed anonymity. Jain Smith was worse, a stupid intentional hillbilly misspelling by her meth-addicted Lisa-mom. Research in her air-conditioned apartment revealed that she could easily change her name in court and shed Jain, and hopefully, Lisa, forever.

She was already converging with Hannah, and even though she loved Eliza, Hannah would become her first name moving forward. Eliza would get the unoccupied middle spot, and the last name was a no-brainer. She changed it slightly so it would be hers, and hers alone, but it was based on the foundation the Kramers had set. Camille and Bobbie were impressed as she laid out the paperwork on the kitchen table.

While she wasn't particularly close to her roommates, they seemed to understand her need to redefine herself. They knew what it was like to live a life of lies, and they, too, had reinvented themselves in a way when their families became aware of their sexual orientations. They gave her efforts loving support, yet when they asked why the name change, she responded with, "I just never liked Jain," leaving a distance between them.

In the heat and humidity of central Florida's summer, everything slowed—even the cicadas droned long and loud. But when she filed the documents with the help of legal aid, the hearing came quickly, and the judge smiled as he read the history of her name and the reason she wanted to change it. By autumn, before classes marked the start of her sophomore year, she was legally Hannah Eliza Cramer. Jain Smith was relegated to a name, hopefully forgotten, alongside "Hana" and "Liza" on the child's stick figure canoe picture in the Box where she placed the judge's order. Some peace came with her new name. Going forward, she resolved to make Hannah's life count by doing good with it, not harm.

CHAPTER FIFTEEN
WATERSHED

As SHE ROUNDED out her undergraduate education, she homed in on contraception. She began to wear a copper necklace with a small copper IUD model that resembled a cross. Copper because copper, in her native Ozarks, was known to be a healing metal. A cross because a cross represented religion so meaningful in her youth. Passion for contraceptive science and the freedom it offered was starting to fill the void left by the church she'd pushed away. It offered freedom from the consequences of creation in lives here and now, not nebulous, unfulfilled promises from a silent God.

Pete's veterinary influence led her undergrad path towards animal, rather than human, contraception. She had internet-spied on the Kramers once or twice over the years and knew his clinic still ran low-cost spay/neuter clinics. She also remembered all the late-night emergency calls Pete had taken, often for injured stray and abandoned animals brought in by the humane society and animal control in Joplin.

Stirring ties to both her abandonment and her early life with the Kramers, animal overpopulation and the plight of unwanted animals touched her at a deep level. Through St. Francis Pet Care, she learned about volunteer positions at a non-profit, low-cost spay/neuter clinic put on by the College of Veterinary Medicine at the University, where her favorite job was easing the dogs and cats as they recovered from surgery.

As their comforter, she found fulfilling the child-like trust of the animals deeply satisfying. Unlike the homeless and their pets at St. Francis, compassion towards just animals involved no human emotional reciprocity and was much less threatening. She would sit with several post-op canine patients at a time on the floor of the recovery kennel, whispering sweet nothings in their ears and gently stroking their foreheads or shoulders. It made a real difference in their spay/neuter experience and cost her nothing from a spiritual standpoint.

Late in her sophomore year, and technically a junior, she met Terri Jackson. Terri had graduated with her degree in biology and started as a research assistant in a human contraception research project in the Population Control Program at the Center for Population Studies (CPS). Her PhD work was related to a new molecule called RU-AT-677 that showed a great deal of promise as a trans-mammalian form of birth control. They were both volunteering at the spay/neuter clinic, and Terri's brilliant blue eyes, reminiscent of Dr. Skinner's, caught Hannah's attention.

Terri's skin was a translucent alabaster that set off the dark course of her veins. Her short, straight hair was ebony and often covered with a floppy sun hat to protect her fair skin. Their paths crossed in the recovery area when Terri was sent to help Hannah, who was momentarily overwhelmed by a dozen recovering dogs, some of which were trying to get up clumsily and needed to be moved to kennels to complete their recovery. It was like herding drunk cats, and Hannah was doing her best to minimize their collisions with the cabinets and falling over other dogs.

"It looks like your life has gone to the dogs!" Terri joked. There were slip leads for each patient, and Terri led or half-carried the more awake dogs to their waiting kennels while Hannah moved from dog to dog as she monitored them. There were over a hundred dogs that Saturday morning, and Terri and Hannah worked well together as they handled each patient with genuine caring.

Owners showed up after 3 p.m. to begin picking up their dogs, and Terri and Hannah brushed and bathed where needed, making sure each owner received their aftercare instructions and paperwork. When the last dog went home after five, they were pleasantly tuckered out. A friendship quickly developed as they discussed music, science, and life over the next two Saturdays.

As they finished up on their third weekend shift together, Terri asked Hannah if she had ever heard the Indigo Girls perform. "They're going to be singing at this little bar venue called Charlie's tonight."

"Umm, that sounds like fun, but I'm not twenty-one yet."

"Hey, no problem. If you wanna go, I can getchya in."

"Well, if you say so. Where is it?" Hannah's reluctance was overcome by Terri's enthusiasm.

Terri smiled warm encouragement. "Over off West University Drive. I'll pick you up."

"Sounds good!" Hannah was happy to be able to get out with someone who wouldn't be after just one thing. It would be relaxing, and she looked forward to a night of music and good company. She walked to the local thrift store and, for the first time in years, chose light-colored, more form-fitting clothes. She wore a trim skirt and a green and white sleeveless button-up shirt and was waiting outside the apartments in Birkenstock sandals when Terri pulled up in her old F100. The door gave a hollow metallic clang when she slammed it, and they were off, laughing when Terri missed a gear on the worn column shift.

The "little" bar was actually a three-hundred-seat venue with straining A/C and a raised stage area at one end where an opening band played Neil Young's *Down by the River*. Terri had a red, "over twenty-one" wrist band for Hannah and found them seats at a small table near the stage. Hannah sat to save their seats while Terri got Jack-N-Cokes.

The opening band finished with a long version of *Millworker's Daughter*, and the lights went dim as they cleared the stage. It was thirty minutes until the Indigo Girls would start, but the bar was filling up, mostly with women it seemed. Clearly, some of them knew Terri, and it took a while to make her way back to Hannah with the sweating glasses in her hands. She was beautiful in just jeans and a t-shirt, and Hannah felt a little overdressed with her cool, tight-fitting skirt, but it was still nice to not have men gawking at her. The Jack's warmth mellowed the nervousness she felt at being out in public without her loose clothes and Gothic touches. It was a tight venue, but there seemed to be a comradery that also made the closeness less stressful. She slid closer to Terri to make more room, and there were only a few clumsy bumps as women moved around them.

"Do you come here often?"

"Once in a while. The Indigo Girls are my favorite. I think you're going to like them."

"Well, I hope so. I'm missing sitting at home reading tonight!" Their laughter came easily. Terri's soft hand felt good on her forearm as she leaned close so Hannah could hear.

"Trust me, they're good. They write almost all their own stuff, and both play acoustic guitars. They brought some extra musicians tonight to add some depth," she pointed to a woman moving a bass into position on the darkened stage. The house lights suddenly dimmed, and over-bright stage lights came on strong.

"Guess it's time to start then!" The small crowd cheered. The lights adjusted, and the performers got together. For Hannah, the music was amazing. It was as if they were singing directly to her, and she was transformed as she began to realize her deepest thoughts and emotions were shared not just by Amy and Emily, but almost everyone in the room. Many sang along with the songs.

Hannah leaned into the table on her forearms, holding her drink, mesmerized by the lyrics, and swaying slowly in time to the music. She put down her drink and crossed her arms on the warm wood of the small table. Terri sensed her feeling and leaned forward some as she watched the emotions running across her face. Hannah leaned back, her hands flat on her lap beneath the table, a faint smile on her lips.

"This next song is by Emily," Amy announced with laughter.

"Ya gotta laugh to keep from cryin'. Here's *Watershed*." Emily started right in on the chords, and the peaceful tones were like a balm to Hannah, the lilting lyrics speaking straight to her heart.

> *When you're learning to face*
> *The path at your pace*
> *Every choice is worth your while.*

As the music and lyrics flowed, they roiled and filled her with a depth of emotion and oneness she had never experienced before. Tears boiled over when she shut her eyes as the music continued, and the lyrics poured into her soul.

I'm not alone. I'm not alone. I'm not alone.

Not part of the song, the mantra repeated from deep down inside. She felt Terri's hands surround her own, squeezing gently as their fingers intertwined. Cycling to dim, it was as if the stage lights were giving them privacy in the moment.

Hannah slid her right hand over where they joined and held gently as the lyrics played out. Her heart pounded in her chest, and she felt a flush of emotion and sensual thrill as color rushed to her chest and neck. As the song wound down, Hannah felt strangely safe as Terri's spirit seemed to surround her heart. She couldn't move as the performers decided which song to play next from their setlist. She leaned over and into Terri, feeling her lithe frame as their hands remained clasped.

They released, and Terri shifted to hold her in a gentle, encompassing hug. She sensed Terri inhaling her scent, and her eyes locked momentarily with Emily's on the stage. Clapping and cheering from the crowd drowned out all other sounds. Emily leaned towards Amy, speaking into her ear, then back to the microphone with another glance at Hannah, "This next song is for what comes after the watershed. It'll be coming out sometime in the next year, but here is your preview!"

The powerful lyrics of *Hammer and a Nail* were what let Hannah regain her composure that night, especially the stanza ending with:

Now I know a refuge never grows
From a chin in a hand in a thoughtful pose...

She knew she had to rebuild her life—there was no other option. She wanted a life based on the foundation of her true self, if she could ever find that.

They walked from the venue to the truck that night, but Hannah felt as if she were floating. Her teeth chattered as they got in through the driver's door. Hannah slid to the middle of the old bench seat, and she couldn't stop shaking as Terri pressed against her.

"I'm not gonna leave you alone after all of that," Terri said as she drove them to her small house on the edge of Gainesville.

Hannah didn't want to be alone. She needed someone she could trust. She was reminded of the cats and dogs waking up from their surgeries, needing comfort as they returned to the harsh realities of the world. She felt safe with Terri, holding her hand whenever it wasn't shifting gears. And the soothing, warm night air washed over them as the old F100 carried them through the night.

Out on the edge of town, the evening was cool, and a light breeze whispered through the needles of the tall pines around Terri's small white clapboard house. The Jack-N-Coke had long worn off as Terri held her close on the walk from the truck into the house, and their clothes slipped off as they descended into the sheets on Terri's deep king bed.

The silence was broken only by their ragged breathing and whispering linens. Their faces were together, but Hannah was aware of the hot dark points of Terri's areoles as they dragged across her olive skin and the rise of her own against the warmth of Terri's breast. Terri's translucent skin seemed to glow in the faint moonlight of the darkened house.

Tongues explored mouths and hands explored coarse hair and warm, moist folds between labia. Tasting and touching their most intimate places brought a luxurious velvety feeling as they cupped and caressed for what seemed like hours. Hannah couldn't tell where her body ended, and Terri's began. She gasped when Terri's thumb was suddenly inside her, and she rode the waves of climax, crying out as she went places she had never been. Anxiety was absent as she rolled towards Terri, doing with her tongue whatever her imagination thought she might like herself.

Afterwards, she traced the fine blue veins that coursed beneath the skin of Terri's breast as she drifted off to sleep with her head on Terri's thigh, sighing as *Hammer and a Nail* played gently in her brain.

Hannah glowed with discovery and release as dawn brought gray light to the room. Terri seemed to sense her consciousness and stirred slightly, and Hannah could feel her warm breath between her shoulder blades. When she awoke the second time, dappled Florida sunshine streamed through the white curtains in the small bedroom. The A/C was blowing through the vents as the Sunday morning heat took hold. Self-conscious about walking around naked but wanting to dwell in the previous night's wonder, she wrapped a sheet around herself and tentatively explored the house. She found Terri in the kitchen wearing a dark blue robe wrapped loosely around her body, making coffee while a bagel toasted. Their eyes met, and Hannah was again startled by the brilliant blue.

"Hey," she said, suddenly shy. This person knew things about her body that even she didn't know.

"Hey, Hannah. I let you sleep. You were so peaceful…and beautiful."

Hannah was used to men admiring her beauty, but she didn't know how to respond to Terri's intent gaze when the sheet parted for a moment. She suddenly wanted to fling them off so Terri could devour her again. Only her innate modesty stopped her, and maybe fear of completely losing herself in another.

"You want half a bagel? I've got some almond spread, and the coffee's almost ready."

"Sure, thanks," Hannah smiled nervously.

"I have soymilk. I guess you should know I'm a vegan, minimal impact and all. Is soymilk okay?"

"Sounds good." She had never been vegan but had considered it might be a step that moved her further from the bad parts of her past. Hannah sat at the round oaken kitchen table and said, "I've considered going vegan, but it seems a little intimidating."

"I could help you; it's not that hard." Terri gave her an encouraging glance.

"You've already helped me!" She could look into Terri's blue eyes forever.

"Was I your first time…with a woman?" Terri sat across from her, lithely straddling the chair, letting her dark robe open slightly to reveal her ivory chest and belly before they were hidden by the chairback.

Hannah felt color blooming on her cheeks and neck. She took a bite of bagel and sipped her coffee, then swallowed. "Yes," she answered.

"Are you okay?"

Hannah's lips curled slightly upward as her eyes went down for a moment, then rose to meet Terri's piercing blue eyes. "Yes… I'm kinda blown away, actually. I've never felt so close to someone. It feels so natural." She put her hand across the table and took Terri's. "I don't know what I'm feeling exactly. Scared? Normal? Gay?"

"Oh, Hannah! Yes, normal, if you want to label it, or gay, or whatever. I call it *ecstasy*, and you're clearly a natural. I'd say you were feeling yourself, maybe for the first time? If your heart's leading, what else matters?" Terri smiled gently, and Hannah couldn't help but look down again.

"It's like the Watershed song. What you've discovered is milk and honey: the stuff that satisfies your soul. You went over the watershed last night, girl. Mentally, physically, and soulfully." Terri laughed before adding, "Hell, you took me with you, and we landed in each other."

Hannah giggled as well, and it became easy to meet Terri's eyes again. "It was something, wasn't it?"

"It was the first day of the rest of your life. Now it's time to get a *hammer and a nail*," she sang the last few words of the last song the Indigo Girls played that night.

Terri took her hand back and started eating again. Hannah followed suit, and the interruption returned introspection. Her eyes turned inward, and her face fell as she chewed.

I'm gay, she thought. *I'm gay?* She tore off another bite of bagel and chewed slowly. She felt Terri's eyes but didn't look up as the mantra circled. She felt free and wondered if she looked different. *Will the world treat me differently? Am I gonna get hurt?* Terri finished her bagel and took her coffee cup to the sink, then came to sit beside Hannah and pressed in close.

"Where are you?"

She glanced up at Terri and shrugged. "I don't know . . . My whole world's different. It's like I've been asleep for twenty years, and now there's a new reality." She'd started fiddling with the IUD cross and looked down at it.

"You sure don't need that. At least not with me."

"Yeah," Hannah gave her a lopsided grin. "It's like my whole life was a dream up until now, and this is real." She put her bare foot on top of Terri's, and Terri gently put her other foot on top of Hannah's. They sat for a long time, holding each other in silence.

*

Hannah rarely wore any black at all after her first night with Terri and began to work towards becoming vegan. In the weeks that followed, the glow of what seemed like first love faded as Hannah realized Terri was already in a relationship with someone else. She began to notice this when she saw two toothbrushes in the bathroom. Other hints quickly followed: Terri was always careful to keep her phone locked. She declined having lunch together during the week and was often distracted when Hannah called her just to talk.

Discovering that Terri had another lover felt like reliving her first clumsy intimacy with her older foster brother. A part of her had opened then, only to be hurt: first by the separation imposed by circumstances, then the realization that he had not been willing to fight to maintain what was between them. Deeper heartbreak had followed with the loss of her baby. Never again had she let her heart be swept into the sensations her body shared with others until the night with Terri. The circumstances were different, but she felt like that clumsy thirteen-year-old again.

Fantasies of Terri somehow declaring fidelity drove her to continue the relationship. Hannah pushed to go out the following Saturday, wanting to talk; to recreate the magic of their first encounter. They ate vegan Indian food, and afterwards, the intense spices brought a relaxed dreaminess as they went back to Terri's house in the old pickup.

Sunset's glowing splendor was made almost holy by the breeze whispering in the pines, and the quietness of their footsteps in the sandy soil left damp from an earlier thunderstorm. Shoulders bumping gently, they walked to the house fell into the crisp sheets of Terri's big bed. But Hannah had a reticence that hadn't been there before and was clumsy in her acceptance of Terri's experienced petting, which became slightly less gentle as Terri became impatient.

"It's okay, Terri. It's okay." She rolled gently towards the window, frustrated at the hot tear that rolled down her cheek and the anxiety clouding their intimacy. Their previous bliss seemed unattainable.

Terri snuggled against her back, her lips in Hannah's hair as she slid her arm under Hannah's neck and pulled her close; softly, but somehow it seemed to Hannah, not tenderly.

"What's going on, Hannah?" Terri's breath was warm and sweet-smelling as she caressed her ribs, brushing Hannah's breast lightly. Hannah felt her areola's involuntary tension build, but she stopped the shiver rising in response.

Terri stiffened when she finally replied, "I fell in love."

"Dammit, I knew it! I'm so sorry, Hannah! We shared the closeness of your discovery, and I'm so glad we did, but I'm in a relationship." Hannah heard consternation in her tone, but no regrets.

"I know. I saw the toothbrushes." *Like revealing that would somehow change things.*

"We've been together a couple of years since my senior year, and he's very good to me."

Hannah spun in her arms, gazing intently in the dim room. "He?!?"

Terri drew back in surprise. "Yes, he."

Hot shame flushed Hannah's face as a new reality crystallized. She realized there had been no reciprocation of the deep emotions she'd felt. She'd been naïve to think the relationship and its initial encounter had been anything other than an intense fling for Terri. In just a few days, she'd found forever and lost it.

She slid from the sheets to the hardwood floor, turning to face Terri. "I'm sorry, I'm such an idiot. Can you just take me home?"

"Hannah, you're not an idiot. We had a great time, and you discovered things about yourself. I'm in a relationship with someone else, but he doesn't own me. Our loving was *free*." Terri sat up on the edge of the bed and tried to give her a hug, but Hannah turned away and mechanically started pulling on her garments.

The breeze lingered faintly, cooler now, and the sunset's glory was a purple memory as Terri followed her out to the truck. The creaking metal door sounded hollow and empty now as she firmly pulled it shut. Terri drew up, then walked around the hood and got in.

She just sat for a moment, then Hannah heard her sigh. The truck came to life, and they rolled away. Hannah noticed potholes now for the first time as the old truck bounced and swayed.

"Just because you're hurt doesn't mean your feelings weren't real, Hannah. I felt blessed to be a part of what happened in you. It was a beautiful thing." Hannah leaned against the far door, her feet on the dash, watching the scenery flow by.

"It's okay, Terri. I'm not mad at you. You didn't do anything wrong. It was my fault." Hannah's bitter words sounded like forgiveness and healing, but her heart was screaming as she realized the revolutionary nature of their deeply personal intimacy was hers alone. She had assumed an exclusivity that Terri never implied.

She involuntarily jerked when Terri's hand squeezed her shoulder before she reached to shift. Tears ran down her face again, and she swiped them off.

"Our friendship was more than a one-night stand, at least to me," Terri said.

Hannah snorted and looked back out the window. "Yeah, me too," she whispered.

Terri pulled up to her building, and the cicada's call was muted in the cool evening. Hannah got out, shut the door, and leaned in through the open window.

"Take it easy, Terri, and thanks for the Indigo Girls."

As she crossed the apartment to her room, Camille and Bobbie laid feet to feet on the couch, watching a movie. Seeing their comfortable relationship jarred her further as she realized straight or gay, people were people, and she had let her walls down with the wrong woman. She waved and ducked in front of them, going straight to the shower.

Water rained down, and she made it hotter until steam filled the stall. She hadn't realized how lonely her life had been until it wasn't, and sobs came thick and silent. The room fogged, and her tears were washed down the drain, but she didn't feel cleansed as despair and loneliness returned.

CHAPTER SIXTEEN
OSAGE ORANGE

FLEEING TERRI AND her easy companionship left her alone and doubting everything she knew of sexuality and intimacy. Being Hannah seemed as bleak as being Jain, so she chose the safety of solitude. For several months, her roommates—brief encounters required to maintain harmonious living—were her only one-on-one contacts in the world.

From the IUD necklace to her jean shorts, loose cotton shirt unbuttoned over a camisole, and light rope bracelet to the Birkenstock sandals that let her tread almost silently, everything had changed in her accouter since her last encounter with Professor of Biology, Dr. Aaron Skinner. Drawn by another email, she raised her knuckles to once again assault his doorjamb. Her churning stomach felt dreadfully familiar.

Worse, just before she knocked, she could see over his shoulder an image of Jain, holding up her name on a sheet of paper like a mug shot. Her knuckles made muted noise as the knock dissolved in reticence. He turned, unstartled this time, and those dark blue eyes met hers, puzzled beneath a tanned brow and black hair.

"Ummm, Dr. Skinner?"

He quickly rose, as many men did to her beauty. "Yes…Hannah?"

"Yes." Her last contact with his hand had brought an unexpected thrill. This time there was only fight or flight, and she wanted flight. But circumstance and the necessity of their meeting fought against her emotion as she squeezed the hand whose accompanying face was so like Terri's, but swarthy. Like Terri, he also knew of her past. His eyes drilled a question into hers. She managed a nervous smile, "I was Jain before; a failing freshman."

"Ah," he paused. "Growing, perhaps, but not failing. In fact, the record shows quite the opposite. Your junior year is almost done. Thanks for coming by…Hannah." They sat the same as before, hypervigilance pressing in on her.

"Didn't you have a wedding band?"

"I did." He glanced at his hands. "Sadly, all good things…"

"Must end," she finished, startled at her quick familiarity.

"Well…yes. I guess." He didn't meet her eyes, looking at the computer screen a little too long.

"I'm sorry." She felt awkward, but empathy calmed her.

"No, no. It's okay." He looked back up. "We need to update your photo."

He turned to grab a sheet of paper from his printer and a marker from the cup on his desk. "Write your name on this." He clicked on the computer screen and had a sudden live link to the webcam on his desk.

Hannah Eliza Cramer. She made her neat block letters large and held up the page. Dr. Skinner adjusted the camera slightly, then clicked, getting it right the first time. He saved the photo.

"I was puzzled when your new name came up in the system, but my pictures never lie."

"Unless they're not updated—" she stopped, not meaning to be impudent. "No offense."

A smile flitted across his face. "None taken, *Hannah*," he paused, seeming to focus. "Now, thank you again for coming."

"You're welcome."

"Dr. Replonge gave me your senior thesis proposal. Did you realize I oversee the animal contraceptive research that falls under the Center for Population Studies' authority?"

"Ummm… Kind of? I thought she was in charge of everything CPS." Hannah's senior thesis and research proposal were directed at answering several important questions about 677's side effects and efficacy in companion animals. Terri's involvement on the human side, and her veterinary past, had driven her to the animal side where they hopefully wouldn't cross paths as much.

"Well, she is, technically, but I handle all the veterinary research and coordinate with her. That's why your proposal landed in my inbox." He looked down at the file on his desk. "All the money and glamour are on the human side, but you've got a veterinary family in your past, so you already know that, right?" He looked back up at her expectantly.

She was suddenly afraid, not wanting to go back there. "Right. My first family owned a vet clinic." Her voice quavered at the first mention of the stories they'd shared. He bit his lower lip, then nodded.

"I liked your proposal, but it's more long-term than senior year." The "but" rang loud in her ears.

"Yes, I was concerned about that. I know it was supposed to be a *senior* thesis paper, but I couldn't come up with any short 677 projects. There are so many implications and facets that need to be explored, and none of the answers are quick," she explained, more comfortable and focused when discussing science.

"And your appreciation of that is what caught my attention. I've spoken with Dr. Replonge and reviewed your work here with my RA's. Part of this could certainly apply to your Bachelor's, but what are your thoughts on making this a PhD thesis? I would become the primary advisor on your faculty committee since our interests are similar." She absorbed the implications, not quite trusting her ears as an angry leaf blower chased leaves outside the window, interrupting their conversation for a moment.

"So…I would automatically be in a PhD program?"

"Yes, with generous funding," he beamed, seeming pleased with himself. "You'd have to apply and be processed in, but you'd be accepted. The funding comes after your undergraduate scholarships run their course."

"Funding… Materials *and* a stipend?" Hannah's eyes widened.

"What I have is grant funding for *graduate* research on 677. You'd have to work some, graduate TA-type stuff, but yes—materials, a stipend, and even travel to the PBCA conference."

Wow. Maybe no glamour, but money's *available.*

Just in the last few years, Hannah had heard about new grants that made research into canine and feline contraception a priority across the country, and the presence of a veterinary college alongside the CPS made UF a natural epicenter to pursue those grants. They resulted from a wealthy family's effort to reduce the number of unwanted pets that were euthanized in the USA each year. The Challenge, as it was called, included a huge financial reward for whoever was first to perfect a single-dose contraception solution for dogs and cats. It also funded millions in grants to help achieve that goal, and a collaborative organization called the Pet Birth Control Association (PBCA) that held conferences to share information and stimulate discussion.

Before The Challenge, the primary focus at UF was on human contraception and RU-AT-677. 677 was a contraceptive molecule that would generate billions in profit in the protected US human market alone, and third-party payers—with the insulation they provided from market forces— would ensure profitability throughout the world. Dr. Aaron Skinner's team was always sucking hind tit because the potential for returns from the veterinary market was tiny in comparison. Full financial consideration usually only came where the veterinary research projects overlapped into human work. Until The Challenge grant, her proposal would not have even been viable.

Lab facilities were funded by money from the grants program, and there were already advancements on the concept of the RU-AT-677 being used in companion animals. The compound appeared to safely render female and male mammalian test subjects sterile in one dose by any delivery method: oral, injected, or even transdermal. 677's efficacy was proven, but there would be years of safety and field studies because as it stood, there were many potential dangers in administration and implementation. The potential of effects on non-target populations and species had to be carefully investigated as well. Environmental impact studies alone could take years. Animal implications aside, its human contraceptive properties could change the future of the world, perhaps even saving it from the ravages of overpopulation.

"Of course, you can take some time. I don't know what your plans are after graduation, but this would pretty much take up the next several years from an academic standpoint." His tone was cautious; expression bland as if he was giving her room to decline.

"This is very intriguing," she said evenly. "I had no idea about the availability of the funding. It's definitely the direction I was hoping to go."

"Well, consider it and let me know. It's the middle of April, and finals are upon us, so how about a decision by May 15th?" They rose together, and her hand met his. The implications of his missing wedding band were distracting, and they had a common past. She felt alone, and he might be ready for a friendship.

"May 15th it is." She looked back up and nodded.

"Call me if you have questions or need to talk. Anytime." He bent to write his cell number, then held out a card.

"Thanks," she smiled as she turned towards the door.

As she walked home through the Florida humidity—no stops to puke in the woods this time—she could feel the little sweat beads on her upper lip again. Shadows from the mossy live oaks eddied across her face as she followed the sidewalk across Norman Lawn. Her pounding heart seemed happy, and she stepped lightly as she entered the apartment. In her room, she laid back on the bed to reflect as her sweat dried in the air-conditioned coolness.

Memories of the Kramers had always fostered her pursuits of science and contraception. The seeds they planted were foundational as her love for science led her to try to save unwanted puppies and kittens from the cruelness of a world offering only euthanasia for so many. Before their rejection, it was the only place she'd ever felt deep abiding love, until Terri.

Terri's shared passion for pets had allowed her to lower her walls and experience the newness of Terri's skilled tenderness. Their female/female reference point had gently eased anxieties that kept her from trusting male intimacy, causing a profound illusion of closeness. She'd touched what felt like forever in Terri's bed, but it was fleeting, leaving her more isolated and unsure, even cynical, than before.

To assuage loneliness, she'd twice, early on, used her beauty to lure random partners for sexual release: once male, once female. But anxiety ruled, and her encounters lacked bliss, even in the moments afterward.

Solace held in Terri's arms could not be replicated without the intimacy from which it derived. And intimacy, as she'd learned so long ago and again with Terri, meant loss.

Now here she was, with something that needed celebration, and she was alone. She fancied herself an Osage orange, an Ozark tree quite attractive from a distance with intriguing fruit-like adornments, but its robust spines were like her anxiety: acutely painful if you tried to climb into her limbs. Terri's blue eyes became Dr. Skinner's as she languidly dozed off.

She woke at five, feeling unsettled and unrested as a vague dream of Dr. Skinner touching her arm faded. Walking helped her find center, so she set out for the paved path around Tumblin Pond, not far from her apartment. It was a short circle, so she made it bigger, briskly following Sixth Street up to Second Avenue, across to Second Street and up and across to Main before coming back south through the old Porters Community and over to Tumblin Pond again.

CHAPTER SEVENTEEN
HE REMEMBERED

HEAVY CLASS LOADS had created the slack in required undergrad hours that allowed the mixing of graduate work into her upcoming senior year. Twenty-nine credit hours meant some unfamiliar studying for the spring semester finals. It was a little challenging, but the payoff was worth it. She'd been using Dr. Aaron Skinner's card as a bookmark for two weeks, remembering his touch and considering his offer, which she'd become fully inclined to accept.

On the way to her chemistry final, she bumped into Dr. Skinner as she cut through Bartram Hall. His large frame blocked her way as she rounded a corner near his office. He smiled as their eyes locked, and she grinned back, breathing a little hard from the hurry. He stepped aside politely.

"Hello, Hannah."

"Dr. Skinner." She waited, trying to control her breathing.

"Have you come to a decision?"

"Yes. I mean, yes, I would love to join your team, but I'd like to talk about it more."

"Great! We never did finish our conversation, did we?"

"We should do something about that. Finals are over for me this afternoon."

"And for me in a few days. Let's get together." He shaped his hand like a phone and wiggled it by his ear.

"I look forward to it!" She smiled and walked away. Already certain she had straight A's, Hannah felt the need to celebrate now, not in a few days, and serenity took effort as she sensed his lingering gaze.

She was left with time and waited impatiently after her last final. She knew he was busy with grading, so she took daily walks through west and central Gainesville to expend her energy. Her thoughts, undirected by academia, ground in a circular groove from the Kramers, to her foster brother, the father of her baby, to Terri, to her PhD thesis, to Dr. Skinner, and then back to the Kramers. Loneliness almost overtook her, and on Friday, she stepped to her balcony and called the precisely printed phone number on the back of the card.

He was free for supper, and they would meet at Reggae Shack Cafe that evening.

*

Warm rain made Hannah wet from her walk over. Her flaxen hair had coalesced into brown wavy strings and fell across her face as she pushed through the door. She flicked her head to clear them, and droplets spattered his face as he rose from the bench. He blinked then smiled, and she grinned back, "Sorry!" He left the water on his face as they hugged lightly.

The room was loud with music and bustling with the end of finals at UF, but the table they landed in the corner was just quiet enough to talk. They moved together with a fluid comradery as the greeter led them, but they both jerked when their bare legs brushed under the small table as they were seated. Coarse hair on his calf gave Hannah a small chill, and she saw desire flash in the shift of his eyes as her wet shirt revealed erect nipples. He caught himself and looked at her face while she looked down, pretending not to notice. She sensed his small grin and felt her lips curl up slightly in response.

A waiter brought the menu, and then stout lemonades. Neither had tried seitan steaks, and the spicy-sweet preparation sounded good, so they ordered the same thing.

Previous conversations and maybe desire overcame inhibition as she sat forward slightly, resisting the urge to somehow cover herself. Skinner held back, letting her set the pace.

"So, what do you think about sex before marriage, Dr. Skinner?" She smiled nervously at her awkward attempt to avoid needless small talk, feeling foolish. But when her stupid line brought spontaneous laughter, she joined it in relief—the ice was broken.

"It's Aaron, please. And timing sexuality in relation to marriage really doesn't matter in a world with adequate access to contraception. To me, not even marriage matters. Why do mature adults need to make a vow expressing mutual commitment just because they're enjoying their bodies?" Playing along revealed his interest in the subject so clumsily and prematurely raised.

"And why does a relationship even have to be committed to, Aaron?" testing out his first name. "There's no need to own someone you love in today's world. After the stuff I've lived through, I'm not even sure people should be allowed to reproduce." And she realized she meant it all. Reproduction meant commitment, and commitment in her world always seemed to hurt.

"Well… Maybe they should be allowed to try." They smiled and clinked bottles as their eyes played lightly on each other's faces.

Aaron swallowed nervously, "What *have* you been through?" He leaned back and watched her face turn inward.

She took another sip and looked down. It wasn't okay, the sudden depth in their conversation, but she *was* the one who'd brought up the past. The lightness of the moment was sabotaged… *Did I do it on purpose?*

She considered whether to go left or right—truth or lies, follow or parry… Their conversation had been of free love, a negotiation about an impending possibility, yet here they were at intimacy. She took another bigger sip, briefly meeting his eyes as she swallowed. Her tongue slid out to clear her lips. Still, she was silent, like a third-grader trapped under the principal's intrusive gaze. Truth or lies?

Truth.

She closed her eyes and forged ahead. "A lot." She could hear a warning bell in her head as flashing red light momentarily blinded her.

He waited. She glanced up into his eyes, seeing intent interest and, yes, compassion. "I...wouldn't know where to start." Could she trust those eyes?

"Tell me about your name change, Hannah Eliza Cramer. How about there?"

He remembered Eliza.

"Did you just look that up? Eliza?" she asked.

"No." He looked down, seeming chagrined. "I saw it when you were in my office."

In April, you mean. But she let it go.

Reluctantly at first, she explained how the name Jain from her biological mother had made her feel until she'd hated it and come to claim her identity using the properly spelled imaginary names of her long-lost wombmates. She took another sip of hard lemonade, licked her lips, and look back up. Now that she was revealing, she wasn't sure how far she wanted to go.

"So, Hannah and Eliza were the names *you* gave your sisters?"

"Yeah, and they're spelled right because I named them. My belly mom, Lisa, never even mentioned them to me. Ever. I became them so I could be free of Jain and *her*." Saying 'Jain' almost doubled the sour after-taste left by speaking Lisa's name out loud.

"I can't talk about this stuff. At least not here."

His eyes showed compassion, intent interest, and something else: dangerous intimacy. "That's okay. I, of all people, can understand."

Delivery of the seitan steaks brought aromas that heightened their appetites and eased the tension. They ate quietly at first.

"This is delicious. First time I've ever dared to try a vegan steak." She took another bite, her mind chewing on his last words.

"Amen." Aaron shoved a big chunk in his mouth, chewed, and swallowed.

"Understand *what?*"

"Your reluctance. My biological parents were fuckin' drunk dopers, always looking for the next high. My dad was a mean motherfucker, too. I was four when an ER doc did the right thing and hotlined my spiral fractures and broken ribs. Dad went to jail, mom went to meth, and that was the last I saw of them. I have no idea what you went through, but foster lives are never pretty, are they?"

Suddenly, she wasn't hungry anymore. Her fork went down. "How can you talk about it so easily?"

"Who said it was easy?" he countered. "I spent years in counseling, and obviously, I'm not over it. I can talk to you though, don't know why. But I wouldn't call it easy." His eyes suddenly brimmed.

"How'd you get counseling?" She pulled a napkin from the holder and handed it to him, acknowledging his feelings without calling them out.

"A teacher realized I wasn't autistic, just traumatized. She was able to get me into some counseling, and I had a good foster family who made sure I went for a few years. Did you get counseling ever?"

"No. I just bounced placements." Afraid to be exposed, she quietly parried back to keep the conversation on him, "Did you stay with that family?"

"Nope. Acted out; got moved." He leaned back, his steak forgotten, and continued, "I attracted molesters, one in particular. He was a pastor-like guy at a boy's and girl's club. His hell was my reality, and no one in the real world noticed. Life seemed like a farce."

"I get it. I want things to be real, but real hurt. Over and over." *Too close.* She parried again, "Did they ever notice? Is he still out there?"

"I don't know. I finally lost him with a move. Is yours?" He thrust the two words unexpectedly.

"No… Yes…" Hot tears began to burn her cheeks, "I don't know!" She covered her face with her palms as she collected herself and looked up, feeling like a little girl. "Let's get out of here."

Aaron had his car, but Hannah's place was within walking distance, and her roommates were out of town. Emotional intensity drove them, and they bumped shoulders gently as they walked and talked in the fading light. The air was slightly cooler, but their skin was shiny from the humidity.

"Aaron Skinner's the only name I ever remember having, and I don't think anyone ever changed it. No one ever cared enough to. I was blessed with brains, like you. Scholarships got me through undergrad, and research has kept me here."

She gladly followed him to lighter topics. "Where'd you come from?"

"Union County, just northeast of here. In the piney woods near Raiford."

"My interest came from the past I told you about before. I came here because of 677 research. Do you remember?"

"Yeah."

They bumped lightly as she glanced over at him and asked, "Where'd you get your interest from?"

"My undergraduate minor in sociology."

"What does sociology have to do with biology?"

"The Population Bomb is real, and at the current rate of reproduction, the world is going hit a brick wall when Malthus's positive checks kick in. I saw the biology of reproduction as a key to defusing the bomb. We have got to put the Earth before people, and I believe 677 can help save the world. It's my only reason for living at this point. Everything else is distraction… or therapy." He gave her a sideways glance.

She ignored the glance. "We studied that in Gubera's sociology class, sophomore year . . . Ehrlich's book."

"Yup. He was my professor, too. Did you minor in soch?" Their hands brushed.

"Nope, I just like to learn. The overpopulation stuff is terrifying. We'll wipe out all the species and then ourselves, and no one seems to care." With passion, but less intimacy, this topic was much easier.

Hannah led as they clomped up the steps to her apartment. Aaron stood close as she opened the door, and the cool air washed out over their bodies, warm from the walk. Goosebumps rose on their legs, the physical effect bringing back the tingle that lured them together earlier. And yet, the mood was different, sensuality precluded by the lingering emotions raised by childhood pain.

Hannah could feel his desire still probing as his eyes drifted across her bare legs. Her erect nipples were back, but his eyes didn't linger. Their past loomed unspoken as she handed him a beer from the fridge and took one for herself. He sipped as she lit some candles on the table and then sat across from him.

He spoke first, directing the conversation in this more intimate setting, "You and I seem to be damaged goods, and maybe that's why we can see the threat of overpopulation more clearly. The world sees a child as an expression of love, but we know how empty that sentiment is. I think our past gives us better vision to help solve the problem."

She was glad of the drift away from the bedroom; she needed the breathing room. "I guess with my background, I was only focused on doggy and kitty overpopulation. I thought that was your focus, too."

"It is, and pet overpopulation is a big problem, but too many dogs aren't going to overconsume and destroy the world. Our work supports development on the human side and expands the base of knowledge to benefit pets, but we gotta stop humans. Nigeria, for instance, is going to overtake the US as the third most populous nation in the next decade or so. They aren't going to stop on their own. No country is, except China, maybe. And they actually *overdid* the population control thing."

"Yeah, but how can *you* stop the reproduction?"

"My department is a part of the CPS, right?"

She nodded, watching his eyes.

"So, the Center works on projects for ethical, voluntary population control, right?"

"If you say so."

"I say so." He smiled, then his face became serious, and he continued, "But there are people in the department and around the country who are quietly devoted to stopping the bomb from destroying the world. They say saving the planet trumps people's right to reproduce. Preventive checks are required, just not voluntary ones like Malthus advoc,ated, but the world ignored. 677 gives the possibility of involuntary preventive checks, but no one needs to know, at least not until it is a *fait accompli*…" He waited while she digested this, watching as recognition dawned.

Her eyes widened. "But people would call that cruel."

"Would you?" His blue eyes rose to an intensity that was captivating, and she couldn't look away.

"Sadly, no."

His head tilted to the side. "Why sadly?"

"I remember how badly my foster mom wanted kids, and their whole lives were changed when the option was taken away. They became obsessed with having a child to the point of letting foster kids ruin their lives." She gestured with her bottle, then took a sip.

"Well, some people will be hurt when they no longer have a choice, but the alternative is either extinction or, at minimum, a massive loss of life and collapse of world social orders."

She nodded in agreement. His intense passion was attractive to Hannah, filling a need for significance and attachment. And it was based on something safer than their pasts.

She scooted closer to the table as she sipped her bottle, and almost unconsciously extended her calf to his under the small table. Still, she held back, not touching, but her other hand went involuntarily to the IUD cross on her neck. His eyes flickered, acknowledging her tell.

"I agree completely. It's just that the world around us may not. Look at all the antiabortion freaks and the Christian agenda. How do you get around that in a public institution?"

"Certainly not with public action."

"So...private action?"

"Maybe." He touched her hand as she set down her bottle, and they stood, drawing together.

"Like this?" She pressed her loins into his and drew him close with her left leg as she wrapped herself around him, pulling him close as she tasted his mouth. She yielded back to him as his desire rose, and despite herself, she slipped back behind the protective shield of anxiety that was like an invisible film between them.

It wasn't just mindless fucking. He was a gentle, firm leader in bed, deep inside as she approached climax, their mons connecting and reconnecting in wavelike movement as they flowed together. She felt her reticence rising with their passion, and as he came, she withdrew from the moment, unable—or unwilling—to let go completely. Uncomplicated and uncommitted didn't mean ignoring barriers to ecstasy, and she knew for them to get it completely right, she would need to unload, or at least circumvent, some baggage.

"Actually, it's not baggage," she said as they lay in bed side by side, letting their sweat-slicked bodies slowly cool and dry, the top sheet up to their waists. "I'm a thorny bitch, and I kinda like it that way. I'm not sure why I can't completely let go, but I know it's safer that way in this life."

"Maybe, but why bother if you're gonna hold back?"

"You didn't enjoy it?"

"Oh, I enjoyed it, but I felt you holding back at the end. It seemed deliberate."

She rolled up on her side and leaned on her elbow, pressing into his side. She placed her hand gently over his heart and looked up at his face. "Look, smarty pants. Take me like I am or don't take me." That sounded harsh, and she didn't want to sound rude. She was anxious—scared, she realized.

His arm cupped her gently as he said, "It seems like you do relax all the way at first, then you don't." He tenderly kissed her hairline, then lowered his voice to almost a whisper, "How'd you get hurt?" He cared enough to keep pushing, and he didn't make her sound like a victim.

"I fell for the wrong person. It seemed like everything, at least to me, then it was nothing." She really didn't want to talk about Terri. "I don't know… It's not because I don't want to be hurt again. I just can't relax all the way. Anxiety? Fear? I don't know."

She considered the conversation. She didn't wanna chase him off. "Don't get me wrong, I really liked what we did, and I like sex, but it is what it is. Sorry you came?" She smiled at the double entendre, then laid her head against his chest and asked, "Sorry you asked?"

"I asked because I care about the woman I was just with. Sex shouldn't equal anxiety, not for anyone, and not for you. It's not a lifetime commitment; it's just momentary respite from the world."

"Doesn't sound like Daddy's advice," she lilted her voice like a little girl's.

He'd been gently hugging her against him, but now he slid his hand down to cup her bum. "I may be older than you, but I'm *not* your daddy."

"You're not old enough to be my daddy, Aaron." She idly moved her hand to his stomach, stroking the line of dark hair as she thought about Pete and Prissy. "My first daddy was a Christian, and to him and my mom, sex meant forever. But I could never be that committed. The beauty of contraception is it frees you from the social tangles Christians, and all religions, create about sex. Sex should stand on its own. You should be able to enjoy it without giving up your freedom. I agree."

"I think Christianity and maybe all religions were created to control that freedom. To make sure babies had a family unit to survive. Society has to move beyond that; we already overpopulate the world and don't need your parents' social structures anymore because we don't need to be reproducing. Many of us believe the time is nigh for mandatory birth control. I mean, commitment's an option, but it's not for everyone, and it certainly shouldn't be based on creating more children."

"Maybe commitment's a threat, and I hold back just cuz I'm afraid, but it feels deeper than that. It's like a limit switch." She slid her hand lower, following his hair past where it turned damp and kinky under the sheet. "Doesn't mean I don't know what I like and can't enjoy it *within* my limits." She found the cause of the tent that formed as her hand teased its way down.

Afterwards, she lay against him again, yearning. When she awoke before twilight, he was gone. Much had been revealed, and she feared what the entanglement of a deeper relationship might bring to both of them. The potential for more pain made the empty bed a relief in a way.

She got up and cracked the balcony door to let some heat in, listening as a car rolled slowly past on the street below. She gave herself the release she couldn't accept from him and was soon curled beneath the sheets, her mind drifting as she considered Aaron's thoughts on contraception and Christianity.

She'd cut them off with her sexual moves despite her fervid interest in the social implications of both issues. Perhaps she'd wanted to buy time since both involved her childhood, and her parents had already come up in the conversation. Unless she lied to Aaron, the conversation had been about to take them to her past and directly back to Jain, and maybe to Terri. It was an intimacy she wasn't ready to fully establish, not without some boundaries. Maybe never.

As she began to understand the evening, the blissful high faded, and she fell into a peaceful rest that carried her until the morning breeze moved her curtains and sunlight flooded the room.

Her roommates weren't due back for two weeks, and she enjoyed spending time alone in her apartment, excited about the future. She showered and ate some toast as she thought about Aaron's level-headed logic and the quest to save the world. She also considered their loving and the yearning that remained.

Similar life experiences and perspectives made it seem safe so far, but fucking her advisor did have its risks. Negotiations the night before helped preclude a more passionate intimacy that might have overcome her anxiety-driven resistance. Maybe that distancing was an unconscious form of protection. Lingering desire bothered her nevertheless. She wanted to be able to throw caution to the wind and embrace passion's reckless drive to ecstasy.

CHAPTER EIGHTEEN
NEXT STEPS

SHE GREW IMPATIENT as Monday afternoon rolled around with still no call from Aaron. Finally, she swallowed her pride and went through the biology offices after her work-study job. His dark hair and large frame were unmistakable in the hallway, where he was talking with a student. He spotted her, and they smiled as their eyes met. He immediately broke off the conversation and approached her. "Hello, Hannah Eliza."

"Aaron." His strong gaze brought a flush of desire, and her heart jumped as it had with Terri. "We never really finished our conversation."

"We should do something about that. What part of our conversation are you referring to?"

"All of it." She grinned.

His eyes twinkled. "Your place again?"

"Do you know Civilization?" He nodded. "How 'bout meetchya there? 7:00?"

"Sure, is next Saturday okay?"

She felt her face fall, but she didn't own him, right? "Sure. See you there."

"I leave this afternoon for a conference and don't get back until late Friday. Sorry, Hannah." He seemed sincere, but not quite as yearning as her heart felt.

"It's okay. See ya later." She tried to sound upbeat.

They touched hands, but she found herself wanting more as she walked calmly away.

*

She rode the bus to Main and 16th and walked up to Civilization the next Saturday evening.

He was waiting on the porch of the restaurant and stood as she approached. "How the heck are you, Hannah Cramer?"

"Hi, Aaron!" They embraced firmly. She was relieved he didn't try to shake hands again.

"Let's get some soul food!"

They sat and ordered a bottle of wine, and then he selected Thai Green Curry and she the Old Florida Harvest. They toasted when the wine came, and each sipped. He asked for an extra glass, and when it came, he poured some wine. "From this glass of scientific endeavor, let us both drink deeply." He took a big swig and handed it to her.

"To scientific endeavor." She drank the rest and refilled the glass. "And now, passion." She drank deeply and handed the glass back to him.

"To passion." He met her eyes, emptied the glass, and set it aside.

She recalled the distance she'd perceived at their last meeting and instinctively gave him room, switching back to the safe topic of science. "So…tell me more about the private action," she said.

"You mean our bedtime activities?" He grinned.

"Work before play," she laughed in return but pressed out of curiosity. "You said other people share our beliefs."

"Yeah, I know what you meant," he paused, thoughtful. "What I was talking about is a way to speed implementation of our work so we can actually do something to benefit the world. Our research is important, but we know enough to start making a difference now, not in ten or twenty years when 677 is fully approved."

"So, what does that look like? Doing something now?"

"It doesn't look like much because we fly below the radar. Mostly it's scattered professors and grad students around the country who believe in the cause," he replied, idly watching the greeter arranging some flowers near the door.

"I can't believe you're doing something. I thought everyone wore blinders." She was pleasantly surprised, unconsciously leaning forward.

"People wear blinders, Hannah. From a scientific standpoint, the risks of 677 are worth the benefits. From a social standpoint, people scream eugenics and genocide. They raise the specter of side effects to slow down progress. For most people, action now isn't worth the risk. There's too much at stake: jobs, families, their futures," he explained, glancing over her shoulder as the greeter approached.

She turned and smiled thanks as he set the freshened vase on their table and left, then returned to the subject. "But if we stand by and hold back on the most important tool I've heard of, they aren't gonna have a future."

"Or at least their children won't," he said. "Taking action now, though, holds personal risk."

"I got nothin' to lose, Aaron." And she meant it.

"People like us don't. I mean, we're operating below the wire because we have to, but I do value my freedom and don't want to lose that if I don't have to. It means we'll never be able to take credit if we're successful."

She paused for a moment to absorb that. "So, how do we meet and organize to make sure everyone is on the same page and knows the bigger picture?"

"Certainly *not* on the internet. We leave no digital footprints; that's how we cover our tracks in the internet age. We only talk in person, and where we need documents, we try to only keep them on offline storage. But there's always a risk of detection. Can't help that." He shrugged.

"How do you know who's part of it?" She lowered her voice. More people were coming into the busy eatery, and she didn't want to be overheard.

"There's no secret handshake or anything. We scientists try to attend the Pet Birth Control Association (PBCA) annual conference so we can all meet face to face. That way, everyone knows who's pursuing what, and it gives us faces to go with our names."

Hannah sipped her wine.

He leaned in, lowering his voice as well, "Right now, we're trying to get a manufacturing site up and running because we think the molecule will be ready to use within a year. Planning how to implement it and making enough product to *do* it are two different things. It's not something we can do overnight, but it can certainly be done sooner than decades from now."

Her eyebrows furrowed. "So, who's coordinating everything?"

Aaron hesitated. "Actually, it's being coordinated right here at the U. 677 is the most promising molecule by far, so the movement naturally centered here." He suddenly leaned back as the food came.

As they ate, they savored the flavors and continued to sip their wines.

"The next conference is in less than three months, you know."

"Uh-huh."

He smiled. "You should present your proposal there, get some feedback early on. I think your work is promising enough that they might even select it for some additional grant money."

"I haven't really started yet." But she was excited at his encouragement and was thrilled it seemed genuine.

"Yes, but you could refine the proposal and have it ready for submission in plenty of time. Your thesis work might help speed our final preparations, you know." Aaron wiped his lips as he finished his plate, glancing around at the now full restaurant.

"Well, if you think it's good enough, that says a lot." She replied before draining her wine.

"I do." He emptied his and fixed those blue eyes intently on hers, making her heart jump to attention. "Was my work good enough?"

She raised her eyebrows, inviting confirmation.

"For you to want more?" Her heart said yes, and so did her smile.

After dinner, they got into his Jeep and drove to her apartment in silence. When he wasn't shifting, he gently touched his hand to hers on the console.

Upstairs, she opened more wine, poured them each a glass, and then sat, legs crisscrossed, on one end of her roommate's couch. She wanted to jump off passion's cliff, but anxiety rose in her heart.

Aaron sat facing her in the opposite corner, concern on his face as he watched a tear of frustration roll down her cheek. "Is it something I did?"

"No, Aaron. It's not you at all," she sighed. "The past keeps knockin' on my door. I'm having a hard time, and I'm not sure why."

"What part of the past?"

"Well," she hesitated a moment. "The part I don't really want to talk about."

"Oh, *that* part," he smiled softly. "Look, Hannah, forget about sex. It's not an issue for me, and don't let it be for you. If you wanna talk, then let's talk. We have a commonality in our backgrounds, and I can be a good listener."

"Yeah, I noticed that. But I don't want to bore you...or run you off."

"You're not running me off." He slid closer, lightly touching her knee in emphasis. "But your face is all crinkled and anxious, and your spirit is, too. It would probably help to talk about it. Do you have anything for anxiety? Anything you take?"

"Just staying busy...and sometimes sex. Why?" Her head tilted slightly.

"Meds can help a lot. I know. Remember when I mentioned counseling?" She nodded. "Well, I use benzos sometimes. They can really help with anxiety. I don't tell everyone this, but I always carry some alprazolam. If you want to try one to help you relax, they can be very therapeutic." He dug in his pocket and pulled out a small pill box, clicked it open, and popped one out. He smiled tentatively. "See? My little blue pills."

She picked it up and studied it.

"Worth a try." She shrugged her shoulders and popped it in her mouth and swallowed.

"Oh. Usually, I just take half a pill... Two milligrams is a lot. You might start to feel weird."

"Oops." She made a funny smile.

"It'll be okay... Don't get anxious." They both laughed. "What part of the past don't you want to talk about?"

She slowly opened up, telling him about the affair with her foster brother, the abortion, and even about the foggy memories from her earlier years, and how it troubled her that some of them were pleasurable in a way she couldn't rediscover in adulthood. She felt like she should hold back more, but the alprazolam gradually relaxed her, and she let her shields down as she never had before, with anyone. She flipped and backed up to him on the couch, and they spooned as they talked.

He talked, too, but not with as much depth as she did. His years of counseling had helped modulate his emotions; still, tears wet his face too. His arm fell asleep, and she turned to face him when they shifted to restore his circulation. The gentle words soon became tender kisses, and the tender touching became sensual petting as they tasted each other's tears, sweat, and mouths.

Hannah was falling into his caresses, and no klaxons sounded, no lights flashed. She swallowed his tongue and breathed in his hair as he explored her open body. She yielded to him, gasping for air and clutching for traction on his shoulders as he moved above her, gentle, then hard, then gentle, then still. His blue eyes were a traction beam, drilling into her mind, and they both started coming with intense pumping waves before they started moving again, then faded away in what felt like a mist to her. She realized her short but sharp nails were hooked into his shoulders and straightened her fingers as he groaned lightly in awareness of the pain she had been inflicting.

"Wrap your legs around me," he whispered in her ear.

She held tight, unembarrassed as they managed to roll over without falling off the big couch, and she collapsed on his chest as she straddled his legs, his still-twitching penis squished against her belly. Their sweat mingled as she brushed his hair gently away from his face and gazed up into his eyes, lingering by his ear to caress it. "You da HooDoo man," her voice was languid.

"HooDoo what?" he mumbled.

"That pill. It was magic." Her skin felt like a luminous blanket, shimmering with pleasant tingles. She faded into his warmth and let the mist envelop her.

Late in the morning, she awoke with a vague memory of floating into her bed and a sheet descending like peace around her. She thought he said he was going to stay the night, but her bed was empty. A cardinal gave its shrill call again from her balcony, waking her all the way. Summer air drifted gently over her through the open door. He shared her preference for the breeze, and she smiled as she realized she wasn't alone.

"Coffee, tea, or me?" He was in the doorway, holding orange juice and a coffee with a smile on his face, "Or orange juice?"

She sat up with the sheets held around her shoulders, taking a sip from the orange juice she chose before setting the glass on her nightstand. "I've never slept this late."

"I'm just glad we got it right this time. You are amazing."

"Better living through drugs is my new motto." She smiled smugly.

"Well, hopefully, they will just be a step on the path to freedom. It *was* a benzo, you know," he cautioned.

"Yeah, but it's not like I would need one that often. Unless benzos make me a nympho."

"I'll leave a few with you in case you need one, and I'm not around."

"Well, thanks. But that doesn't mean I'm playing the field. I don't think I could handle two lovers like that." Her smile was almost carnivorous.

"I like that, but don't feel like a prisoner, not ever." He sat, and she saw the deep scratches on his bare back. "Anyway, it was about all I could handle, too."

"I am so sorry! I barely remember that. I felt like I was falling and needed to hold on!" She leaned forward and gently kissed the dark red grooves. He flinched, then laughed.

"They aren't as bad as they look, Hannah. They're just love scratches."

They talked some more, but both were starving, so she got up and dug the makings for fruit smoothies and bagels out of her kitchen, and they both ate their fill. Hannah walked him to the Jeep so he could get the last of his grading done, then walked down and around Tumblin' Creek Pond in the quiet Sunday air. She realized it was probably the lingering effect of the alprazolam, and maybe the fullness of the sex she shared with Aaron, but she felt an openness and innocence that changed everything she saw: A reality free of anxiety and perceptions that chained her to the past.

Her body warmed while walking a big loop through west Gainesville, and a pleasant smell of sex rose around her whenever she paused to cross a street. She passed seven churches, feeling a pull of the morning gatherings yet fearful of entering. She feared judgment from people, but she realized she really feared going before God after having lived so long away from him. As she passed the seventh church, the Shady Grove Primitive in Porters Neighborhood, an usher in a worn black suit and tie over a white shirt pushed the doors open. The closing hymn, *Blessed Assurance*, resonated in beautiful acapella harmony into the narrow street. Their eyes met, and Hannah looked away, feeling suddenly unworthy and unclean as her past came knocking again.

Convoluted visions of childhood mingled with the night before and were dancing through her brain. Aaron felt right, even though she wasn't as sure of her sexuality after her experiences with Terri. She thought the Kramers would have considered it a sin, but they'd never discussed it. She yearned for the innocence of childhood and its closeness to God, but it felt like she had grown up and could never return. She picked up her pace until she was back at Tumblin, skirting the south side of the pond as she made for her apartment.

*

Summer months flew by, with a few more intense benzo-modulated lovemaking sessions with Aaron mixed in with summer work-study, volunteer work at St Francis, and preparation of her full grant proposal for the PBCA conference in August. Terri didn't come to the spay/neuter clinics that summer, which suited Hannah. She didn't feel animosity, just sadness at the loss of her innocence, and really didn't want to see Terri at all. Then one Saturday in late July, her cell rang as she was finishing up at the clinic. "Hey, Aaron!"

"Hannah! How are you?"

"Good."

"I'm calling you because we need to get together to review your proposal and get it submitted for the conference proceedings. Deadline's coming up."

"Sure, I'm about finished."

"If you email it, I'll read it, and then we can get together. Maybe Monday at my office, say ten o'clock?"

"That works for me, Aaron."

A pang of sadness passed through her as he hung up without any terms of endearment.

Though he'd given her a small bottle of benzos with the clear implication that she could use them for sex with other people, she had no desire to be wildly active with anyone but him. Sharing wasn't her style, and she hoped he felt the same, but didn't quite dare to ask—his answer might hurt.

CHAPTER NINETEEN
BUSTED

HANNAH ARRIVED EARLY at the biology department and went down the narrow hall. She could hear Aaron's voice and a woman's reply—intimate intonations that broke into quiet laughter as she approached. She paused to knock before rounding into his office and heard a rustle of clothes and the sound of a quiet kiss. Suddenly, she was face to face with a nicely tanned Terri exiting the small office. "Hannah!"

She stepped back and felt color rising on her cheeks, and she was sure on her chest, too. "Terri? Wha...?" Her mouth quit working.

"I hear you're going to the conference, too. To present?" Terri looked at her squarely.

"Ummm, yes. That's why I'm here." Her brain spun as she tried to grasp what she'd heard from the hall.

"Well, that's great! I look forward to seeing your proposal. Maybe I'll get to watch you present." Her blue eyes were intense, playing on Hannah's.

"Maybe. That would be great." Hannah looked behind Terri as Aaron stepped into the hall, looking caught.

"Hi, Hannah. You can come in." He stepped aside to make room as Terri started walking down the hall.

"See you later, Terri," he said in a professional tone. He stepped back into his office, where Hannah was already sitting, avoiding his eyes. "You look flushed. Everything okay?" He quickly glanced at her before sitting behind his desk.

"Yes. No… How long have you been seeing Terri?" He wasn't looking directly at her, so she stared at his eyes, their blue seeming suddenly cold rather than captivating. She shuddered slightly.

"About a year, off and on." His tone was even. "We aren't committed any more than you and I are, but we're friends."

"Oh… But *I* was seeing her until I found out she was seeing someone else. I thought I was in love until she slipped and said she was seeing a man—you, I guess," she kept her voice quiet, remembering the second toothbrush in Terri's bathroom.

"Most likely… Are you two still friends?" He pursed his lips and finally met her eyes.

"I haven't seen her since April, and she was amazingly pale then." She looked down and continued, "We haven't spoken since she broke my heart. I was discovering myself, but from what I could tell, she was just having fun."

"Well, I hope this doesn't affect us too much. I really enjoy our little times together."

Little times? Those were little *times?*

"I hope not, too, but it's kind of awkward. How'd she get so tan?" Hannah kept her knees together, and her hands were glued to her lap.

"She was working on a special project in Africa for the summer in Nigeria."

"A special project?" asked Hannah, looking up again.

"If you're still on board, you'll find out about it at the conference." His eyebrows raised in question. *How could I not be on board? It's my life!* And now it seemed there would be little else unless she was willing to share him…with Terri.

"I'll still be on board for the conference, but honestly, I'm not sure about us." Hannah felt herself blushing again, and she felt like screaming. Instead, she asked, "Have you and Terri discussed me?"

"What? No! Of course not." His quick downward glance said otherwise. She squinted her green eyes and waited for him to meet her gaze again. He ran his hands through his hair and looked back at her with a sigh.

"Well, just your research and that she knows you from the spay/neuter program. Nothing personal about us, or her and you." Hannah listened as he prattled, barely registering his words.

Aaron had managed to get Dr. Replonge's approval for Hannah's travel and registration for the conference so she could present her thesis proposal, but they didn't prolong the conversation as Hannah departed with a curt 'thanks.'

Her mind raced from the visceral effects of seeing Terri and Aaron together. A weird blend of desire, revulsion, jealousy, and hurt spun unbidden as she walked home fast, raising a sweat that made her feel alive. She popped an alprazolam and lay abruptly on her bed. Slowly, the calming mist came over her, and she touched the moistness between her legs, gently at first, then more vigorously, fantasmically violating Terri and Aaron's relationship. She came quickly, was spent, and fell into a fitful sleep.

CHAPTER TWENTY
CONFERENCE/ABALAND

In August 2013, the PBCA annual conference was still small as conferences go, and the hotel that year was in Dallas. Hannah presented her research proposal for 677, with Aaron as her primary investigator, and it was very well received. Though they had flown from Florida with Terri and a few others, Hannah didn't see Terri anywhere the first two days of the conference. On the second evening, Aaron invited her to dinner, and she asked about Terri. He assured her they would see Terri the following evening. Neither of them brought up sleeping together.

Early the following evening, they were the last to climb into a fifteen-passenger van full of other conference attendees. Hannah recognized a few from UF, including Dr. Replonge, the head of the 677 project. A short, broad woman, Hazel Replonge, MS, PharmD, was always dressed impeccably. Today, she wore a crisp white blouse and a calf-length navy skirt. Her hair was a tight silver bun, and little makeup graced her plump, pasty face. Practical black ankle-high laced shoes finished the picture. Hannah had no idea someone like the grandmotherly woman who always brought homemade cookies to staff meetings was a part of the cause. She always thought of her as Mary Poppins.

"You didn't say this was a *group* meal," she whispered.

"That part is a surprise. We will talk about it when we get there.

Remember, this is just a group with common interests that meets every year at this conference."

Hannah got that she wasn't supposed to ask questions in the van, so she sat back and tried to relax as they drove to nearby Meadowmere Park, where a picnic pavilion had been reserved. Terri was already there and had set up a vegan meal on the center table. She smiled at Aaron and Hannah as they walked up. "Congratulations on your presentation."

"Thank you, Terri."

Hannah felt an intense flash of jealousy as the man with whom she'd endorsed free sex gave Terri a tender hug while everyone exchanged greetings. There were researchers from Davis, Madison, Harvard, Yale, Universities of Texas and Washington, NYU, Northwestern, and others. After they ate, Dr. Hazel Replonge stood and took the lead. "Okay, folks, we're here to discuss the Nigerian project and update each other on where we are now.

"We have one new person, Hannah Cramer, vouched for by Aaron. She's just starting her senior year in the biology department at UF and is combining her senior year with the thesis proposal she presented today in competition for a MERCY Grant. Hannah, please stand so everyone can see you." There was spontaneous clapping as she stood. "Your excellent proposal will certainly be selected as a recipient."

"Thank you." Hannah sat, embarrassed and thrilled by the attention.

"Now, as you know, we meet out here for security, and what is said in this meeting stays in this meeting."

Aaron stood with a grin and said, "My name is Aaron, and I'm here to save the world." Everyone laughed as he sat quickly.

"And my name is Hazel. Thank you, *Aaron*," she said with a tiny eye roll. "Now, if you would update us, Terri."

Terri stood and outlined her activities over the last two years. She and Aaron, with Hazel's help, had set up a system to pilfer hundreds of grams of raw RU-AT-677 that had been formed into sweetened vitamin pills with the help of their industry contact. Acceptance was excellent as the compound itself had little taste.

In May, she and Aaron traveled with a large Gainesville church on a medical mission to a poorer Christian town with very high fertility rates in

Abaland, southern Nigeria, and distributed the pills to everyone who came into the clinic. Placed in smaller bottles with real vitamin pills, they received wide acceptance. The safety margin meant there should be no side effects from excess dosing. Terri had worked for several weeks, developing contacts and monitoring for signs of immediate side effects. None were seen.

Terri paused while a couple walking by lost their terrier's leash, and the little dog ran to the shelter, looking for scraps. Everyone ogled the little dog, and the owners lingered in small talk about the conference, which they hadn't heard about. Hannah was learning by example how to remain cool and act normal, even when they were discussing momentous events in world history. Finally, they moved on.

"So, we were able to distribute at the clinic and locations around the town: Churches, markets, and government buildings. We distributed eight thousand bottles with three doses added to each bottle. Some of the bottles were labeled for men, some for women. Our hypothesis is there will be a noticeable decline in fertility in the town. While we won't be able to follow up from a scientific perspective, we should be able to gather enough information to draw some conclusions in the next year. Thoughts, anyone?" Terri sat, and Hazel stood to moderate.

"Sounds like you've done a good job. This should allow us to monitor unanticipated side effects and see if any alarms are raised in the community. A big thanks to Terri and Aaron on a job well done." Applause was immediate, followed by discussion.

"So, let's say this shows promise. How are we going to get this done on a scale that will make a difference on the world scene?" The question came from a professor at the University of Washington. "That's gonna take a lot of doses. What's the long-term plan? Where are we on that?"

Aaron rose. "Several critical steps are involved. At UF, we continue to skim and store small amounts of raw product in a safe location and are almost ready to set up a remote mass production facility." Most of this was news to Hannah, who was seeing him and Terri in a new light. Her eyes studied his face as he spoke. "The long shelf life means we don't have to worry about a timetable unless it's longer than twenty to thirty years.

"Since 677 has various safe routes of administration, there are multiple delivery options available. We currently doubt it will ever be approved in the US, and if political solutions are not found that would allow significant distribution, we'll be forced into covert administration. We're looking at several options if the political system doesn't come up with a solution in the next few years. By then, we'll have close to a half a billion doses secured off-site unless we have to stop for some reason.

"Personally, I don't see a political solution that would work, and that means that distribution is the biggest challenge at this point." Aaron sat back down.

Hazel stood, dipped her chin at Aaron, and fielded several questions about monitoring in the Nigerian village. There was discussion on how to distribute the billions of doses needed to dent world growth, and a population biologist also discussed the most efficient distribution schemes.

"If there are no other questions or comments, I would just like to say thanks for everything you all do and have done to support this project and help the animals, which is what this conference is all about. Everyone police your trash, use the recycling bins, and we'd better start heading back," said Dr. Replonge.

Back at the hotel, the four UF people gathered in Dr. Replonge's room. She let Aaron drop the bombshell. That spring, some senior faculty had pointed out the dangers of the compound, as well as the research being done during a Homeland Security administrative review.

Besides its potent ability to sterilize humans and pets in very small doses, it could affect any species; the smaller the animal, the smaller the exposure required. The drug worked by effectively killing germinal sex cells, but a big unknown was how it affected other germinal and stem cells in the body.

Suppression of the immune system, cancer, early aging...these were just a few of the potential real-life side effects. In the environment, whole species could be rendered extinct if they lost the ability to reproduce. 677 could also be used as a tool of terror or a tool of warfare, wiping out entire nations by attrition. As the slow arm of government realized the threat, alarms were raised, and it was decided to make their research center a secured facility.

Unfortunately, the only way to do that was to apply the newer

Department of Homeland Security classification, which would affect the entire Center for Population Studies.

All personnel, even maintenance, would have to be background checked, and biometric data would be collected in order to establish secured entry to the laboratory facility. They would all be retina scanned, fingerprinted, and asked to submit DNA swabs.

No specific plan was made from that meeting, but since Aaron already had all the production details, they would be able to manufacture 677 even if they had to go offshore. He assured them the method for skimming product was bulletproof and would circumvent security efforts. He didn't elaborate, simply telling them they really didn't want or need to know how it was happening. Their possible way to change the course of human history seemed safe, even if they might experience some inconveniences.

As the UF group gathered at DFW for the flight home, a heightened sense of purpose lightened their mood. Hannah felt it too, but excitement couldn't fill the hole of betrayal that lingered, leaving her bewildered. Free love philosophies weren't resolving feelings from her heart either. Each interaction she witnessed between Terri and Aaron stirred her emotions again.

I'm a fool.

On the partially filled flight home, Aaron sat in an aisle seat while Hannah leaned against a window. The rest of the row was empty, and the ambient noise gave privacy to their quiet conversation. They folded up the armrests and leaned inward as they talked. "I know I'm not supposed to, but I still feel jealous. Jealous about you, jealous about her. You're the only two adult people I've ever let my walls down for, and it feels like you both betrayed me."

"But we discussed this. And I haven't betrayed you; I'm right here."

"I said it *feels* like you betrayed me. Terri, too." She wasn't looking at him, but his shoulder pressed against hers, and she could smell his mild cologne.

"As far as I know, she only stayed away because she sensed your pain. She didn't intend to betray you."

"I thought you didn't discuss me with her."

"We love you, Hannah—we never meant to hurt you." *So they did talk about me! Out of love, or was it guilt?!?* Just discussing it eased her a little, even if she had to process the feelings at some point.

"That doesn't change what I feel, but a drink might since I'm out of blue pills." She looked at him, but he didn't offer. They both took Jack-N-Diet Coke from the passing flight attendant. They sipped silently for a while.

After a moment, he looked at her and said, "We both want you to continue with your program."

"I agree wholeheartedly," she nodded, "I probably just need to grow up."

"No, I'm not sayin' that. You need to deal with the bad feelings. It's not a matter of growing up." It was like he was reading her thoughts again. Aaron looked at her hands, which were still holding the cup. "We're in this together, and hidden resentments can hold back everything. We need to work through feelings and work together because the project is bigger than us, right?"

"Yeah, I guess…about the project." She wasn't ready to entrust her feelings to him again. Not yet.

"Yeah, and "I guess" about your feelings, too." He looked back up, trying to catch her eyes.

She sighed and drained her plastic cup. "My feelings are that I don't feel as betrayed by you as I do Terri," she conceded, briefly meeting his eyes "Even though you've taken me where no man ever has, and you mean a lot to me, we've said all along…" She stopped with a lump in her throat. He silently took her hand in his; the gesture made clumsy by the airplane seating.

"You never promised anything, but it was different with Terri and me. I had no idea she was seeing you or anyone else. I thought it meant something real, something special," she said as she studied his empty cup.

"I doubt you're not special to Terri. You know you are to me. And I'm sure neither of us wanted to hurt you," he said earnestly. She pulled her hand away, placing it around the cup again.

His words rang hollow to her, not because she doubted his honesty, but more because she doubted Terri's. Trusting anyone was hard when everyone betrayed you. "Whether you wanted to or not, you did."

"I'm sorry, Hannah."

"I'm sorry, too." It wasn't heartfelt, so it sounded condescending. They journeyed in silence awhile as she struggled in her heart. She realized one passion remained that could fill the hole in her heart even if she was unwilling—or unable—to accept his apology. "Like you said, 677 is bigger than us, so let's focus on that, and I'll try to get along."

Forgiveness might come later, if at all.

CHAPTER TWENTY-ONE
BALANCE

Stop by my office after work today. I have something for you.

It was a text from Aaron, and she went as bidden. His hallway brought memories, and he turned from the computer screen when she knocked quietly on the jamb. "Hi, Hannah," he said as he met her eyes.

She threw her voice, trying to keep it light, "You rang?"

Aaron slid open the file drawer on his small desk and handed her a small brown bottle. Busy with the start of the fall semester, they'd had little time to interact, yet he remembered. She leaned into the hug he offered, thankful she didn't have to ask him for more pills. Her response was visceral but surprising as she felt him breathe in the scent of her hair.

Seeming to expect nothing further, he stepped back when she made no moves. She kept her voice steady, "Thanks, Aaron." He smiled.

"You, me, and Terri need to go to a meeting of balance."

"What's that?"

"It's a 677 sub-group, and you'll find out more at the meeting." She raised her eyebrows. "Just more of our secret ways."

It turned out 'balance,' always lower case, was purposed to produce and distribute 677. Hannah saw how compartmentalized the 677 effort was when the group met in a small room at the public library. Aaron, Terri, and now she, were responsible for production, but no one else from UF or the PBCA conference was there except Mary Poppins. The rest of balance were anonymous upper-level contacts from WHO, US Customs Enforcement (ICE), and a generic vitamin manufacturer that contracted with WHO and UNICEF. A "billionaire" no one had met checked in by speakerphone, assuring unlimited funding, but urging haste in a somehow superior tone.

She learned that once they produced five hundred million doses, insertion of the RU-AT-667 pills into bottles was going to be handled by the vitamin manufacturer. She knew nothing of how the pills were going to be delivered to the company and subdivided into millions of bottles, nor was distribution discussed. The meeting was brief, unlike committee meetings at UF.

Aaron dropped her off at her apartment afterwards, and as she climbed the steps alone, she remembered making that climb together, buzzing with anticipation. She imagined him heading for Terri's now, face lit with the spark they'd somehow lost. Her stomach sank as she realized she still had to get used to the shifted reality.

They were going to be together a lot this year, working on getting production up and running—how would she handle that? She picked at a frozen dinner she'd microwaved as her feelings circled. After a cool shower, she lay in her bed, the sheet light on her sweat-damped skin. Closing her eyes, she listened to cicadas drone in the August night. Bobbie and Camille came home later, their quiet, comfortable communication needing few words. Missing the intimacy of love talk, she rolled over and drifted off to sleep, helped along by a little blue benzo.

August went, September too, with autumn wavering as it does in the South. Work and study were there to fill weekdays, while St. Francis took up Saturdays. Saturday nights brought solitude relieved only by her brief encounters with her roommates, her fantasies, and the little blue pills. But without the bliss she'd found with Aaron, ancient yearning returned each Sunday morning.

She filled those Sabbath dawns by walking the same path she followed after her first benzo. Parking lots were empty as she passed the seven worship houses on her 6-7 a.m. walks, but from her childhood, Pete Kramer's morning song mix filled her head, unbidden:

Good morning, good morning, good morning!

It's time to rise and shine.

Good morning, good morning, good morning!

I hope you're feelin' fine.

The cows are calling in the corn, the rooster's crowing up a storm!

Good morning, good morning, good morning...

It's time to rise and shine!

Rise and shine, give God the glory, glory.

Rise and shine, give God the glory, glory!

Rise and shine and give God the glory, glory...

Children of the LORD!

Back when she was taken away, and they didn't seem to object, her loss was profound. And yet, she yearned for the love they'd shared. She feared she'd never find such love again.

CHAPTER TWENTY-TWO
JULES

OCTOBER BROUGHT COOLER mornings and a text from Aaron to meet again. Together now in the privacy of Aaron's office, she was sure Terri and Aaron were still sleeping together. Their love glances did not include her, and she sensed electricity when they touched. And neither had called her before this, seeking intimacy. Desire smoldered inside, but a benzo and a half helped dull her passion.

Outwardly, there was détente. Inwardly, she struggled with lust, pain, fantasies, and anger. Autumn's cooling always heightened her desire to cuddle under covers and taste the pleasures of the flesh—their flesh. Yet her jealous heart resisted an intimacy that would be shared three ways. It helped keep her motivation all about 677 as they quietly discussed progress to date.

Aaron had located a small warehouse for lease in Union County near Raiford, where they would begin mass production. She was sure the location brought back foster care memories for him but didn't bring up the subject she hoped was still their separate intimacy.

"The location's isolated, and there's no active zoning in the county, so no one'll come poking around," he said. "It's perfect for us. Once we get the go-ahead, we'll be ready to fly into production."

"Do you have all the equipment detailed?" Terri asked.

"Yep." He pulled out a hand-written outline and some sketches, pointing to the outline. "We can get almost everything through online sources. I've located a pair of three thousand-gallon bulk milk tanks at a dairy doing upgrades. Nothing is raising any eyebrows."

Hannah looked thoughtful. "So, what about safety equipment?"

"We haven't discussed that much, but it's a big issue. If we don't want exposure from inhaling and absorbing the 677, we're going to have to have level four biosecurity, just like at the school." He paused as that sunk in. "We'll be able to cut lots of administrative and personnel steps, of course, but we do have to get the biosecurity part right."

"And we can do all that without attracting attention?" Terri looked at him intently.

"I think so." He sat back and scratched his head. "I've worked through several of the steps in the construction process on paper, and we can compartmentalize enough that it shouldn't generate too many questions when we order supplies. If anyone asks, our cover is that we are a vaccine research facility for dog influenza."

"What about my thesis and your academic work?" Hannah wanted to know. She leaned in slightly, raising her eyebrows.

"It's on hold, unofficially," Aaron explained. The distribution of the 677 to Nigeria was their highest priority—academic work paled in comparison to saving the world.

Her thesis fell behind through the autumn and winter as they pushed and pushed to get the facility set up for production. Mary Poppins rode interference for their academic work, signing off on submission delays throughout the year. She also made sure funds were available to cover their work at the warehouse.

Terri's old F100 was perfect for hauling supplies and materials to the Union County warehouse, and the three would often ride together to the location. The smell of an oily engine and hot antifreeze brought back her first encounter with Terri on each trip. Riding in the middle of the big bench seat, with Terri driving and Aaron riding shotgun, it was hard to keep their legs from brushing, but the jeans that now separated bare flesh, and benzos a little more often, helped her cope.

Aaron had many talents, as it turned out, and Hannah and Terri were like his apprentices as they gradually plumbed and wired the warehouse and readied it for production. Walls were formed with sheets of heavy plastic stapled onto a flimsy wooden framework to form airtight rooms where production would be staged. They made a rodent-safe storeroom, they hoped, and spread several tubs of rodenticide throughout the warehouse.

Terri's pickup was able to move almost everything. When the dairy tanks were delivered to the building's dock on a big truck, they used a pallet jack and piano dollies to get them moved inside. Working hard, feeling her muscles strain, and the underlying intensity driving them almost made Hannah forget the hurt that she'd let pull them apart.

Aaron kept her supplied with benzos, but she worried he might come to see her as an addict. She could quit anytime, of course, but she didn't want her emotions to hinder their work. Regardless, it didn't seem to bother him.

At St. Francis one Saturday, she saw a street-person in the bathroom turn her bird eyes away and feign indifference after catching her swallowing a little blue pill. As she left the bathroom, she realized her habits were making her careless.

When bird eyes, named Jules, approached her the following Saturday as she left St. Francis, she was instantly wary. "Hi, Jules. What's up?" Jules was pushing her shopping cart of belongings down the sidewalk, and her little wiener dog rode on top. He growled, and Jules slapped him lightly and said, "Hush, Booger!"

She turned to Hannah. "Yeah, so, I was just wondering where I could score some oxies? If you know?"

"I wouldn't know, I don't use oxy, Jules."

"I saw you swallow the little blue pill last week." Her bird eyes shifted, looking Hannah over.

Her reply was an exasperated whisper, "It wasn't oxy."

"So, it was a Zannie?" Her little eyes now said *gotchya!*

"What if it was?" Hannah realized she was getting sucked into something and turned to leave. "I have a script." But she was never good at lying.

"Yeah, you do," Jules cackled like a crow. "If you ever want some... I know where to get it."

Hannah kept walking, but now she had a source if she got desperate to hide it from Aaron. Her lie about the script made her realized she could possibly get some legally as well, although probably not in the amounts she was currently using.

She'd been sleeping in a little later each Sunday, and with less incentive to avoid the heat, her Sunday morning walks, now ritualistic, grew gradually later over the winter. She began to see people gathering at several of the churches she passed, and a need for connection began to stir inside as her heart reached out for their calm camaraderie and gentle intonations, a community intimacy that could fill the hole left by Terri and Aaron.

Shady Grove Primitive, the last on her route, was always empty. Somehow, the old man's gaze and *Blessed Assurance's* slow acapella cadence had formed a weak but real connection to her soul's missing song—had the church died? Was God real, or just a crutch to prop up meager existence on this planet?

Spring came, and Hannah noticed some Easter events posted on the church marquees she passed, as well as pots of lilies on the porch of Shady Grove Primitive. The tiny marquee board near the front door changed, too, for the first time that she'd noticed. Someone had arranged the little plastic letters to read "EASTER SERVICE 11:30".

She realized then their service was always late, and most mornings, she walked too early to see anyone. She stepped lighter, knowing the church was still alive, and chords of *Blessed Assurance* began humming unbidden in her throat.

Hannah, Terri, and Aaron all worked long hours, trying to get production up and running before the August PBCA conference. If they'd been able to use contractors, preparation for the lab would have taken months instead of almost a year, so far. Even Hazel came some days to provide an extra hand, and every spare moment was taken by the project.

May Day brought demonstrators in the street near Hannah's apartment. Hannah, and even Terri and Aaron, saw them as an inconvenience since they were already behind schedule on production. They sat in the truck for ten minutes one day, waiting to get past the perennial May Day protesters that were chanting almost unintelligible demands for immigrant rights and apparently abortion rights. Terri and Hannah's eyes met, and they both laughed at a poster of block letters one marcher displayed:

BRING BACK THE McRIB!!

Aaron, however, was impatient. "We're doing something about *real* problems, and they're slowing us up."

"They're doing something, too: protesting," Terri laughed.

May turned into June then July, and sweltering heat in their warehouse brought exhaustion and easier sleep, helping to fill Hannah's emptiness. Because Terri was presenting an update on the human side, and Aaron had review responsibilities for papers being presented, they couldn't get 677 production ready before the August conference.

Dr. Replonge continued to provide funding and covered for their absences. She also updated the balance sub-committee without them, reporting back everyone's satisfaction with the progress—except the self-important billionaire, who wanted everything done quickly.

Hannah continued St. Francis Saturdays and some work-study. Summer also brought irregularity in Hannah's periods, but as people often will, she tried to ignore the symptoms, minimizing them in her mind. She'd had lifelong irregularity but finally grew impatient as the symptoms persisted.

At the campus clinic, a routine battery of tests for STIs and pregnancy were all negative, and the junior resident attributed the irregularity to stress and possibly the medication wearing off in her IUD. It had been five years, and they decided to change her IUD to a copper-only one. Hannah liked the idea of copper only, and they scheduled a follow-up to make sure everything returned to normal.

Then the 2014 PBCA was finally upon them, and they made final preparations for the conference, which was in Kansas City that year. Distraction from her melancholy was a welcome relief.

CHAPTER TWENTY-THREE
MEETING PETE

THE NON-STOP FLIGHT to PBCA was uneventful, and Hannah's small bag was now in the closet of the "Honeymoon Suite" at the conference hotel. A call to the hotel operator verified the suite was hers, and at no extra charge because of a room shortage. A bottle of Champaign on ice was labeled complementary, and the covers were already turned back. She hesitated in the bathroom; only one pill left in the little brown bottle. It had been several days, and a mild withdrawal of nausea and faint dizziness seemed to be over, though her appetite was down. Unfortunately, it was too late to ask Aaron for more before they left. Haunted by Jules's cackle, she decided to break it in half.

Looking in the mirror, she saw a flaxen-haired beauty that simple clothes couldn't hide. Anyone could drown in those green eyes, but she knew their depth was a lie and was almost repulsed by the emptiness and confusion she felt inside. She loosened the top button on her chambray shirt to reveal the small IUD cross lying against her fine olive skin. She shrugged and finally smiled as she practiced a confident look.

She went back down and checked in at the conference welcome tables, collecting her packet and slipping a name lanyard over her neck. She grabbed a cup of coffee from a table loaded with vegan hors d'oeuvres and headed to an atrium where people were gathering.

As she approached an area of table seating, a handsome man caught her glance. She held his eyes, so he glanced at the open seat next to him and half-stood. Everywhere else was filling up quickly, so Hannah nodded.

"Thanks," she said. His face was open, craggy, and thick blonde hair hung across his forehead. Her knees weakened, and she sat quickly, hiding an involuntary gasp when she saw his name tag. She needed something to distract her, and fast.

"No problem. There aren't many seats, Hannah from Gainesville." His voice was smooth as he read her lanyard and closed his program schedule. "I'm Pete from Joplin, Missouri."

She took a sip of coffee to buy time, wincing as it scalded her tongue.

"Let me grab a water." He was up before she could stop him and returned with a bottle from the hors d'oeuvre table. "Here." He cracked the lid before handing it to her, and she swallowed a deep sip, her mind racing and heart thundering. Fortunately, the benzo bump seemed to help, but she wished she'd taken the whole thing.

"Thanks, Pete from Joplin. Why're you at the conference?" Nervousness sharpened her tone, making it inquisition-like. He blinked.

"I'm just a vet who can't get surgeries done fast enough to satisfy the need, so I'm looking for solutions." He glanced around at the roomful of scientists.

"That makes sense." How could it be this man, her father figure from so many years ago, was before her today? Her attraction lingered, undeniable, and he was familiar at the root of her being. But she was distracted by other feelings of resentment, love, fear, and joy that were expanding inside. Her surroundings briefly faded against memories of his kindness. She realized she must have blanched as warmth returned to her cheeks, livened by his obvious attraction, but she couldn't look away. "Most people here aren't practicing veterinarians."

He shifted, unsure, and she realized her attention was unnerving him. She finally blinked, and he replied, "I noticed. How about you?"

"I'm here with my research team from UF." She took a breath and smiled nervously, regaining eye contact as focus on her work established breathing room. "I'm not ready to present, but some of my team is. We're working on an oral toxin that induces sterility in mammals, essentially for life."

"Do you plan to try it in dogs and cats?" Pete asked. He seemed captivated by her eyes and the crisp, youthful intensity she knew they held.

"Eventually, but we're having some issues with dosing. The compound's extremely effective in sterilizing both males and females, and it's probably permanent. We're trying to find a more temporary dose, but the amounts are very small." She was able to regain composure with the familiar subject. "Right now, on the human side, there's a desire to have reversibility so that once someone decides to have a family, they can. Our compound's not reversible, so far, and the route of administration is still a concern. Oral dosing makes it very accessible to laypeople."

"I see." His eyes remained on her face, but his tone was no longer flirtatious. "I've been reading for several years that this vaccine or that medication is about to come out for sterilizing dogs and cats, but then nothing. What other issues are there?"

Hannah paused a moment, looking up at the ceiling to mentally access her project files. "I think the significant thing holding up the veterinary release of 677 is the regulatory process. It's already proven to work extremely well no matter how you give it—orally, SQ or IM injection, and even trans-dermally—and it's simple to produce. It's patented now, but the formula and cookbook are available in the research world if you know where to look." She looked back at him, jarred now by the juxtaposition of her childhood feelings against the mutual visceral attraction she sensed and shared with him.

"As far as other approaches go, there are a lot of problems with a lack of safety studies and efficacy. For the most part, it's not as easy to stop the reproductive process as we would like to think. Millions of years of evolution are hard to overcome, or as they say: Evolution's a bitch. Our compound is exceptional and already proven safe in some ways, but long-term studies haven't been completed."

"So, what's your take on how long it'll be before we have something practical and effective for spay/neuter? How much longer do puppies and kittens have to keep dying?" His focus and passion seemed unchanged as he remained on subject, undiverted by his attraction.

"I would still say about ten more years, possibly longer. It *will* happen, it's just gonna take time."

"Thanks for sharing that. Ten years is too long, though." Pete sipped his coffee. "I need to look at the schedule to see where I want to go."

"Right now, it's pretty easy." Hannah leaned towards him. She could smell his scent. "There are only the paper presentations in the general conference, or you can go to the flash presentations and thesis critiques, which is where I have to go to support my guys. There's a pretty good opening dinner scheduled tonight, and the keynote speaker's the president of one of the big sponsors."

"That makes it easy then. I'd like to see your team in action." He seemed eager and watched as she tried to hide a smile behind her coffee cup.

"Well, I have to get to the thesis defense if you want to come. I'll introduce you to my colleagues. This is only my second year, but they've been coming here since the beginning." She moved to stand up from the table.

Pete Kramer rose too, and they walked to the meeting room.

They were huddled together, preparing for Terri's thesis defense as Hannah introduced them. "This is Terri, who's on the human side and presenting this afternoon, and Dr. Aaron Skinner, my faculty advisor. He's a vet too."

They exchanged greetings, and Pete sat at the rear of the room while Hannah stayed with Aaron and Terri. "Nice." Terri winked. Hannah felt guilty when she wanted to agree. He *was* good-looking. Aaron looked away, but Hannah could feel him listening.

"You okay?" asked Terri.

"Yeah. He's nice, that's all," said Hannah as she realized her attraction was showing. Terri smiled knowingly.

"You go, girl!" Terri punched her lightly in the arm.

The presentation and following questions were interesting and set the tone for the conference, which was basically a desire to find an effective way to safely sterilize animals in one dose. It was very important that the treatment not spread to other animals. For pets, the dose had to be essentially permanent or only reversible by a pre-planned method, and the simplicity of administration and minimization of side effects were essential.

After the session, Hannah had to hang with the team. With nothing to present this year, she'd been elected the official photographer for their group. Pete wandered off, but she was determined not to lose track of him. At five, the combination of visceral tension of meeting her old "father," long day of travel and presentations, and crisp sheets calling from the huge bed drew her into an unmedicated nap. She awoke and showered to freshen up, then headed down to the keynote dinner.

Table seating was not assigned, and she watched for him as she sat at a mostly empty table for eight. She caught his eye and felt her heart speed up as he sat next to her. Aaron and Terri found seats nearby, but they were deep in conversation with some people at their table.

"How was the afternoon?" he asked.

"Very good. Everyone was quite pleased with the progress." She remembered his frustration with the timeline and added, "It still looks like it'll be a long time before we will have something to take to market."

"It doesn't make sense, the delays. If it's a single-dose toxin, what's the danger? It's not like it could spread to another animal or something." He was a little irritated.

"They still want to make sure it can be safely distributed and used in real-world situations, and it takes a lot longer to complete the studies required for human approval." She leaned back in her chair. "What you have to remember is that even with the MERCY grants, the veterinary side is still small potatoes. The market potential on the human side isn't in millions of dollars, but billions."

"Ain't that the truth. So, it holds up 'our' product, and the euthanasias continue." Pete's cynicism about the mass killings of unwanted pets, accompanied by pursed lips and a slow head shake, brought back a flash of childhood memories.

He had been holding pretty intense eye contact with her, and she was fully focused. Pete looked at the small placard at each place that noted 'All vegan offerings. Non-vegan options available, see server.'

"Cool," he said, then looked at Hannah. "Are you vegan?"

"Actually, I'm thinking about it. They always try to serve vegan."

Pete shrugged. "Well, it doesn't matter to me. Just different than back home."

Noise increased as the tables filled in, making conversation difficult. Then the keynote speaker rose and gave a pep talk on the need for contraception solutions in order to help solve the pet overpopulation problem. He emphasized the need for interim solutions since the actual production of the contraceptives for commercial release was still a ways off.

He finished, and everyone started rising to leave. Hannah stood as well, and Pete followed suit. "Good pep talk, but it doesn't sound very promising," he commented.

"Yeah." Hannah stepped closer, looking up at him, wanting time with him. "There's a good blues player at the bar across the street unless you're too tired."

"It's only nine, and I love blues. Who is it?"

"Janiva Magness."

"Never heard of her." He looked thoughtful.

"She's amazing. If you like blues, she's that and maybe a little folk mixed in. We can talk, just you and me."

"Just you and me?" he asked, suddenly nervous. She could see a slight flush, and she felt her body return it.

"Yeah, no interruptions. Why not? Let's go now, so we get a good seat." She linked her arm in his, and the brush of their forearms gave her a thrill.

They crossed the street a moment later, walking in time with each other. "So, who's Janiva Magness?"

"She's a blues slash soul singer from Detroit." Hannah hopped up on the curb. "Her parents both killed themselves, and she ended up in the foster care system. She kind of grew into the blues naturally."

"I guess so," he agreed. "My mom was a foster parent, and I grew up with foster kids all around."

"Really?" Hannah looked up at him to make sure it was true. "Were you a foster kid?"

"No, not at all. My mom was just devoted to the cause. I have two belly siblings and had lots of foster brothers and sisters growing up." There was no line yet at the venue, and they landed a small booth in the corner and ordered merlot and a bowl of figs, strawberries, dark chocolate, and cashews.

"So, did you ever do foster care yourself?"

"Well…yes. I used to with my wife." He hesitated, trying to gauge her reaction. "We had a bunch of kids over the years before we stopped but were never able to adopt."

"Is that why you fostered, so you could adopt?"

"That was part of it. We had tried and tried to make babies of our own to no avail. Had fun tryin' though." He grinned at the memory. "But we wanted to help kids, too. We believed—and still do—that as Christians, God wants us to change our world. Kids are in our world now; they're the future, and we can make a difference one life at a time by helping them when they're down."

"Why'd you stop?"

Pete didn't answer right away. His eyes looked distant to her as he watched Magness and her crew starting to take their places. She slowly sipped her wine, watching him intently.

"I guess you could say it was because of a broken heart if you wanted any one reason. We lost several pre-adoptive kids over the years to the vagaries of the system, but the last one broke Prissy's heart…and mine…" He met her gaze.

Hannah placed her hand over his, gently touching, wanting more as she remembered the river house couch, where Pete read them the Bible each night. She was surprised at how clearly the memory suddenly returned—it had been dormant for years.

"She was a crazy sweet little girl named Jane, but her belly mom misspelled it J-A-I-N. Her mom was a hopeless meth head who knew how to work the system. Despite Jain's seven years with us, the mom used connections to get a judge to order Jain moved closer to her, two counties away near Springfield, which was an hour east of us…" He turned to face her more, swallowing hard.

He cupped her hand inside his as gently as an egg, then continued, "…to unite Jain with her and her other children; reunification, they call it. It didn't matter that she'd never even met her mother. We spent a fortune on attorney's fees, trying to fight it…" He shook his head at the memory, his voice choking. "We tried to foster again after that, but our hearts went cold."

"Ouch." Hannah swallowed more wine. "Both of you were done?"

"I could have done more, but I couldn't see Prissy destroyed. She never really recovered."

Maybe this was God's attempt to rescue her: get him talking about Prissy, so this thing with their hands would stop. They both picked a fig, and she had never considered it a sexy fruit until she watched his mouth take it in. "We haven't been close in decades." *So much for the God thing.* She had a sudden desire to comfort him, to hold and be held.

"So these days, my focus is on de-sexing dogs and cats to stop the carnage. That's why I'm here. But it dun' look like there's any salvation from science comin' soon, do it?" She smiled at the vernacular, listening at two levels: Heart and mind.

"Hardly. It seems like the delays are endless. So, how did you get interested in spay/neuter?" At this point, Hannah was an expert at parrying to keep from revealing too much about herself.

House lights suddenly dimmed, and stage lights lit Magness and the band as their blues started flowing loud and smooth, flooding their senses.

Hannah slid nearer to Pete, shifting her arm to the inside of his as she intertwined their fingers. She quit struggling and chose to give and seek bodily comfort. He didn't resist as Magness opened with "I Don't Wanna Do Wrong." She didn't want to do wrong either, yet here she was with deep spiritual stirrings and music, once again focusing her passion and carrying her forward.

As they sipped their wine, with him a little awkward using his left hand, she leaned in to pick a fig and strawberry from the shallow bowl and offered them in her open palm. He took the fig, and she delicately bit off the strawberry, dropping the stem on the table. Its juice and pulp filled her mouth as she gently traced the veins on the back of his hand, seeing wetness in his eyes.

She slid closer, bumping hips, and they leaned into each other as the rest of the set took them on an emotional journey through their past lives.

The last song of the set was "I Won't Cry," and they both felt the raw pain and strength in the music and lyrics.

She decided then to follow where the night led, remaining anonymous to Pete. The attraction was mutual in the way they pressed together—their bodies, their arms, their hands . . . Electricity tingled where their fingers intertwined.

She was willing to offer her body in unspoken thanks and healing to this man whose kindness had carried her and given her purpose through the years. He was alone, she was alone, and everything outside the moment was fading in the bloom of shared desire.

She laid her head against his shoulder and looked up, unhesitant once she decided. Her voice was loud enough just for him, "I'm in the Honeymoon Suite."

His sigh sounded relieved as he looked back intensely. "Let's go."

Words weren't needed as they crossed the street. She inserted the key card and was already breathing faster than normal as they went arm in arm over the threshold. Neither hesitated as the door clicked shut. Hannah faced him and pulled his head down, her tongue dancing with his as their hands explored, testing, caressing, probing, guiding. His scent was intoxicating, and her taste was exotic, exciting. By the time they made it to the bed, she was only wearing her IUD cross, and she paused to remove that when it hung up in his hair.

His body was heated with passion, and his musk rose up around them, making her feel safe and secure. Opening to him was like falling into a pillow, and she soaked his passion into her every pore. They laughed together when they went the same direction and concentrated when one led. He groaned as he was unleashed for the first time in years, and she basked in his explorations that were like adorations.

There was urgency but not emergency in each tiny caress, brush, and taste. Everything about them seemed to mix into one massive feeling until she ended up lithe and light on top of his thighs, his penis against her belly. She rose and slid her legs up his hips, taking her weight on her hands as they mingled in the silvering hair of his chest. She dipped her head to line him up with her wetness, then looked back up at him as he slid in fully for the first time.

They both closed their eyes, brains overwhelmed with the input from below. In and out faster, fitting perfectly, and his moan became a growl as he began to pump deep inside her. She had never ridden a man like this and heard ragged breathing, realizing it was hers, then came around him with a pulsing she had never experienced before, grinding into his mons. Her orgasm was like a tidal wave, leaving her arms weak and trembling. She collapsed on his chest with a sigh, fanning her damp hair across his face and watched as he slowly pulled a cord of her hair into his mouth, savoring her. She wanted to melt.

Their panting subsided as they lay on the sheets. Hannah laughed—only half a little blue pill, and here she was atop a stallion, exhausted by her unabashed passion for this man she knew to be safe. Her laugh brought a caress in the small of her back, and little else. She felt her labia starting to twitch again as she listened to the steady cadence of his heart. "Relax and enjoy," he whispered as he rolled her over and began to caress her most intimate parts, slipping up and down, in and out, leaning in with tongue and taste occasionally, taking her up, up, up, up, and over again…and again, and again for what felt like an eternity until she was fully spent, a first for her as well.

She quit breathing for a few moments from the hyperventilation, long enough to spark his concern she realized as he reached to feel her chest, then she let out a deeply satisfied sigh. He smiled and pulled the sheet and top cover over catty-cornered, and they lay head to thigh as a deep post-coital sleep gently surrounded them.

CHAPTER TWENTY-FOUR
MORNING AFTER

"Uggh!" Pete jerked awake, scrambling for his cell phone and pulling the tangle of sheets with him. She automatically jerked them back, covering herself but leaving him nude. She was momentarily confused by her surroundings, but came to the present when he said, "Prissy!"

Prissy's voice was tiny through the phone but loud in her head as Pete quickly went into the bathroom. She registered the time on the bedside clock, almost 10 a.m., and realized she'd overslept for the first time in years. Listening to the murmured conversation from the bedroom, Hannah couldn't help but feel guilt.

Even in her distant memories, she had always felt close to Pete, wanting to be held by him, following him around when he was home, and singing songs with him when no one else would. She didn't realize until last night how deep and weirdly sexual her attachments to him had been. She'd always blamed Prissy for letting her go, and even hearing Pete speak her name brought no emotional pangs. Still, her memories of Prissy were of an attentive mother who provided for her needs and showed her love.

Hearing Prissy's voice and the familiarity in their mundane conversation, she realized she was fucking with a real family, and perhaps the only part of her past that *was* real. It brought a sudden tangle of emotions and an unfamiliar moral reset. She willingly gave her body in hopefully restorative loving, but she knew it would have to stop there. She couldn't destroy what Pete and Prissy had, nor did she want to. They were the rock upon which she had built her past. While she would gladly give her body to Pete again, his body belonged to someone else.

In the passions of the night before, Hannah felt no personal downside in loving Pete with all she had, ignoring the stakes for him. Even now, he had much more to lose if their encounter were discovered. His apparent dissatisfaction with Prissy as a lover and her ability to fulfill him last night gave her satisfaction. And certainly, she was spent at the end of the evening herself! Some part of her wanted to spend her life with him, but she couldn't bring herself to act further towards that end. He was her father, really, and his wife was her mother… Her only hope was to walk away.

Hannah was sitting on the edge of the bed, wrapped in the top sheet when Pete came back into the room. His eyes said they found her just as distractingly and naturally beautiful as the night before, but Prissy's call ended any hope of rekindling the fire. Hannah had to get to her group for their day's scientific presentation, and they separated their clothes from the strewn piles on the floor so she could shower.

Hannah found him wrapped in the sheet this time, only his hair visible where the back of his head poked out at the edge of the bed. She kneeled alongside the bed and placed her hand on his shoulder. She kissed his hair gently, then put her forehead in the curve of his neck, feeling his warmth through the still crisp sheet. He pressed back with a tilt of his head, then relaxed. "I've never done this before," he whispered through the sheet.

Neither have I! Lingering guilt precluded the closeness of the night before. Empathy suddenly felt clumsy, and all she could manage was, "It's okay. Accept it as the gift it was." She took one more breath of his hair, then wanted no more and stood, letting her fingers slide wistfully down and off his arm as she turned towards the door.

She could feel it, and she was sure he did, too: It would be their last intimacy.

CHAPTER TWENTY-FIVE
677 MEETS AGAIN

IN THE YEAR since the last 677 group meeting, their cynicism had grown towards the reproducing populations in the third world. Christian fecundity in Nigeria had drawn ire from several organizations concerned about the future of the planet. Many reports told how burgeoning populations like Nigeria's, soon to replace the United States as the third largest, were accelerating climate change.

It was a threat to the wealthy and, in their own eyes, the responsible tribes of the world—a threat exaggerated by the reductions (in almost everything) mandated by proposed climate change interventions. Wealthy elites believed desires for big families were selfish, and Nigerians couldn't understand the threat their overpopulation implied for the rest of the world. It wasn't right those Africans could draw on resources made scarce by climate change mandates. The wise rich should not have to sacrifice so that the un-informed poor could choose babies, and 677 was the secret weapon to save the first-world from third-world ignorance.

On a small lake with adequate privacy, Shelter 4 in Antioch Park in the nearby City of Overland Park, Kansas, was where the 677 group met on the last night of the conference to exchange information and insights. Dr. Replonge started with a concern about libido that had been raised since the last meeting. In humans, elimination of sexual desire would probably not be a welcome side effect.

Ya think? Hannah smiled slightly as she remembered the night before.

So far, short-term studies in primates and other species had shown shrinkage of the gonads in both genders, and it might reduce levels of sex hormones or sexual performance. Long-term studies were planned. Mary turned to Terri and said, "And now, maybe Terri can give us an update from Nigeria?"

"My pleasure," replied Terri as she rose. "A case report from Nigeria at WHO details a sharp fertility decline in a small southern town called Akwete... Christian, like small southern towns in the US." Her sarcasm brought chuckles.

"A cluster of early-term spontaneous abortions preceded the decline. Human Herpes Virus HHV-6A, known to be spreading in the region, is speculated to be the cause. HHV-6A is very easily spread and certainly is associated with many other conditions, so they propose testing in the region to at least establish a baseline," she finished.

Dr. Replonge nodded curtly, looked over her reading glasses, and reassured her by adding, "The report is observational in tone and lacks any urgency. Regardless, we feel it would be impossible to trace it to us."

"They don't even suspect intentional population interventions," said Terri. She raised one hand, praise-like, and continued, "Just the hand of God." Derisive chuckles came again.

"Are there fertility services in the area that could end up biopsying or ultrasounding gonads?" The question came from a Davis professor.

"Great question! I'm not aware of any significant fertility service in that part of Nigeria, and the low-income nature of the distributions makes it unlikely there will be any gonadal changes detected in the subject population," Terri replied. "But that question raises an important point. The uniform loss of fertility layers in the gonads is a hallmark of only 677. I think Dr. Replonge has a few words to say about that." She gestured to Hazel, who stood ramrod in her dark, impeccable clothes. Hannah still thought of her as Mary Poppins.

"Thank you, Terri. Bottom line, we're okay for now, I suspect. It is very doubtful there will be any blow-back from this trial, but this needs to be our only field trial, and time is of the essence. Once we are able to widely distribute, and a serious inquiry into the resulting infertility is made, all histological biopsy findings from the treated subjects will point to our molecule, and those of us at Florida," she paused, face stern as she looked at her trio from Gainesville.

"After detection, you can bet there will be much tighter control going forward. It will probably be a one-shot thing—one chance to save the planet. After that?" She looked around, then down. "677 will become a tool made ineffective by other political players, or else a tool of terror and/or warfare."

"What about the abortions? Are they caused by the destruction of the corpus luteum?" It was the same professor.

"Yes. Thanks for that," said Dr. Replonge. "On the human side, there has been a lot of discussion about the corpus and whether 677 would kill luteal follicles. Early abortions would indicate the destruction of the corpus, and any pregnancy not beyond the six to ten-week window would likely terminate. We think that is exactly what happened."

"But after that, the pregnancies should be self-sustaining without a corpus?"

"Correct. Any other questions?" Dr. Replonge looked around.

There was silence, then Hannah's internal thoughts burned to the surface. Pete and Prissy had desperately wanted children. "Are we doing anything for the mothers?"

"What?" Terri spoke, and Hannah saw her barely suppress an eye-roll.

"The Nigerian mothers who are trying to build families. Is there any counseling, or something, to help them cope with infertility?" An uncomfortable silence drew out. Hannah was embarrassed and felt a flush, but she continued to look at Terri.

Hannah thought of Pete and Prissy. Before, she'd been known to make anti-Christian jabs herself, but they struck home this year. It was Christian families like the Kramers that took in most foster kids like her, and it was real people in Nigeria who were now struggling with infertility, something Hannah now understood had devastated Prissy and hurt Pete deeply.

"That's an admirable point." Mary Poppins broke the moment, her tone conciliatory.

Hannah, implacable, plowed ahead, "I'm worried about the women who *wanted* to conceive. Having babies is their whole life, their culture. If it were everyone, or almost everyone, who was infertile, it wouldn't be *as* bad. But it wasn't everyone, and these women will feel like they're cursed or something." There were a few thoughtful nods.

"Really, it's the Spock thing," began Terri. "The needs of the many outweigh the needs of the few. How can we possibly provide counseling for millions?"

"Millions aren't a few," Hannah insisted.

Terri glanced at Aaron for support. "It's a few compared to billions starving and unable to breathe."

"Do you hear what you're saying? We have to consider the personal impact in so many lives, don't we? Don't you think it might come back and bite us in the butt?" There were still a few nods, but she saw Terri drum her fingers briefly, seeming annoyed, and Aaron shifted slightly.

Dr. Replonge looked thoughtful. "We certainly have folks working on environmental impact assessments for the potential commercial product. Maybe we need to commission a social impact assessment as a group."

"Or consider the social impacts for a minute, at least. That's all I'm saying."

"You think we haven't?" Terri asked.

"Maybe, but a Star Trek metaphor didn't sound like consideration." Hannah was softening her tone as she realized that if they were going to act, there would be consequences they could do little about. Acknowledging that didn't mean they were callus. She remembered what she and Terri had shared, though, and how little it had meant to her. It seemed Terri lacked empathy in all areas of her life. Still, they had to work together if they were going to accomplish their goals.

"Any other thoughts?" Dr. Replonge asked. Everyone seemed quiet, thoughtful about the maturing plan. "If not, we'll see you all next year or sooner if the need arises. Police the trash, use the recycling bins, and don't forget our veterinary mission. Remember the animals put to sleep today."

What about the mothers feeling depressed today? But Hannah knew better than to say more.

CHAPTER TWENTY-SIX
GOD HELP ME

TIME FLEW BY after the conference while getting production up and running remained their highest priority. Sleep was limited as they configured the systems at the warehouse in preparation for a test run, and Hannah was irritable as she tried to avoid the blue pills Aaron had replenished for her. Certainly, she had no prospects for sex, but nighttime recollections of her encounter with Pete led to guilt, tossing, and turning. Anxiety prevailed, worsened by another irregular period, and she needed the benzos to sleep.

It seemed each time she tried to limit herself, she grew more irritable, restless, and sick to her stomach. She'd fallen asleep in the wee hours one Sunday, slept late, and woke up puking. She vaguely worried it might've been from the benzos—maybe from trying to stop them?

Whenever her roommates were home, she always gave them room, taking care to preserve relations in the apartment. Now she experienced an uncharacteristic irritability whenever they were at the apartment sharing little intimacies—a touch, a look—during their daily routine, clueless to their effect on her. It accentuated her loneliness. Rather than start the day with the benzo she'd skipped the night before, she quietly set out on her old morning walk, hoping it would help.

She made her rounds by habit, and at this late hour, most of the churches were entering service. But then, she saw the same man she had seen before at Shady Grove Primitive coming out of the old house across the street from the church.

On previous Sundays, she'd seen him a time or two in his worn and rounded black suit and tie. His ebony face was set off by a white shirt as he opened up the church. His fringe of hair was silvering, and he moved with the deliberate care of an octogenarian. But his skin was smooth, and today, she saw his clear, dark brown eyes as he studied her intently when they met in the street. She nodded to him, not slowing her step.

"I seen you go by here all summer and fall, honey. Only on Sunday, like you lookin' fo' a church."

"Why would I be looking for a church?" She stopped and faced him, then looked down.

"We all need a church, honey. It hep us be right with God."

"What makes you think God even cares?" She checked his eyes again, looking for a fight. Seeing only kindness, she looked away again.

"Oh, chil', God cares about you. He made you a beautiful tent and a beautiful heart inside. But you troubled 'bout sum'thin' you holdin' on to. Sum'thin' you need to give to him."

"Why don' he tell me hisself, din?" Her anger mocked, leaving the old man to watch, saddened as she upped her pace towards home.

Through the week, she worked by day to save the world; by night, she stewed over Pete. And not just Pete—her long-held resentment of Prissy's abandonment had been a lie. She realized the Kramers had tried to ease the court-ordered separation by encouraging her to embrace it. They must have been in shock at a sudden order from a callous authority protected by a bench of "justice." They never wanted her to go, fought it with all they had, and she had blamed them.

Even now, she wanted retribution—what they must have felt back then! Especially Pete, impotent and unable to protect his family. Then slowly dying as bitterness ate away, burning at first, then cooling as the years passed without resolution. Now winter clearly held Prissy's soul, leaving Pete isolated and yearning for connection. And Hannah certainly made a connection, knowingly yet not considering, and realized that connection risked breaking theirs completely.

What if she'd revealed to Pete who she was? What if instead of flying home, he'd driven her to Joplin? What if a thaw came between Pete and Prissy? What if love rekindled what they'd all lost so long ago? But instead, she'd chosen herself, and by secretly sleeping with Pete, herself only. Her momentary physical desire had been justified by the illusion of healing him with her body. But his body wasn't broken, only his spirit, and the healing needed was between him and Prissy, where she had no right to be!

If she'd considered, if she'd acted with love, her presence could have been a healing balm. Instead, the truth of her choices now left her and everyone else desolate. If only she could right her wrong, but she saw no way out. Her only solace were the little blue pills that brought rest each night, while each day's activities brought distraction.

Weekdays were filled with academics and preparations for 677 production. Saturdays were reserved for St. Francis, and the benzos let her sleep in on Sundays, but they couldn't last forever. Even with no alarm, she awoke before mid-day.

The following Sunday was cloudy and cool for Florida, and she almost skipped over two blocks to avoid Shady Grove altogether. But it didn't matter—she was running late, and late services were already started, including Shady Grove's. As she approached the old building, there were a few cars in the vacant lot across the street, and she could hear voices raised inside with a song she knew from the river house days:

> *What a friend we have in Jesus, all our sins and griefs to bear!*
> *What a privilege to carry everything to God in prayer!*
> *Oh what peace we often forfeit, oh what needless pain we bear,*
> *All because we do not carry everything to God in prayer!*

It was as if the old man had arranged to sing that song as she was passing. She gave a wry smile and sped up as a cold drizzle started falling in the still air.

She went back to her apartment and snuggled under her covers as the gray light filled her room. She'd run out of blue pills but didn't want to ask Aaron for more. He was always looking at her with concern, and it was driving her crazy. She knew she'd eventually have to go to him for more, or else ask Jules at St. Francis.

She lay in bed most of the day, reviewing scientific articles for her thesis. She, Terri, and Aaron were supposed to meet Monday morning to begin a test run at the lab in Union County. Production required a full day on Mondays, then afternoons on Tuesday through Friday. If the test run worked, they would be ahead of schedule. Along with the 677 Aaron still pilfered and hid in his office, total production would take less than a year.

Without the blue pill, she had a hard time getting to sleep after she set the article on her nightstand, her mind circling endlessly between her encounter with Pete, the sterility they were bringing to the Nigerians, and her sexuality. She began to wonder about exposure to 677, even though they weren't making it yet. Her periods had been irregular, but that was probably the medication in the old IUD wearing out, right?

Round and round they went, then a new thought jumped into the whirl... *Am I bi?*

Certainly, she'd felt attracted to Terri despite hurt feelings, but she'd wanted Pete with everything she had. Was that okay? Was she a freak? Was it a sin? Surely, sleeping with her father figure was frowned upon, but it had been so good–for both–until the phone rang with Prissy's call. She realized she was trying to justify sleeping with Pete and instead circled back to Terri again, then Aaron, and then to Eddie, her eighth-grade foster brother. The milieu that was her life wouldn't quit swirling. She wrapped around her blankets and one pillow, bare leg on top, and scrunched her eyes shut. Eventually, she just prayed: *God, please help me.*

She didn't know what else to say or do, but it seemed to help. Sleep finally came.

CHAPTER TWENTY-SEVEN
TO INFERTILITY

Monday found the sky, her head, and her stomach clear as she waited by the bus stop for Aaron and Terri to pick her up. They came together from Aaron's apartment, where Terri had been staying. It was a rare, cold morning in Gainesville, a crisp forty-five degrees under a deep blue sky. Bright sun coming through the residual morning mist in the pines helped her suppress the anger she still held towards Terri, and she was able to forget her struggles as they drove. Today was the beginning of the test run, and Hannah allowed herself to be buoyed by the excitement.

Union County was beautiful, and once they got off the 231, the road was empty. Bound together with a level of commitment much higher than before the conference, they were almost jovial in the morning sun. "Funny, fighting overpopulation in the wilderness," noted Aaron.

"Yeah, well… If it gives you pause, Nigeria used to be a wilderness. Look at the shithole it is now. Just remember, this is what you are trying to preserve." Terri was adamant.

Hannah thought about how those third-world Nigerian women and men would have to suffer so that first-worlders could rest at night, knowing their way of life wasn't threatened. Every time she became cynical because of the human suffering they were going to inflict, and already had, she had to remind herself it wasn't just protecting their way of life—it was saving the whole planet from the ravages of climate change.

Climate change was the thing that mattered, the rock of truth that established moral high ground for the involuntary intervention they were preparing. It made the work worthwhile and justified the suffering of some, and their misery would inform the world that interventions could work, and that science did hold planet-saving answers that brought no *actual* pain or suffering. At least, none that was visible… Not like starvation.

Terri turned the pickup past the large "No Trespassing" sign and down the narrow dirt road. Hannah hopped out and opened the gate, and they pulled up to the facility. From the outside, it looked like an old Florida pole building, slowing rusting away, but that was only a shell covering the bio-secure lab they'd built within. Heat was their enemy, and while the tall pines blocked the sun part of the day and big fans brought fresh air to flap the plastic walls of their workrooms, it began to get oppressive inside as afternoon sun warmed the sheet metal.

Afternoon chores required HAZMAT suits, enhancing the heat effect. They decided to go almost naked as they changed in the small locker area they'd constructed at the entrance to the production rooms. Aaron had purchased water packs, and they strapped them on before the suits, so they wouldn't have to decontaminate to get a drink.

After she'd fitted her suit, Terri sang out, "I gotta go to the bat-roooom!" Her voice mocked a child's, "Just kidding."

Despite the suits' circulating fans, all three were wet with sweat by the time they entered the production rooms.

"Stay hydrated, stay hydrated, stay hydrated," Aaron teased. "It's gonna be a long day, children."

Terri played along, "Yes, Daddy."

They all smiled as they looked through their face shields.

Written together with Dr. Replonge, the five-day production protocol's first day required almost sixteen hours to complete. Stopping only for a quick lunch of fruits, crackers, juice, and "bat-roooom" breaks, they finished Monday evening and returned home exhausted. Hannah had a headache from mild dehydration and made a mental note to bring extra underwear—the ones she had to put back on after showering out at the facility were still soaked with sweat.

"We should've arranged the wet work for early mornings, then we wouldn't have to sweat so much," said Hannah as Terri drove them over on Tuesday. They found her wet-work reference to the sweat lodges they worked in each day cute, and she didn't dissuade them. But in her mind, women had the right to choose, and making the choice for them still bothered her. Killing was wet work: killing dreams, killing hope, killing spirits… Even fetuses. Her sarcasm helped her cope.

"Yeah," Aaron agreed. "Too bad we can't flip the hours so that we work in the mornings, but we can for the next round."

"That would be a relief. Not sure I can get up that early, though. I'm not a morning person," Terri said. She rested her hand on the inside of his thigh. "Maybe if you made coffee…"

"I'm not a coffee person," said Aaron. He smiled as she started to squeeze his knee and said, "But for you, I'd do anything."

Their familiarity didn't bother Hannah as it had before. Her silent prayer seemed like a type of reset, and she wasn't dwelling on sexuality as much as she had been, but the loss of intimacy with Terri, then Aaron, and then Pete, left a yearning she didn't yet know how to handle. Back at her apartment, Hannah crashed.

Morning found her in senior seminar class in Bartram Hall, working on her thesis. With only half days required for the rest of the week, they decided on afternoons in case the work went longer than they expected.

Blurred by activity and excitement at the first run, their week flew by. Academic responsibilities were fulfilled as best they could in the mornings, with Dr. Replonge covering for Aaron and Terri, and Aaron covering for Hannah. Each afternoon, Terri drove them to Union County for the half-days required by the last four days of the protocol.

By Friday night, a one-kilo slug of 677, enough for one hundred thousand doses, was screened out and drying. It would be ready to powderize by morning. With the equipment they had gathered, they could do ten kilos at a time, which would mean fifty weeks until they hit the half a billion dose mark.

Two runs a week were possible, but it would require at least one additional worker since two persons had to be there for a run, and they couldn't all be gone for six months straight without really raising some eyebrows. As it was, all the half days away were hard to cover for, and one year was within their original timeline. It would take time after that to get the product into the vitamin production line, and there was some talk of putting the compound into protein supplements being marketed through the same relief agency chains as well.

Civilization would be a good place to celebrate the first week's success, so they went to shower out and don street clothes. Hannah had been avoiding being in the shower room with Terri all week by finishing clean-up while Terri showered, but tonight they were eager to get to dinner, and it was almost an hour drive to Gainesville. All three helped clean up the work areas, and there was no easy way to avoid the shower room together.

Terri's tan had faded, and despite herself, when they slipped out of their HAZMATs in the airlock, Hannah found her just as attractive as the first time, but the pain and shame were still sharp. A smirk flitted across Terri's face when she saw Hannah blush and avert her eyes.

"There's nothing wrong with being bi, Hannah. It's okay." She mistook Hannah's shame for lust, yet Hannah wondered if maybe she was right about being bi.

"I didn't say there was."

"And just because we both like fucking the same guy doesn't mean we can't still be friends."

"You hurt me, Terri. You changed my life, but it was nothing to you. You laughed." Pent-up anger seeped out, and Terri drew back.

"It wasn't nothing. You think I didn't feel your soul too? Being with you was everything to me." Terri was facing her and had moved closer, but Hannah turned to step into the shower without meeting her eyes. "We never discussed being exclusive," Terri spoke louder.

"I'm sorry I was so naïve. I'm learning." Hannah wanted to run, but remnants of attraction lingered, and the shower hindered her.

Terri stepped into the adjoining stall and spoke loudly over the flowing water.

"I'll say. Trying older men now, right?"

How the hell could she know that? "Were you spying on me?" Hannah's heart was beating hard, and her voice was sharp.

"Hardly." She shooshed the idea away with a gesture, saying, "I was leaving my room while you were going into the honeymoon suite. Good-looking guy, but the *honeymoon* suite?" Terri's sing-song tone made Hannah smile despite her horror at Terri knowing.

"You don't know him, *too*, do you?"

"Never saw him before in my life, Hannah. Really. I don't usually go for older guys. But if I did . . ."

"Goddammit, Terri."

They finished bathing, and Hannah was first out and already wrapped in a towel. She waited and watched while Terri dried and wrapped her towel around her creamy body. This time, Hannah let their eyes meet, which had the same effect as before.

Terri spoke before she could, "Look, Hannah. I'm sorry. I really wasn't trying to hurt or use you. I had—I still have—feelings for you. If I ever laughed, it was just at the irony of the situation. How could I have known you'd been with Aaron? I really am sorry!" There were tears in her eyes as she continued, "You can't keep holding on to that. Why can't you forgive me?" The electric rush of her body and her innate empathy overcame her resistance and fear.

"I can, Terri." They hugged, and Hannah was surprised by the relief forgiveness brought, but more so by the involuntary wetness between her legs. She couldn't reconcile that with her attraction to men, but it showed that Terri was right. She let the attraction hold a moment longer, and Terri kissed her wet hair before they separated.

"Let's go get some food and celebrate the milestone." Terri moved on without hesitation.

At dinner, Aaron could feel the decreased tension between the two women, and they discussed the project quietly as they sipped wine. Terri and Hannah voted him designated driver since they were in his Jeep today. They were into their third glass while Aaron was nursing his second when Hannah changed the subject. "So, there's something that's been bothering me..."

"What? A ménage à trois?" Terri was quick to respond in her funny voice.

"Really?" Hannah wasn't laughing. "No. Something serious."

"What's not serious about a ménage à trois? It would be a big step, but we're all obviously mutually attracted to each other." Terri *was* serious, Hannah realized.

"Yeah, but not committed." Hannah punched her playfully in the arm, and looked at Aaron, "We made up earlier, and now Terri's ready to move in together. I'm not, for the record."

"Hmmm," Aaron's tone was noncommittal. "So, what's on your mind?"

"677 destroys luteal follicles, as we've now established. So, how is it right to abort women without their consent?"

"Good question, Hannah." He used his professor's voice with a grin, the drink making everything funny. "As you should know, it's the price we have to pay to act. It isn't pretty, but there you are."

"You're okay with that?" Hannah kept her composure, and they all swallowed more wine.

"It will take years for 677 to get approved for anything but lab animal testing, and the totalitarian nature of the drug means it is unlikely to ever get approved for use in pets, much less humans. We have this opportunity now, and we could lose it if we wait. Then, the population bomb will continue to explode, with all of us suffering. Nigeria alone will surpass the population of the US in less than a decade."

"Assuming there's not some positive check we can't foresee."

"What are the odds of that, Hannah?" Aaron sounded slightly impatient, but the alcohol let Hannah persist.

"What about just targeting men?"

"Right on, sister," laughed Terri.

"We could, but the downside is that one man can impregnate many women, and it'd be impossible to hit enough men to make much of a dent." Aaron let a couple pass the table, then leaned forward as he continued, "The way we're doing it will hit men too, but women will be the main target."

"Like always," Hannah said sarcastically. She didn't consider herself to be a feminist or anything political, but the history of the world was clearly to put women first in blame and second in recognition.

"That's not where we're coming from, Hannah. This is about an amazing compound and the chance to use it to save the world from vast suffering," Terri insisted.

"I share your passion; I just feel bad about all the mothers losing their babies." Hannah spread her hands in front of her in defense.

"They're just a fetus at that point, Hannah. It will be sad, but it's not like they lost a living, breathing baby," Terri's voice was kind, and she gently stroked Hannah's thigh under the table. Hannah sighed as she let her.

"Well, it's buggin' me, and I need to talk about it. I know you're right; I'm just struggling with the abortion part." Hannah swallowed the rest of the glass and grabbed the bottle for a refill. "And if they were us, would we still accept the side effect of abortion? Would we even test it in us?"

Food came, vegetative delights, and it did little to negate the effects of the wine. Both Terri and Hannah had a fourth glass, and Aaron nursed a third. Hannah's questions made the undertones more somber as they ordered desserts. She was, after all, questioning much of what they'd been working toward. "You say it's wrong to treat the others but not ourselves, right?" Terri returned to the thread.

"Well, yes, but that doesn't mean I'm not committed... To the project, not to you, Terri," she tried to lighten it up a little.

Terri smirked. "That's okay. How committed are you?"

"To the project? One hundred percent."

Terri pulled a small Ziplock out of her pocket and slapped it on the table, and Hannah and Aaron leaned in to look at the three pills inside. They weren't blue.

"If you're really committed, we can deal with those concerns here and now." Hannah and Aaron both shifted uncomfortably. "Boom, there it is. What do you think?"

Terri covered them with her napkin while the waiter delivered the desserts, and Hannah sat quietly, thinking about the choice Terri had thrown out.

"I'd do it, but I don't have to worry about menopause." Aaron looked at Hannah, then Terri. "You probably would."

"I already feel like I'm going through menopause or something, so I'd be glad to get it over with." Hannah slowly nodded at Terri and said, "It only seems right."

Terri dumped the pills into her palm and held them out. Still, they hesitated, so she pushed a little harder, "No reason not to; not if we're committed." She took one in her other hand, then offered the rest to them.

Hannah thought about the troubles she'd faced as an unwanted child, the nature of the world, and what they were working towards. "Why not?" She shrugged and took the second one, and Terri held her hand out to Aaron. He wavered, but then took the offered pill.

"Bottoms up!" Hannah popped the pill in and glugged her wine. Terri followed suit, then Aaron, choosing to sip his wine instead.

After a moment, Terri held up her glass. "To infertility." They toasted, and both women finished their wine. Aaron still had to drive. They were the last ones out of the restaurant, and as they made their way to the little Jeep, they were sobered by their impulsive action.

Hannah and Terri sat in the back, pretending Aaron was their chauffer. "How about my place for a nightcap?" Terri winked at Hannah.

"Ha. I'm up past my bedtime already." Hannah wasn't ready for anything beyond their new entente. Forgiveness only went so far.

"Your place it is," Aaron said, glancing at Hannah in the rearview.

Mist was already drifting across the road in places, momentarily bright in the headlights, and Hannah was reminded of stories of angels, haints, and saints from her childhood. The mists were haints, looking for something they lost but could never recover. She didn't resist as Terri reached over and held her hand, but she disconnected at her apartment and went up quietly to her room.

She'd been vomiting less and sleeping better with the exhaustion from the long hours, but now she tossed and turned, circling the same issues and unstoppable sterility coming her way. Benzo desires went unfulfilled again, but finally, the wee hours she knew so well brought sleep. As she drifted off, she realized Terri had been carrying the pills with her. Her decision had not been impulsive at all, but calculated.

CHAPTER TWENTY-EIGHT
CLEAN-UP TIME

SHE WOKE UP late, dry-mouthed and foggy from lack of rest. Showering quickly and almost running, she made it to St. Francis only a few minutes late. She was the opener that day, and there were already several homeless gathered on the sidewalk with their pets. Waking came early when you lived outside, especially with a pet. She squeezed through the small group of people and let everyone in. "I'm so sorry I'm late!"

Jules was there and followed her into the bathroom that also served as a locker room. "You okay, Miss Hannah?" Her bird eyes probed Hannah's face.

"Yes, Jules. Fine."

"You look like you dint' sleep too well." Her tone was hopeful, like a circling buzzard.

"Just out partying last night, nothing crazy. Why?" Hannah played dumb, but she needed a fix.

"You ain't foolin' me. You want Zannies, you let me know."

"You can get them?" She tried for idle curiosity, but her eyes were tightly focused.

It made Jules cackle, her suspicions confirmed. "You want 'em? I got 'em out in my cart. Clean bars, right from the stock bottle."

"Bars?" Hannah felt stupid.

Jules cackled again, "Bars. Two-milligram bars. Same as your little blue pills, but they break four ways. Thirty for one hundred and twenty."

That would be a couple months' worth, hopefully. "I'll have to go to the cash machine…"

"That's fine, just be cool about it. Leave the money behind the mirror. Next time I see you come in here, I be watchin', and I'll trade the Zannies for the money, K?"

"K." Hannah pushed out the door to start preparing for the volunteer vet coming to see patients.

"Don't say tanks, din."

Hannah heard and poked her head back in, "Thanks, then." She began to wonder if this made her a junkie but was soon too busy to think about it.

I'm not a junkie. Idleness gave her thinking time that evening. Bobbie and Camille were home, so she made popcorn and tried to watch a movie with them. Normal interaction didn't deter the thoughts intruding and circling inside, so she retired to her bedroom, claiming fatigue.

She crawled under her covers and curled up but couldn't stay still, tossing and turning as her brain reviewed the purchase of the benzo bars. *Was* she a junkie now? Junkies bought drugs on the street from dealers. Until now, she'd accepted what Aaron freely offered, but now, refusing to ask for his because of the appearance it gave, she was buying her drugs from a street dealer.

Her thoughts circled to the sterile solidarity she'd chosen with the African women. While it was part of their group effort to change the course of world natural history, the rash act set up by Terri changed the course of *her* history. She'd never intended to leave a personal legacy of family, but now she didn't even have the choice: 677 was ruthless!

Her life was a legacy of pain and hurt. She'd been conceived by an unholy ghost of a father she'd never even met, disrupted her belly mom's quest for the next whim, and, even though she had no say in the matter, destroyed the Kramers when she left—especially Prissy.

Once old enough to be in control of her life, she'd allowed an abortion, was now forcing sterility on a whole nation with two lovers (who'd not chosen her in the end), and was floundering in her very identity. She'd tried to heal Pete, at least, by using her body, but she hadn't done that just for him. Who even knew how that would turn out for his relationship with Prissy, the one couple who, as it turned out, had cared? Cared like she was their own.

The anxious circling of her life took her later and later into the night, but she stubbornly refused to take one of the new "bars," or even half of one, or even a quarter.

I'm not a junkie, cuz I can say no, she thought. But sleep wouldn't come. Finally desperate, she took a half tablet: one milligram. It was enough, and she woke late Sunday. Her hair was cold and damp from her shower as she walked in the crisp, sunny November morning. There were golds, oranges, and browns in store windows and turkeys on electronic signs. Thanksgiving was nearly upon her.

She did her habitual round, which might vary by a block or two, but she always passed the seven churches, driven by a habit, a quest for something unknown, and a call from memories of her youth with the Kramers every Sunday.

She wasn't ready to go into a church again because she knew she wasn't worthy to be in God's house amongst Christians. She'd lived so much, and carried so much baggage! As she approached Shady Grove Primitive, the old man she'd mocked stepped inside and was closing the doors as the service began, and as they shut, the sound of their singing was cut off.

He seemed to be watching her through the glass, and she knew her expression must've looked defiant as she began to round the corner towards Tumblin Pond. It wasn't defiance, but ambivalence. Suddenly she stopped, turned back, and stared. Her sudden shift caught his eye, and he stepped out, looking toward her with his head slightly tilted. Something drew her, and she began to walk to him.

There was really no one else to call or go to. She felt dirty, overwhelming shame, and regret. Shame that she had lived a lifestyle that had led to loneliness, and regret for the children she would never bear and never even knew she wanted to bear until she took the white pill. Then more shame for joining in taking that ability away from so many innocent victims in Africa!

As she walked up to the steps, unsure but following her need, she met his eyes and realized there was only kindness. He seemed to sense her void; a barrenness only God could fill.

"Welcome home, chil'." He handed her a folded sheet of the morning's service. She took it and looked down, remembering her previous rudeness. But there had been no reproach in his stance, no grudge. She walked past him and stood in an open spot in the darkly stained pews at the back.

A few people—mostly older—looked around at her, and never had she felt so white. But their looks, too, were gentle and without judgment, and their song continued with joyful expression. They were singing from memory, and Hannah could only listen. After the song was a greeting time, and the old man approached her again.

"You been comin' past here a long time 'n we've never been properly intra'duced. I'm James Weldon Foxx. Folks call me Weldon."

"My name's Hannah." She met his gentle brown eyes and added, "I don't know why I'm here."

"God knows, honey. God knows. You safe in dis' house." Only kindness returned to her.

She broke eye contact and sat, not wanting to meet a bunch of other people. The feelings in her heart and voices in her head were reeling, reaching, searching—for what, she wasn't sure. The service continued with singing and preaching, but Hannah just sat, letting the spirit of the place wash over her, feeling unworthy to enter in. The preaching somehow involved the threat of Solomon to cut a baby in half to find who the true mother of the child was, and her soul opened.

She'd let her baby get cut in half, sacrificing what they had called a fetus on the altar of convenience. She could have stopped the abortion, which destroyed an act of love, but she chose expediency and would never see her baby again, and now would never have another. Loss and depravity were upon her, and she leaned forward against the pew in front of her, tears silently dripping on the shiny hardwood floor and the seat as she slowly rocked. The closing hymn began in the Primitive acapella voices. It was a song she remembered from childhood, and she silently joined in:

Softly and tenderly Jesus is calling

Calling for you and for me
See on the portals He's waiting and watching
Watching for you and for me

Come home, come home
Ye who are weary come home
Earnestly, tenderly Jesus is calling
Calling, "O sinner come home"

The words surrounded her heart and soul, and she began to pray to a God suddenly known, begging forgiveness as she looked up to the dark open rafters. Bright light came down through the roof, and a silhouette looked down on her, a girl she knew to be her lost child, whose gaze held only love and forgiveness. Suddenly, startlingly, she found she was freed from guilt.

The light grew warmer, and she sensed another presence filling her heart. She dumped everything that had held her prisoner and felt the burdens gently lifted as she gave them over. She put her head in her hands, feeling strangely warm. Suddenly, she knew what she had to do. As the song finished, she rose before anyone else with a lump in her throat, her face wet with tears and joy shining through. Weldon, seeming to know her intention, was watching her closely. She felt other faces turn towards them as he stepped down from the small stage, his face offering peace.

She addressed him with a direct, intent gaze as they met, "I need to be clean; I need to be baptized."

"The baptismal is right here under the stage, but it's empty." The singing was dying down.

"I need to be clean," she repeated, her green eyes shining. "Now?"

"Well, I got a big bathtub and a brand-new hot water heater. We can go do it at my house, across da street," he said. "What's your whole name, child?"

"Hannah Cramer. Hannah Eliza Cramer."

"Folks, Hannah Cramer just came here today, and she laid down her burdens, and she wants to be baptized, so we gonna do it after da service in da bathtub, praise the Lord," he declared, his face beaming with joy.

Exclamations of praise broke out, and the song leader began to belt out "Glory, Glory, Hallelujah." Soon, the congregation joined her. The service ended as Hannah stepped to the narrow altar rail at the front, knelt, and prayed again, and she felt hands on her shoulders and back, hearing the prayers of saints.

More than could fit walked her over to Weldon's house, and soon she was baptized in his old clawfoot tub. Weldon put a chair beside the tub, and as he dipped her under, she was aware of his words, "Hannah Eliza Cramer, I baptize you in da name of Jesus Christ!"

She didn't really know what happened, but she came up clean, fresh, and new. The warmth was still upon her as she was wrapped in a huge white towel and sat on his living room couch with two of the older women as he dried her clothes. Others stood wherever they could.

She told them about the abortion and her upbringing, but not 677. She realized there were a lot of things she had to go make right now. "Just give it to Jesus, he'll show you," they encouraged her, and all nodded in agreement. She realized quite some time had passed, yet there was no shifting impatience. She went back to the bathroom to get dressed, then they all prayed together, with Weldon leading. When he finished, he went to the side of the room and found an almost new Bible on his bookshelf.

He wrote inside and handed her the book. "Start with Psalms and da book of John, cuz you gonna wanna know more, chil'. Psalms'll help ya sleep at night." She was disinclined to accept a gift from this humble man but had no choice after he wrote in it. She smiled and took the book. "Really, dey will. And John's book'll gitchya along in da story of Jesus."

She opened the cover and read the inscription. His tiny, neat script read:

Hannah Eliza Cramer, baptized in Jesus this day by my hand.
May you hold God close and know his blessings each day.
Rev. James Weldon Foxx, November 19, 2015

She'd not received a personal gift in many years. Her heart overflowed with love and gratitude for this little church.

"Thank you, thank you all." The lump filled her throat again as she looked around Eldon's crowded living room.

"Don't thank us, thank Jesus," one of the younger women spoke kindly. They all hugged her and made plans to see her next Sunday as they went out into the yard and parted ways.

She floated home past Tumblin in the early afternoon and back to her apartment, empty because her roommates had left for Thanksgiving. She cried tears of joy and relief on the couch until she had a headache. She had an overwhelming feeling of thankfulness that turned into a prayer and inexplicable, wonderful joy. That evening, as she circled bedtime, she realized that while her burdens were lightened, anxiety remained.

"Read Psalms for sleep," Weldon had said, and she did, but sleep didn't come. She turned to the book of John and continued to read words made suddenly clear, but her mind kept returning to old ruts slick with the muddy troubles of the world. She tried to escape them, but they stuck like river bottom clay. Prayers and calling to Jesus had cleansed her heart, but she couldn't get this mud off her feet.

Her intellect knew anxiety didn't always have an easy cure as she hesitated, then downed a half a bar of Zannie. Her heart said she was going to have to get counseling if she was going to get rest any time soon, but for now, the Zannie would have to do.

When she awoke a few hours later, she felt rested but still foggy. Yet her deceptions, what she'd done to Pete, and what she, Aaron, and Terri had done to the Nigerians, remained. She knew forgiveness had been granted in heaven, yet guilt called for action towards resolution, somehow, of these earthly crimes. She was sure, in that moment, that action was the path to peace, a path marked by the Spirit she now felt inside. If only she could follow.

She got up and went to the bathroom to wash her face, which looked swollen and tired in the mirror. She ate, took another half a bar, and sleep came more gently. Monday morning followed, and the week rushed by again, unabated by the holiday. It was weird, she thought, when her vomiting and irregular periods stopped completely. The few hot flashes she was having were nothing, almost imaginary, and it made her wonder if God had miraculously healed her last Sunday.

Aaron seemed normal as well, but Terri was looking rough, her easy flippancy gone as she rode the sudden waves of menopause brought on by the (ovarian germinal) endocrine slaughter that was 677. Without her usual comic relief, their work was more focused, and they finished early each evening. Terri was no longer carefree as she dealt with the biology of menopause and the impact it was having on everything about her.

"Having some rough days?" she asked Terri one afternoon.

Terri nodded firmly, "Sure am. This change of life stuff's not so great. Glad it's only once in a lifetime." She looked at Hannah, "How're you doing?"

"Apparently better than you. I actually feel guilty… You seem to be taking the hit for both of us, or maybe all three cuz Aaron seems pretty much okay, too." Hannah still felt new and invigorated. Every moment still glowed precious and sacred, filled with purpose. Glad menopause hadn't stolen that, her heart wanted to smile, but she hid it from Terri so it wouldn't be an annoyance.

Terri tried to keep a positive attitude in the shower each day, but her heart wasn't in it. Hannah didn't miss the shower room sensuality driven by Terri, and she wasn't interested anyway.

"How are *you* doing?" she asked Aaron as they waited for Terri one evening outside the showers. She'd sensed increased attention from him as Terri's interest in anything sexual waned.

"Well, I haven't noticed anything, except my semen seems watery."

"How would you know?" They both smiled at her question. She could tell Aaron was relieved she seemed "normal," and felt her body return the desire in his gaze for a moment. But the uncleanliness she'd left behind helped her resist the call of momentary pleasure. She knew free sex wasn't free, and the Spirit reinforced that knowledge. She didn't want to let the old chains return. Her smile faded as she looked away.

Moving forward, she knew the resolution of her relationship with Pete would have to wait. While Hannah didn't quite know how to intervene to stop the 677 project, she knew it was a priority. She would need information to present to whatever authority she determined was the most appropriate to begin the process. Detailing that information would become her first step, and she'd take it from there.

Hannah used her time before the Christmas break wisely. She carefully wrote summaries of where she was in her thesis research on the pet contraception and filed them in her cabinet at the University. She then wrote a summary of everything she knew about what Aaron and Terri had done in Africa, and what was planned for the year to come. Her first draft sounded almost like a lunatic conspiracy theory rant, so she had to start over several times for it to make sense to someone reading from the outside. The outline of their work on campus included the pilfered raw product. As far as she knew, only the three of them knew it was hidden behind a panel in Aaron's office closet. She made no effort to justify her own actions, making it clear she was a willing participant.

As she began to detail the meetings at the conferences and how the RU-AT-677 would be packaged in vitamin supplements, she realized how compartmentalized the whole thing was. She only knew a few names, the folks at UF, and several from the PBCA meetings. The balance sub-group people were just positions and resources to her, mostly anonymous. Insertion of the RU-AT-667 pills was going to be handled by an executive at a production contractor, but she had no idea how they were going to be delivered and subdivided into millions of bottles.

Despite the compartmentalization, she felt like she had a lot of information. She also included Google aerial images of the warehouse factory, a few pictures of the setup inside, and a photo of the three of them together at Civilization after the first production slug. She saved all the information onto two mini SD cards, one of which she put into her cell phone. The other she taped to the inside of her bed rail.

During the time it took to do all of this, she continued her regular schedule but remained withdrawn from her colleagues. Guilt made it feel wrong, but her spirit said it was right. She avoided socialization with Aaron and Terri, claiming she'd felt fatigued since taking the 677, and it was true, she did feel tired much of the time. Terri seemed to be feeling better and didn't seem to mind now when Aaron's hand rested on her thigh as they drove along, with Hannah riding shotgun.

Each Sunday, she went straight to Shady Grove and sang her heart out with the Primitives. The sermons were old-fashioned, but surprisingly applicable to the world she knew. Hannah's motives, seeking God, were clear to her new church family as they became closer. But sometimes she felt awfully white in the brown-skinned congregation even if they were bound by faith. Regardless, she was determined to savor the fellowship even though it probably wouldn't be lifelong.

CHAPTER TWENTY-NINE
OOPS!

On Friday morning, Hannah returned to the campus clinic for a follow-up from her visit before the conference, which resulted in orders for an ultrasound to evaluate her reproductive tract for endometriosis, cystic ovaries, and the like. When the call about results came, it was a nurse who wanted to arrange for Hannah to meet with the new resident and her staff doctor. "Why can't you just give me the results over the phone?" Hannah said, irritated. "It's not like I don't understand reproduction."

"I know, but they want to meet with you to review the findings. Do you have time next week to come in?"

"Whatever works best for you," she sighed.

Hannah met with the two doctors on the following Tuesday morning. Monday was their longest day at the warehouse, but fatigue and half a Zannie had provided good sleep the night before. She was fidgety in the waiting room but became still as the resident explained the findings in a small office. "The ultrasound showed atrophy of your ovaries. Atrophy is when—"

"I know what atrophy is," Hannah's voice was quiet, intense.

"Okay…so there was atrophy of your ovaries, which is compatible with menopause," she stated bluntly. Hannah expected that from the 677, but not what came next. "But it turns out you're also pregnant."

"Wha…? How?" She immediately knew how stupid she sounded but was too confused to care—her world was reeling. *Pregnant? Menopause?* She knew pregnancy required a corpus luteum at least for the first ten weeks. "How far along?"

"It looks like fourteen weeks." The doctors watched her closely.

"How can I be in menopause, have an IUD, and be pregnant?" She assumed they were mistaken and couldn't help but sound slightly annoyed.

"You tell us. Never seen anything like it," said the attending, Dr. Roberts. "We can certainly run hormonal assays, but the only other way to see what's going on is to biopsy your ovaries, and I would advise against that with the baby. We do need to remove your IUD, though, and it appears to be accessible."

"I've checked the string; I know it's in place." With all the irregularities she'd had, she had checked everything she could think of…except for a pregnancy test. As reality set in, she couldn't help but think it might be a miracle she was carrying, and a strange smile flitted across her face.

"We can remove that today if you'd like. It's riding low in your cervix, which is probably why you were able to get pregnant. Is it safe to assume you're keeping the baby?" They had noticed her smile.

I have to; it's my last chance. The thought came unbidden, and she realized how deeply the loss of options had affected her after she took the 677.

Removing the IUD was simple, and afterwards, the doctor droned on about further diagnostics, but Hannah wasn't listening. She agreed that close follow-up was important and scheduled another appointment to monitor hormones and the baby's development before escaping to the street.

Her head was spinning. She was effectively a clinical test of 677 and early pregnancy. The timing must have been perfect as far as not causing an early death of the corpus luteum and spontaneous abortion. Pete's baby inside her changed things, but who knew if the baby would survive or even be normal? Everything in babies grew from germinal stem cells.

For Hannah, Terri's little group experiment now reinforced just how flawed the whole plan to save the world was. This waking nightmare of not knowing if her baby would be normal was proof that saving the whole world could wait for something less hideous.

CHAPTER THIRTY

REELING

IT WAS HANNAH'S turn to be distracted and irritable as they worked each afternoon. Even though Terri was obviously feeling better, Hannah avoided and resisted any in-depth interaction. On her bathroom mirror each morning, Hannah looked at the picture they'd given her of the bump in her womb, and it drove the sudden deep concern about the potential effects of 677 exposure on her baby. She took extra care about her protective gear and had little to discuss in the shower.

Reeling from the knowledge of the baby, which also made her try to stop her self-prescribed meds, she was sleepless. Finally, she restarted just a quarter of a Zannie bar each night, and clarity started to return after a good night's sleep on Wednesday night. They were planning to halt production for the holidays, and the only thing she could think of was to buy time. She'd call in sick next Monday, the beginning of the last full week before the holiday, and buy an additional week to consider her options and figure out what to do.

She acted distracted and irritable throughout the run Friday evening. When she called in sick for Monday, it would be more convincing. Saturday, she stayed busy at St. Francis, and Sunday morning, she was back at Shady Grove, singing and praying with the believers. Weldon preached about Matthew 18, where Jesus talks about correcting a fellow believer, and Hannah listened closely as she sought help from God.

"As believers, we are called to go to our brothers and sisters first, face to face, as we seek to correct them. After that, after trying twice even, then Jesus calls us to treat them as you would anyone else, however that might be. You have done your duty." Weldon preached with clarity, not with his conversational vernacular, which Hannah had grown used to.

Hannah wondered if his words were the guidance she was so desperately seeking from God, and pondered that off and on until a Zannie brought sleep.

CHAPTER THIRTY-ONE
TRACKING HANNAH

AFTER SHE'D CALLED Aaron on Monday morning, sick and full of apologies, she went to the used bookstore to scope out baby books. She was about to decide on one when she smelled Jules before she saw her. Hannah hadn't noticed the odor while at St. Francis with all its rich animal smells. Jules had crept up and was looking at Hannah's perusals and cawed, "Who's having a baby?" Hannah felt her beady eyes sliding up and down her body and realized those hands had touched her pills.

"Not me," she said too fast. "Missed you yesterday at the clinic."

Jules cackled, ignoring her implied inquiry. "Whose foolin' who? You go right by me on yo' way to Shady Grove." She leered knowingly and added, "Not many things make a junkie go to church."

Dammit! Somehow, she could see the truth in Hannah's eyes, sensing her discomfort. "I'm not a junkie," she whispered.

"I seen you goin' by, walkin' in that place like a Zombie. A Zombie on Zannies!" she whispered back loudly. Then she leaned closer and lowered her voice again, "Don't worry, honey, your secret's safe with me. I won't tell old Mr. Weldon what you up to." She cackled again. "Gotta take care of each other."

Hannah was infuriated, but Jules sensed her cue and quickly scuttled out of the store. Hannah watched her untie her little wiener dog from the bike rack outside and look back through the glass with a wink before pushing her cart down the sidewalk.

Hannah looked around to make sure there was no one else she knew, then bought the book, *Mayo Clinic's Guide to Your First Baby*. She made sure it was double-sacked so that the title wouldn't show through the plastic.

As she came down the block towards her apartment, she saw a stranger emerge from the stairway and go sit in a car across the street. Hannah slipped her cell phone out of her pocket, ready to dial 911. As she approached her building, the man just sat. She sensed him getting out of the car after she passed her stairway entrance and glanced back at him, her heart starting to race.

"Miss Cramer?"

She turned to face him. He was tall and slender, wearing jeans and a button-down shirt, and silver hair showed under a straw cowboy hat. He was vaguely familiar. "Yes?" She held up her phone and unlocked the screen.

The man put his hands out and pointed to a badge pinned on his belt. "I'm a Deputy Sheriff, ma'am." He then slowly approached and said, "Newton County Sheriff's Office, Deputy Allen Miller." He held out his hand, his face friendly. Hannah stepped back, eyes narrowed, looking for danger.

"Do I know you?" She was sure she did.

The deputy let his hand down, and she saw his gun now on his right hip, along with a badge shining on his belt. "I don't know, ma'am, unless it was through dog training, and I think I'd remember you if it was." She blinked at the compliment. "I'm from Newton County, Missouri, near Joplin."

Uncle Allen? Pete's brother!

Amazement opened her mouth as she remembered, and he looked concerned. She shut her mouth but couldn't help blinking several times before she asked, "Is everything okay?"

"Yes, ma'am." He studied her. "I just wanted to ask you a few questions about a case."

"Is it Pete?" she asked.

He blinked. "Pete?"

She realized he didn't know who she was, but there was no going back.

Something tied to her childhood, or he wouldn't be here. She crossed her arms. "How'd you find me, Uncle Allen?"

As a child, her hair had been light blonde, not the shimmering flaxen he saw now, but she had the same intense green eyes. He blinked again as recognition dawned. "Jain? Little Jain? Jain with no last name? I'll be damned." He was the other reason she liked dogs, and memories of riding in his pickup with a dog lying in the back seat suddenly seemed like yesterday.

She leaned into him, and they hugged tightly. "You made it." He stepped back to look at her again. "To adulthood, I mean." They were both smiling as they stared at each other. "Pete's okay; everything's okay. I'm working on a cold case. The detectives were all busy, so they sent the old guy."

She realized they must look silly, standing out there in the street when she was supposed to be sick.

"Come inside. You gotta tell me what's going on." She led him up the steps and around the inner courtyard, breathless as she trotted up the stairs.

"This is beautiful." Allen was admiring the huge old oak that shaded the courtyard and building.

"Yeah. I'm blessed to get to live here. I have roommates, but they're gone for the holidays. Down to Key West this time." As she talked, her mind raced. She expected his did too and gestured to the table. "Have a seat. You want a glass of water or a Diet Coke?"

"No, thanks," he hesitated and smiled, "Ma'am."

"You can call me Hannah; that's my new name. Hannah Eliza Cramer, with a 'C.'" She grabbed a can of soda, popping the lid as they sat at the table. "I'm a senior now at UF, and I'm working on my PhD thesis. Animal birth control."

"Time flies! Hard to believe little Jain is about to graduate college." He shook his head, then continued, "And already workin' on a thesis! It sounds like you're keeping the faith on spay/neuter." His face beamed.

"Yep. How are you doing?" She was mentally sorting possibilities for his visit.

"I'm doing great." He pulled out his wallet. "This is Dutch, my old dog. He tracks and does HRD." He showed her a picture of the big old red dog alongside an adolescent pup of the same breed. "The younger guy is the next generation, Butch."

"What's HRD?"

"Human remains detection. Sorry."

"Oh, no problem. I love Redbones."

"You got good taste," he paused, smiling. "I want to catch up, but I bet you're wondering why I'm here."

She laughed nervously. "Yep."

"I think I know why I'm here, now that I know who *you* are. I'm trying to identify a body we found awhile back. We know she's a she, and her DNA recently matched to yours in the Homeland Security database. Actually, Hannah, she was your mother. So here I am."

"My mother?" Hannah felt relief that Pete and Prissy were okay, but she wasn't sure how she felt about her mother. She stroked her face absently before focusing back on him. "So, my belly mom is dead. Why couldn't you ID her?"

He explained about the body's discovery several years ago, and Pete's role in that. "The reason she's in the DNA database enough to pick you up is that she was a murder victim. We haven't had any leads until now."

"We had to go through high-level security for the project I'm working on, and DNA submission was a part of that. Supposedly voluntary, but not really."

His fingers unconsciously tapped his Camels. "Now that we know who you are, we can begin to trace back her moves. Do you happen to know your biological mother's name, and if you had sisters?"

"Lisa Hartley, and my dad was Leonard. And I know I had brothers and sisters, but I never really knew them. I don't know how many kids my dad had with other women, either. I guess I don't really even know if he was my dad."

"That's okay, Hannah. Just having her name will be a big help. Before this, we had nothing to go on." He pulled a small notebook out of his shirt pocket, where it shared space with his Camels.

"Pete's going to flip out when he hears about you."

"How is Pete?" Suddenly eager, she added, "and Prissy?"

"Well, about that…" He leaned slightly towards her. "They split up not too long ago. Pete cheated on her, he says for the first time, and he couldn't keep it secret."

She swallowed nervously, knowing she was the cause and asked, "What happened?"

"He went to some conference in Kansas City. It happened there, some young girl. It was preyin' on him, and I told him not to tell her. He did anyway, and Prissy flipped out. She still lives at the river house, you remember?"

"Of course," she said, trying to keep her voice even. "Where did Pete go?"

"He's living in that small apartment at the back of the vet clinic. Says it makes life easier for emergencies."

"Are they divorced?"

"No, but they filed. It's maybe just as well. They haven't been close ever since… Well, ever since you were taken away. Prissy never got over it. It's like something died inside her. My Janice died from cancer, but Pete lost Prissy to a broken heart." His hand made an involuntary reach for his pocket of Camels.

It was worse than Hannah could imagine. What she'd given Pete–shared with him–was for them, not Prissy, but it was now a nail in the coffin of her foster parents' marriage. She needed to gather her thoughts, and they were running wild.

"Uncle Allen, there's something else I need to talk to you about. Do you want to go outside on the balcony or out somewhere for lunch so you can smoke?" She knew her nervousness was coming through, too; couldn't help it.

"Uh, sure, I wouldn't mind a smoke."

"Those things'll kill you," Hannah laughed, remembering how she used to try to steal his cigarettes and hide them. She got up and said, "There's plenty of room on the balcony, and I have salad makings."

"Sure, why not."

She led him through her room to the balcony with its small table and said, "I'll bring you an ashtray."

Hannah could immediately smell the familiar sharp tobacco as he lit up and sat at the small table. She brought him an empty bean can to catch his ashes, then went back to the kitchen while he smoked.

Hannah came back out with two big bowls of salad greens and ranch dressing, and they sat to eat. He crushed out the cigarette and then removed his hat while she prayed, his head shiny and bald above the hat line.

Allen waited for her to talk as they ate, occasionally looking over at her face as she watched a squirrel in the tree near her corner balcony. He was eating some, but she just picked.

Finally, she gathered her thoughts and courage, meeting his eyes. "I've done a couple of things I'm not proud of... I don't want you to judge," she paused, looking at the tree now instead of him.

"It's okay, Hannah, I'm out of my jurisdiction." He gave her a wry smile, encouraging her to continue. She returned his smile nervously, then looked away. After a second, Allen leaned back in the rattan chair and looked at the tree, too, waiting again.

"I'm the reason they broke up." She felt immediate relief but waited for him to attack as she watched his face.

He digested that for a minute, then turned to look at her. "That was years ago, Hannah. You can't—"

"No." She made a little cutting motion with her hand, met his eyes, then looked down at the bowl in front of her. "Not that."

He waited. Nearby, the squirrel flicked its tail and hopped to a closer branch.

Hannah sighed before continuing, "I mean, I'm the young girl. The one who slept with him." She still couldn't look at Allen. Finally, he pushed his salad bowl aside and lit another Camel.

"I need one, too." He looked at her, then lit a second off the end of his and handed it over.

"Tell me what happened." Both took a long drag, and she felt tears, suppressing a cough at the unfamiliar burn. She realized he must have heard worse over his many years of policing and was encouraged.

"I mean, first, I wounded their marriage as a kid, then I finished it off this summer." She wiped her eyes with her hand and left them shut. Then she blinked back up at him and waited for a response.

"The first time wasn't your fault," he tapered off with pursed lips, nodding slightly.

"Maybe not, but it feels like it. And the second time…" She told him the story.

"It takes two to tango. It's not all your fault, Hannah Jain." He paused to consider, "Did he know it was you?"

"No! Of course not. I never thought I'd see him again. He said it was all but over between them, but it's never going to be over. I was trying to heal him." She felt trapped and took another drag. The burning in her throat was penance, the toxins in her blood a punishment. He took a drag as well while he paused to consider.

"Look, Hannah, I can keep a secret. He'll never know I know." *Allen the priest*, she thought. "And you should probably move on."

"That's just it. I can't." She waved the ciggy. "I'm pregnant." Despair and frustration washed over her as she said the words aloud. She looked at him dry-eyed, feeling like she was going to lose her mind, but he remained calm as he swallowed, took her remaining cigarette, crushed it out in his bowl, and slid it carefully back into the pack.

"I don't smoke anyway." She shook her head in disgust at herself, then leaned back in her chair, mirroring Allen as they both watched the squirrel for a while.

"Are you going to tell him?" he finally asked.

"I don't know. It was an accident. I had an IUD; they're supposed to be foolproof." Allen seemed embarrassed as he looked down, his face a little red—TMI.

"I wasn't accusing you. I was just wondering." He glanced at her. She realized her tone had been sharp.

"Sorry," she said. "I maybe had a fantasy of giving them the baby once I found out, but not if they aren't together anymore."

He considered that while he smoked. "Maybe the baby could still bring them back, like a Phoenix."

She tried to picture a situation where that could happen. Her deep embarrassment kept her from thinking too far along those lines, though, because each scenario meant facing Prissy. "Doubt it," she said.

Allen nodded slightly but said nothing as they sat and ruminated on her options. After a minute or so, he carefully crushed out his cigarette, too. "Second-hand smoke ain't good for babies either," he said as he carefully slid it back in the pack as well.

She wasn't about to bring up Zannies and babies.

Finally, he stretched his leg and reached into his pocket, shifting things around. His hand came out with a large coin. It was worn, and he flipped it slowly between his fingers while he considered.

"When my wife, your Aunt Janice, died of cancer years before you were born, your…" Allen paused. 'Father' didn't seem right. "Pete… gave me this coin a few months later. It's silver and has a Phoenix on one side and a cross on the other. He explained that it meant you could rise from the ashes of anything through the power of Christ." He took a deep breath before continuing, "I ain't much on church like Pete is, but I see God in things like that squirrel and the beautiful tulip tree he's climbin' on. And I talk to God in the forest, and at sunset, and places like that. Never felt comfortable in a church filled with people, though." Then he sat back for a few moments, letting all that sink in.

Then he leaned more towards her and said, "You must feel pretty burnt to ashes right now, overwhelmed. I want you to have this coin and remember why Pete gave it to me. I was able to rise from the ashes, and it's been a constant reminder. With God's help, you can rise too. He has the answers." Allen set the coin on the table, then slid it over in front of her. Hannah remained silent but fingered the coin.

"I don't even have to tell him right away who we found in the river bottoms. I can just say it was a drug thing, which it'll probably end up being." She listened but didn't speak.

"I'm not at all sure what you should do, but think about things and give me a call if you want me to tell him. I'll let you know when I find out more about Lisa's death." He could wait all day, but it was hard without a cigarette. He silently tapped his finger on the table.

Suddenly, the squirrel started chirring loudly, and a jay swooped by, screeching. Hannah jerked out of her reverie. Allen wasn't in one.

"It's the cat on the next balcony over," she explained. She picked up the coin and studied it, then stood and put it in her pocket. "Thanks, Uncle Allen. You gonna be okay without it?"

"You need it more than me right now, Hannah Jain. You can give it back to me when this is over. Hope it helps."

If only he knew, she thought about the 677 mess. "It already has... You already have. Who knew when I woke up this morning we would be meeting here, like this?"

"Same here." He smiled slightly, picked up his hat, and placed it carefully on his head, looking thoughtful.

She saw him to the door.

"I don't know what I'm going to do, exactly, but we'll probably meet again soon. Maybe I should come home for Christmas?" She looked up at him.

"If you do, I'll be there for you, Hannah." They hugged tightly.

Hannah walked him down the steps, watching as he drove away. She heard the blue jay around the corner and realized she'd left the salads on the table. It was probably too late, but she trotted back up the steps anyway.

CHAPTER THIRTY-TWO
SEEKING COUNSEL

HANNAH GAVE A deep sigh at seeing bits of salad strewn across the tabletop, but nothing had been knocked off. She knew the jay was probably the culprit and shot him a dirty look. He'd figured out long ago that the cat couldn't get over to her side, but the squirrel wasn't that smart and stayed away when the cat was out.

As she dumped the salad and washed the bowls, she felt an urge to get out, to fly away like the salad-stealing bird.

She walked east towards Tumblin and Shady Grove, away from campus. Between her baby and the 677 project, the baby was more urgent. Production runs of 677 had almost a year to go, and the baby had six months, but she was gonna be showing a lot sooner than that.

The Primitive was empty in the early afternoon sun, but a dog was barking from the overgrown porch of an abandoned house across the street from Weldon's. There was movement on the porch, and through the winter-thinned bushes, Hannah recognized Jules staring out. She'd never seen her there before, but she'd never walked by during the week, either.

Jules had a clear view of the front of Shady Grove and Weldon's little house. *No wonder she'd seen everything.* The dog stopped suddenly, and Jules hunkered down. Hannah kept walking, fighting the urge to rat her out. She might need Zannies again, just to sleep. Jules was her source now, which freed her from asking and accepting from Aaron. Yet Jules had called her a junkie. Was that true?

It wouldn't be if she were in counseling, and the meds were prescribed. They didn't rule her life. She was sickened by the thought of putting something in her mouth that had been touched by those hands. And yet…she hadn't thrown out her purchase.

She walked faster, heading east instead of swinging north along her usual route past St. Francis, empty on a Monday, then turned south. News of Lisa's death freshened memories from her seven-year-old self, and Jules's similarity to her mother made her wonder if she was becoming her mother. Jules's cackle rattled in her mind. Dealers, junkies, and the fog of benzos were familiar thanks to Lisa, but were distracting from things brought by Allen that demanded her attention.

She realized she needed to ask God for help; that's what Weldon would advise. She needed a place to pray, here and now, and another church was coming up. It was a long, low rectangular building surrounded by shade trees, not unlike Shady Grove, but a generation or two newer. The double front doors had burglar bars. Undeterred, she walked up and gave one a try.

To her surprise, it opened easily into a dim interior. She looked around the simple rooms, noticing a foyer that led directly into a preaching room with folding chairs arranged in rows facing a small stage. Everything seemed empty, so she walked up to the kneeling rail in front. She was aware of the new weight in her womb but still moved gracefully to her knees and leaned forward on her elbows, hands folded, trying to clear her mind.

God… God… God… nothing else came. She pictured Pete, Allen, Prissy, Terri, Aaron, the warehouse, the baby bump, Jules, Weldon… She tried to picture Nigerian mothers, too. *God… Jesus?* She realized all those people in her life were loved by Jesus, to whom she was calling. Lisa, Lenny, all her foster families, too. She couldn't focus on Lisa, and Lenny was a shadow, but several fosters passed through her mind.

Pete and Prissy loomed large, surrounded by a mass of dark Nigerian faces glowing in a warm light that, weirdly, seemed to connect to the baby in her womb. *Jesus, help me. I'm sorry I've hurt Pete and Prissy. Lord, I've hurt so many. I don't know what to do, where to go, or how to live. Please help me make it right. Just help.*

Just help.

She was without thought, just waiting. Weldon's sermon about going to a brother or sister if you have an issue came to her: Talk to them. It didn't feel like a revelation, but it was the only thought she had, the only nudge. And right now, she had issues hidden from Aaron and Terri, and Pete and Prissy.

What she knew was that God would be with her, and she needed to act. Nothing in her life would change or stop on its own. Her heart suddenly knew the path led to Joplin. For what, she didn't yet know.

Thank you, Jesus. The gratitude for direction came from her heart, and she leaned back from the rail, then stood.

As she left the building, she realized the neighborhood wasn't the greatest, but no one seemed to notice her leaving. It was like she was a ghost, and she didn't even recall exactly how she got there. She walked quickly past boarded-up houses, following her instinct on which streets to take.

As she came to Depot Park and then Main Street, she was relieved to cut back over to familiar Tumblin Pond and make her way home.

CHAPTER THIRTY-THREE
JOPLIN BOUND

GAINESVILLE TO JOPLIN could take a day if you didn't need sleep or rest, but Hannah needed both. She'd downloaded an audiobook to help make the drive time pass, but so far, she'd just listened to Indigo Girls and other music as she rolled down the highway. Farms and forest passed, and her mind kept returning to her last meeting with Aaron before she left.

He'd been protective and fatherly as she'd told him her plans to travel home for Christmas. Not knowing about the baby, he didn't understand her sudden need to go home, but she'd stayed upbeat and positive. As she told him goodbye in his office, his final words were distracted, "We'll be hitting it hard after the New Year, so be ready to roll when you get back, and call if you need anything on your trip."

"Yeah," she'd replied. "I'll be fine."

His reminder didn't sit well. She didn't want to return and face the wrongness of the project whose passion, for her, had morphed into a desire to stop it. She just wanted to leave it all behind, even blow it up. But until the baby, it had been the culmination of her entire college career, even her entire life, not something she could just walk away from.

It had been a way to fight back against the wanton procreation that had brought her into the world, a type of atonement to erase her personal history. She wanted to counter the pain that Lisa had inflicted, pain that forged the floundering reality that had been hers, despite her name change and new start in Florida. Pain that had driven her to barren relationships with people who seemed unable to really love. Ultimately, though, that pain led her to Jesus, who was founding a new reality deep within her: a child, forged in human passion but purposed by the loving discernment of her new heart.

She realized her current reality had become hunger as she approached Birmingham, and her little rented Nissan's needle pointed to empty. Exiting I-20, she drove until the neighborhood improved some, and she smelled barbeque in the cold December air. It was coming from a family-owned gas station/restaurant, and on impulse, she swerved in.

She stretched as she filled the tank, then entered the little store. The smell of smoking meat made her stomach growl, and barbequed smoked sausage was the afternoon's special. When the large, long-skirted and bonneted lady behind the counter offered her a taste, she almost refused.

Being vegan, or at least vegetarian, had been common in the radical contraceptive movement. Even before that, she'd tended towards the more enlightened who chose the countercultural vegan culinary evolution. Now, on this journey to her childhood, memories of barbeque pulled hard at her stomach strings.

The woman smiled in triumph as Hannah took the sample piece and delicately pulled it off the toothpick with her teeth. Decadent flavor burst into her mouth, and she chewed the sample thoroughly before she swallowed.

"Our sausage plate today is only eight-fifty and includes your water there," the lady said, pointing to the bottle Hannah had selected.

"How can I resist?" she asked, smiling ironically. There were two sides, and Hannah selected deviled eggs and baked beans with bacon, feeling a little triumphant with this freedom she'd claimed.

She took a seat in the corner of the empty dining area along the windows and savored each bite. She could go back to being vegan tomorrow, or not. For today, she would enjoy this further rejection of the 677 society as she journeyed home on an unknown mission from God.

Unable to accept the extreme sugar load of regular soda but still nourishing the freedom from dietary rules, she'd bought a 44-ounce Diet Coke.

She hoped it would overcome the sleepiness brought on by the unfamiliar but comforting meal. If nothing else, bathroom stops would keep her awake as she proceeded westward.

As she drove, though, sleepiness was overcome by the thoughts returning to her head. She realized Lisa had been stalking her all her life and was the force that had succeeded in yanking her from the Kramers. She'd thought her trust had been destroyed by the Kramers, and she'd been unable to form healthy bonds with any family that followed.

She'd believed her family wasn't waiting, that they'd given up and moved on. It was an evil deception caused by the snaky tendrils of Lisa's vain intent, an evil she imagined was nothing more than Lisa's attempt to validate herself and her motherhood using the power of the family "justice" system.

If the system said she deserved her child, then it must be so, but Hannah was just a pawn in Lisa's game. A mother who truly loved her could never have yanked her away after all those years. Anyone with even an iota of compassion couldn't do that to the Kramers, much less their own daughter. Layered thick with evil and fancy words like reunification and family, it was a sick endorsement of nothing more than Lisa's vanity.

As she thought about it, Hannah realized that it wasn't just Lisa, but a whole system. One that didn't just allow Lisa's evil perpetrations, but hardily endorsed them with random orders that must grate at the very foundations of heaven's justice. Thinking of trying to change that system almost made her head explode. She had to focus on righting *her* system, her family, and the journey today.

Her family was too messed up by Lisa, and really by her, she realized, to ever make right. Something was going to happen when she got to Joplin, but she had no idea what that would be. Certainly, Jesus, who had motivated her to travel there, would guide her in love. The closeness and trust she felt in him was the one thing she knew for sure to be real in all this. Somehow, he would see her through. For today, that would have to be enough.

The bigger stuff, like changing the system, was beyond her.

CHAPTER THIRTY-FOUR

BACK IN TOUCH

"Yes?" Pete always answered unknown numbers carefully. He hated spammers.

"Pete?" It was a young woman's voice, and he wasn't expecting a call from any young woman, let alone one who would call him Pete.

"Yes, this is Pete. How can I help you?" he was terse, clipped.

"Pete… It's Hannah."

"Hannah?" He was taken off guard. "From Gainesville?"

"Yes, me. I hope there's not a lot of Hannahs," she laughed.

"Oh, no. You're the only one, Hannah. It's great to hear from you." Pete was surprised at the relief in his voice. He'd missed her more than he'd thought, dreaming of her often. She had his entire attention. Theirs was his only intimacy in years, and the brevity of their encounter belied its profound impact. "What're you up to?"

"Well, actually, I'm on my way to Joplin."

"Here?" Disbelief mixed with excitement made his voice pitch upwards.

"Yes." He could hear her smile, but as she continued, her tone became more reserved, "I'm staying at a hotel in Ft. Smith tonight. I was hoping we could meet tomorrow. Maybe for supper?"

"Of course. Prissy—my wife—and I are fully separated, so my nights are pretty quiet." He'd longed for their blissful ecstasy and would do anything to see her again despite the lingering guilt. "Right before Christmas, business tapers off. I'd still have to take an emergency if it were critical… But otherwise, yes, I'm free." Hopefully, he didn't sound desperate.

"Okay, great. You have my number now, how about you call me when you finish up tomorrow night?" Her tone remained more reserved.

"Well, yes, that'd be fine. I missed you." Each heartbeat thrummed in his chest. He never thought he'd see her again, and now her voice brought a firmness in his groin. "How'd you find my number?"

"Actually, that's a long story. I'll tell you tomorrow night." She was about to hang up.

"Okay, sounds good. I guess I'll see you then." He wanted to keep talking but didn't push.

They disconnected, and Pete laid back on the couch where he'd been. His mind was racing. He hadn't even had the chance to ask how she was before she'd cut off the conversation.

By nature, he considered himself to be fairly neat, but as he looked around his studio apartment through a woman's eye for the first time, it was clearly a bachelor pad. He spent the rest of the evening cleaning it up. He had been going to a laundromat down the street, but he washed his sheets and clothes in the clinic washing machine, hoping it wouldn't make them smell doggy. He was around it so much and had gone noseblind to it years ago.

He finally laid down around midnight, trying to sleep. But of course, his mind wandered. Why was she back? Did she think of him often? She hadn't said she missed him, and her tone was familiar but not yearning. Certainly, if he was going on a trip to see her and was as close to Joplin as she was, he would have kept driving if he was intent on resuming a relationship.

The truth of that hit him: He couldn't assume anything. Maybe she was here on a Christmas trip, and he was an afterthought—a courtesy call. He could've been her father, but she wasn't too embarrassed about his age to call and get his hopes up.

He realized thoughts like these could go on all night and decided to read the Bible some. Often, it calmed him. When the Bible didn't work, he went online and started worked on a continuing education course he'd been studying. "Feline Diabetes: A Clinical Update" was not exciting at all, and he slogged through it until his lids became heavy.

He didn't even think of praying and hadn't in months. Other than a brief "God help me" during surgery here and there and a ritualistic thanks for his meal each evening, he'd not even been praying for Prissy and their relationship. When he drifted off, he was thinking of Hannah and their one night together.

Even the challenging and funny things were just marking time the next day, and Mikki, his lead Registered Technician, wouldn't let up.

"Hot date tonight?" Her tone was sarcastic. He knew she didn't approve of his break-up with Prissy, and they all knew he was staying in the clinic's intern apartment.

"Nunya." He gave her nothing more than a smile.

She smiled back and presented a big orange tabby for an exam. "It must be something, cuz you sure ain't here today."

"It's just that Christmas is getting close. Been thinking about family." In a way, Hannah was family.

Her dark eyebrow raised in Spock-like inquiry, "It seems like you're more distracted than that."

She knew him too well. If he said 'nunya' now, she'd know she was right, so he silently examined the cat with the attention he could muster. When he finished, he asked, "So, why is this kitty here today?"

"Maybe for the mass on his shoulder?" Mikki smirked at him.

Pete was flustered as he palpated a mass he'd missed. It was only a half-centimeter, but he never missed things like that...or hoped he didn't. If it *was* cancer, it may have spread to the lymph nodes, which could then be swollen, so he was deliberate as he carefully reexamined the kitty. Thankfully, his fingers found nothing more.

The error cleared his mind, and he focused on work the rest of the day. Even Mikki couldn't fault him. He said his goodbyes earlier than usual after checking with her to make sure nothing was forgotten. "So, is it a hot date, doc?" She pressed, eyes narrowing as she assessed his reaction.

"No, just a colleague from the birth control conference stopping through town. I'm hoping to get an update; learn something new. She's working on the birth control medication I told you about. Might make spay/neuter obsolete."

"She?" Mikki smirked. "Have fun with your *update*." She made little quote signs in the air around the word. Pete faked a little growl, but he was too excited to be mad.

He went to his apartment, not even having to leave the clinic. It was still strange to him after all the years of driving home to the river house. He thought of Prissy, alone, and then pushed her out of his mind as he got ready to shower.

The little built-in shower was annoying every time he used it. It was too narrow for him to even bend over, so he had to lift each leg to wash his feet. The cheap shower curtain flapped in the breeze, letting water run out on the floor, and the head gave off little more than a trickle.

But the anticipation of meeting with Hannah made all those annoyances fade. He kept thinking of her face, her wonderful hair, and mostly her intense, loving, almost admiring green eyes. He'd longed for her, but never expected she would re-enter his life. It was time to call her back.

"Hi, Pete," her voice was measured, clear.

"Hi, Hannah." Her tone gave him pause, and he left off the "from Gainesville." "Did you make it to Joplin?"

"Yes, Pete, I did." She sounded awkward now, "I met with your brother, Allen, this morning, and he thinks we should meet you at your clinic. I thought I'd bring take-out."

"My brother? Is something wrong?" Allen being a cop, it was the first thing that came to his mind. "What's up with my brother?"

"No, nothing's wrong, really. I met him when he was down in Florida, and we wanted to share a few things that came up." *An affair with my brother from another father?* Pete didn't know what to think. *Obviously, she goes for older men. How'd she meet my brother?* His mind jumped into overdrive. *Has she done something wrong? Is she in trouble with the law? Is she connected with the body Allen found?*

"Oh?" He tried to keep his inflection from rising, but it did.

"Yeah, I know that sounds cryptic." He heard a nervous laugh. "There's nothing wrong, so don't panic. We'll be at your place soon and explain. We'll get Chinese." He and Allen always went out for Chinese.

"We? He's coming, too?" He couldn't stop the disappointment that crept in, making him feel like a teenager in heat.

"Yeah, he wants to join us tonight." She was matter-of-fact.

"Oh," Pete said again. He didn't understand what was happening and reluctantly added, "Okay. Well... He knows where the back door to the apartment is."

Pete paced around his rooms while he waited for them. Finally, after he heard the last of the staff members leave, he went out and sat on the tailgate of his pickup, swinging his legs some as he watched the evening come. It was cool out, but he didn't really feel it. Finally, two cars rolled up: Allen in his pickup and Hannah in her little rented Nissan. They got out, and he slid off the tailgate.

"Hi, ya'll." He nodded slightly at Allen, then looked at Hannah, who smiled gently.

"Hi, Pete," they replied together, and Hannah exchanged a brief, nervous smile with Allen.

It was a little awkward, hugging Hannah. She hugged him back but didn't melt into his arms, nor did he want her to with Allen there. Her green eyes were the same, her hair soft where his hand tangled lightly, and she looked intently into his eyes for a moment, then stepped back.

He looked at Allen, recalled his earlier thoughts about Hannah and older men, then stepped over to give him a brief bro-hug.

"Let's go inside. We got Chinese. On me." Allen didn't usually buy, either. Allen and Hannah seemed comfortable together. *Were* they lovers? He couldn't help but wonder.

He resisted the urge to ask or confront them and led them to the door instead.

Inside, the food smelled great, but his appetite was gone. Allen and Hannah took off their jackets and sat around the little kitchen table. He grabbed them beers, but Hannah declined, so he offered her a Diet Coke, and she took it. He sat, and they faced each other, all a little hesitant. His leg bounced furiously, causing little waves in their drinks.

"So, what gives?" He tried to sound casual but knew his tone was accusatory. He looked at Hannah, who looked at Allen.

Allen cleared his throat. "Remember years back, the body we found on the river?"

"Yes…"

"Well, a DNA match finally came up."

"Really?" It had been a long time. He looked at Hannah, wondering how this related to her. She smiled nervously and looked back at Allen.

"So, I had to follow up because it was a parent match. Long story short, Pete, it was Hannah's mom. Lisa Hartley." He waited, then said, "It looks like a drug deal gone bad."

Lisa? It started to dawn, but he couldn't take it in. He looked at Hannah, who looked back, her green eyes afraid. *Green eyes.* Recognition came, and he abruptly straightened.

"I'm sorry, Pete," her words were sincere as she reached out to comfort him, but he slid his chair back, and his mouth hung open, unable to process what her apology was even for.

"No." The rebuff came automatically, followed quickly by derision, despair, horror, confusion, and finally, hurt, as only love can. His response was visceral and unfamiliar, and he shifted in his seat as if to rise. He wanted to lash out, to take control of his confusion. Allen put a gentle hand on his shoulder, and he sat, dumbfounded, looking from Hannah and Allen to the ceiling, then the floor. He shut his mouth.

He'd started the evening anticipating adultery with its momentary, and maybe longer, comfort. And now here he was, incestuous and lost. "Jain? How could…" He laughed nervously and ran his hands through his hair.

"Pete, I'm sorry. I was trying to help—"

"*Help?*" The revulsion of knowing his daughter—literally inside and out—competed with his love for her as a father. He started to get up again, wanting to run. "You had to know."

Allen gently pressured his shoulder down. "Pete, there's more she needs to tell you."

"What else could there possibly be?" But he realized it could only be one thing because they'd really only *done* one thing: mated.

Then she said it, "I'm carrying your baby."

"My baby? You mean *our* baby." He began to think again, brain whirling, in fact, and smiled as a memory returned, and things clicked. "Don't tell me it's triplets!?"

Hannah laughed, snorted, and relief showed on her face. He couldn't hold on to the anger part, as the joy of fatherhood began to overcome his shock. He looked at her belly, which was slightly poochy.

He then looked at Allen as his disjointed thoughts formed and said, "The three pennies. The bracelet. It was for the triplets, Jain and her sisters!"

"Probably. That's what me 'n Hannah Jain thought, too." Allen nodded, looking at Hannah. Pete's eyes followed, and now he met her eyes more gently, his momentary revulsion fading fast.

"Hannah Jain. Is that your name now?" He realized there was much catching up to do, and much to discuss.

"Actually…" Hannah began to explain about her name, and then about the project, the miracle of her pregnancy, and about finding Jesus in the little Primitive church near her apartment.

Talk of Jesus brought Pete back to his sin, their sin, and Prissy, and how long it had been since *he'd* talked to Jesus. He realized that not talking to Jesus was part of how he'd come to be living like this. He looked at Allen. "Can we pray?" Allen had been very quiet, listening as Hannah retold her story. Now he nodded, and they joined hands.

In his prayer, through his prayer, he was able to forgive Hannah Jain and Prissy, and even began to accept forgiveness for himself. He knew through grace, Jesus and his Spirit would guide them forward. He thought of Prissy as he opened his eyes, his mind cleared somewhat by the deep prayer.

Feeling the Spirit, he stood and went to the counter, where there was a corked bottle of merlot he'd been working on. They watched him pull the cork and pour three paper cups, one with just a sip, and pull out a heel from a loaf of rye bread he kept in the cupboard. He brought it all back to the table and sat. "Will you two take communion with me? I feel the need."

"Sure," said Hannah, and Allen nodded reluctantly.

Pete handed Hannah the cup holding the sip, and he and Allen took the other two. He bowed his head, and Hannah and Allen followed suit as he prayed, "Lord, we come to you seeking to be clean and restored and remember the blood you shed as we drink this wine."

He held up his cup, and they toasted and sipped. They followed his lead as he took the heel of rye and bowed his head again and said, "Lord, as I break this bread, we remember your body broken for us. Please be with us tonight."

He tore the heel in two, then let Allen and Hannah tear off what they wanted before he took a piece, and they all ate. He stood and raised his cup, and so did they. He toasted once more, "To babies and Jesus, and what he's gonna do." They all drank, finishing the wine.

"And I need a cigarette." Allen sounded resigned to his addiction as he tapped the package in his breast pocket and added, "I'll be right back."

Pete and Hannah were finally alone, and he faced her. They fell into a hug, and he breathed in her hair again as he kissed her head, holding tight. He was immediately aroused, and she felt it but didn't pull back. He could appreciate her baby bump now, pressing into him. They both stepped back, unsure, and took a deep breath at the same moment. It made them smile.

"Where's this gonna go?" Pete asked her softly. She'd had a lot more time to consider the future, he realized. He'd only had time to find some forgiveness in his heart.

She shrugged, looking at him with a hint of a half-smile.

"What, Mona Lisa?" He spoke to her with familiarity now, less guarded.

"I know where I think it should go." The half-smile lingered.

"Where's that?"

"You keeping the baby might go a long way to healing both you and Prissy."

"Us?"

"Yeah. If it could wrong a right, I would gladly let you adopt her. As long as you didn't sleep with her later." She snorted again, and he laughed. "Seriously, I've had a lot of time to think about this."

They heard Allen coming back in, and he stepped into the kitchen a moment later. "There's someone here to see you." It was hardly the time for visitors, and Pete was annoyed, but his whole life had been work interruptions. He headed to the door, but Hannah stopped him.

Allen stepped aside so Prissy could come in. She looked afraid, but recognition was immediate as her eyes met Hannah's, and Hannah moved forward to hug her. It was coolly received. Prissy didn't look at Pete, and he quietly stepped back. "Jain," her voice was measured, like she was holding back. "Allen told me, but I would have recognized you." She looked at Pete with disdain, "Obviously, Pete didn't. You're grown up and beautiful, and he's a man."

"Mom." Hannah was tearing up. "I'm so sorry." She gave an involuntary sob. "I knew what I was doing." Pete knew what he was doing, too, just not who he was doing it with.

"Quit trying to make me out like a victim. I was wrong, and I said it before. I'm sorry, too," he said. He wanted to hug Hannah and Prissy, but he was frozen. These were two women he loved, one as a wife, one as a daughter, both deeply, and both as lovers. They stood, looking from one to the other, but Pete could only look down when Prissy looked at him, his shame not relieved by communion with Jesus.

Allen cleared his throat, "I'm gonna smoke another cigarette." He stepped back outside.

Pete realized the three of them did love each other, sharing a deep spiritual commitment even though he and Prissy hadn't shared a friendship love, or even a sensual expression of their love, in a long time. Their being here together meant there was hope for that to happen again, even as any hope of a future sensual love with Hannah was forever fading.

Hannah grabbed them both by the hands, and they automatically balanced her as she suddenly knelt and looked up. "Can we pray together? I don't know what else to do." She pulled gently at their hands, and when Pete looked at Prissy, their eyes met as parents. Prissy shrugged slightly, and they knelt and closed the circle of hands. Pete was startled by Prissy's warm, sweaty palm, realizing and appreciating her stress for the first time. He'd only been focused on his.

Hannah looked intently from one to the other, her face wet with silent tears. "I am so sorry; deeply sorry. We need help." Her voice was urgent, intense. Her eyes flicked upwards, and her countenance became peaceful despite the tears. She closed them, and Pete and Prissy followed suit.

"Father God." Pete opened his eyes and looked up, sensing a presence, then bowed his head again as the prayer continued without pause. "Thank you. Thank you. Thank you so much for bringing us together. God, I'm so sorry I haven't been living right. I'm so sorry for the hurt I've caused with Pete"—she squeezed his hand—"and Prissy." Pete sensed Prissy shifting on the floor where she knelt. "Please forgive us. Please show us a path forward to righteousness. Please, God, help us. I know you can. I know you will." Hannah scooched forward on the hard floor. She turned their hands and drew them to her belly, pressing them firmly against the bump under the soft fabric layers. Pete opened his eyes and saw recognition dawn in Prissy's.

In their sudden closeness, he could smell Hannah, and Prissy's familiar scent venerated their old love. He gently, tentatively, pushed her hand over on top of Hannah's, and then put his on top of hers. Slightly off-balance, they leaned against each other. Hannah's head went down, and Pete and Prissy put their foreheads on her shoulders. He could feel her tears steadily dripping on his arm.

Hannah continued, her voice cracking, but her prayer strong, "Lord, please accept my offering of peace: My baby as a gift of love. And help Prissy and Pete accept her for who she is." Hannah laughed, "She is a girl, isn't she, Lord. Your gift. A healing gift. We can't do this on our own, Lord, but only with your help." Hannah stopped, breathing deeply.

Pete withdrew his hands and carefully encircled both women, tentative at first, allowing room for either to pull back. Instead, they both drew closer in his embrace, and he felt Prissy's arms tighten around him and Hannah—it was going to be okay. Tears of relief and joy now filled his eyes. "Lord, thank you for being our friend; always there when we call. Lord, thanks for forgiving our sins, as well as my sins against you, my wife, and my daughter. I'm unworthy, and yet you listen. Please, Lord, bless this baby, bless these women, and guide us forward in this life together." He felt Prissy suddenly draw them even closer.

"Jesus, please. Forgive me for not being the wife and mother I should have been. I clung to grief and hurt instead of love. Forgive me for being self-righteous, and for pulling so far away from my husband and from you, Lord. Thank you so much for your hope. Thank you for this baby, and if raising her is your will, then please make it happen and make me a better parent, wife, and…mother."

They kneeled like that, holding each other, crying, and rocking gently for what felt like an eternity. It had only been a few minutes.

Pete's knees suddenly complained, so he released his hold and rose, then helped the others stand. Their faces were wet.

"Need to fix that leaky roof," said Pete.

But Hannah was looking at Prissy. "Before you accept this baby, there's more we need to talk about. Allen needs to be here."

A weight had been lifted, but practicalities remained. Pete asked, "Why Allen?"

"You'll see." Hannah smiled gently, looking at him now.

He went to get Allen and found him sitting in his truck with the window cracked, smoking. He got out as Pete approached.

"Sorry to catch you off guard. Hannah and I were improvising on this whole thing," he said. "How'd it go?"

"I think it went great. Prissy accepted the adoption proposal, but of course, she and I probably have some things to resolve. Hannah says there's more to talk about, and she wants you to come in," explained Pete, watching Allen's face for a hint of what else there might be. *Surely it can't get any crazier!*

They went back and joined Prissy and Hannah at the table. It should have been awkward, but somehow it wasn't. "I've told Allen some of this at his house, and also met Dutch and the new guy, Butch," said Hannah, "but there's a lot more I need to explain." She looked at each of them and began to tell them about 677, its ramifications for birth control in pets and people, and then about the secret groups subverting it to attack the Nigerians and what they'd already done.

Finally, she told them about her intentional exposure and its unknown effect on the baby. "That's the part you need to think about before you accept this baby. I really want you to have her, and I feel like she'll be fine, but maybe she'll never be able to have kids, or something worse. Is that okay?"

"How could I not accept Pete's child? I realized tonight that he and I are one, even though he's joined to you in the same way now, and that makes the baby ours. Ours collectively. I have no choice but to accept your gift. We'll help her cope with whatever defects she may have, as we have with all our kids." Prissy took a deep breath and looked at Pete. "I don't know how I'm going to accept you back, but I think I am. I think, somehow, through Christ, it's going to be fine."

"Pete?" Hannah looked at him intently.

"What choice do I have? She's a miracle child."

Hannah smiled. "People are never gonna understand all this, and we'll never be able to tell the whole story."

"Nope. But we'll know, even if we don't fully understand either."

"Sounds pretty gnarly." Allen asked, "Especially this 677 stuff. What are you gonna do?"

"I don't know, Uncle Allen. What should I do?" She shrugged helplessly.

"It has to be stopped." Prissy's voice held no doubt as she interjected.

"It does, but how?" Hannah looked at Allen again.

"I have no idea, Hannah Jain. It's above my pay grade, honestly."

"Well, I haven't told you this yet, but the balance subgroup I met had people very high up in government agencies, including law enforcement. One was an associate director at ICE. Who knows who else might be involved?"

They all digested this. "You realize you sound crazy," said Pete. He had no idea how they could help Hannah fix the 677 situation. He knew he and Allen could go fix things with the cunning application of brute force—guns, fire, and physical intervention like in a Mel Gibson movie. But that wouldn't stop the bigger movement, and probably wouldn't be blessed by God. "No one is gonna believe you."

"Maybe, but what I know right now is I'm gettin' hungry. I'm eating for two." Hannah stood and looked at the untouched bags of food on the kitchen counter. Prissy stood, too, and they started warming the food. Pete's intern-sized microwave was tiny, and they had to heat the plates one by one. It clicked with Pete that nothing was vegan, something Hannah had surely noticed.

"Sorry, Allen didn't get any vegetarian food," he said.

Hannah smiled. "I'll savor every bite!"

He realized she was putting beef and broccoli and pork fried rice on every plate. "Allllriiiighty then," he replied in his funny Ace Ventura voice.

After they ate, they all agreed more clarity would come with sleep. Pete couldn't take off work because tomorrow would be busy as people tried to get their pet's medical issues taken care of on Christmas Eve, ignored in the run-up to the holidays. Christmas was on a Friday this year, making a long weekend when the clinic would be closed.

Allen couldn't take off work because the law never sleeps, and crime never stops, nor do the numerous depression, drug, and alcohol-related issues that arise in every season.

Hannah and Prissy realized they alone were free, and as everyone said their goodbyes, they decided to meet tomorrow at the river house and prepare things for a Christmas together to celebrate anew the birth of Jesus, whose healing power had been so active in their lives that night.

CHAPTER THIRTY-FIVE
HANNAH'S SONG

HANNAH WENT BACK to her hotel, feeling all Christmassy and glowing with the love she'd found but didn't deserve. After a shower, she draped a towel over her shoulders and sat on the end of the bed, facing a big mirror. She saw her belly peeking out between the edges of the towel and glanced down as she cupped its form, feeling its weight. Looking back up, she realized the lost and drifting girl had changed. She saw a woman, heavy with child and filled with supernatural purpose.

Her child would have hope and a home now, and she had a mission to redeem herself by shining the light of truth on the work she'd been doing in Florida. Now she only had to help save the Nigerians. Her goal was clear, but the path wasn't.

What she knew now, more than ever, was that gratefulness was still burning in her heart and that God would see her through. She smiled at the woman in the mirror, thanking God for where he'd brought her, then went to her suitcase and dug Weldon's bible out.

She'd hadn't made a regular habit of reading it and felt a little guilty as she sat back on the bed. It opened to a section at the beginning of Luke, and Hannah knew it wasn't a coincidence as she read the words:

Mary's Song

And Mary said:

"My soul glorifies the Lord
and my spirit rejoices in God my Savior,
for he has been mindful
of the humble state of his servant.
From now on all generations will call me blessed,
for the Mighty One has done great things for me—
holy is his name.
His mercy extends to those who fear him,
from generation to generation.
He has performed mighty deeds with his arm;
he has scattered those who are proud in their inmost thoughts.
He has brought down rulers from their thrones
but has lifted up the humble.
He has filled the hungry with good things
but has sent the rich away empty.
He has helped his servant Israel,
remembering to be merciful
to Abraham and his descendants forever,
just as he promised our ancestors."

Mary stayed with Elizabeth for about three months and then
returned home.

What Hannah knew, as she took in the words, was that she was supposed to return home to Joplin to have the baby. The knowledge was a revelation she knew God would bring to pass. And she knew he would scatter the proud who stood against her, but she sure didn't know how.

She found a pen and underlined the whole passage, marking the treasure and storing it in her heart.

She didn't need a Zannie that night as she fell asleep praying thanksgiving to a crazy God she was coming to know as a friend.

CHAPTER THIRTY-SIX

BACK TO THE RIVER HOUSE

IT HAD BEEN almost sixteen years since Hannah set foot in the river house. It was a pleasure to see the flora and fauna unchanged as she drove up the long driveway past stately sycamores, black walnut trees, and fields tinged green with winter wheat. There were deer and honking Canadian geese near the creek. Lingering nervousness calmed to an easy peace as her heart and spirit recalled life spent on the river.

The house itself was up on stilts now, having been elevated to mitigate future flood losses, but the front door was the same, and so was the familiar creosote smell from the original underpinning that mixed with Prissy's cooking when she opened the door. Prissy hugged Hannah tentatively, and Hannah hugged her back.

"You can just hang your coat on the rack." It was the same one as always.

Hannah looked around for a dog, another thing often in her childhood memories, and asked, "Where are the dogs?"

"It's been a while. We haven't had a dog in a few years, and no new ones since you were taken away. After the last Golden died from cancer, I just never wanted another, and Pete's always too busy taking care of other people's dogs to keep one of his own."

"I thought you would always have dogs; you loved them." Hannah couldn't keep the disappointment out of her voice.

"I did, and still do. Pete did try to get me one he'd rescued to replace the outside ones, a little foo-foo dog, but I wasn't interested, so he found someone else to take it in," Prissy replied as she led Hannah towards the old kitchen with its many memories.

"I hope it wasn't my fault." She stopped as she said this, looking at Prissy.

"Like you could help it." Prissy didn't deny it as she looked into Hannah's green eyes. "After they took you away, I didn't want a dog around anymore. I didn't even want to live. Pete buried himself in his work, and I…" she faltered, choking back tears, and Hannah touched her arm lightly.

Tears came, but Prissy swallowed and continued, "I just buried myself in the house, the clinic, and…myself…my self-pity, maybe. It's so good you came back, even with the circumstances." She hesitated again and sobbed, "I missed you so much!" She looked Hannah up and down now as if seeing her for the first time.

Hannah's heart was thumping, seeming to pound out the truth in her next words, "God *brought* me back, and he's making it right now. I'm carrying *your* baby. I feel that with everything I am!" Prissy's hug wasn't tentative this time, and Hannah hugged her back tightly before they separated. "And I missed you, too," she hesitated, then added, "And your smell."

She watched while Prissy pulled some tissues from the box on the kitchen island counter, then handed one to her.

"Why don't you join me in the kitchen while I'm getting things ready for tonight and dinner tomorrow?" Prissy invited. Hannah followed her to the warm smells of pie cooking and stuffing being prepared for the turkey thawing in the kitchen sink. She stopped at the edge of the island counter that separated the kitchen from the rest of the great room.

"It's like nothing's changed," Hannah said wistfully as memories kept flooding back.

"We always were boring, but routine and consistency seem to be what all kids need to thrive," Prissy sighed. "We tried to give that to you."

"You did," Hannah replied. "That's probably what made it so hard to leave. This was home, and a kid's paradise." She couldn't go on as she remembered her childhood. Coming home for Christmas was a cliché, but the memories were real.

Hannah realized it was the Box, that old plastic file box Prissy had prepared so long ago, that had kept her memories of this place so real, and asked, "Do you remember the Box you kept for me, with important documents and little mementos from my life here?"

Prissy looked at her. "Yes. Of course," she smiled. "It was like my version of a baby book. I made one for all the long-term foster kids."

"I still have mine." Hannah watched Prissy's eyes widen as she nodded and continued, "It was a constant, little anchor. It kept me grounded by letting me know my memories of my 'real' family were just that: real."

"I can't believe you still have it."

"I do," she said and looked down as that brought a sharp pang of guilt. The Box was a gift from the woman who'd said 'I do' to Pete, a vow she'd knowingly violated, kicking Prissy when she was down. "It was wrong." Her voice was almost a whisper, distant.

"What?" asked Prissy, dismayed. Hannah snapped out of it and focused back in on Prissy's eyes, realizing what she'd said.

"Sorry! Not the Box!" Hannah stepped into the kitchen and grabbed Prissy's hands, holding them to her chest. "No, no. I was thinking about what I did to you and Pete, how I violated *your* 'I do.' How wrong that was!"

"Oh, Hannah." Prissy took her hands back and placed them on Hannah's shoulders. "We went over that last night. I will never be able to forget all that, but I can only forgive you once, and I did." She stroked the flaxen hair, pushing it behind Hannah's ears and said earnestly, "You're forgiven, and the Bible says God doesn't just forgive you—unlike me, he forgets. It's over at every level."

"You're a better woman than me." Hannah hugged her in relief for a few moments, breathing her in again.

They both stepped back, mildly self-conscious. Prissy shooed Hannah around the counter, saying, "Now get back. I have work to do here."

Hannah smiled and stepped out of the kitchen and moved around the counter.

"Who all's going to be here tonight?"

"Pete and Allen, for sure. We really hadn't invited anyone else since we were separated."

"Suits me." Hannah shrugged as she sat at the counter, facing Prissy. She wasn't sure she wanted to explain things to a lot of people anyway.

"What are your plans? Are you entirely serious about the baby and us adopting her?" Prissy had accepted Hannah's gender determination without question.

"Yes, which is really why I came here." Her sincerity came through in her tone.

"We've always wanted a baby to raise from scratch." Prissy checked Hannah's eyes with a quick smile.

"That's what I wanna give you." Hannah grinned and watched her as she returned to mixing what looked like cookies in a bowl. "It's kind of a package deal. I'm hoping I get you guys back, too."

"That could probably work if you don't sleep with my husband again." Prissy's tone wasn't harsh, but Hannah's cheeks flushed, and she heard the undercurrent of lingering pain.

"I won't, *mom*," said Hannah, trying to sound like a kid. Prissy just smiled slightly as she kept working the dough.

As Prissy worked, Hannah mostly watched and finally stated, "After this break, I really need to stop this 677 project I'm working on. That's the most important thing for me right now. This baby changed something in me, this baby and God, and now I want her to come so I can fight back. What we're going to do and what we've already done to the Nigerian women is so horrible, I have a hard time thinking about it."

"Let's get this baby out safely first; that's most important here and now. Then we can stop 677. Uncle Allen might have some ideas on how to go about that." Prissy looked at her pointedly.

"He might," Hannah nodded. "I know next to nothing about law enforcement." She carefully made no comment on the timing of stopping the 677 project in relationship to the baby's birth, but Prissy didn't seem to notice. She didn't talk about her benzo habit, either, but since she'd been home, she hadn't needed one.

Later that afternoon, after they both took a nap, Prissy came from her room with a file folder.

"I didn't have time to add this stuff to the Box when the judge tore you from us back then. I didn't even have some of it yet; things went so fast. It's a record of your court hearings and my story to you of what happened that day and in the week after—it's your history. I'd forgotten how hard we'd tried to get the decision overturned, and that's in there, too." She handed Hannah the folder. "It wasn't right."

"But you tried," Hannah soothed, trying to sound hopeful. Sounding genuine was hard, though, because the old feelings of abandonment were real even if the internal narrative that had driven them so long had been in error.

"Yeah, but it wasn't enough. I've always felt guilty, but as you'll see, there was nothing we could do." Prissy shrugged as she slowly shook her head and added, "The way the system works is just plain wrong."

Hannah went back to her room with the records, to the small desk that had been hers, and truth began to sink in. As she read the backstory of her early life, she realized how deeply her scars were shared by the Kramers, and how God's healing balm was now working in their messed-up lives.

CHAPTER THIRTY-SEVEN
CHRISTMAS

IT STARTED SNOWING as they got to church for the midnight Christmas Eve service, and when they came out, everything was white. They rode home together in Pete's truck, and after Allen left the house, Prissy invited Hannah to spend the night in her old room. Prissy wasn't quite ready to invite Pete back to her bed, so he was left to sleep on the couch alone.

Morning was cold, sunny, and beautiful. It was like the whole world was starting from scratch. Hannah heard Pete start playing *White Christmas* on the Bluetooth in the living room. It brought back childhood memories of him always playing music to accompany the events of their lives.

Things were different between Pete and Prissy that morning. They were interacting as a couple: touching, smiling, and intimate. Hannah realized Pete hadn't spent the whole night on the couch. She'd noticed it empty in an early morning bathroom trip, one of many that affected her sleep these days, but hadn't realized what it meant. Even though she had never intended to stay with Pete, she had a pang of jealousy as it sunk in.

She was on the outside looking in, which was how it would be, how it *must* be, from there on out. Somewhere inside, she'd held a fantasy of them both being wives, but this morning it was clear to her that she would be a daughter.

She didn't talk much as morning grew into afternoon, and it wasn't uncomfortable as she slipped more fully into the role of a daughter. This baby she carried could 'right her wrongs and save her world, even restore it after the years of separation brought by the justice system and the capricious decision of that judge so long ago.

It was obvious that judges were given too much power with too little accountability when it came to matters of fostering and family justice. She was positive a jury of her peers, or even of Pete and Prissy's peers, would never rip a child from her forever home at the whim of a junkie mother after so many years. And yet some judge had done just that and never looked back. She was sure it happened with startling regularity. And if a foster parent tried to cry out to the world, they were slapped with confidentiality rules and blah, blah, blah.

God was righting her wrong, but look what it had taken, and look at the damage the world and to the people involved. She and Aaron were victims of the same system, she realized. Aaron, like her, was without a healthy life mate or long-term relationship, at least not healthy by most standards. And like her, he had an antipathy towards producing children cloaked beneath a veil of social responsibility.

As far as Terri, who knew? Their relationship had been an intense animal-like interaction, never reaching any personal connections that mattered. Despite the hurt she'd caused Hannah, it didn't have the marks of deliberation that so often heralded a personality disorder. What seemed to be emptiness in Terri was probably just a cover for pain as well. Maybe she was a victim of the same system, a bird of the feather.

If a brother sins against you, go to him privately... had been Jesus's words from Weldon's sermon. To her, it sounded like a directive, and she thought she would have to try, once more, to reach out to Terri and Aaron. She needed to reason with them before she walked away and tried to stop the secret project. Probably in vain, she hoped she could at least get Aaron away from the evil, and that there might come a way to work together to change the foster care justice system once this first battle was over.

Allen came back in the afternoon, and over Christmas dinner, they discussed several possible courses of action. Hannah wanted to get away from the project and out of Florida. The side effects of 677 were unknown, and she wanted to keep the baby safe. Before, she had crazily kept working in the warehouse, which showed just how evil the whole thing was for her. Leaving it behind seemed almost urgent now.

Finally, after Pete and Prissy learned of her work at St. Francis and the Spay/Neuter project at UF, it was decided that Pete would come back home now, not in three months, and she could live in the intern apartment or in her old room at the river house, whichever felt best. The clinic could always use another veterinary assistant, and her employment there would cover health insurance.

To Hannah, the clinic apartment felt best. She knew she was weak, and there was every possibility she might reach out to Pete in her loneliness despite everything that had transgressed. It would only be worse if they lived under the same roof.

They would have to play it by ear once the baby was weaned, but certainly, she could resume her graduate education at Missouri Southern, Pittsburg State, or any of several universities in the area. Over dinner one evening, they decided Prissy would go back to Florida to help Hannah move.

It all came together nicely until they came to the part of the plan where they stopped 677. For Hannah, the baby she carried was in the way, but she still didn't know how to stop what was happening in Florida, even if she wasn't.

CHAPTER THIRTY-EIGHT
ALL OPTIONS

"Let's say you went to the authorities today. What would you tell them?" Allen asked. "I'm thinking like a cop. Waddya got?"

"Funny you ask, officer." Hannah held up her phone. "I just happen to have an SD card chock full of information."

Allen's eyes widened in appreciation. "Well, let's see."

"It'd be better if we looked on a computer."

Pete led them over to the home's computer in the corner of the great room. Prissy started clearing the table, insisting on doing it alone. "I can hear from here. You guys do your thing." It was the old Prissy, deeply interested in the details of her family's lives, but not so much actively participating in their projects. *Monitoring*, if you will. A mom, through and through.

They inserted the micro SD card into the computer with an adapter and opened the file browser. "I have this in one more place back in the apartment, but would it be okay to back it up on to your computer, Pete?"

"Sure. We wouldn't want to lose anything."

Hannah moved all the files onto the Kramer computer and ejected the SD card, putting it back into her phone. They looked through the pictures of the warehouse and Hannah, Terri, and Aaron together at Civilization, celebrating the first production slug of 677.

Hannah had also snuck a picture of the panel in the back of Aaron's closet, behind which sat the pilfered 677, and they read her summary of the events and people Hannah had seen and been involved in.

"So," Allen began, "what does the product actually look like? Do you have pictures of it?"

"No, it's been hard to get away from them to get pictures like that." Hannah considered this a moment. "I don't think it's intentional; it's just that we're all together when all that is happening. It would look funny if I took my phone out and started shooting pictures."

"So, as a cop, I have your story, which I might believe and might not, and really nothing else, right?"

"Well, there are my atrophied ovaries and a baby despite that."

"But you could have been exposed to 677 a lot of different ways?"

"Yeah… I guess." Hannah was thinking about where he was going with this.

"Well, from my perspective, as local law enforcement, I'd want you to get more before I could go ask for a search warrant, for instance. I don't know what the feds would need, though. And it's most likely going to be a fed case because I don't see how even a state agency would have the resources to pursue all this. Nigeria is a long way from Florida…or Missouri."

"So, what would 'more' be?"

"More pictures, maybe? Pictures of the actual product would definitely help. Maybe a recording of one of those meetings you talk about? I don't know." Allen paused. "If I'm going to give you any advice, what I'll need to do is talk to someone who would know. The best thing is probably going to be just to go to the FBI and see where that leads."

"But they have people in ICE and who knows where else in government, remember?" Hannah tried not to sound skeptical, but her tone was instinctive.

"Yeah, but a local agent's not going to be involved, I don't think. That would be the place to start. It's probably gonna be your only choice, but still, if you could get more pictures or a recording where they talk about it…"

"So, I have to go back inside the facility?" She frowned and looked down.

"I don't know. How else could you get the information?"

Prissy, still listening, spoke up, "I don't think you should do anything that might harm the baby. She's innocent, and she's already been exposed."

They looked at her, and Hannah knew she was right. "Don't worry. I'm not gonna go back in there to work, but I might be able to get some pictures. I have an access code to the door lock, and the inner walls are just plastic." Hannah crossed her arms and paced around the room.

The construction was pretty primitive, and there was an exhaust fan always keeping a slight negative pressure so that the walls were always bowing inwards. She knew she could stick her phone through a taped seam and get some pictures, but she'd have to get there when no one else was there.

"I think I could get some more pictures at the warehouse, and probably in Aaron's closet. His closet would be the hardest because it's in the biology department, and it might look weird if I was diggin' around his closet and got caught." She stopped, placing her index finger on her chin as she thought it through.

"I have to go back there to get my stuff anyway if I'm gonna come stay here. I can use my phone to record any conversations where I explain my plans to Aaron. Maybe he'll talk about the project some." She had to try to get him to stop, too, but she didn't mention that—she didn't know how she was going to approach it.

"Just remember, our baby is innocent and has already been exposed," cautioned Prissy with motherly concern.

CHAPTER THIRTY-NINE
BACK TO GAINESVILLE

TRAVELING BACK TO Gainesville went much better with company, and it gave Hannah time to reacquaint with Prissy. The weather and landscape grew warmer and greener as they drove, and their relationship grew as well.

At first, being alone in the car was more than a little uncomfortable, and Hannah could sense that Prissy felt the same. But as they talked about the future and the baby, it became more and more natural. They spent one night on the road and arrived in Gainesville in the early afternoon on Tuesday after New Year's Day. After turning in the rental car, they rode the bus back to her apartment.

The green live oaks, pine trees, and moss hanging down seemed far removed from Joplin and winter, even though it was cool. Seeing it with Prissy, who kept admiring the beauty, made her realize how nice her life had been. Her internal struggles had diminished her appreciation until now.

Hannah was afraid Prissy might feel weird, but they were both tired from the travel and fell into a slumber on Hannah's big bed when they got up to her apartment. Two hours later, they woke up to the muted sounds of her roommates through the bedroom door.

Camille and Bobbie had been very understanding when they had texted back and forth about her need to go to Joplin to have the baby. After waking and taking quick trips to the bathroom, Hannah introduced Prissy as her mother, then quickly changed the subject to her departure, "I'm so sorry I have to go. I'm glad you aren't mad at me."

"You gotta take care of that baby now, Hannah." Camille's smile was sincere and kind as she said, "It's not an issue for us. We'll be able to get a new roommate."

"After all, your room has a balcony," Bobbie added. "Who gets to have a room with a balcony?"

"Good luck with the whole thing, girl. You'd better bring that baby back to see us!" Camille smiled and touched Hannah's belly lightly.

"You know I will." Hannah meant it.

She and Prissy packed her few possessions and quickly came across the Box tucked in the back of Hannah's closet. She watched Prissy's eyes widen as she realized what Hannah was holding up. Hannah smiled and asked, "Remember this?"

"How could I forget?" She took the Box from Hannah and held it up, turning it slowly. "You've added a few decorations."

"Yeah." Hannah shrugged apologetically and said, "I was young."

"No, it's beautiful! At least to me." Prissy gave her a motherly look that reminded her of Grade Nine foster mom. Memories of Eddie followed, then Terri, then Aaron, and that led back to the her past once again. She looked at Prissy, so tenderly holding the Box on her knees as she sat on the edge of the bed.

In that moment, Hannah felt the press of all her years, the tangle of all their lives, and the direction her future must take. It wouldn't be any easier going forward, but she would be led by righteous purpose, and she felt her burden lighten. It was like sailing out of the fog and into the sun with a fair wind blowing, but knowing storms were forecast.

She sat on the bed by Prissy. "This'll be your Box now," she said. "You'll need it for the baby. You can use it to help her understand her past one day, maybe."

Prissy looked from her to the Box, and back again. "It's your Box...your past. I made it for you." But Hannah shook her head.

"No, it needs to go with you." Hannah knew it in her heart and insisted, "I'm never going to have another kid or a family. I'll take my birth certificate and name change stuff, but you made the Box, and it's part of your past and her future."

Prissy's lips pursed. "We'll see, okay? I can take it for now."

They ordered pizza that evening and went to bed. Hannah was hoping for a clear head to deal with tomorrow and the partings it held. She prayed for peace. Later, when she could tell Prissy was still awake too, they prayed together, and sleep finally came.

CHAPTER FORTY

ST. FRANCIS WITH PRISSY

PRISSY CAME WITH her to St. Francis the next morning, and Hannah was aware of Jules in the background as she spoke with her supervisor, a veterinary student, letting her know she would be leaving soon. Wednesdays were administrative days at the clinic, so there weren't many people around.

When they left, Jules was walking down the block, pushing her cart and taking up the whole sidewalk. As they approached, the wiener dog watched carefully and gave a couple of growly barks before Jules shushed her, then cackled as she scooched over to make room. "Don't mind him, he's all bark and no bite. Sorry!"

Turning back to the dog, she slapped at him and said, "Shut up, Booger! I raised you better than that." The dog alternated between growling at them and glancing at Jules and wagging his tail. Hannah realized Jules was going to be cool and just let her pass with Prissy, but on impulse, she decided to engage her.

"Hi, Jules," she said. "This is my mother, Prissy. She's visiting from Missouri."

Jules frowned, then smiled at Prissy and replied, "Well, hi, Miss Priss. Yo' daughter's real nice. She always takin' care of me and my little Booger." Her shrewd bird eyes turned to Hannah, adding, "Ain't you, Miss Hannah."

"I try, Jules." Her guard was suddenly up. "I just wanted you to meet my mom. I'm going to go live with her pretty soon."

"Oh-oh! You gonna go have dat baby, ain'tchya! Well, if you ever *need* anytin', you just let old Jules know, ya hea?" Jules cackled loudly, and Hannah instantly regretted stopping to talk to her. "Babies can be *real* stressful. Lots more stressful than a puppy, huh, Booger!" She patted Booger's head, and he wagged his skinny tail.

"Well, I'll be a long way away, Jules."

"Dats okay, baby. Jules got her cell phone, and she can reach out true da mail. I know how to send a letter, ya know wat I'm sayin'?" Jules cackled again when she saw fear in Hannah's eyes. "No worries, baby."

"I don't have your number," Hannah said without thinking.

"Dat's okay." Jules reached into one of her bags and pulled out a scrap of paper and a Sharpie. She wrote her number down and handed it to Hannah. "You call ol' Jules if you need to talk."

"Okay, Jules. Thanks." Hannah was relieved she didn't have to give Jules her number. She wanted to run, but at the same time, she knew how important the Zannies were. Important enough to where she kept her remaining bottle carefully hidden in the inside zipper compartment of her purse, even though she hadn't needed one since she'd arrived in Joplin. She'd even stuffed some cotton in the bottle to keep the pills from rattling around.

Jules winked at her and looked at Prissy, "Yo daughter be *real* faithful at church, Miss Priss. I see her go every Sunday almost."

"That's good to hear, Miss Jules." Prissy followed Hannah's lead and started to move on, adding, "It was nice to meet you."

"See you, Jules. I just wanted to say goodbye."

"I'll sure miss ya, Miss Hannah." She cackled again as they moved on down the sidewalk. Hannah was kicking herself for even stopping.

As they walked away, she explained, "She saw me picking out a baby book one day at the used bookstore. I told her it was for a friend, but she's pretty sharp."

"She seemed a little creepy to me," Prissy sneered a bit.

"Well, she's not as creepy as a lot of the homeless we serve." Hannah was just relieved to get the discussion away from any hint of her true relationship with Jules. The Zannies she kept became weighty as anxiety fought against her desire to quit them for the baby's sake. The peace she'd found in Joplin was suddenly elusive.

"I'd like you to meet Weldon, the man who baptized me. He's having a Bible study tonight at the church I go to. We could go." Hannah figured that would go a little better than meeting Jules had.

CHAPTER FORTY-ONE
HARD GOODBYES

They went home and had lunch, and after a nap, Hannah went to see Aaron alone. She didn't really want him to be involved in her new life and wanted the transition to go as smoothly as possible. They were scheduled to resume production the following week, but she planned to be back in Joplin by then. If they were going to continue production, it wouldn't be easy to find a replacement for her.

As she walked down the familiar hall towards his office, she realized what a stress the wrongness of it had been, and how her belly mom Lisa had rescued her in death. Still, she felt the weight of the Nigerian women and men, and the evil that had been set upon them. Stopping that, righting that, was everything. She didn't know how she was going to do the stopping part, but she knew the light of truth would somehow bring the righting part.

She did know that she had to do something. Feeling duplicitous, she pulled out her phone in the hallway, set it to 'record,' and let it fall back down in her pocket. She knocked casually on the door jamb, and Aaron looked up. "Hi, Hannah! Glad you're back." He stood and gave her a hug, and she sat in the usual chair.

"So… How the hell are you?"

"Great!" Her response was automatic. Suddenly, she wished she'd taken a Zannie. The only thing that had stopped her was the thought of Jules's dirty hands on the pills. Their eyes met, and she looked down.

"What's up, Hannah? How was Joplin?" Concern was in his voice, and her emotions roiled; thoughts flew through her brain. She'd known his love, and a desire to save him was overwhelming. She fully appreciated how her parting would hurt him, and how what she was doing would probably drive a wedge between them forever. It was suddenly much more than just telling him she was leaving, and she knew she had to try to get him to see how wrong the whole project was. Making a recording and turning him in wasn't what Weldon had preached about.

Going to him and trying to get him to see the error of his ways was the message of the passages in Matthew, and what Weldon had seemed to insist on. In her earnestness and anxiety, she'd failed to appreciate that Jesus and Weldon were talking about a fellow believer, a fellow member of the family of Christ. She didn't consider that the rules might be different when dealing with a non-believer. Still, her desire to enlighten him was almost overwhelming.

She looked back up at him and said, "Joplin was great. I found my old foster mom and dad."

His eyes widened. "Really! So, how'd *that* go?"

"Better than expected," she replied. "A lot better."

He nodded, waiting.

"There's something I need to tell you, Aaron," she hesitated. Her resolve waned a moment, and then she plunged ahead, "I'm pregnant."

He slowly nodded again, and then his eyes widened in alarm as the whole import of her statement hit him. "*Pregnant*? Are you sure?"

"Yes." It was easier now, and added, "I'm due in about four months." She unconsciously put her hand on her belly, and he looked down.

"I… I hadn't noticed."

"No, I'm carrying it well." She smiled at that, then sensed his mind racing. He showed no reflexive joy, just alarm and concern, maybe even fear. "Nevertheless, she's coming."

"But…what about the dose we took?" his voice was lowered.

"I guess I was just far enough along to not need a corpus anymore.

My ovaries are definitely shot, and the doctor couldn't understand it, but it doesn't matter." She leaned forward. "What we don't know is if she'll be affected."

"Who's the father?" She still found him attractive as he unconsciously ran his hands through his hair. "Me?" He met her eyes, and for a moment, she couldn't look away.

She smiled weakly and broke the gaze. "Not, it's not you, silly. It was a guy at the last conference. In Kansas City."

"Does he know?" He hadn't sighed in relief and wanted to know more. He seemed to genuinely care, but she then thought of Terri.

She decided in that moment not to tell him who the father was and looked briefly back into his eyes. "No, and he never will. It was a one-time deal. I'm going to adopt the baby out."

He seemed relieved, but then looked concerned. "You can't keep working at the warehouse."

"Actually, that's why I came to meet with you." She wanted to say, *No shit, Sherlock*, but that wasn't fair. "I can't work there anymore. In fact, I'm moving in with my old foster family in Joplin. I'm going to have to put my academic career here on hold, Aaron."

"Oh, man. I get it, but it's sure gonna throw us off, not to mention your thesis." His chair creaked as he leaned back and looked at her, clearly thinking. "I thought you had an IUD?"

"I did! Kinda ironic, getting pregnant with an IUD while attending a conference on birth control," she said, unconsciously touching her necklace. "I think it's a God thing."

He peered at the small cross hanging from her necklace, and she saw him realize that the IUD pendent had been replaced by a real cross. He scoffed. "You're not into religion now, are you?" She was surprised at the revulsion in his face and tone. It was as if she suddenly developed an odor, and she resisted the urge to sniff her pits.

"What if I am?" She was just curious, not trying to be confrontational, as she adjusted to this new side of him.

"Well…" He was taken aback, looking at her like she was a stranger. "It's so…lame."

"I'm not lame, Aaron, and neither is God."

"Well, no. *You're* not. I just mean…"

"It's okay. I used to feel that same way, I think," she paused. "But God is real, Aaron, and yes, I'm a believer now. The baby helped me realize that."

"So, the baby made you believe… I think I understand." Aaron seemed to be collecting himself as he processed her new reality.

"No, I chose to believe, but the baby helped me see the truth. The truth of Jesus." Hannah knew how horrible that must sound to him. She had been there herself just a short time ago. She softened her confrontational tone, "I don't expect you to understand that, but it is what it is."

He gave his head a tiny shake, "I noticed you didn't need my little blue pills anymore. Was that cuz of the baby?"

"Kind of." She didn't want to lie, but neither did she want to mention Jules. "I'm trying not to use them anymore. Not when I'm pregnant."

"I see." He stroked his chin, like a professor evaluating an inferior student.

She really wanted to bring up the Nigerian mothers, but now she was worried about him blaming her Kelli. "So, what do you think you're gonna do when I leave?"

"Obviously, we'll have to find someone else to trust. Hazel can help, but I don't think anyone else at UF knows about the warehouse. You're setting us back a bit, but we'll figure something out." He let some accusation into his tone.

At least he didn't bring up abortion. She took a breath, gathering her courage before diving in. "Maybe it would be a good time to pause production. Think about the impact on the people in Nigeria, what you're doing to them."

"There you go again. This isn't about them; it's about saving the world." He looked at her intently. "Is your sudden concern for them part of your God thing, too?"

"It's not a God *thing*. I'm talking about real people who are going to have real suffering."

"I realize that, but if we give them a choice, this isn't going to work. Their beliefs…" He looked at her again. "They think it's their Christian duty to make babies. There's no practical way to convince them to voluntarily stop."

She realized she had forgotten about her recorder. "So, we should just give them the 677 and volunteer for them then."

"Yes. It's the only way." He dropped a fist lightly on the desk.

"I can't be a part of that anymore." She stared at him, but he evaded her eyes. "It's just wrong, Aaron. It really doesn't matter that I'm leaving. You would've had to find someone to replace me anyway." She realized she still had feelings for him as guilt began to rise in her chest over what she was doing with her recording and how she was leaving him alone with Terri in the project.

"Maybe getting yourself pregnant was just your way of getting out," he retorted sharply, meeting her eyes now.

"Like I knew I could get pregnant with an IUD! It's supposed to be impossible," she paused when a realization came to her. "Maybe it was God's way of getting me out. Maybe it's his way of getting you out, too—by sending me to talk to you. What do you think about that?"

"I think God is a construct you've bought into."

"Uggh!" she exclaimed. "Can't you see you're on track to becoming a mass murderer?!"

He blinked. "Taking away reproduction ability is not mass murder. How can you even say that?"

"The babies! You're killing their babies."

"They are *not* babies; they're miscarriages. It's not *murder!*" He shook his head. "*I'm* not a murderer or a killer. I'm using science to do what's right, Hannah. If anything, we're *saviors.*"

Her guilt was assuaged somewhat by his insistence on the heroics of his task. She sat back, stunned, looking out the window over his shoulder and into the trees beyond. The revulsion she felt towards the position he'd staked out brought the pain she'd felt when she discovered his relationship with Terri to the forefront. It was a whole lifestyle she'd embraced, a whole philosophy of living, and she realized it was all grounded in this world without any connection to heaven.

It was an attitude that spoke of spirituality without realizing the one eternal Spirit who inhabited everything on Earth. It denied the transcendence of human existence and made her, and all humans, prisoners in the here and now, desperately seeking meaning from a reality they evolved without God's hand and the love he brought. A reality that made love just another human emotional construct, powerful but worldly.

It ignored—or was ignorant of—the ordered reality only God's unrestrained love could bring. A love that couldn't discriminate or prevaricate but flowed unrestricted in all people and things that welcomed it, and could become all-consuming if unresisted. A love born of life, not the death Aaron and his friends were so persistent to perpetuate.

If unresisted, this God-love became irresistible, but by its very nature, it was polite, never forcing itself. Patient, kind, gentle, faithful…it could wait an eternity to be requited, and she realized that it wasn't hers to force upon Aaron or anyone else. But God had placed her, she knew with all her heart, into this time, place, and situation so that she might stand for the innocents.

Her passion for them was becoming all-consuming. She knew at that moment that her passion wasn't hers, but an expression of the very love that had saved her and brought her to a realization of its truth. She had become an incarnate vessel of his love, and to restrain it was not even thinkable anymore.

She had become a prisoner of love, but not a captive. The thought to leave her cause of justice and walk away to have a baby and continue her life in a new place crossed her mind, and she knew she was free to do just that. There would be no penalty. But neither would she obtain the blessing of unabashedly serving God's needs as he led her.

It no longer mattered to her where the path led or what she might suffer for standing against Aaron, Terri, Hazel, and everything they were doing. It didn't even matter if she succeeded; all she knew, deep inside where her spirit mingled with God's, was that she couldn't remain silent.

The 677 group was not her family, and never had been, and everything about them was "no longer" to her. She realized Aaron was staring at her, waiting for a reply.

She didn't choose her words; they just rose up from her heart as she stood. "Science belongs to God, and He does know right from wrong. You, my friend, are lost." The tears on her cheeks seemed to confirm it.

She turned and went back down the hall, needing sunshine.

CHAPTER FORTY-TWO

WEDNESDAY NIGHT AT SHADY GROVE

"THIS IS WELDON, the man who baptized me," said Hannah as they entered Shady Grove for evening Bible study, "and this is Prissy, my foster mom from my early years."

"Pleased to meetchya, Mrs. Prissy," Weldon welcomed them. "It's sho' a pleasure having yo' daughta' in fellowship with us. And she do know how ta sing. Come on and take a seat, we ready ta start."

There were seven besides them gathered to study, and once again, God spoke to Hannah through Weldon as he taught about Esther from the small podium. In the near-perfect diction he used for teaching and preaching, he focused on doing what you were called to do, and Esther 4 especially, where Mordecai speculates that Esther was raised up for "just such a time as this." A time to fight injustice even if it meant risking your life.

Hannah knew the message was for her, and she could see amazement in Prissy's eyes at the appropriateness of the passages. God was sending encouragement. Clearly, she was on the right path.

They discussed ways God used people and places, and Weldon related how God had used the Shady Grove Primitive church during the civil rights movement as a place where NAACP members, supporters of MLK's Freedom Movement, met to plan the steps of desegregation for Gainesville's public facilities.

"Everyone in the NAACP knew that when a meeting time was publicly announced, no matter what church it was announced to be at, the real meeting would be one hour earlier in this very building. Shady Grove was a sanctuary, an incubator for the plans and ideas of the civil rights workers." His shoulders straightened as he related the proud history.

"They had to do this because if they'd met where they'd said, the haters would show up, and there would be violence. We were deep in the Porters Neighborhood, and the haters either didn't know about us or were afraid. Don't really know. But when it was built, no one knew it would come to serve the civil rights movement in such a way. Only God.

"And since it's still here, who knows how God will use it in the future?" He stepped back slightly and looked over the class, inviting discussion.

"He sure used it to lead me in," Hannah said.

"Indeed, he did, and we are so glad you came!" Everyone nodded in agreement.

"There's something I need to share with you all." Several people leaned forward, and Weldon saw the struggle in her face.

"Go ahead, Hannah. You safe here."

"I'm gonna have to leave you. I got pregnant with a man I love, but he isn't mine." Tears came, and her sentences were short and choppy. Prissy handed her a tissue. "My foster mom and her husband took me in years ago." *Dammit! Why was this suddenly so hard?* She wiped her eyes. "I've done bad things, but they're gonna adopt my baby. Anyway, I'm gonna go to Missouri, and I won't be seeing you guys for a while. I don't know why this is so hard!"

One of the others spoke up, an elderly woman who had quietly witnessed Hannah's journey there, "It's hard cuz you found love here, honey, at Shady Grove. But you can take that love anywhere. It be okay if you got that. You only leavin' for a little while, and we all gonna be together forever after that."

There was a chorus of amens. Weldon stood and said softly, "Let's pray to close and pray for Hannah, her baby, and her mom."

She and Prissy marveled at the timeliness of the Bible study's subject as they walked home, bugs and frogs gently calling in the warm Florida evening.

CHAPTER FORTY-THREE
JOMO BOUND

ON THE TRIP back to Joplin, Hannah had transferred the recording of her conversation with Aaron onto the micro SD card she'd pulled from the inside of her bed rail and put it into the empty slot in her phone. She also emailed the file to Uncle Allen. Throughout the week, she ignored an email and several texts from Aaron, resolving not to be distracted from her preparations.

They had visited the UF spay/neuter team at the clinic, and Hannah introduced Prissy around. She was relieved there was no sign of Terri; it would just be one more thing to explain to Prissy. The clinic was sad to see her go but wished her well on her journey to Joplin.

Now, as Prissy drove the rental past Atlanta, she'd decided to check the messages, texts first.

Hazel isn't happy. You need to call me so we can work this out.

Are you resigning? Call me.

Call me, please. Your roommates said you moved out.

The email was more like a write-up, informing her that by not reporting to work, she was in danger of losing her stipend and scholarships. She knew she would have to respond to this one to protect her academic career, even though it seemed secondary to the higher purpose of stopping the 677 group.

They had decided Hannah would move back into her old bedroom at the river house, but Prissy was still a little hesitant about having Pete come home for good, so he was going to stay in the apartment for the time being. Once she was settled into her room with her few belongings, they decided to invite Allen and Pete for a meal and worked together in the kitchen to prepare it.

Scents were strong to Hannah nowadays, and her heart warmed at Allen's raw tobacco smell when she hugged him in greeting, feeling small against the tall man despite her protruding belly. Allen brought Dutch and Butch this time, the old and the new. Prissy allowed old Dutch inside because it was dry out, and his feet were clean. But the new dog, after relieving himself, waited in the back seat of Allen's truck.

Dutch smelled like clean doggy outdoors when Hannah knelt to hug him, too. His drool strung across her arm, but it was worth it, and she wiped herself on the bandana he had around his neck. He went to lie in the middle of the great room floor.

Hannah moved to Pete, and they hugged. It was a little awkward, not because of the baby bulging between them, but because their relationship had shifted. Despite what they had created, there was no longer a sensual thrill, at least for her, but neither were they father-daughter. She went back to the kitchen area to keep helping Prissy.

As they were finishing meal prep, the big hound passed through the kitchen, patrolling for scraps from the floor. He was out of luck otherwise because, in a veterinarian's house, no dog gets to eat people food.

Hannah loved the feel of his soft red ears and floppy skin, and she reached down to pet him as he passed. She knew this white-muzzled old dog was the scenting machine that found Lisa. If he hadn't, she expected she would still be in Florida. Hannah gave him one last ear rub, then shooed him out of the kitchen.

Prissy looked at her, and she knew she'd better wash her hands before returning to shred the lettuce. Hannah looked at Allen sitting across the sink at the kitchen bar counter and asked, "So, did you find anything about what happened to Lisa?"

"Not much so far. She had been living over in Springfield, apparently, but still had connections here. She'd been reported missing, kind-of. The report was vague and not persistent, most likely because she hung out with dopers." Prissy looked at him, eyebrows raised.

"That's what they are. It's a fact, not judgment. They just don't like to call the police, so they let it lie, I guess. She had an extensive drug and petty crime history, including prostitution."

"So who killed her?" Hannah went back to the lettuce after wiping her hands off on a kitchen towel.

"Don't know yet. I'm still looking, and so are the Springfield police, but it may take a while. At some point, we'll probably get someone to trade information in exchange for reduced charges on something. We don't have any direct leads so far."

"It'd be interesting to know. She apparently still cared about us, the triplets." She said it like a question. "I'm assuming that's what the three coins were, right?"

"We can only guess, but I think so, Hannah."

"Too bad a good dog had to die, though." Pete was still bitter but shut up when he got a look from Prissy, too.

It was a simple meal, and they sat around the living room afterward to share more information. Hannah played her conversation with Aaron, and they were all silent after listening to the impassioned recording. Prissy explained that they had decided not to go to the warehouse to try for more pictures because it was too risky.

"Well, he's certainly convinced he's doing the right thing." Hannah saw Allen's subtle cigarette tell and smiled to herself as he continued, "I think you definitely got enough to show his intent. I'm not sure about Florida law, but in Missouri, the recording should be admissible in court."

"So, what else do you have, Uncle Allen?" asked Hannah.

"I did go talk with Jared down at the FBI. Sort of explained the situation and shared the information you gave with him. There was a lot of head-scratching, and I wasn't too good at explaining the science part. He didn't seem to get the connection to Nigeria, or at least had a hard time processing the connection between animal birth control and Nigeria."

"Apparently, the animal part is making a good smokescreen for the human side," Hannah commented, feeling frustrated. "Do you think they'll investigate further?"

"I think so, but we'll just have to see. They'll be calling to interview you, too, but we won't be privy to their investigation, I'm afraid."

"What I do know is there's a whole lot of evil going on, but nothing ever seems to get done to save the animals. It drives me crazy," said Pete. "It seems like this 677 stuff could be used in pets *now*. Do you have any idea of the amount of resources we're devoting to spay/neuter surgeries? Or how few we can actually do because of the time it takes?"

"Don't blame me. I'm a cop, not a scientist." Pete had been looking at Allen as he spoke. They both looked at Hannah.

"Hey, I was sucked into the human thing, too. Overpopulation is a real issue, but my thesis was designed to answer a question about applications for pet sterilization. I think everything in academia and government goes slow these days because everyone wants to protect themselves against lawsuits and crazies, so it moves forward in little steps."

"Well, animals are still being euthanized by the millions in the meantime." Resignation was in his tone.

Hannah burped. "I'm just glad I don't have to be vegan anymore!" They all laughed as she forked in the last of Prissy's spaghetti and meatballs.

"It does seem to be a common characteristic of everyone at those conferences, doesn't it?" asked Pete.

"It's like a symbol of counter-culture."

Hannah met with Jared the next week and was extensively interviewed. She gave the recording to him, but the outcome was as frustrating as the meal had been. She wanted action, but they told her little, and all she could do was wait.

CHAPTER FORTY-FOUR
677 RETALIATES

JANUARY IN THE Ozarks can only be described as bleak. When snow comes, it dresses up the browns and grays for a day or two before it melts, returning the landscape to its dreary oneness. It's cold enough to require coats, but certainly not bitter. On rare days, warmth brings a cruel hint of summer, but cold returns a day later. Winter seemed to drag on forever.

Hannah longed for Florida's green landscape but tried to focus on her life in Joplin, which was looking to be where she'd stay at least until the baby was born, and maybe longer. It was Valentine's Day, and she made her way to the back door of the clinic. "Bye, Mikki, I'm out the back!"

"Bye, Hannah! See you later." Mikki and Hannah became fast friends. Both had a penchant for the unloved and a dedication to comforting animals in their care, taking the time to give them extra words of kindness and gentle pettings as they underwent treatments or recovered from their surgeries.

She was able to make friends at work, but the younger ones liked to go out drinking, and the more mature ones were busy with families of their own. As she walked to her car, she mused over the fact that her main free-time activities had come to mostly involve the Methodist church where the Kramers were members. Her alert suddenly went to high as she approached the parking lot.

A man had been sitting in a pickup and began to get out as she approached in the dusky light. She prepared to hustle back to the clinic when she realized it was just Allen without his cowboy hat. He popped open the back door, and Dutch jumped out and bounded over to Hannah, wagging his big tail.

"Sorry if I scared you!" said Allen.

"Oh, it's okay," she laughed. "I just went into early labor, though!" He'd never come to the clinic at quitting time. "What's up, Uncle?"

"Hop in, and we'll talk." He pointed, and Dutch jumped back into the back seat as Allen walked around and let Hannah in the passenger side. "We can talk somewhere else if the smoke bothers you."

"No, I actually love the smell. It always reminds me of you." Hannah smiled at him and the harsh, lingering smell of Camels.

"Well, that's a first." He shut the door and went back around and got in behind the wheel. "Are you warm enough?"

"Sure."

Allen wasn't a big one for small talk, so he dove right in, "I got back from visiting with Jared down at the FBI office." Hannah's heart jumped. She was excited to hear what they had been doing to investigate her report. She'd heard nothing, and Aaron had never replied to her email of resignation.

"It wasn't what I expected, Hannah. They said you had been expelled from the university for cause. And your advisor, Aaron Skinner, had been fired and charged with theft of university property."

Hannah was stunned. She didn't know what to expect, but it wasn't this. She couldn't speak.

"There's more, but the program head, the Hazel person you wrote about, said you hadn't completed your senior seminar courses last semester and weren't showing up for your work-study." He looked up, checking her reaction.

"On the details you provided, there was some product like you reported in Dr. Skinner's closet, but the warehouse was a bust. They sent a team to check out the property and found an unsecured, empty building. There was nothing there. The pictures of the inside you had didn't match anything they saw."

Hannah began to get angry as realization hit. Everything she'd done had been in secret, and all the assurances that her academic record would be protected were verbal and from Aaron, reporting what Hazel had told him. She had almost nothing to prove her allegations, nothing but her word, and now she was looking like a disgruntled dropout and a foster care fuck-up.

"There's more, Hannah. Dr. Skinner threw you under the bus. He says some drugs they found in his car were yours. It was Xanax, and the fingerprints on the bottle were a match."

And now, she was a prescription drug abuser. Her heart raced, and she felt herself flushing in a mixture of embarrassment and anger. She had been playing checkers while they were playing chess. She tried to find her voice and realized her mouth was opening and closing like a fish out of water.

"I don't know where to start," she fumbled, shaking her head. "I figured they would investigate more before taking action. Gather more information . . ."

"I don't know the whole story, but I think they went to the head lady when they found out Skinner had been fired. The Terri woman denied everything, and Skinner said she wasn't involved at all in the thefts. He said it was all your idea."

"You don't believe all that, do you?" She pleaded with her eyes.

He looked at her sharply, his eyes angry. "I don't know who to believe, Hannah Jain!" He fiddled with his hat on the console between them. "You fucked my brother when he was weak, split their marriage, and came back pregnant with a baby you claim is his. You didn't complete your degree, you've been expelled from college, and you abuse prescription drugs," his voice rose throughout his tirade. "Who the hell do you expect me to believe?!"

A playback of Jules's cynical cackle seared through her brain. Why would anyone believe her? She wanted to cry for someone to hold her, but tears wouldn't come. She hadn't earned comfort, and certainly not from Allen. She realized her only hope lay in the truth and turned in her seat to look at Allen, her tone anguish mixed with intense anger.

"Believe this, Uncle. I'm sorry about what I did to Prissy, and I'm trying to make that right. I'm sorry I let you down, but I didn't do anything *to* you. As far as me, Prissy, and Pete, God's trying to make that right. That's between us. I know this investigation is making you look like a fool right now, and making me look like a messed-up child of the system…and I guess I am." She looked out the windshield at the gray, bare limbs of the scraggly trees bleakly rattling in the cold wind behind the clinic. They matched her mood.

"But the Xanax was the only true thing they told you! I did use Xanax for anxiety. Aaron was the one who got me started, but I was uncomfortable getting it from him, so I found another source. He must have had my old bottle, the one he'd given me. I had terrible anxiety for years but never got help, and when he gave me some, it was like magic." She dug in her purse, pulling out the bottle from the inner pocket. "This is it, the stuff I bought. And I haven't needed it since I've been here." She shoved the bottle back in her purse.

"I promise that is the only true thing they told you!" Now tears of relief came; relief that she had emptied the only real garbage she carried. "Those other things are lies. They're trying to destroy me, and I don't even matter. What matters are all those women and men in Nigeria."

She realized she had done nothing to help the Nigerian women, which was her whole reason for coming forward. Now there were at least two hundred thousand doses of 677 missing, and everyone had disappeared like cockroaches scattering in the light. And all the fingers were pointing towards her. She broke into sobs, "God. Oh, God, help me."

She shrugged off Allen's comforting hand, so he sat, fiddling awkwardly with his hat while she gathered herself.

She heard Dutch's big tail slapping the back seat, and he poked his head between them to sniff Hannah. It was her turn to leave mucous and tears all over him, so she wrapped her arm around his neck as he nuzzled her breast. His unconditional love was like a hug from Jesus. She wiped her nose on him and could smell his floppy dog ear smell. "I gotta go."

She opened the door and left Allen with his thoughts.

CHAPTER FORTY-FIVE

PSALM 40

SHE FOUND COMFORT in the 40th Psalm in Sunday School the following week. It was a plea for help and forgiveness.

Pete and Prissy still seemed to accept her story for what it was, despite the outcome of the initial probe by the FBI. The clinic was so busy she really didn't have a lot of time to think about how to approach the problem beyond what they'd already tried with Allen.

Her belly continued to swell, and life at the river house fell into a steady, predictable pattern. Work, eat, and sleep, with betrayal, anger, and embarrassment always in the background. One evening in early March, Hannah exited the vet clinic to find Allen sitting in his F150 out in the parking lot again. He got out as she approached and opened the back door again to let Dutch jump out and greet her.

"You're back." She moved a little awkwardly as she stooped down to hold Dutch's head by his ears, giving them a good scratching followed by a hug.

"Yep." He flicked his Camel across the gravel. "I was wondering if we could talk."

"Of course. I hope you don't think I hate you."

"I don't think you hate me, Hannah Jain, and I hope you don't think I believe everything I hear." 'Hannah Jain' had become his pet name for her, and she'd given up correcting him.

"Fair enough." She put her hand out, and he helped pull her up. It was her turn to be drooled on, and he handed her a handkerchief so that she didn't have to bend down and use the bandana. They watched Dutch trot to the side of the parking lot and pee on some weeds.

"I've got some information about Lisa." He walked her around to the passenger door and let her in, then let Dutch hop up into the back seat.

When Allen got back behind the wheel, he said, "Thought you ought to know what I've been able to find out about her death. It ain't pretty, but I think most of it's true. Are you ready to hear about this?"

She gave a little impatient sigh. "Yes, I've wanted to know."

"Well, she was still using and abusing prescription drugs." He looked at her cautiously, but she just shook her head in reply.

"I'm not. Using, that is. So, don't worry."

"Well, apparently, she was dealing, too, along with your original father, Lenny. There was an altercation about territory with a group called the Quattros. They arranged for a buy from her, and she agreed to meet at the old Tipton Access at the end of Ortiz Lane.

"This was back in December before last. She thought it was just a routine buy, but they wanted to warn her out of their territory. Push came to shove, and she ended up getting shot. They tried to weigh her down and threw her in the river right before the Christmas flood.

"From what we can tell, no one knew she was over here but Lenny, and he was afraid to say much to the police, but her mother did report her missing in Springfield. There were so many priors, it wasn't deemed important, so the delay in finding her body meant the missing persons report was pretty cold."

"What about Lenny?"

"He didn't even bring you up when we talked to him, and he must have already figured out what happened to Lisa because he wasn't surprised. Our source was a Quattro we'd arrested for something else, and he gave us Lisa." Allen automatically started to take out a cigarette but stopped himself. "I'm sorry, Hannah."

"No need to be sorry; she was never a mother to me." Hannah knew the lightness of her reply belied the processing she would have to work through. "Lenny wasn't even my dad."

"What do you mean?"

"I did a DNA test just to see what came out. I am all European and Persian." She looked at Allen with her green eyes, "Lenny was at least half Choctaw. His mother is a full-blood member of the Mississippi tribe, so Lenny couldn't be my dad."

"Huh." Allen looked down.

"Pete was the closest thing to a dad I ever had, and I slept with him. I've used prescription drugs, too. I'm not much better than Lisa, am I?" she sighed. "Apple from the tree, and all that."

"Aw, I don't know, Hannah Jain. To be honest, I believe you about everything."

"The FBI doesn't."

"Oh, Fart, Barf, and Itch. What do they know? They're a federal agency. I'm not even sure they can think."

"So…speaking of them…" Hannah looked at Allen.

"What?"

"I saw Hazel Replonge's name come up in a strange place the other day. Remember her?"

"Of course."

"Well, I was looking through a magazine last week and saw that she's on a global board of the Methodist church. Her name stands out anyway, so I couldn't help but notice it. She's part of the United Methodist Women, and she's on a board advocating for birth control in Nigeria and other African countries."

"This is the woman who expelled you, right?"

"Yup. It turns out the church that Terri used to sneak those first doses into Nigeria is a United Methodist affiliate. That was how they made the connection to get on that mission team, and why it was so easy for the team to get into Nigeria. The Methodist church is very active there. 677 is working it from the inside."

"Oh, man. How are we ever gonna stop that?" Hannah was glad to hear him say 'we.'

"I don't know, Uncle Allen. It's not gonna be easy." She hesitated for a moment, then continued, "A lot of people in the population control community would probably support using 677, especially on the Nigerians. All I know to do is pray. God is the only one who can fix this, and if he wants our help, he'll show us. I have no doubt. And I'm ready to help." Allen looked wryly at her five-month belly, which truth be told wasn't crazy big yet. "Really!" she insisted.

He laughed. "So am I. I guess we can't give up."

"No, we can't. There're at least two hundred thousand doses hiding somewhere, and they're probably already making more. Can you get any more out of your FBI friends?" It seemed their only hope at this point.

"I can try, but don't expect miracles from them."

"No… Only God does miracles these days."

CHAPTER FORTY-SIX

DALUCHI

When Hannah first noticed Daluchi at church one Sunday, she sat alone. Hannah was standing by the bathroom entrance before the late service started when she saw the tall, stately African woman stride into the sanctuary. She had deep ebony skin and fine high-cheeked features, and her hair was short kinky coils tight against her skull. She wore jeans, but her blouse was a woven wrap that looked more African than American. It hung loosely, hiding her figure, but Hannah thought she moved like an athlete. She wore a brightly colored beaded neckpiece.

Something about her seemed tentative despite her confident stride, and she sat alone. She didn't look around at first but down at her folded hands, and Hannah realized she was a newcomer—if you had friends in church, you looked around. Hannah watched and saw her glance up and around and back down, looking quiet and contained.

Pastor Chris always said to greet newcomers, so Hannah headed over to say hi. After getting over her fear of being judged for being pregnant without a husband, Hannah had made a few friends but was still a newcomer herself, and she sensed newness in this woman.

She sidled down the aisle, put out her hand, and said, "Hi, I'm Hannah."

"And I am Daluchi." Daluchi's teeth flashed white. Hannah didn't recognize the slight lyrical accent. Daluchi's hand was cool and smooth, but the skin had a thickness that came from working hard for many years, though she couldn't be much over twenty. She looked a question at the seat next to Daluchi, who gestured with an open hand to sit, so Hannah did.

"Are you new here?" Hannah asked.

"I am. This is my first time here, but I am a Methodist. I have been looking for a good Methodist church."

"Well, I'm pretty new too. I was raised a Methodist, but now I'm just a Jesus gal. I've been coming to church here for a few months. It's where my parents go."

Daluchi looked at the baby bump, then looked around. "Does your husband go here, too?"

"No, no husband. What about you?"

"Ha, ha! Fair question. I have no husband. None would have me in my homeland." Then she looked away, seeming embarrassed at her over-eager revelation.

Hannah looked her up and down. "Why not? You're a beauty."

"Ah, thank you, Hannah!" She looked Hannah up and down with an ironic grin. "You are too. But I cannot have babies, and in my country, that means I am *no good* as a wife."

"I can't have babies either; this is my first and last." Hannah patted her belly. "I got lucky with this one. Or blessed, really. But I could still get married…if I wanted to."

"Oh, then, you should. It is not good to be without a husband."

"A lot of women here would disagree with you, Daluchi. They don't want a mate." Hannah made her tone stern, like an encouraging mother.

Daluchi blinked. "I think I have heard about that. Do you mean for being a bride of Christ, or do you mean homosexual?" Her voice sank to a whisper.

"No one wants to be a bride of Christ anymore—or hardly anyone," Hannah smiled. "I meant gay people: lesbians. Folks like that."

"Yes, I see. LGBTQ. Alphabets. In my country, the prison sentence is seventeen years, or even death, for being homosexual." Daluchi widened her eyes in humorous emphasis when she said 'homosexual.' "Or any letter of the alphabet," Hannah laughed.

"Why do you laugh? I am serious!" Her accent grew stronger when she spoke with emotion. "In my country, we struggle for our lives, while here, in this country, you struggle for a label!"

"No, no! I just laughed at your eyes. Your expressions are funny." Hannah touched her hand as she said this. "I didn't mean anything by it."

Daluchi widened her eyes again and jerked her hand away. "You want me to go to prison?" Then she smiled. "It is true, though. More in the northeast and central parts than where I am from, but still very true."

"Where are you from?"

"Nigeria, from near Akwete. A little town near Aba. Port Harcourt, too, you might recognize." Daluchi noticed Hannah's sudden intensity, and she widened her eyes again, making Hannah giggle. "What? Are you afraid of Nigerians?"

"No, no, I'm sorry." *Nigerian? A 677 victim?!* She didn't want to reveal too much too fast, but she felt like Daluchi was easy to share with, like an old friend. Nevertheless, she made her voice light, like in idle conversation, she hoped. "I just had a friend go there once. I'm very interested in Nigeria. I hear there are a lot of people there, and a lot of Methodists."

"There are. I think there are more Methodists there than there are here." She looked around at the almost full sanctuary, which wasn't really a sanctuary, but a large room with a big stage in front and portable chairs set up on the floor, which doubled as a gymnasium and a dining hall. There were three hundred to four hundred people.

"And this is a lot of Methodists!" said Hannah. "Most Methodist churches are dying in this country."

"Oh my! I hate to hear you say that." She shook her head sadly. "Our bishop tells us that back home, says we need to send missionaries here. Maybe I am a missionary!" Daluchi made a goofy stern face and crossed her fingers in front of her.

The service was starting, so they couldn't talk further.

Chris, the pastor, gave a sermon about Job and his trials, and the theme was based on the Bible verses in Jeremiah 17:

But blessed are those who trust in the LORD and have made the LORD

their hope and confidence. They are like trees planted along a river-
bank, with roots that reach deep into the water. Such trees are not
bothered by the heat or worried by long months of drought. Their leaves
stay green, and they never stop producing fruit.

And the main point was to use adversity to endure and be fruitful, letting your response to adversity be an ardent fragrance to God and the world
around you. It felt like God was talking to her, and she noticed Daluchi also
listening intently.

When they sang, Daluchi swayed as Hannah did, and when their shoulders bumped every so often, it wasn't uncomfortable. Hannah felt like she
had a friend for the first time in a long time.

"Would you like to come to our house for lunch?" Hannah invited
after the service.

"And be seen with a pregnant woman with no husband?" She feigned
terror. "Oh, dear! Jesus would not approve, and neither would my embassy!"

Hannah giggled, feeling like a kid. "It's not catching!"

Daluchi was still smiling, but it suddenly turned wistful as she said, "I
only wish it was."

She led Daluchi back to children's church, where she knew Prissy was
working, pushing against a steady stream of noisy children and parents.
Daluchi was a tall, regal bean pole, towering above the children and even
most of the parents.

"You have turned me into a fish!" Daluchi puffed her lips into fish lips
and made like she was swimming, "A salmon no less."

"Good thing you can swim!" Hannah laughed.

She introduced Prissy once they broke through the queue of children
and parents, and Hannah told her she would be riding home with Daluchi,
who would be staying for lunch.

CHAPTER FORTY-SEVEN
FELONIOUS ALPHABETS

PRISSY HAD A pot roast in the slow cooker, and its aroma filled the river house. Hannah felt like drooling.

"I am hungry, a starving African child. We must eat now!" Daluchi sucked in her cheeks and begged.

"We have to wait, little child, for the parents to get home." Hannah tried for the sing-song cadence Daluchi used.

Daluchi lifted the lid, sniffed, and used the serving spoon to ladle a small amount. She held the spoon up and raised her eyebrows at Hannah. "May I?"

"Yes, but don't let Prissy see you. She's proprietary about her cooking," she warned with a mischievous grin.

"Mmmm. This looks like nwo-nwo, but it is not peppery. It is very good, though."

"Nwo-nwo?"

"Goat peppersoup. It is a delicacy where I am from. This is a delicacy, too."

Hannah tasted from the spoon Daluchi offered. "We call it pot roast, and it needs salt."

"I wanted to say that, but I did not want to sound rude." Daluchi picked up the saltshaker. "May I?"

"Of course." She watched as Daluchi added salt, stirred, and tasted again. She gave Hannah a new taste as well. "You're at home in the kitchen, aren't you?"

"It is the duty of all Nigerian women, but especially if you cannot have children. If you want the women, and even the men, to accept you, you must do other things well and work hard. Otherwise, you can be treated like a leper."

Pete and Prissy came home, and Prissy took over in the kitchen as Daluchi and Hannah set the table. Daluchi made funny eyes at Hannah behind Prissy's back when Prissy tasted the pot roast.

Hannah laughed. "We added salt, Mom." She'd been calling her that lately. "Or rather, Daluchi added salt." Prissy caught her making a wide-eyed fearful face at Daluchi, and they all laughed.

"I'm sure she warned you, but I'm not that bad," said Prissy. "It tastes good."

"It does, Mrs. Kramer. Hannah told me I could do it." She met Hannah's eyes as she ratted her out.

"Really, it's fine. I'm glad you like to cook. Maybe you'll cook us some Nigerian food."

"Oh, I would love to do that! We cook a little spicier than you, though."

"That would be great!" Pete had been listening from the table. "I love spicy!"

"Ah! A kindred spirit." Daluchi pressed her hands as if in prayer and bowed gracefully towards Pete.

Then they moved to the table, where Pete gave a prayer of thanks, and Prissy insisted they sit while she served them. She cut up a hot baguette and served it with butter, and they dug in.

"So, what're you doing in America, Daluchi? School?" Prissy asked.

"Yes, I am studying biology, and I hope to get into the new medical school here. I think I have enough brains." She tapped her temple, which made Hannah smile again.

"I've heard there's a real need for doctors in Nigeria," said Pete.

Daluchi didn't answer at first. Instead, she looked hard at Hannah for a moment, then at Pete and Prissy, and spoke with exaggerated caution. "If

I went back as anything else, I would not be accepted. But I do not want to go back."

"Why not?" Hannah asked.

"I was not kidding at church, Hannah. In most of my country, being barren is a curse. There is no man to take care of you, so you must go live in a hut with other barren women." Daluchi spoke passionately with emotional gestures, and her face darkened with anger now, "So for that reason alone, I do not want to go back.

"Your president was right when he called it a shithole. Maybe I could get out of the stigma if I lived in a big city. Maybe. But who wants to live in a country like that?" She softened her tone and looked at Pete, "You are right, Mr. Pete, our country desperately needs doctors. It is not a shithole, and pardon my language, but I am quoting *your* president. Our country needs love, too. I am here because there was no love for me there."

"Just because you weren't fertile?" asked Prissy, who wasn't fertile herself.

"There are other things. If I tell you, I could lose my visa." Daluchi's face was suddenly fierce. No one spoke.

Hannah gave silent attention to her food as the dark flash of Daluchi's sudden mood faded.

Finally, Hannah said, "They can keep a secret." Daluchi looked at Pete and Prissy.

"Why could you lose your visa?" Hannah wanted to know and ignored Prissy's daggers at her rudeness. "You brought it up."

"LGBTQ or whatever, those are your labels. We say *Alphabet*. It is a felony to be an *Alphabet* in my country. Here, Alphabets struggle for a label. In Nigeria, we struggle for our lives." Now there was defiance. Daluchi looked at each of them carefully, then her expression melted into fearful resignation, "A law was passed, called SSMPA: the Same-Sex Marriage Prohibition Act. It outlawed being Alphabet, or even associating with Alphabets, not just gay marriage. In Christian areas, there are long prison sentences. In Sharia areas, it can bring the *death penalty*." She made her wide-eyed funny face again, but Hannah wasn't tickled. It was a very serious situation that she'd heard of, but not fully appreciated.

"So, no one there knows you're gay?"

"I hope not. I could either take a husband and get pregnant or become a bride of Christ. When a disease went through our area, and I became infertile, no man would have me anyway. I was cursed." She seemed relieved to be telling this. "My mother and father may have suspected about the Alphabet, but it is not talked about. The consequences are too high." She couldn't reach the baguette basket, so Prissy helped her out.

"How'd you end up here?" Prissy asked.

"I have been called to church ever since I was a little girl. When the curse came upon us, it was almost a relief to me. No man wanted me, and because I was always at the church clinic anyway, everyone assumed I would serve the church. Women rarely get to come here for an education, but I had brains and could not have children, so it was accepted that I would come to study. It helped that my father is an elder in the Methodist church."

Hannah swallowed her last bite and asked, "Why Joplin?"

"Your university has medical and nursing colleges and a very progressive international policy. It is that simple." Daluchi gave a one-shoulder shrug.

Pete spoke up, "But if you go back, you can be imprisoned if they find out you're gay."

"Yes, and your president before this one helped a Muslim get elected, and he wants to extend Sharia law even further, so I can be killed. Supposedly, Sharia doesn't apply to Christians, but in practice, they both come for you at night. Christian *and* Muslim haters. You are raped to teach you to like men, or killed if you struggle too much." Daluchi ran a finger like a knife across her throat. Her face imitated fear, "Usually with a knife, so it is kosher, I guess. Or halal."

"Our politicians are mostly idiots," Pete interjected.

"How about no politics," Prissy said as she started clearing the dishes, raising a brow at Pete. Hannah got up to help.

"So, what about your dad? How does he feel about you being gay?" Pete asked.

"Like I said, Mr. Pete, we haven't discussed it." Daluchi leaned back in her chair and stretched her long frame. "He has talked about the battle inside the Methodist church here, and about gay marriage and pastors. All

I know about that is that we could no longer be Methodist if gay marriages were done in Nigeria. The SSMPA outlaws such religions."

Hannah and Prissy brought pecan pie and ice cream. "Hope you like dessert, Daluchi!" Hannah set a big piece in front of her and a smaller piece for herself.

"Indeed, I do!"

"So." Hannah looked at Pete and Prissy, then said, "Tell me about this curse you mentioned."

"Oh, the curse," Daluchi's face fell dramatically. "The curse changed my life forever. I was pregnant and would have had to marry a man. God saved me, but he took my baby." She stopped as her eyes teared up. Hannah handed her a napkin, and she wiped her eyes.

"I would have married the man if it meant I could keep my baby. I miscarried at home, and only my family knew. I never had a cycle again. Excuse me." She blew her nose as Hannah, Pete, and Prissy exchanged glances. Daluchi noticed and waved her hands in front of her. "Don't worry! I am not contagious. It never spread to anyone else." Hannah smiled briefly.

"I'm not worried. How many were affected?"

"Thousands. I don't know how many, but it was men and women all across our area. They became infertile. If women were pregnant, they had miscarriages."

"Was there a church doing mission work there?" Hannah tried to keep her voice casual.

"There is always a church doing mission work in the area. Why do you ask, Hannah?" Daluchi faced her squarely, curious.

"Oh, nothing." Hannah was deep in thought. She looked away. Surely this was from God. "Did anyone figure out what caused it? The abortions?"

"Abortions?" Daluchi pondered that for a moment but seemed to accept the medical term. "No. Who cares about infertility for a few thousand in Nigeria if no one is dying? When I went to the clinic here, they sent me to the ultrasound, and all they said was that I have bad ovaries. They are atrophied. I could get a biopsy, and they did blood work, but everything was normal. I did not even have HIV, and everybody in Africa has HIV, right?"

Daluchi looked the three of them and added, "Why are you all looking at me so closely?"

"Sorry. We're not trying to be rude." Prissy gave her a soft smile. "Hannah, why don't you explain? Show her, then we can go from there." Normally, Prissy took a nap after church, but no one was napping now. "Pete and I will clean up."

"Explain what?" asked Daluchi.

"Our ovaries match. It's a long story, Daluchi. Do you have time?"

"Of course. I am a Nigerian exchange student. I have no social life." Her inflection rose, and her lower lip went out, pouty-like.

Hannah led Daluchi to the computer where she had backed up the miniSD card in her phone. "It'll be easier if you read it yourself. Then we'll talk."

She pulled up the summary she'd given to the FBI and then gave Daluchi her seat. "Read it and weep." Concern, not flippancy, toned her comment.

Daluchi furrowed her brow and began to read while Hannah sat in a second chair behind and to the side, where she could watch.

Once Daluchi was finished, she was visibly upset. She said something in her native Igbo, then looked at Hannah. "*You* did this to my people? To me?" She drifted off into a few more Igbo phrases. Her anguish cut to Hannah's bones, and Daluchi looked down, head shaking.

"Yes, me and the others." Hannah knew she should say sorry, too, but it seemed weak, and the words wouldn't come. She nervously reached out a comforting hand, cupping Daluchi's shoulder from behind. Daluchi reached up and held Hannah's hand silently, continuing to stare at her lap, as if studying her other hand resting there.

Hannah was almost afraid to move, afraid of what might come; certainly, she deserved Daluchi's wrath. Her instinct said to freeze, and she shuddered slightly as she tried to make her breathing undetectable. She closed her eyes. *Lord, help her know my heart.*

Daluchi sighed, gripped Hannah's hand, then grabbed her other hand and turned to face her squarely, almost forehead to forehead. They were close enough to where Hannah could see Daluchi's pupils getting slightly bigger and smaller as they searched each other's souls. Hannah knew Daluchi deserved to be upset, and the wait seemed interminable.

She flinched when Daluchi finally spoke, but held her gaze, blinking involuntarily.

Daluchi's voice was measured, precise, "There is a reason God brought me to your church today. We must stop this thing; the authorities must wake up, and your colleagues must be exposed. You are a hero then, and not a criminal, Hannah." She waited, and her stare seemed less threatening. She realized Daluchi's eyes held love, and her words were a balm. But it didn't seem right.

"Thanks for the sentiment, but I'm not a hero." She felt her head shaking in rejection, her eyes still locked with Daluchi's. "And the authorities don't agree. They don't even believe me." She glanced down, then up, not wanting to do anything to draw further comfort she didn't deserve. But now Daluchi's head was shaking slowly and definitively. Her eyes were still locked on Hannah's.

"No, Hannah. Anyone acting righteously for God without regard for the consequences is a hero." She gently moved her hands to Hannah's cheeks, cupping her face. "You are not guilty. I say so, and so does Jesus." There was still only love looking back at her.

The words she'd been resisting suddenly came as a whisper, "I'm sorry... So, so sorry." Daluchi's blink was slow, deliberate, and she leaned close until Hannah could feel the warm breath in her ear.

"You are forgiven." It was like a blessing, sealed with the gentlest kiss her ear had ever felt, and a weight was lifted. She could sense the lightness in Daluchi, too, as they hugged.

Daluchi's voice returned to its sing-song cadence as they headed back to the dining area, "Justice flows like a never-ending stream, and God will direct its course for us. There is no need to worry." She'd gently tugged Hannah by the hand like a playmate, but now let go.

They sat with her around the table and explained what had happened, how Hannah hadn't been involved until later, how they'd tried to report the plot, and how the 677 Nigeria project was now deeper underground. It wasn't going to be easy.

"Let me think about this, and let us all pray and meditate on it. God will find a way." Daluchi's diction was even more clipped and proper when she was excited. "And thank you for the fine pot roast. Next Sunday, I will cook Nigerian pot roast for you. I must go now; I have to think."

CHAPTER FORTY-EIGHT

DALUCHI'S WORLD

DALUCHI WALKED WHEN she was upset or needed to think. When she was in her Igboland village of Akwete in Africa, she walked for miles and miles. Even as she matured into a full-grown woman, she roamed unafraid through the forests, palm groves, and pasturelands of her tribal lands. Harsh, even lethal, penalties for assault and rape protected her from human threats, and most animals respected humans and gave them a wide berth.

In other parts of Nigeria, there was regular warring between factions, and a single woman or man could easily end up being murdered or taken as a slave, which was worse. It had become more dangerous in those areas of the country over time, and who knew what the big cities were like (she'd heard stories), but her traditional land remained fairly safe, except for Alphabets.

When she first arrived in Joplin, she tried walking to clear her head. It was a mile to the closest walking trail, a beautiful path through the woods along Turkey Creek, just north of Ozark Cemetery. The late August sun was moving west, and the shadows started to grow long, but the pavement, which was everywhere, kept the heat very much alive as she walked along Newman Road towards the trailhead. Cicadas were calling long and loud, becoming hypnotic in their cadence.

She walked to the end of the trail and found a shaded sitting place on a cliff edge about thirty feet over Turkey Creek. Some kids were swimming but didn't seem to notice her as she closed her eyes, processing her first days in the USA. She found herself pining for her homeland and secret places she used to go to in the jungle and along the Imo River.

It was her habit to meditate on Bible verses she'd memorized since childhood, and Psalm 42 was strong in her head as she struggled with her emotions. She played it over and over: *As the deer pants for water, so my soul pants for you, oh God... As the deer pants for water, so my soul pants for you, oh God...* And that first time, far from home, she found comfort from a God who was everywhere at once.

He was there and also in faraway Nigeria, and that was all she needed to know. Walking back toward the university, she became aware of others keeping parallel on a secondary trail, hearing male laughter. She hoped they hadn't noticed her as she picked up her pace.

But their pace picked up, too, and she could see them through the brush. Fear rose when they started taunting her. "Hey, nigger gal...you ever had a real man?"

Suddenly the solitude of the trail became dangerous. She began to trot, remembering a clearing ahead, where they would either have to stop or show themselves. She returned to the Psalm in her head, repeating *Like a Deer* to herself over and over when she burst into a run as she hit the clearing.

Her stride was long, and she heard a few hurled insults, but they didn't follow her into the open. *Like a deer, like a deer, like a deer. Oh, God...* There was a convenience store just past the trailhead. She was sweaty and panting in the heat, and her heart was still pounding. She ignored the glances of the patrons and went inside for a bottle of water.

She had never felt blacker as she approached the clerk to pay. He was a big white man, rounded and greasy-haired with doughy features. She feared the worst but finally looked up to meet kind, concerned eyes. "You okay, ma'am? You look out of breath."

"Yes, yes." She was annoyed at her quavering voice. "I was just running."

"I saw that, but it looked like you were being chased."

She didn't want a scene. "No... Yes, there were some boys, but I ran away. I am okay now."

"I can call the police."

'No, really. I think I will be fine. How much?" She made her voice steady, her face inscrutable.

She paid and, embarrassed for showing weakness in the first place, went back outside to escape his help. It was still light, and she remembered a car dealer and a small fire station just down Newman Road towards the university. She walked towards home against the traffic like she'd been taught. It should be safe.

After passing the car dealer, she crossed busy Range Line Road, then started down an isolated stretch after the railroad crossing. She heard a car approaching from behind, and as it went by on the far side, the same voice as before yelled out, "Hey nigger! Go home, bitch!"

The car, a small sedan she didn't recognize, sped away towards the university, and soon, a police car passed as well. She made it back to the dorms unscathed, thanking God. But the devil had brought a fear of walking, and the lazy droll of cicadas would never sound the same.

CHAPTER FORTY-NINE
AWAITING GRACE

HER QUICK FRIENDSHIP with Hannah grew, and the friendly church gave her a hope that matched the promise of spring brought by blooming forsythias and red buds all around. Relief from the gray-brown of North American winter monotony was coming, but the revelation about 677 was still jarring. Learning the truth of her menopausal malady was like the hatred exposed by the call of 'nigger' from the passing sedan.

She still needed to think, to walk, so she'd found a place on campus, down past the biology pond along Turkey Creek, where she could walk in safety. There was no road nearby, and it was almost always deserted. The trail wasn't smooth or well-kept, but she felt safe there. She could circle back along the soccer fields and repeat the circuit covering about a mile, and usually saw no one else. Today, she took the 677 revelations, and all the emotion and anger they called, to the soft base of a tamarack tree that grew near the creek. Its soft needle bed peacefully deadened sounds and was like a mattress in the woods.

It was easy to climb to the branch she'd previously found that made a seat where relaxation and meditation were possible. Tiny leaflet buds on the secondary branches of the big deciduous conifer held the promise of spring. She leaned back against the smooth bark, clearing her brain with another memorized Psalm, number 40, repeating part of it as a mantra:

Be pleased, O Lord, to deliver me: O Lord, make haste to help me. Let them be ashamed and confounded together that seek after my soul to destroy it; let them be driven backward and put to shame...

Her mind began to clear, and her spirit was guided to consider what Hannah and her parents had related. Their reliance on authorities seemed to be inhibiting their problem-solving skills. She realized they did not appreciate the lack of reliance on "authorities" in her home country. Where there were authorities, they were hopelessly corrupt. Police are not called on to resolve most matters because they usually don't come anyway.

Rape, kidnapping, beatings, and street justice are common ways to resolve "crimes." Homosexuality is punishable by imprisonment, but street justice was usually swifter. Gay men are stripped and publicly humiliated and sometimes mutilated, while lesbians commonly suffer gang-rape to teach them to appreciate men. Abductions, murder, and torture of Alphabet people were common and without repercussions.

When imprisonment occurs, prisons have horrid conditions and are hopelessly overcrowded. Alphabet people are denigrated and at the bottom of the social order, often dying of disease and malnutrition if they are not assaulted to death first. The average wait for a trial is measured in years, and many prisoners are not even charged for several years after their arrest.

In her village area, where she could roam safely even today, the forces of common good emanated from the people, not from elected or employed authorities. The almost universal presence of faithful Christians in her little community served as the glue that sealed them all together. They also acted as the authority protecting her from most evils. Other religions served similar functions in other parts of the country.

Usually, the forces of love brought justice and safety. Though it wasn't perfect, it worked most of the time because it was driven by the law of love, which was always perfect. God called humans, despite their imperfections, to bring his light into the world through the application of that love. Still, many Nigerian Christians would watch, or even participate in, attacks on Alphabets. Even she would not be safe in her hometown if it were known she was an Alphabet.

She would probably end up gang-raped, murdered, or kidnapped and made into a sex slave somewhere. She hoped the Kramers appreciated her warnings about keeping her sexuality confidential. As it was, the inability to have a child made her unacceptable to be a wife, and she was forced to rely on the beneficence of her family or devote her life to the church as an acceptable childless alternative. No self-respecting man would have her, and jobs were not available.

She shifted, taking pressure off her lower back by leaning forward and resting her glowing forehead on her arms, which were crossed over her knees. She studied the long, stringy-soft strands of bark, still reflecting. It was these things that led her to study in the USA and seek a long-term work visa. Now, she was faced with knowledge of 677, knowing it had already affected many and would affect many more if the experiment continued. Being silent would mean she was a part of the coverup, and ultimately a part of the crime. She had no choice but to act; the question was, how?

In Nigeria, the swiftest justice came from turning to the Sharia system in the northern parts of the country, or vigilante action elsewhere. But she knew Nigerian authorities would not likely respond to her if she tried to report what Hannah had revealed, and the 677 participants had proven amazingly adept covering their tracks.

She realized the answer lay in letting God's light shine through the people affected by the 677 experiment. She must bring them a voice, and the way was suddenly clear to her. She had only one close friend, and she leaned back to pull her phone out and pressed Hannah's speed dial number, not bothering with a greeting.

"Hannah, we must meet!"

"Where are you?" Hannah didn't question the urgency of the request.

"In a tree!"

"What?"

"In a tree, thinking. But now I am calling you. We must meet; I have had a revelation."

"What kind of revelation?"

"A good kind. It is a God thing, I think. We need to talk about it."

"In a tree?"

She laughed at the thought of Hannah climbing the tree. "No, silly. I am just here thinking. Are you at home?"

"Yep. I have no car and nowhere else to be on a Sunday night."

Daluchi climbed down and almost ran back to the dorms. She had to concentrate so that she didn't speed through Duquesne village and get a ticket on her way to the river house.

Hannah, Pete, and Prissy were all at home. Hannah hugged her, and she felt the baby against her stomach. Daluchi stepped back, holding Hannah's hands. "I have an idea I need to bounce off of you."

"Well, let's go sit at the table. Pete and Prissy are here."

They sat down, and Daluchi eagerly began, "You are having no luck with the authorities. That is much like my country, but for different reasons. But the ending is the same, right? No justice."

"Right," Hannah agreed. Pete and Prissy nodded, too.

"In Nigeria, when there is a serious crime, like murder, rape, or being Alphabet, our authorities ignore it almost every time because they are completely overwhelmed. That is why group justice is so common. If something needs to be done about a crime, the men usually gather to capture the one responsible and administer punishment. Often, they get a police officer to help."

"We call that mob rule," said Pete, raising a brow at her.

"Yes, but it is the only way to get the guilty one. If you follow the legal system, nothing will happen. Only in the Sharia system is there rapid hearing of cases and administration of justice. That is why even Christians, both accused and victims, sometimes prefer it when it is available in Nigeria."

"So, the republic's justice system doesn't function well," Pete replied, beginning to understand.

"Right, Mr. Kramer! But in my area, in Abaland, we do not have the Sharia option. We are all Christian. We must take action ourselves if we want something done, and I think there is an action we can take to expose and fight 677." Daluchi paused for effect as they leaned forward.

"Mob action through social media! We can have the victims tell their stories and post the videos here on Twitter, Instagram, Facebook, and any other platforms we can think of."

"That could work," encouraged Prissy.

Pete chimed in, "If the news media picked it up, and hopefully they would, it'd bring pressure on our government to investigate further."

"Especially if you can show how many are affected," Hannah agreed, and Pete nodded, too.

"Does that mean you'll have to go there to make the videos?" Prissy wanted to know. "I don't want our baby to be in danger."

"Mom. I wouldn't hurt her." Hannah sounded like a girl again.

"I do not think we should travel there if we can help it. I do not have many friends at home, but the few that I do have are good ones. I have been thinking about getting them to help. It would not be that hard to send the videos here," said Daluchi.

In the end, they all agreed that if they had to go to Nigeria, it would be after the baby was born.

CHAPTER FIFTY
EBONY AND OLIVEWOOD

Delivery came by surgery after hours of pushing, and though all the blood and sweat were Hannah's, her work product belonged to another. Back at the river house, she nursed and pumped without reservation, knowing Prissy was ready and experienced. She didn't need Hannah's help. Hannah was just a vessel and would never carry another.

Although nursing evoked a surprising pleasure in her bosom, flooding her heart with the warmth of deep affection, motherhood failed to lure Hannah. She had never intended to have children. It still seemed somehow natural and fitting that God's baby was meant for Prissy—and Pete. Yet something was lacking, and it left her spirit unsettled.

One morning, as dawn dimly lit the mist, moving like a mystery over the lowlands outside her wind, Hannah and the baby drifted peacefully in the lull that follows nursing. She realized the child was a love offering from God, a manifestation of his grace to everyone involved. Though she had worked for years to find God through institutions and physicality, his amazing grace had always been there. It was the child, her Amazing Grace, that matured Hannah's faith enough to allow her to give her freely—a gift, back to God. Peace rested gently upon her as daylight slowly came.

Pete and Prissy's names went directly on the birth certificate as the adoption was completed, and the baby took the name that had become Hannah's private endearment: Amazing Grace Kramer.

Recovery in those first days meant time with Prissy, Pete, and the baby. Grace smoothly transitioned to formula, making Hannah redundant. Prissy was joyful in motherhood, even as Hannah began to emulate Pete's long hours at the clinic. She gradually drifted from Grace, lured by Nigeria's cry resounding in her heart.

Daluchi and Hannah often met to work on what they'd come to call Operation Infertility, and became close friends in the early months of summer. There was no internet in the valley where the river house lay, and the dorms and university library offered little privacy. It made sense when they decided to share an apartment near the school that solved both problems, and leaving Grace was easier with Daluchi's steady presence.

Both worked during the day, Hannah at the vet clinic and Daluchi at her work-study job. By night, their synergy worked to develop a plan to shine the light of justice on what 677 had done and was planning to do in Nigeria.

Daluchi's childhood friend, Maryam, proved to be a valuable resource. Maryam was also gay, but her school performance had not provided the same options. Left behind when Daluchi escaped to the United States, she ended up in Port Harcourt, where judgment against Alphabets was more muted. She couldn't live openly, but she no longer feared for her life if discovered.

Akwete, their home village, didn't have internet like Port Harcourt, but she traveled to the area and recorded testimony from affected people. Videos began coming in as Maryam worked, careful to just gather information and perspectives and not create attention by sharing the truth locally—not yet, Daluchi kept telling her. Her interviews included men and women of almost all ages affected by taking the 677-laced vitamins. From spontaneous abortions to de-sexualization by menopause, the stories were heart-wrenching.

A picture began to emerge of a new generation of Nigerian eunuchs. Intentionally or otherwise, the 677 group had targeted rural Nigerians. With no medical records to document the alterations forced on them, they sounded like paranoids speaking of alien abduction. Decreased libido came unbidden, and desire faded: intimacy forever altered.

Passion became a memory, friendships became languid, and much of life's urgency seemed to recede. Deeply personal changes, with no knowledge of cause, brought introspection rather than a focused movement for justice. All this became clear from the videos and their sometimes-lengthy discussions on WhatsApp. But Hannah and Daluchi had knowledge, and the passion to address the injustice rose within them as that knowledge grew.

One evening, Daluchi's scent drew Hannah as they edited Maryam's videography at the laptop. Turning slightly, she gently inhaled Daluchi's still exotic odor as they watched a clip. She could feel Daluchi's warmth, and memories of passion sharpened a yearning to hold and be held.

Daluchi didn't pull away as Hannah swallowed, then reached out to touch the hair she'd been longing to feel. When the video ended, she remained still as Hannah continued to stroke ever so gently, following the coiled rows, springy and tight, against her fingertips.

"Are you sure this is what you want, Hannah?" It was a whisper. Daluchi was still leaned forward towards the laptop.

Hannah turned her chair towards Daluchi's stool, and warmth sharpened as she leaned to rest her cheek on Daluchi's shoulder, fingers following the rows down to the warm softness at her nape. She'd imagined it would be roughened from long exposure to the sun as a child. She turned and brushed her lips against the tender hair there and sighed a gentle "Yes."

She watched Daluchi's eyes close, and her lips parted slightly as she began to follow the underlying muscles of her neck and shoulders, gently kneading through the ebony smoothness. She rolled behind Daluchi and brought her legs to either side, leaning forward to massage more thoroughly as Daluchi rested her head onto her now folded arms on the edge of the desk and purred.

Hannah paused when her arms fatigued, and Daluchi finally turned to face her. Daluchi's gentle touch on her thighs was electric. Feathery fingertips, then palms, then flattened fingers caressing, said Daluchi had been yearning to touch her as well. Hannah realized she was as exotic to Daluchi as Daluchi was to her.

It wasn't ebony on ivory, but ebony on olivewood as they moved to Hannah's king-sized bed. Loving was slow and unhurried, and Hannah unabashedly allowed Daluchi to caress and kiss her Grace scar. Hannah was startled at Daluchi's genitalia, smoothed by female circumcision, but her curiosity was mostly satisfied as she sought to give pleasure even as she received it.

Even though their climax was muted, it was enough. Hannah was acutely aware of the change in her sexuality from the 677, and she knew it had to be different for Daluchi as well. Post-coital bliss erased all tension as they snuggled close under the sheets. Daluchi's arms wrapped around Hannah as they spooned, while Hannah's arm draped over the thigh Daluchi slid lightly across her.

Hannah, languid but curious, couldn't help herself. "Did it hurt? To be altered?"

"Altered?" Daluchi's voice was dreamy, but her mirth brought focus as she continued, "You make it sound like I was a puppy." Hannah, embarrassed at her ignorance, squirmed closer.

"I just—"

"You are just curious. It is okay." Daluchi's diction became precise again, and her usual sing-song lilt returned, but her voice still had wisps of dreaminess, and her body remained relaxed against Hannah's back. "I *was* just a puppy, and they used anesthesia. I have no real memory of it. For me, it is just how my body is made." She had lifted her head slightly to speak, and now Hannah felt her snuggle back against her neck and relax her head as she breathed Hannah's hair. "And you made my body feel good."

Hannah was still lightly glowing across her belly and pudendal regions and thought of another round, but the bliss returned, proof there was life after menopause, and she drifted off without reply. Golden August afternoon light made everything beautiful.

Allen's call was jarring when it came, and Hannah jerked awake. "Allen, what's up?"

"Did I wake you?"

"No, no," she lied. "I was just dozing."

Daluchi rolled away, and the sheet slid off with her. Its crispness felt delicious.

"So, 'yes.'" She heard Allen laugh. "I have something for you and thought we could meet. It's about Lisa."

"Sure." Her focus sharpened. "Tonight?"

"Yeah, that works for me. How about the river house so that I can update Pete and Prissy at the same time?"

"Sounds good. I'll head over there now." Daluchi drove her right over.

Allen was sitting in his pickup in the drive with the windows down when they pulled up, smoking a Camel. He took one last long drag as he got out and flicked it to the ground where he crushed it with his heel. Dutch poked his big head out the back window, ears cupping forward then back as he recognized her voice and scent, and dog-smiled a greeting. His big tail whacked against the back seat as Hannah scratched behind his ears and introduced him to Daluchi, and then Daluchi to Allen: first things first.

They left Dutch and walked up the long stairway to the front door of the stilted river house. Inside, they were greeted by Prissy and Grace. Hannah took Grace and gave her a bottle Prissy had prepared, and they all sat at the kitchen island bar. Pete soon joined them, hair still wet from the shower.

"So, what do you have, Uncle Allen?"

"Things went better with the investigation once your mother was identified…"

"My biological mother." Prissy was her mother, now more than ever.

"Yeah. Like I said," Allen smiled. "Once she was identified, I was able to piece things together with information from the Springfield and Ozark police departments, and some help from the drug task force and the Highway Patrol.

"Do you remember ever hearing about a guy called Poonboy when you were a kid?"

Hannah kept her composure, but the name was like a fist in her stomach. Her tiny cringe was involuntary, and she blushed faintly. She could suddenly smell booze, and Allen's tobacco odor recalled weed. Dim rooms, terror, pain, helplessness, and memories of guilty pleasure suddenly swirled beneath her surface.

She felt Prissy's gaze, and Daluchi shifted, but Hannah focused on Grace quietly sucking down the formula. "Yes?" her voice was small.

"He was on and off with Lisa for quite a while. Lenny was in the picture, too, still cooking meth for cash. They were small-time dealers, and Lisa was in and out of street prostitution.

"It looks fairly certain that Lisa died in an altercation at the end of Ortiz Lane just before the Christmas Eve flood the winter before Dutch found her. The big rain had already started."

"You probably don't remember, Hannah. That's where we used to put into the river for floats back to the farm here when you were a kid," interjected Pete. "The Tipton Ford access."

"I remember the floats." Hannah kept her focus on Grace, only glancing up at Pete and Allen briefly. She didn't trust herself to say more, afraid her voice would crack as her throat tightened.

"What we know, more or less, is that Lisa ended up getting shot in an altercation with a local dealer, a Quattro. Tipton's always been a place for dealing, but no one ever bothered anyone. Don't know why the wrong paths crossed that night, or why Lisa ended up dead. It looks accidental: manslaughter or second-degree murder.

"They knew it was supposed to be a big flood, and they threw her body in the river with the gun, probably figuring everything would disappear. That's why she was never really reported missing until later. Everyone but Lisa's mother knew where she ended up."

"It was a drug deal gone bad?" Hannah asked bitterly, looking up to see Allen nodding. "Seems fitting."

Allen reached to his shirt pocket, and Hannah could see a baggie poking out behind his Camels. He pulled out the bag and flattened it on the table so she could see it contained three coins and a battered coppery chain bracelet. Everyone leaned in to look except Hannah, who kept feeding Grace, who was slowing down. The bottle was almost empty.

"This is the bracelet and three coins she was wearing, the ones that killed

Catniss," said Allen. He looked at Hannah, then around the table. "Poonboy said she always wore the bracelet." Hannah gave a derisive sniff.

"Her other biological kids stayed in the area, and she was able to keep tabs on them, but she was never able to track you down again." Hannah was burping Grace now, focusing on that to mask her emotions. Escaping her past was the whole point of changing her name and moving away. She felt no guilt, only the idle interest of a child poking at a corpse on the roadside.

Allen continued, "We don't need 'em, and if you want 'em, they're yours."

She touched the bag, and it was like turning the corpse over to reveal maggots and stench. She felt revulsion and despair at the same time—revulsion at the memories being brought forth, and despair at the convoluted path of her life and its dead-end in Florida. It was as if she was back at the start of it all, having traveled far, but only in a circle.

And yet…here was Grace, burping on her shoulder and cooing. And Prissy. And Pete with Prissy *and* her, together by Grace. And this new thing with Daluchi. All of it had been facilitated by Uncle Allen and Dutch's big nose. *Thank you, Lord, for bringing good from the bad.* She felt her soul calm.

She rearranged Grace, and, since Allen made an effort to bring it, picked up the baggie in her free hand to studied its contents. Everyone was watching her but trying not to.

The bracelet remains were green/black stained copper, and the three coins were battered and corroded. She almost gave it back to Allen, but then she smiled at the irony. Lisa probably didn't feel love like a mother should, yet she had carried the three of them her whole life, apparently. Similar to how Hannah carried her lost sisters in her name everywhere she went. Hannah felt a strange, bittersweet connection.

The bracelet was her history, and she realized she would keep it forever. Not as a treasure, but as a reminder of where she'd come from, and a motivation for moving forward. Her battered life mattered enough to God, to these people who'd forgiven her past and taken her in, and even to Lisa, who'd once worn this battered bracelet, that suddenly she knew *she* must matter. Really matter, in the tapestry of the universe in which her life had been woven.

She looked at Allen, noticing his concern for her as he delivered this emotional information. A half-smile played across her face as she thought of the phoenix on the coin he'd given her in Florida. She could emerge again, stronger than before.

Grace shifted, and she automatically bounced her slightly, holding her close. She looked in Daluchi's dark eyes. Folks might judge her sexuality if they knew, but they were purposed together to bring God's light to the situation in Nigeria, and he would take care of everything else. With Jesus, she knew the only judgment she had to fear was the misguided hatred of people, both here and in Nigeria, whereas the threats against Daluchi and Maryam were life-altering and even deadly.

God, she realized, had always been taking care of her details. She only had today, and here she was with her new friend, her only true family, and the next generation. Tomorrow was a distraction, limited only by the measure of her faith against her fears. She felt a sudden, profound love for Daluchi that rivaled her love for Grace and the Kramers and silently gave thanks.

She set the baggie with the bracelet close in front of her, accepting it in her spirit. "Thanks, Uncle. I think I'll keep it."

He nodded and looked at Pete and Prissy, then glanced at Daluchi. "I was able to clear Lenny because he was in jail that night. And Poonboy probably isn't long for this world. I found him in a long-term care facility. He's got bad cancer, stage four, and we're paying for his treatment."

Hannah nodded absently, distracted by the mention of Poonboy again. She was glad he was dying, but knowing was of little comfort. She'd never be able to confront him, or any of her past for that matter, and probably wouldn't have even if he lived. His death might bring more closure than meeting face to face, but a confrontation might bring forgiveness, which she knew from her own recent experience to be the only way to peace.

She had been feeling Grace poop, and now she could smell her. "Poonboy doesn't break my heart. I barely remember him, and what I do remember, I wish I didn't."

She got up to change diapers, and Prissy followed her to the nursery.

"I wish there was nothing to remember," said Prissy, her face a mask of worry. "I'm sorry we lost you."

"Me, too." Hannah changed the diaper and re-bundled Grace. "Even though we never should've been forced apart, we're back together now."

When she handed her back to Prissy, they hugged together with Grace cupped in the middle, cooing softly. Hannah knew then that God's peace could be hers forever, no matter what things swirled in the spiritual and material world around her and those she loved. It might be messed up, it might be hard, but she was home, and it was good to hug her mom again.

EPILOGUE
ANOTHER WORLD

DR. KIMBERLY FIRKOVITCH thought she had seen it all after eight years of providing medical care in Abaland, home to the Igbo people. One of the worst problems she had encountered was a widespread condition known as Vesicovaginal Fistula (VVF), which is when a woman's birth canal tears during the birthing process and creates a permanent opening between the bladder and the vagina. A constant leak of urine results, and affected women are often divorced and ostracized. Hundreds of thousands of women were affected, and Firkovitch tried to get them all to a surgeon who could repair the defect, so they didn't face a life of isolation.

But the infertility crisis now facing her was overwhelming. Women and men throughout the communities she served had become infertile, and their gonads were shrunken and fibrosed. It was a malady she could see even on her older ultrasound machine, and it made eunuchs of both genders. Men who were willing to provide semen samples, a social taboo, had mostly clear semen with little or no sperm cells. Women were experiencing menopause and secondary hormonal problems.

Working long hours in the primitive conditions, she tried to ignore her own symptoms. Yet they persisted, and when she used her old ultrasound machine to check her own ovaries, she found the same problem. She could understand why affected persons were considered cursed, and calls to her colleagues when she got within cell range provided the devastating news that thousands were affected in the Nigerian states around her. Her colleagues at the WHO were somewhat aware of the situation and thought it was due to a form of herpes virus called HHV-6A.

Just going through early menopause herself was bad enough, and she knew the social ramifications doubled down on the personal loss felt by the women and men of the nation she served. Adolescents of both genders faced a barren future in a country where large families were highly prized. Knowing she wasn't alone didn't help as the depression and anxiety she had suffered for years were worsened by the hormonal swings and concurrent loss of status that came as western doctors were unable to help the social fabric being torn by the plague.

Social media contributed to the devastation as insensitive trolls posted memes blaming western medicine and doctors like Firkovitch. Gleefully derisive comments by self-proclaimed western population control advocates—who had never even been to Africa—further inflamed attitudes against western aid organizations. While the good doctor might have once worked to overcome the hostility generated in the general population, she was finally defeated after an encounter that shook her to her core.

She was staying at a small mission clinic in Okoloma, a Rivers state town near Akwete. It was after two in the morning when a persistent tapping woke her. She heard urgent Igbo voices outside the door, "This woman needs help! We found her in a road ditch. She's been raped and beaten!"

Unable to resist, she opened the door to admit six young men and women carrying a battered and semi-conscious woman. "Why didn't you take her to the emergency room?"

"We couldn't. She's a lesbian, you know! They would probably let her die."

Kimmy sighed and gestured towards an exam bed in the treatment room. They deposited her on the bed and made to leave. "Wait. I'll need someone to stay and help me!" The six looked at each other, all hesitant. Finally, one of the men shrugged his shoulders.

"I can stay for a little while." He didn't look happy about it. The others started to leave.

"Thanks for caring." Kimmy meant it. They could have just left her wherever they found her.

"What's your name?" she asked the man.

"Yibo."

"Yibo, don't let her fall off the table. I have to lock the door." She was acutely aware that whoever attacked the woman might have followed her here. She went and carefully re-bolted the door and returned to the small room.

She began to examine the semi-conscious woman who said her name was Maryam before passing out. Yibo helped her as she started an IV, completed an examination, and then cleaned the woman. They moved her to an old hospital bed in the small room where Kimmy was staying, and Yibo left them alone.

As Maryam recovered over the next several weeks, Kimmy learned that she'd been outed as a lesbian while working on a film project nearby. A "justice" mob, led by a police captain, had attacked her and taken her to an old warehouse where they taught her to appreciate men by repeatedly raping her after choking and beating her into submission.

She'd suffered facial fractures, and several teeth were missing. Her body was horribly bruised and battered. A cross they had cut into her belly was scarring in slowly with proud flesh, leaving a distorted symbol of the Christ she followed. Her faith remained strong, but her will to live was gone, and she longed to go to heaven.

It was through her that Kimmy learned about 677 and all its ramifications. She even remembered the vitamin distribution Maryam told her about. Kimmy had been a part of it and knew that was where she'd been exposed. She'd used those vitamins herself.

While Maryam had sent a few videos to Daluchi and Hannah, the rest had been backed up on her cell phone. It, and all her possessions, had been taken by her assailants. Both her spirit and work were destroyed. Kimmy, too, was becoming disillusioned with Nigeria, and could see no way to effectively bring light to the 677 attack, and doubted it would make much difference if she did.

After Maryam healed enough to move back to Port Harcourt, Kimmy left the country and returned to a private practice near her family in St. Louis, never to return.

Back home, Daluchi and Hannah began to worry. To them, Maryam had simply disappeared, leaving them with insufficient information to drive any kind of social media campaign. When she later contacted Daluchi by WhatsApp and explained through many tears why she'd disappeared, it became clear the campaign had been over before it began. They had to come up with a better way to expose the movement.

Both Daluchi and Hannah had started back to school full time in September, careful to appear just as roommates because the consequences were dire if their relationship was discovered by any unfriendly Nigerians.

They struggled with what direction to take. Many options could easily involve Daluchi losing her visa, and none provided assurance of stopping the 677 movement.

Then, it didn't matter. First, there were reports by the WHO of a viral outbreak profoundly affecting human reproduction in the Abaland area. Hundreds of thousands had become sterile, and many pregnancies were spontaneously aborted. It was a humanitarian disaster of historic significance that finally brought a media frenzy.

Epidemiologists soon determined the "disease" was foodborne, and then a chemical contaminant was discovered in a flavoring widely used in both plantain and potato chips and crisps. Hannah and Daluchi knew they'd been outsmarted, and they all knew the world would never be the same as 677 became the most dangerous weapon of mass destruction ever imagined.

ACKNOWLEDGMENTS

Who really knows what dogs think? Notions abound!

Travis Walthall reviewed, helped adjust, and then approved the thoughts and work habits of "Dutch" in this book. Travis is the best dog man I've ever met. Dr. Stephen MacKenzie at SUNY Cobleskill, who developed the first four-year degree program in canine behavior and training in the United States, also reviewed those chapters. He's the best dog man I never met! Shane Eckhardt's skills were proven when his dogs found the children at Moore. Shane trusted me with his heart so I could better understand a handler's soul. All dog people are eccentric. Shane is the most eccentric, and I love him.

But this book is about a lot more than dogs. People caring for the lost children helped us come to know and feel their struggles, and the children continue to make us see things in a different light. My mom and dad took in Harris County, Texas children through the system—and sometimes off the street—while we were growing up. Case workers in Jasper, Newton, and MacDonald Counties in Missouri trusted us with their children over the years and stuck with us through thick and thin. I couldn't write about Hannah without their help.

There are good workers and bad, soft children and hard, and they all struggle in a system that seems worse than the lives it dictates. That gut-retching and randomly pitiless system is forming our future. Even though we must sometimes step aside—with hearts broken or scornful—a CASA volunteer on an airplane helped me see anew that we can't give up, no matter what! God will help us, and know in your heart he will provide a path to healing for the hurts we couldn't prevent. Counselors and pastors stand in testimony to his faithfulness to all his children. It isn't up to you or me; it's up to us. To all of you who do your best: your best inspires me daily.

For those who kept the faith on our journey through veterinary medicine, I am eternally grateful. While you may recognize some scenes and settings herein, they are generic to our profession for the most part, but you were always an inspiration to me. We accomplished so many things together over the years. We couldn't change the world, but we certainly changed our world and, I think, made it a better place when we were together. For your loyalty and love, I thank you.

Many work in the field of pet birth control, inspired by the ongoing slaughter of unwanted pets. Like me, they dedicate much of their lives to finding a way to stop it. If there are those with nefarious intentions, I never met them, but the potential for harm from contraceptive research is real. It is the most dangerous bioweapon ever conceived, but no one seems to care. Calling attention to the threat also helped inspire this book.

For my early readers and encouragers, your care, insights, and corrections were a big part of making this book possible. You endured the early versions…ewe. Dr. Anna Blick hand-edited the entire manuscript with loving care. Two of my daughters (Whitney and Coco), Rhonda Sloan, Beverly Bieber (thank you Jeff), Bird Janhonen, Tiffany Artinger, Tim and Carol Ferguson, Ellen Pendley, Amy Sperling, and Thad Sperling all provided early reading. Richard Leavens, my brother from the same mother, read the manuscript and helped make sure police protocol was accurate. Whitney, Beverly, Rhonda, and Bird all provided more extensive feedback that helped shape the final book.

Whitney was tireless in her edits and feedback and helped write all the ancillary parts and submission letters for the book. I thought her work was great, but almost 40 agents said, "no thanks!" I say thanks, Whitney, for never losing heart!

Tennessee Jones, MFA, was instrumental in shaping the early novel, providing insightful editing, pointed feedback, and kind encouragement. Then, God sent Casey Fenich of Thoth Editing when I was on the ropes. She's a part of the future of the publishing industry. She rocked out the final drafts in record time and believed in the book from the first day. Her referral to Damonza provided the final touches needed to go live with Ortiz Lane.

There are others, like Dick and Patty Kruse who gave me a place to work for a spell, but the most important of all is Becky, my partner in this journey through life. She is my first and last reader and my compass. You cannot write without your spouse's support unless you are willing to choose writing over your relationship. Becky never made me choose, even for a second. And while so many others helped with the polish, it is her input above all others that makes this book something worthy of publication.

I hope you enjoyed it, and if you did, please give it a review on Amazon. If you didn't, please don't! Either way, I always appreciate your feedback.

Feel free to email me via joplinvet@gmail.com

ABOUT THE AUTHOR

Even though Ortiz Lane is his first novel, Benjamin Leavens has been writing stories, articles and commentaries since the fifth grade. A friend submitted one of his columns in college and it won Best in State at the Missouri College Newspaper Association competitions in 1985. It was the only writing contest his work has seen. Level 1 trauma medicine as a Registered Respiratory Therapist, a later career in veterinary medicine and animal abuse investigation, and a lifelong devotion to foster care inform many aspects of his writing.

Ben and his wife Becky live in the Ozark foothills community of Joplin, Missouri near their constantly growing family, a beloved church family, several pets, and around 250,000 folks that call the four-state region home. Ben continues to serve in rescue and recovery, bible teaching, and divorce recovery workshops. Sometimes, it is hard to tell the three apart!

Retired from medicine, his work time is devoted to writing another book, which is scheduled for release in the winter of 2021.